THE
RELIC GUILD

For Jack …

DOUBT & WONDER

In the long game, defeat was only part of the strategy.

Alone and beaten, Fabian Moor strode across a narrow bridge of stone. Cold purpose drove each of his steps as his path arced over a chasm so deep that light itself was swallowed into an endless void. He looked up at the luminescent stalactites that hung from the ceiling of a vast cavern like the spires of an inverted cityscape, glowing with a violet radiance. With a surge of intolerance, Moor gritted his teeth as he glimpsed something moving among the shadows there. A silhouette, dark and sleek against the pale light, left the cover of a stalactite and sailed down towards him with the slow beating of huge wings.

Without breaking his gait, Moor thrust out a hand. A point of light, no bigger than a pebble, shot from his palm and streaked upward. It hit the silhouette with a flash of silver-blue that illuminated a creature three times the size of any man. The creature recoiled, great leathery wings folding forward, a bellow of pain coming from a gaping maw manifestly designed for rending flesh. As the light faded, a bitter wind moaned around the cavern, followed by the sound of dull creaking. In the gloom, the creature's frozen body hit the bridge several paces ahead of Moor and shattered into a thousand glassy shards which glittered like jewels as they tumbled and spilled into the abyss.

Icy remnants crunched under Moor's boots as he continued onward.

The bridge ended at a promontory, where, before the rough and sheer cavern wall, a stone golem stood sentinel. A thick neck and broad shoulders supported its boulder-sized head. The wall of its chest tapered to a marginally thinner waist; massive fists dangled from powerful arms and hung down past the knees of tree-trunk legs. Hulking, easily twice Moor's height, the stone golem didn't move, but its eyeless sockets seemed to glare a challenge to the man standing before it.

Moor sneered up at its chipped and worn face. 'Well?' he said intolerantly. 'Let me in, you fool!'

The golem shifted its bulk, its joints rasping with the grind of stone on stone as it turned to face the cavern wall. Raising both massive fists, it punched out at the rock. The hard surface accepted the blows, turning to liquid, as if cowering in the face of a greater might. It then solidified, fusing the golem's arms to the wall at the wrists. The golem leaned back and heaved. With more grinding, the stony sentinel wrenched free a great section of the wall as easily as if it were pulling out a plug. Its footfalls were heavy as it bore the hunk of rock back a few paces to reveal a round opening.

Without a word, Moor stepped through the opening. A dull boom confirmed that the golem had resealed the way behind him.

Moor entered a circular chamber whose wall and floor were as smooth as if scooped out of the rock. Above, the domed ceiling was coated with a luminous substance that bathed the chamber in a warm, golden glow. A large round table of stone occupied the centre, around which four people sat. All of them stared at the new arrival, but not one uttered a word as he took his chair among them.

Only when he was seated did Moor acknowledge the pain from the injuries he had suffered to his ribs, and the deep fatigue overwhelming his body.

He felt eyes upon him. Each of these people was well-known to Moor, though he would hardly call them friends. They had all been summoned to this council chamber before, and always in secret, but never under such circumstances as these. Their dark cassocks were ripped and stained as Moor's own, and all but one carried visible wounds.

To his right sat obese Viktor Gadreel; the old man held a bloodied cloth to his left eye, and shallow cuts and bruises decorated his bald head. To his left, Hagi Tabet's glassy eyes stared off into some unknown distance, a thin line of blood running down the side of her face from a head wound partially hidden by her short, matted hair. Further along, Yves Harrow was shaking, gritting his teeth against the pain of raw facial burns.

The one person present who displayed no obvious injuries was Mo Asajad. She sat calmly opposite Moor. Her long, raven hair was straight and neat; her gaunt, porcelain face was blemished only by a patch of scarring on her forehead – the same ritual scarring each of them bore with pride.

'Where is Lord Spiral?' Moor demanded of her.

'We do not know.' Asajad's thin, colourless lips gave him a cold smile. 'How goes your part in the war?'

Meeting her dark eyes with a chilly gaze of his own, Moor remained silent.

'Come now, Fabian,' she said. 'There's no shame in defeat.' Her smile grew thinner and colder. 'Even my own troops were destroyed today at the Falls of Dust and Silver. I thought I was to die, too, but then I was manifested here.'

Viktor Gadreel grunted. 'It is the same for us all, Fabian.' He removed the cloth from his face and looked at the blood upon it. His left eye was nothing more than red pulp. 'I lost over a thousand today, dead to a man at the Burrows of Underneath. I should have fallen with them.'

'So many dead,' Hagi Tabet whispered. With each passing moment, she seemed more and more lost. Whatever wound she had sustained, it had clearly addled her mind. 'It all happened so quickly …'

'We didn't stand a chance,' added Yves Harrow. He closed his burnt eyelids and continued to shiver.

'So you see, Fabian,' Asajad purred, 'each of *our* armies suffered defeat in battle, and with synchronised precision, it would seem. But you didn't lead an army, did you? Your part in the war was of a more clandestine nature.' She gave him a pitying pout. 'I am assuming, by your presence, your mission to the Great Labyrinth was not a success?'

'What do you know of my mission, Asajad?' Moor's tone was guarded.

'Enough to make an educated guess that the little magickers of the Relic Guild proved too strong for even Lord Spiral's most trusted assassin.'

Moor rubbed a hand across his bruised ribs and averted his gaze.

'Oh, poor Fabian.' As Asajad's unhelpful amusement deepened, she looked at each person seated around the table. 'A sorry lot for sure,' she sighed. 'Yet, even in failure, our lord and master has seen fit to spare us from death, to bring us safely to this place. We must indeed be favoured.'

'But are we few all that remain?' Gadreel said. 'Did Lord Spiral save others?'

Before any could speculate further, there was a deep click and a square section in the middle of the round table began to rise.

Moor watched as a glass tank was revealed, slowly rising with puffs of dust and steam. Within the tank stood a small and withered man, his body and limbs wrapped in strips of black cloth. He was bald and pale-skinned. His eyelids were sown together with twine and his lips were fused around a glass tube that connected to a box held in his thin-fingered hands. The box was diamond-shaped and dark, but the symbols carved into its surface glowed with a dull purple hue. A second glass tube ran from the box and disappeared into the withered man's temple. Thick fluid travelled along both tubes.

A second click was followed by a long sigh, and the man in the tank spoke. 'Greetings.' His voice, stony and emotionless, came from all places at once.

Viktor Gadreel was the first to reply. 'Where is Lord Spiral?' he demanded.

The answer was matter-of-fact. 'I am to instruct you in the Lord Spiral's absence.'

Moor looked around the table. They all knew the abomination in the tank, and knew him well. His name was Voice of Known Things, and not one of them would dare refute him, for he had been created by Lord Spiral to speak the truth. Voice of Known Things was incapable of mistake or lie, and his word was the word of their absent master.

'The war has reached its conclusion,' the emotionless voice continued. 'The Timewatcher's army has proved too strong, and Her Thaumaturgists have pressed their advantage. Our allies among the Houses of the Aelfir have been broken and scattered. Even as I speak, the Lord Spiral's enemies are clinching the final victory.'

'Then the war *is* lost,' Tabet whimpered. Her eyelids fluttered, struggling to stay open. 'Lost ...' Blood dripped from her earlobe onto the shoulder of her cassock.

Gadreel growled defiance. 'No. I will not accept that.' He jabbed the bloodied cloth towards Voice of Known Things. 'The Great Labyrinth can still be ours – I refuse to sit idly by while our lord falls.'

Harrow, his facial burns weeping and ugly, hissed between chattering teeth, 'Yes. Better to die in battle.'

Moor remained silent. Only he understood there was more to this situation than his comrades realised – or so he thought until he noticed Mo Asajad, smiling at him through the glass tank. The other three had not grasped the obvious: none of them would have been saved if it did not serve some greater purpose in the war.

'You will do only as the Lord Spiral commands,' Voice of Known Things said. It was simply a statement: the truth. 'The war for the Great Labyrinth is lost, but your master does not lose hope in the face of defeat. Never again will he bow to the rule of the Timewatcher and Her Thaumaturgists, and nor will his generals.'

A moment of silence passed before Asajad said, 'How then can we serve our lord in these times of despair?'

Fluid gurgled along the glass tubes, and Voice of Known Things replied, 'No despair can last forever.' He turned his head to Moor, as though those ruined eyes could see him. 'History will record that each of you died during the final days of the war. That is as intended. That is as it should be.'

He allowed a further moment of silence to pass, and the glow of the symbols upon the diamond-shaped box in his bony hands intensified. 'The plans of your master have not changed, and your orders remain the same.' It seemed his words were directed at Moor alone. Then, 'Your flesh is the sacrifice, but your souls are reserved for the Lord Spiral's will. In this matter you have no choice.'

'And never could we conceive of refusing him,' Asajad said. Her voice had become whispery, excited.

'Indeed,' Moor added.

He felt a thrill that banished his pain and fatigue. Gadreel, Harrow and Tabet seemed perplexed as they stared at the abomination in the glass tank, but Moor understood where they were being led, as he had always known. For the first time, he returned Asajad's mirthless smile through the glass tank.

Once again the stony, emotionless Voice of Known Things spoke from all places at once. 'You are the vanguard of the future. You are the last of the Genii.'

CHAPTER ONE

THE GREAT LABYRINTH

Marney glanced up at the sky as she ran. A thick blanket of clouds obscured the stars and blurred Ruby Moon to a smudge of dull red. The stench of mould filled her nostrils. The air was warm and humid, dampening her skin, promising heavy rain. Already a fine mist of drizzle had slicked the cobbles beneath her boots, and glinted as it clung to moss growing on the black bricks of the high walls flanking her. Surrounded by miles of intersecting alleyways, with only moonlight and shadows to guide her, Marney blocked the pain of her burning leg muscles and headed deeper into the Great Labyrinth.

Tonight, she searched for a denizen lost among the alleyways: a young woman with bad people on her tail, assassins more accustomed than their prey to the kind of danger lurking in this monstrous maze. The girl would only find despair in the complexities of the Great Labyrinth. However, on this occasion, her would-be assassins had more to deal with than a straightforward killing. They had an empath on *their* tail.

As the alley came to a cross junction, Marney paused in the shadow of a buttress. The alleyways of the Great Labyrinth did not differ from each other much: roughly five paces wide, twisting and curving in seemingly impossible ways, with pairs of opposing buttresses every fifteen paces or so. Usually, cobbled ground and mossy brickwork were all that could be seen for miles on end; but across this junction, standing further down the opposite alleyway, were the remnants of a makeshift camp.

A canvas sheet, damp and covered in mould, had been fashioned into a crude bivouac. The top edge was studded to the brickwork. It stretched diagonally down to roughly the centre of the path, where it was held to the ground by heavy weights. There were a few metal storage containers close by, piled on top of each other, rusty and full of holes. Beside them lay a glow lamp, smashed and useless.

A few rats scurried around the improvised camp and into the bivouac's triangular opening. Marney could see the dark shapes of heaped bundles inside. She knew it had once been the shelter of a treasure hunter, someone who had died of his own greed and stupidity, probably decades ago. The camp appeared deserted, but maybe deceptively so …

Marney summoned her empathic magic.

Her awareness shifted, falling out of sync with the world of dark, cloudy sky and misted night air. She could no longer smell the damp of her hair and clothes. Detached now from her intuition, Marney focused on a single moment, a single space, and her magic reached out.

The mossy bricks of the alley walls and the slick cobbles became insubstantial as her senses searched for revealing signs: the emotions of an assassin hiding around the treasure hunter's camp. But the only emotive response was the otherness of rats existing within their simple-minded routines. No ambush awaited her. Marney didn't know whether to feel relieved or offended.

These rodents weren't the only kind of creatures dwelling in the Great Labyrinth; there were monsters too, especially here where the maze twisted and turned like the arteries of a black heart. If she had a mind to, Marney could be the worst monster of them all, yet the assassins had left no trap. Perhaps they didn't perceive her as a serious threat. She was only one old woman, after all …

Marney stopped searching. Her restored awareness once again registered the damp air and foul-smelling alleyways. She took the left alley at the cross junction, leaving the camp behind, and resumed running.

The girl Marney was trying to rescue was known as Peppercorn Clara. Barely eighteen, she was a whore rumoured to have a libido as spicy as it was insatiable. The story was that Clara had killed a client halfway through a job. The man had been a disreputable sort who wouldn't be missed, and according to Marney's information, Peppercorn had been forced into a corner and had no choice but to defend herself. Marney believed that somebody, somewhere, had benefited from the murder of Clara's client. These assassins were on a clean up job.

Marney cut a right and then a quick left. She skidded on damp moss, righted herself and sped down a long alley that stretched straight ahead into the gloom.

Time was running short, and Marney was behind in the chase. Clara was too far away to contact mentally, but her fear left emotional footprints that led clearly through the alleyways. Unless Marney could head her off, and fast, Clara would flee too deep into the Great Labyrinth, to the places where assassins would be the least of her problems.

Between the alley walls, in the little niches and hidden corners of the giant maze, there was a peripheral place that both inhabited the real world and did not. The denizens of Labrys Town called this place the Retrospective; and there pockets of dead time existed – remnants of long gone civilisations. These epochs were a treasure house of forgotten artefacts and secrets, or so it was said. But only the greed of treasure hunters, or insanity, could drive a person to search for the Retrospective. For within that twilight realm dwelt many terrible things.

Manifested as a horde of ghosts, they snaked and weaved through the very fabric of the Great Labyrinth, like tendrils of dark history, remorseless aspects without good or reason; monsters, phantoms from nightmares with names only mentioned in whispers, or upon the pages of secret books. The wild demons of the Retrospective slept with one eye open, always ready to swallow the unwary.

And Peppercorn Clara was heading straight for them.

As the light of Ruby Moon shone brightly through a gap in the clouds, Marney reached the end of the alleyway and cut a sharp right. Somehow, she didn't see the assassin until it almost was too late.

Boldly, he stood further ahead, in the middle of the alley, dressed in a dark, flowing priest's cassock and wide-brimmed hat. The violet light of thaumaturgy glowed from the power stone set behind the chamber of the pistol in his hand.

An instant before the power stone flashed and the pistol shot its deadly slug with a low and hollow spitting sound, Marney leapt aside, ramming her shoulder into a buttress, and pressing her back flat to the alley wall. The assassin's bullet cracked the brickwork a few paces to her right with a spray of stone. A sharp, high-pitched whine was immediately followed by a whirl of icy wind. The noise scrambled Marney's empathic senses, but she retained control and heard a creaking, deep and dull sounding.

Ice was forming where the slug had hit the wall. It spread out over the brickwork, creeping towards her like frosted breath on a windowpane. In an instant, the ice reached Marney's right shoulder. She gasped and gritted her teeth as the cloth of her jacket began to freeze. Just as she thought she would have to break cover, the ice ceased spreading and mercifully began to melt.

Magic: that bullet was designed to capture not kill. A direct hit would have preserved Marney's body within a cocoon of ice. But magical ammunition was rare in the Labyrinth, and no one – *no one* – packed that kind of power into a bullet unless they were damn sure of their skills, unless they were ... *well connected*. What kind of enemies had Clara made?

The assassin still loomed in the alleyway. Marney tried to engage with his emotions, to manipulate him into obeying her command, but he was shielded from her empathy. More magic. There was no way she could get close to him while the gun remained in his hand, so she unzipped her jacket and carefully slipped it off. A baldric of slim throwing daggers was fastened around her torso like a girdle. She slid out a single blade. The silver metal felt cool and smooth in her hand.

Marney waited several heartbeats, and then threw her jacket into the alley. Immediately, the power stone in the assassin's pistol flashed and released a burst of thaumaturgy. The ice-bullet fizzed into the jacket, freezing it in midair. It fell, shattering to shards of ice upon the cobbles. Marney spun into the alleyway and threw the dagger. It sliced the air with a sigh before thudding into the face of her adversary. His head snapped back, dislodging the wide-brimmed hat, and the pistol fell clattering from his hand. The violet glow of its power stone faded and died.

Marney wasted no time. She let fly with two more daggers; one took the assassin in the throat, the other in the chest. He stumbled, but did not fall. Marney readied a fourth blade, but paused before throwing it.

Something was wrong.

Beneath the black cassock, the assassin's body was misshapen, top heavy. His back was hunched and his chest sunken. His limbs appeared overly long and painfully thin. There was no hair on his head, and his face was grotesquely deformed. The hilt of the first dagger protruded from his eye socket; it reflected red moonlight, but there was no blood, not from any of his wounds.

Silently, he began convulsing. There came a hissing sound and the alley was filled with the hot and acrid stench of dispelling magic. Violent spasms shook the assassin's body, bending his already twisted form to hideous angles. The hissing was replaced by a multitude of dull cracks, as if every bone in his body was breaking. Still, he emitted not one single cry of pain. Finally the assassin collapsed to the ground where his heaped bulk lay unmoving on the cobbles.

With the dagger still in her hand, Marney moved forwards cautiously. She inspected the remains. A knot formed in her stomach.

The souls of the dead could still talk, but even the most adept necromancer would get no information from this assassin. The creature had once been human, she was sure, but now it was not even made of flesh and blood. The cassock lay as rags upon the alley floor, and within its black folds the assassin's body had shattered into small pieces of powdery stone. Not enough of the face and body remained intact to suggest that they had ever been part of a humanoid shape.

They said that empaths could never forget, though the Timewatcher only knew Marney had tried. The situation suddenly smacked of something from a long time ago. The assassin's emotions had not been shielded to her senses; it no longer *had* any. Her magic was useless against creatures such as these. She could not feel them coming …

Her basic instincts kicked in. Spiky pulses of warning rushed up Marney's spine and stabbed into her head. From the corner of her eye she caught the swish of a cassock and the violet glint of a power stone as a second inhuman assassin rounded the corner into the alleyway. Marney rolled to one side and the dagger flew from her hand just as the assassin's handgun spat out its bullet.

CHAPTER TWO

RETROSPECTIVE

Samuel had spotted the assassin, passed close enough to see the flash of a power stone and hear the vague spitting sound made by the killer's handgun, but he did not stop to see if Marney had lived or died.

Some fifteen feet above the Great Labyrinth's cobbled ground, he ran along the ramparts atop the alley walls: slick, moss-covered walkways, flanked on either side by low and crenellated barriers. Breathing hard, his hair matted with sweat and drizzle, Samuel pushed his ageing legs with all the strength he could muster.

Samuel was an old bounty hunter and he understood well that those who allowed sentiment to dictate action did not last long anywhere in the Labyrinth. There were no loyalties, no bonds of friendship and honour in this place – not anymore. He had made headway in this chase, and wasn't about to surrender it. Marney's business was her own. Old friendships were dust to him.

In his hand, Samuel carried a spirit compass. The needle ticked and turned and steered his direction true as it tracked the life energy of his prey. The mark was a whore, young, barely eighteen. Oh, she had a name, but that meant nothing to the old bounty hunter; she was a murderer, and the reward for killing her was almost too good to be true. That was the only important detail.

With Marney out of the running, the night's work should have been child's play for Samuel. But someone must have issued a second contract on the whore; there were a bunch of amateurs running around the alleys playing at assassins. Samuel still had the advantage. Here and there, narrow bridges formed shortcuts through the Great Labyrinth by connecting one rampart to another. Like a maze upon a maze, the bridges led to places where those on the ground could not go. While the attention of these amateurs was focused on the ground, they had no reason to suspect that Samuel shadowed them from up on the ramparts – and nor would they, until it was too late.

He came to a halt as the rampart stopped at a T-junction. Down below, the alleyway on his left side came to a blind end; down on the right, the cobbled pathway led to a contained courtyard. There were no bridges at this intersection, and the rampart split into two paths. But which should he follow – east or west? Evidently, the spirit compass was also undecided. Its needle spun and shivered as it remained locked onto the whore's spirit and adjusted navigation inconclusively.

As Samuel waited, the drizzle turned to full rain, and he let it splash against his upturned face. In the humid glow of Ruby Moon, the rain-drops felt refreshing against his skin.

In the distance, Samuel could see a ghostly glow hanging over the Great Labyrinth, as though the lights of a far away land shone through the mist. It was only a trick of the night, he knew; for there was nothing out there except the alleyways that continued on forever, or so it was thought. But there *was* a place, a fabled haven that all the Labyrinth's denizens wondered about, dreamed of reaching. Far beyond the mists, in the deepest regions of the maze, there was a doorway that led to a paradise named Mother Earth. And there, the Timewatcher waited with open arms to welcome all lost souls. Every denizen dreamed of Mother Earth …

Samuel felt a sudden pang of weariness.

Old Man Sam they called him. He was a legend among bounty hunters; the deadliest man alive, some said. In truth, Old Man Sam was one of the last vestiges of a past generation. It was difficult for him to remember the strength of his youth, to remember a time when his actions had carried a sense of duty. He imagined the whore, out in the alleys, praying she could somehow escape this mess, find her way back to Labrys Town at the centre of the Great Labyrinth. Did she dream of returning to the sanctuary of her whorehouse, surrounded by the comforting glow of streetlamps and the protection of friends?

Samuel gritted his teeth and closed his eyes against the rain.

His prey tonight would never see Labrys Town again. Even if she survived Old Man Sam's gun, she was utterly lost. Sooner or later, she would stumble upon the Retrospective, and then the wild demons would have their fun with her. Better to be shot. Better to die a quick death than face the Retrospective. At least then her soul would reach Mother Earth.

The compass gave a solid *click* in Samuel's hand, and the needle shivered on a definite north-westerly direction. In the distance the glow of the mist, the promise of a far away paradise, somehow seemed to mock the bounty hunter.

Old Man Sam they called him …

He took the left turn at the T-junction. After a short distance, he crossed a bridge to a new rampart. From there, a quick series of bridges and walkways followed. Head down against the rain, Samuel zigzagged across the Great Labyrinth, and the chase continued.

By the time he caught up with the whore, some amateur assassins already had her trapped in a courtyard. Samuel crouched behind the rampart wall and furtively peered down at them through the crenellations.

The mark was clearly exhausted. She was dressed in clothes so oversized they barely stayed on her waiflike frame. Her large eyes were round with fear, and her short hair, streaked with red dye, was lank from rain. Fatigue and panic creased the pointed features of her gawky face.

Down to Samuel's left was the mouth of an alley. It was the only way in or out of the courtyard, and an assassin guarded it. He wore a priest's cassock and a wide-brimmed hat covered his face. His body was clearly deformed beneath his dress; his arms were so spindly they barely looked strong enough to carry the silver pistol in his hand. Away from the assassin, closer to the girl, stood a short, grubby man whose clothes were scarcely better than rags. Samuel recognised him and a twinge of anger flared in his chest.

Charlie Hemlock: perhaps the most venal, untrustworthy bastard in Labrys Town. More than once this snake had crossed Samuel, but lived to tell the tale. His involvement came as no surprise.

Samuel slipped his short rifle from the holster on his back, its power stone covered for stealth.

Down in the courtyard, Hemlock made a grab for the girl, but, despite her obvious exhaustion, she clearly wasn't ready to give up the fight. She screeched, clawing at Hemlock's face, dragging her fingernails down his cheek. As she broke free of him, Hemlock clutched his face and stamped his foot, uttering a stream of curses.

'Bitch!' he shouted for a finale.

The girl backed away.

The assassin remained by the alley mouth offering no help to his friend. Motionless, almost statuesque, he seemed content to watch Hemlock struggle with his lacerations. Why were they toying with their victim?

Suspicious now, he looked back to the mark.

Samuel's employer had told him a rumour about this girl – that she was a magicker, a human born with a specific magical gift. She was a changeling, and could shift her form into that of a wolf. Samuel was sceptical of such tales – nothing like a changeling had been seen in the Labyrinth for a couple of generations at least. But that Hemlock and the assassin had not yet killed the girl got him thinking: changeling blood was a potent catalyst in the art of spell-craft, and any mundane magic-user would give his right arm to procure it, however much damage his lackey took in the process. But there weren't supposed to be any magic-users left that Samuel didn't know about, and no matter what he thought of them, the ones he knew wouldn't stoop this low.

Whoever had employed Hemlock obviously wanted the whore captured alive, for some reason. Even if the rumours were true about her, she was clearly too exhausted to defend herself with any metamorphosis into a wolf. Samuel guessed that the assassin's pistol was loaded with some kind of magical ammunition designed to incarcerate her, and that was what triggered his suspicion. The assassin had a clear view of the whore, the power stone on his weapon was primed and glowing, yet he hadn't taken the shot. Even a child couldn't miss from that distance. Why was he waiting?

In his long years in the Labyrinth, Samuel had witnessed many strange and terrible things, and nothing was ever as it seemed. Whatever orders Hemlock and the assassin were under, the instructions for Samuel's contract were clear: kill the whore. Destroy her remains.

Hemlock had recovered somewhat from his pain, but four deep gouges lined his cheek. He began goading his captive.

'Don't be like that, Peppercorn,' he wheedled. 'We don't want to hurt you, honest.' The lie dripped from his mouth like bile.

'Just let me go,' the girl said, in a shaky voice. 'I-I can pay you.'

Hemlock chuckled with smug satisfaction. 'Why would I want that? We're all friends here. You should be more trusting.'

The girl retreated until her back was pressed up against the wall opposite Samuel's position, thus making herself a perfect target. Samuel slid the barrel of his rifle through the crenellations. With his thumb, he primed the power stone set behind the barrel. It gave a small whine, and its violet glow struggled to shine through the thick metal gauze covering it. Old Man Sam peered down the sight at his target.

'Don't be shy,' Hemlock said. 'We could have some fun.'

Samuel's weapon was a police issue rifle. Ordinarily its power stone held such a high-grade thaumaturgic charge that it could spit out a thumb-sized metal slug with enough force to take off a man's arm. But Samuel had loaded his weapon with ammunition that packed a little extra something, certainly not police issue: fire-bullets. One round would incinerate the mark entirely. Proof of kill would be a box of ashes.

'Leave me alone!' the girl sobbed.

The magazine only held four rounds, and that allowed Samuel one miss. Four shots, three kills: the girl, the assassin, and Charlie Hemlock he would save until last. The fire magic would destroy all evidence.

With steadying breaths, Samuel began squeezing the trigger.

'I haven't done you any harm!' the whore pleaded.

Hemlock laughed.

Samuel's finger relaxed.

Strange: the inclination to honour his contract was dulling like the passion of an argument regretted in the cold light of day. All he had to do was pull the trigger, release a burst of thaumaturgy, and the bounty was his. But when he tried again, he still could not summon the will to shoot the girl, and he grew angry with himself.

Nothing was ever as it seemed ...

Then, as smooth as spider silk, a voice whispered inside Samuel's head: *Leave the girl alone, Old Man.*

Marney!

Samuel recognised her voice as easily as his own. Alive and well, the empath was somewhere close, tampering with his emotive reactions.

Her tones, clear and strong, filled his mind once again: *There's more to this situation than you want to acknowledge.*

Samuel whispered a curse.

Down in the courtyard, Marney appeared from the alley mouth. Dressed in simple black jersey and trousers, she crept up behind the assassin, silently. Around her torso was her baldric of throwing daggers – one was already in her hand. She threw it at the assassin. It stabbed into the base of his skull. The man gave no cry of pain or alarm, but instead made a hissing noise as he began to jerk spasmodically. There came a series of dull *pops*, and to Samuel's astonishment, the assassin collapsed with a stony sound as if he had broken apart. His cassock lay heaped on the floor as though his body had fallen through a trapdoor.

Stay where you are, Old Man, Marney's voice said. *Whatever happens, whatever you see, do not show yourself.*

Samuel did as he was told. Not that he had a choice; Marney had his emotions in the palm of her hand.

All this time, Hemlock had not reacted. He was apparently unsurprised by Marney's arrival, and amused. He smiled at the crumpled ruins of his companion, and then at the empath. The girl had hunkered down on the floor, trembling against the wall. Samuel did nothing but watch them all.

'Hello, Marney,' Hemlock said. 'For a moment there I thought we'd lost you.'

'Shut up, Charlie,' Marney snapped, coming to stand within a few feet of him. 'I know who you're working for.'

'Good for you.'

Hemlock held his ground, but Samuel could tell his easy manner was a façade. The snake was stalling for time. His shifty gaze darted around the courtyard, as if looking for something that should be there.

'You know, I'm sure you want some explanations,' he said to Marney. He touched a hand to his cheek wounds and looked at the blood on his palm. 'Make it worth my while, and maybe I'll help.'

'I already have what I need.' Samuel detected a touch of desperation in Marney's voice. 'You have no idea who you're involved with, Charlie. This is low, even by your standards.'

'You think so?' Hemlock shrugged. 'I've been lower. Besides—'

He never finished the sentence. Marney sprang forwards and rammed the palm of her hand into his face. There was a spark of empathic energy, and Hemlock fell flat on his back, his senses scrambled.

The girl had risen from the floor by this time. She looked confused and scared, but she did not shy away as Marney approached her. In voices too low for Samuel to pick up, they spoke.

The old bounty hunter suddenly remembered the rifle in his hands. The grip was coarse and familiar against his skin, the black metal cold, the power stone glowing beneath its cover. Whether Marney's influence over him still lingered, he could not say, but he remained hidden up on the rampart, just as she commanded.

What had she discovered?

After a few moments, Marney stepped forwards and, to Samuel's surprise, pulled the whore into a kiss. There was another, softer, flash of energy, and the girl gasped, staggering backwards. Several heartbeats passed, and then Marney let the girl flee the courtyard. The slaps of her bare feet on slick cobbles disappeared into the gloom – along with Samuel's bounty.

Marney looked up at the ramparts. Her expression was challenging. Even though Samuel knew it was too murky for her to see him, somehow her eyes still burned into his.

It's been a long time, Samuel, her voice said in his mind. *How are you?*

It seemed pointless now to continue the conversation mentally, but Samuel obliged the empath's wishes. He did not, however, deactivate the power stone on his weapon.

That whore is a murderer, he thought back angrily.

That whore *has a name,* Marney countered, just as hotly. *Clara. Remember it!*

What are you doing, Marney?

I could ask you the same thing. Clara's a changeling. She's a magicker, Old Man. Did you know that?

Get to the point, Samuel snapped.

Marney shook her head and moved to Hemlock's unconscious form lying on the courtyard floor. She checked him over, and then sat on his chest, looking down at his face.

Do you ever think about the old days, Samuel?

What?

Do you remember life before the Genii War, before the Aelfir dis-appeared? Marney slipped a dagger from the baldric and toyed with it between her fingers. *Don't tell me you've forgotten about that as well as your duty.*

Her voice carried a measure of dark mirth. Samuel did not care for the way it felt in his head.

Where are you going with this, Marney?

Charlie Hemlock, she replied and held the slim dagger as though it were a pencil. *He has a new paymaster. Nothing surprising there, I sup-pose – whoever's paying the most with Charlie, right? But this time he's bitten off more than he can chew.*

And what has this to do with me?

Everything. You see, Samuel, Charlie's been employed by an old friend of ours.

Marney then leant forwards and used the dagger to cut something into Hemlock's forehead. Even with younger eyes, it would have been impossible for Samuel to see at that distance what she had carved into Hemlock's skin.

In Samuel's pocket, the spirit compass ticked as it continued to track the whore's life energy.

What have you found? he demanded. *Who's Hemlock working for?*

When she replied, Marney's anxiety scratched the inside of Samuel's skull. *The Genii War spawned so many myths, stories that faded like echoes until the truth was utterly forgotten. But I remember the truth, Old Man, and I remember the promises we made. Perhaps you should too.*

She sat back and admired her handiwork. Hemlock's face was smeared with blood that ran down the side of his face.

Samuel felt a shift in the air, a sudden temperature drop.

We sacrificed so much to win the war against Spiral, Marney said, *but if we'd lost, it would have been much, much worse.* She rose and stepped back from Hemlock's body. *I want Charlie Hemlock to understand that. I want him to know what his new employer is capable of.*

The temperature continued to drop, dispelling the humidity of Ruby Moon. Samuel's breath began to rise in clouds. On the courtyard floor, Hemlock's body shimmered, darkening as if drawing the very shadows to it. A breeze picked up bringing with it a sense of hopelessness and the stench of corruption. Samuel understood then that Marney had carved a sigil into Hemlock's forehead, a symbol of summoning.

What madness is this, Marney?

He deserves no better, Samuel, she said calmly. *I'm giving Charlie to the Orphan.*

Samuel's grip tightened on his rifle.

Of all people, Marney understood what terrible things dwelt within the Retrospective. The Orphan – the blood harvester. Summoning such a demon could see them all swallowed into oblivion. But the darkness was already gathering; Hemlock's facial features were now indistinguishable, as if shrouded. There was no stopping the summons. The Retrospective was coming.

I won't be part of this, Samuel told Marney angrily.

You already are! Marney snapped. She thrust out a hand, pointing to the heaped bulk of the dead assassin lying by the courtyard's exit. *That thing isn't human, Samuel. It's a golem!*

What?

That made no sense to Samuel. Golems were facile servants, human victims whose flesh and blood and bone had been converted to stone by the darkest of magics. But a magic-user skilled enough to create a golem hadn't been seen in the Labyrinth for decades, not since …

No. Samuel's thought was as chilling as the snake that slithered around his spine. *That's impossible, Marney.*

Remember your promise, Old Man, she said. *Follow Clara. You need to keep her close.*

The air behind Marney shimmered and distorted, and from the distortion shot a flash of light that slammed into Marney's back. She fell to her knees with a cry. There was a sound like the howl of bitter wind, and Marney's voice was choked off as her body hardened to ice.

The distortion shattered in the air like glass, collapsing to reveal a square portal, a doorway to somewhere else from which sterile light spilled onto the cobbles of the courtyard. Four disfigured golems dressed in cassocks stumbled from the portal and grabbed Marney's frozen body.

Behind the golems, Samuel saw a man bathed in the light of a silver chamber, standing before what looked to be some kind of tree. With long, white hair and pale skin, he too was dressed in the black cassock of a priest. He watched with dispassionate eyes as his servants carried the empath back to him.

Samuel stood on the rampart and aimed his rifle. But he was too slow. The golems had already taken the empath through to the silver chamber, and, before he could fire, the portal closed with a swirl of distorted air. Marney was gone.

Samuel stared into empty space, not quite believing what he had witnessed.

He flinched as a small, child-like form on the courtyard floor caught his eye. A little boy had appeared, crouching over Hemlock's body, short fingers clawing at his clothes. The boy and Hemlock quickly dissipated, turning to shadow that seeped into the cobbles like oil drawn into cracks in the ground.

The Retrospective had been and gone, and the Orphan had claimed its prize.

The night's humidity returned and pressed in on Samuel. In his pocket, the spirit compass vibrated. He fished it out. The needle was still locked onto the girl. There was only one option left to Old Man Sam now.

He followed her.

CHAPTER THREE

LABRYS TOWN

People disappeared in the Great Labyrinth, out in the deep maze where the Retrospective roamed. Wild demons hid between the alley walls like spiders waiting for the tingle of flies on their webs. The demons always welcomed fresh meat, and once they had picked the bones of their victims clean of flesh, they reserved the spirits as offerings to the lowest age of the Retrospective: Oldest Place, where Spiral, the Lord of the Genii, was said to feast upon the souls of the dead.

Out in the Great Labyrinth Clara had thought she would die – if not from an assassin's gun, then by the teeth and claws of wild demons. She had feared her soul was destined for the fire and poison of Oldest Place, and the endless hunger of the Genii Lord Spiral. She had given up hope of ever reaching the paradise of Mother Earth – until she had been kissed by a guardian angel.

By the time Clara left the alleyways, the rain was constant, humid and warm. She felt light-headed and disorientated. Exhaustion numbed the burning in her leg muscles, and nauseating pangs of hunger griped at her stomach. Her throat was parched and cracked; her feet were bare and bleeding.

She entered a wide and square courtyard where two stubby pillars of stone rose from the floor like broken fangs. On the far side of the courtyard, the high boundary wall loomed over her. A hundred feet tall, sheer and impossible to scale, the boundary wall surrounded Labrys Town entirely, and kept it segregated from the Great Labyrinth, protected it from the Retrospective. From where she was, there appeared no way through to the civilised sanctuary on the other side. Clara tried to steady her breathing and gain some focus.

She looked around the courtyard, then focused on the two stubby pillars positioned barely ten feet apart. Clara had learned enough about the old days to know that at one time the pillars had connected to form a tall archway. Forty years ago, long before she was born, this courtyard had been a checkpoint, and the archway had been a portal that led to the doorways of the Great Labyrinth through which the denizens journeyed to the Houses of the Aelfir.

There were many such checkpoints located around the boundary wall, but the entrances to them all had been sealed shut, back when the Genii War ended. Each of the portals had been broken, smashed, and all paths to the realms outside the Great Labyrinth had been destroyed.

Standing in the shadow of the boundary wall, Clara could just make out where the entrance to this courtyard had once been. The bricks were a lighter shade of black, forming a square – large enough for a tram to pass through. The tracks cut into the cobbles were rusty from disuse and disappeared beneath the wall that was undoubtedly solid and seemingly impassable.

As warm rain soaked her, a strange calm descended on Clara. She knew what she had to do next, though she could hardly fathom how she knew it.

Feeling almost as though her actions belonged to someone else, she stepped forwards and placed a hand against the wall where the former entranceway had been. Immediately, she felt heat against her palm that was at once alien yet familiar. Beneath her hand, the mortar between the bricks began to emit a dull purple glow that spread to form a maze-like pattern. Clara felt a vibration, as though mechanisms were turning deep within the brickwork. The purple glow receded and, with a low rumble, a section of the wall depressed and slid to one side, revealing a slim but open doorway.

Her skin prickled. She had heard rumours that there were secret entrances to the Great Labyrinth hidden in the boundary wall, but she had never thought they were real. Until now.

Clara licked her lips nervously and stepped through the opening.

She stood on a narrow path which ran along the boundary wall, skirting the backs of terraced buildings. Directly ahead of her, and crossing the path, the tramline continued along a fat alley that led out onto the streets of Labrys Town. The slim doorway rumbled shut behind Clara, showing no sign that it had ever been there. At last she felt in control of herself, as though she could breathe for the first time.

She turned her face up to the rain and closed her eyes.

The distant noise and scents of life stroked Clara's heightened senses: music and buzzing voices whispered in her ears; a vague stale and dank smell filled her nostrils. She had escaped the dangers of the Great Labyrinth's alleyways. She had been saved by an old woman – a stranger called Marney, a magicker, an empath – and her kiss had shown Clara an impossible way home. Though what *home* now meant was anyone's guess.

Body drenched and foot sore, she followed the alley ahead, happy to discover she had arrived in the northern part of Labrys Town. Clara took a furtive glance from the alley entrance to ensure the way was clear, and then stepped out onto the rain-soaked cobbles of Head Street.

She began walking, her footsteps uncertain. Above, the clouds parted to reveal the full orb of Ruby Moon. The night was still young. There were at least another few hours before Silver Moon would chase its sibling away with blue-grey light. Then the humidity would begin to freshen, grow cooler, colder, until the dawning sun brought the warmth of the day.

Head Street was divided by two shining tramlines. Along its pavements lampposts spilled violet light onto the ground. But like much of Labrys Town it was mostly asleep. The terraced stores and businesses were darkened, the lights of their signs dead for the night. On the opposite side of the street was the confined passage of Elder Lane which cut between a baker's and a confectioner's, and led to the back alleys. Clara stopped to stare down it.

The clouds obscured Ruby Moon once more, and the rain fell harder than before – heavy droplets that splashed upon the street and ran down Clara's face. She heard the rumble of an approaching tram, saw its lights cresting a rise, glaring through the downpour, heading towards her. Hiding in the gloom of a butcher's doorway, Clara was suddenly aware of how disgusting she smelt. Somehow it completed the night's misery. Her over-sized clothes were no better than rags. They were torn, soaked by rain that had only partly flushed away the blood encrusted in the thread – these clothes belonged to a dead man, a man she had slaughtered.

The taste of his blood still lingered in her mouth, the ghost of his screams echoed in her ears, yet she had never even known his name.

Lights glared. The rumbling reached a crescendo. The tram trundled by with sparks of purple thaumaturgy snapping from the power line above it. Clara saw a few nondescript passengers seated inside the carriage, and then the tram had gone. The power line swayed gently in its wake. Stillness returned. Breaking cover, she stepped out into the downpour and, quickly crossing Head Street, ducked into the gloom of Elder Lane.

It was safer to remain unseen, and the back alleys of Labrys Town afforded the best places to hide. But staying unseen in this town wasn't easy. Elder Lane wove between tall and twisted shop buildings, as dark now as those on Head Street. Every so often, Clara passed hemispheres of clear glass fixed to the walls. These observation devices, simply called 'eyes' by most people, were filled with a milky fluid that gave them the appearance of rheumy eyeballs. They were scattered throughout the streets, lanes and alleys, and there was no telling when the eyes were watching you. In Labrys Town the way to remain unseen was to not draw attention to yourself.

Clara moved as fast as she was able. As fast as she dared.

She turned off Elder Lane into Market Square and headed across the open ground towards the other side. The metal shutters of storage lock-ups were closed and locked for the night, the skeletons of empty barrows and stalls stood in front of them. Clara glanced nervously at a stone pillar standing proud at the square's centre, with a wooden bench surrounding its base. Around the top of the pillar were five eyes capable of seeing every angle of the square. Cautiously, she jogged past and headed out into a narrow lane that had no name.

A figure lying prone on a shop doorstep did not stir as she passed. A dim light shone from within a dispensary, but no one could be seen working inside.

A wave of nausea and dizziness threatened to swamp Clara. She placed a hand against a shop window to steady herself and took several deep breaths.

Ahead of Clara, a Chapel of the Timewatcher lit the dimness with soft blue light. The doors to the chapels and churches of Labrys Town were always open to both the faithful and those seeking sanctuary. Clara was tempted to slip inside its welcoming entrance, to sleep till morning under the protective gaze of the Timewatcher. But this was not the time for rest.

Marney's kiss had altered Clara. Somehow, it had transferred a map of the Great Labyrinth into her head, shown her how to navigate the twists and turns of its alleyways. But the empath had left something else behind, too, a presence of some kind ... a message? Clara could feel it, drifting, dormant in her mind like a locked box without a key. A box of secrets? Clara didn't understand why Marney had saved her, or what she had done to her. Clara needed a safe haven to rest and make sense of everything – somewhere more familiar than a random place of worship.

Her dizziness passing, Clara continued on, leaving the Chapel of the Timewatcher and the promise of its sanctuary behind.

She cut through a plaza full of gambling houses and weapon-smiths, and then across a communal garden where she paused to drink cool water from a fountain. She flinched as the angry shouts of a brawl, not too far away, reached her ears. Thankfully, the shouts did not come from the direction she was headed.

After passing a row of lodging houses, she turned left into another alley and slowed to a walk. Reaching the end of the alley, Clara furtively peered out onto Green Glass Row, the busiest street in Labrys Town – especially at night.

The beat of music and the buzz of voices spilled from the open doors and misted windows of clubs and taverns. The smell of sweat and alcohol was strong and bitter in the air. Though rain had lessened the activity on the street, several denizens had gathered under umbrellas and darted through the downpour, eager to be somewhere drier. A tram stopped, and a group of young men disembarked. They laughed and joked and jostled one another as they passed the scrutiny of the big doorman of a nightclub called the Lazy House. Having ushered them in, the doorman then resumed his conversation with two girls who were sheltering under the club's awning.

The five-storey Lazy House wasn't just a nightclub; it was also a whorehouse, and Clara was one of its employees. Clara knew the door-man, Roma, at least as much as she wanted to. She vaguely recognised the girls he spoke with, but they were streetwalkers, not employed by Clara's boss.

It had been three days since Charlie Hemlock had first kidnapped her; three days she had been missing. There would be repercussions, questions she couldn't answer, waiting inside the Lazy House. Exhausted, mentally and physically, Clara could only deal with one step at a time. Step one – she must get to the safety of her room, where she could think and make sense of the night, her own private sanctuary where she could find a little peace of mind. However, she needed to get there without being seen by Roma, without having to walk across a busy bar and dance floor. She ducked back into the shadows as a couple, giggling beneath an umbrella, hurried past.

The door to the Lazy House opened, and someone inside spoke to Roma. While he was turned away from them, the streetwalkers moved off, and Clara seized her chance. She left the alley, ran across Green Glass Row and down the side of the nightclub building to the rear. To her relief she found a back door open and unattended. She slipped inside to a darkened hallway, and crept up the stairs which vibrated from the sound of music pounding through the walls.

Up on the second floor, the telltale sounds of whores plying their trade came from behind closed doors. The place reeked of alcohol and sex. Clara headed for her room, praying that no one would hear her, that no door would suddenly open to catch her with a bright glare of accusing light. But there was already a streak of illumination on the hallway carpet coming from one door that was open just a crack. With caution and a thudding heart, Clara sneaked up to it and peered through.

She saw two policemen standing in the bedroom beyond. Obviously not here for pleasure, they wore the dark uniforms of the street patrols. Short rifles hung from their shoulders, and long batons were holstered at their waists. Their helmets completely concealed their heads and faces in bowls of black glass: receptor helmets, attuned to the eye devices on the streets.

One of them spoke, his voice muffled. 'You know why we're here?'

'Yeah,' replied a girl's voice. 'I know why you're here.'

Although Clara could not see the speaker, she recognised the voice as that of her work colleague, Willow.

The other policeman took over, 'We're going to ask you some questions, and I needn't tell you the seriousness of withholding information.'

'Withholding information?' Willow chuckled dryly. 'I was there when you arrested Fat Jacob. You think I want to be treated like that?'

Fat Jacob arrested? He was the owner of the Lazy House, and a vicious master whom all the girls did their best to steer clear of.

Willow continued, 'Good riddance is what I say. I hope it's as bad as it gets for that fat bastard. I hope you took him to the Nightshade for the Resident to deal with.'

'Miss Willow,' said the first policeman, 'you've confirmed Miss Clara has been missing for three days now. Any further information you might have will help our search.'

'I've only heard the rumour,' said Willow. 'Fat Jacob sold her to that arsehole Charlie Hemlock. It must be true or I don't suppose you'd be here.'

'Quite. Do you know why she was sold?'

Willow's only response was a snort.

Clara understood why. Willow knew as well as any that Fat Jacob's contempt for his employees showed itself in the *acts* he sometimes forced them to perform. Selling off one of his girls would mean nothing more to him than extra beer money in his pocket.

'Have you any idea of Charlie Hemlock's whereabouts?'

Willow scoffed. 'Your guess is as good as mine.'

He's dead in the Great Labyrinth, with any luck, Clara thought.

The policeman continued, 'Then do you have any information on who he is working for?'

'Whoever pays the best,' Willow said with finality. 'This *is* Charlie Hemlock we're talking about …'

Clara had heard enough. She moved past Willow's room and slipped into her own.

The lights of Green Glass Row glowed through the window like an early morning haze and illuminated the chaos of Clara's room. When people disappeared in Labrys Town, they rarely resurfaced. The other whores of the Lazy House obviously thought Clara would never return, and her room had been turned over by scavengers. What remained of her clothes and belongings lay strewn across the floor. Her colleagues had helped themselves to everything that was worth selling, it seemed. But they were welcome to it all – apart from the one thing she needed now.

Clara stepped through the mess of clothes and books, and onto her bed, careful to limit the creaking of the springs in the mattress. Reaching up, she pulled free the grille of a vent above the bed, pushed her arm inside and searched around until her fingers closed on a small tin taped to the vent's ceiling. Clara took it out and stepped back down onto the floor.

The tin was filled with little white tablets. She took one and popped it into her mouth. The taste was bitter as she chewed; her tongue and throat prickled as she swallowed. Almost immediately, a sense of calm descended, and Clara felt a little strength returning. Her thoughts became less cloudy. She closed her eyes and felt a little safer.

Peppercorn Clara: she was a wild ride, they joked; only a real man could survive a night with her. Clara's clients never realised how close they were to the madness of magic; that only her medication prevented a monster escaping its cage—

'What are you doing in here?'

The ceiling lamp glared into life, bathing the room in light. Clara wheeled around to be confronted by a patrolwoman. She stood in the doorway, the black glass of her receptor helmet glinting like the eye of a giant insect. Clara slipped the medicine tin into the pocket of her ill-fitting trousers, fully aware of the baton in the patrolwoman's hand.

'Name?' the officer demanded.

'Uh – Rosa.' The lie came quickly. 'I was just – you know – seeing if there was anything left in here worth taking.'

The patrolwoman was quiet for a moment, and Clara prayed she would find nothing suspicious about her drenched and oddly-matched clothes and bare feet. But she obviously knew the Lazy House catered for most fetishes, and finally said, 'We're investigating the activities of your employer, Miss Rosa. You might want to make yourself available for questioning.'

'Oh, no problem,' Clara said brightly. 'I'll be downstairs if you need me.'

The patrolwoman allowed her to leave the room. But as Clara hurried towards the stairs, the door to Willow's room opened and the other two policemen emerged, followed by Willow herself.

Willow blinked. 'Clara!' she blurted. 'You're alive ...'

Clara bolted down the stairs.

Shouts and heavy footfalls followed her.

The backdoor was now blocked by a fourth police officer. Clara dodged his grabbing hand and burst through the door to the main nightclub instead. Pounding music and flashing lights hit her as if she had run into a wall; the humidity, the stench of bodies, like a thick fluid to swim through.

The Lazy House was in full swing.

Dancers, drunk or high on drugs, swore at Clara, pushed and slapped her, as she clawed a path through the bodies to the other side of the club. As she ran up a wide staircase she saw two of the patrolmen behind her, struggling to follow her through the dancing sea. Then she was through the entrance doors, across the foyer, out onto Green Glass Row ... and straight into the wide chest of Roma.

'Clara?' The doorman caught her by the arms. 'I thought you were dead.'

'Another time, Roma,' Clara panted. 'I have to go.'

'Hey!' he gripped her arms tighter. 'The police are asking about you. Fat Jacob's been arrested. What's going on?'

Through the doors to the Lazy House, Clara could see receptor helmets entering the foyer. Her panic rose. 'Well, it's like this, Roma—' and she kneed him hard in the groin.

The big doorman groaned as he doubled over, and Clara ran into the rain, onto Green Glass Row, with no idea where she was headed.

She hadn't run very far when the patrolwoman appeared from the side of the Lazy House and smacked a baton into her legs. Clara yelled in pain and collapsed onto the wet cobbles in a skidding heap. The patrolwoman pounced, pinning Clara to the ground, roughly cuffing her hands behind her back.

HUNTING TREASURE

The war against Spiral had been raging for two years, during which the Merchants' Guild of Labrys Town had suffered greatly. But Mr Taffin was doing better than ever.

It wasn't as though he was without concern or sympathy for the situation – far from it. He was thankful that Spiral's Genii, and the legions under their command, had thus far been unable to reach the Great Labyrinth; but he regretted that while the threat of them doing so remained, the Labyrinth in its entirety had been isolated and all trade with the realms beyond the boundary walls had ceased. However, unlike most other traders, Mr Taffin did not rely on the import and export industry shared with the Houses of the Aelfir. His business was to provide a service for the merchants of Labrys Town themselves.

When the tram on which he rode arrived in the western district, Mr Taffin disembarked and immediately summoned a rickshaw. The driver was a tall and fit-looking youth, who seemed eager to serve as he pulled his cart over to his client. Mr Taffin climbed aboard, sighing as he sank into the plush, cushioned seat.

'Linker Lane,' he ordered, giving the footrest a tap with his crystal-topped cane. 'Make good time, my lad, and there's a tip in it for you.'

'Yes, sir!'

Mr Taffin smiled as the driver's young muscles bunched, and the rickshaw set off at a pace.

Some denizens would have it that Mr Taffin was a greedy profiteer, and worse besides. But he paid no mind to the insults of jealousy. He could not help it if the war had been kind to him, and his particular business had flourished because of it. What was he supposed to do? Apologise? Close down? No, Mr Taffin would ride the good times as he had the bad. War had not made him so rich that he could afford apartments here in the plush west side of town, among the wealthiest merchants; but it had sufficiently elevated his social standing that he could sit in the rickshaw, unashamedly proud, and with his head held high.

The streets of the western district were busy under the afternoon sun, much busier than they would have been if not for the war. Rich merchants, with little else to do these days, strolled with their children and wives, pretending that all was well in their world. Many of them glared at Mr Taffin as he passed. Mr Taffin acknowledged their disgruntlement by tapping a finger to the brim of his hat and offering a knowing smile.

Let them stare at him, the *greedy profiteer* from the back alleys of the northern district, in his fine, tailored suit, carrying a crystal-topped cane; let these *fellow traders*, with their crumbling empires and dwindling riches, see him travelling among them as an equal. Let them think what they wanted. When the morning came, many of them would come crawling to his doorstep, seeking business under the cover of the early hours. Mr Taffin would feel no shame at his good fortune, even if he had been given a helping hand by those who outranked even the most loftily positioned merchants.

When the rickshaw reached its destination, Mr Taffin handed the driver twenty Labyrinth pounds and took particular pleasure in the young man's reaction when he declined to take the change due. The rickshaw set off in search of a fresh customer, and Mr Taffin walked down Linker Lane with a jaunty stride.

His cane ticking against the cobbles with each step, he passed quaint tearooms and boutiques, and walked on until he reached the grimy exterior of an apothecary's called Master Remedies. A bell jingled when Taffin opened the door. Inside he was greeted by the sickly-sweet smells of potions and medicines that cast a heady atmosphere throughout the room. The shop was small and dingy, the sun struggling to penetrate the thick dirt on the windows. Mr Taffin was pleased – though not surprised – to find he was the only customer present.

'Ah, my good Master Gene,' he said brightly to the shopkeeper standing behind the counter. 'I trust the afternoon finds you well?'

'Mustn't complain, Mr Taffin,' Gene said in that usual lacklustre way of his. He stared at Mr Taffin through wire-framed spectacles, making no attempt to enquire after his sole customer's well-being or to further the conversation in any way whatsoever. Then he added, 'We make the most of what we have during such times.'

'Indeed, indeed, Master Gene – the sun still rises in the morning, and all of that.'

'Ah, but it shines brighter for some than others, eh?'

Mr Taffin tapped his nose and smiled knowingly, but the shopkeeper resumed staring at him.

A small and elderly man, Gene the apothecary always presented a bedraggled appearance. His shirt was never quite white, his waistcoat a little threadbare, and the wisps of his thinning hair always seemed in need of a cut or a good combing. Truth be told, the elderly apothecary was a miserable wretch who set Mr Taffin's teeth on edge; so, as his grey eyes continued to stare out through his wire-framed spectacles, Mr Taffin looked around at the display of ornate bottles filled with colourful liquids, and cleared his throat before getting down to business.

'Master Gene,' he said, licking his lips, 'I was led to believe that our – ah – *benefactors* have left a package with you for my attention?'

A tight smile appeared on Gene's wrinkled face. 'If you would be so kind, Mr Taffin, please lock the door.'

'Of course.'

Mr Taffin kept a sour expression at bay as he turned to lock the shop door. It might have been a mystery to some how one so miserable as the apothecary, and his shabby little shop with its dirty windows and dusty floor, had managed to stay in business in such an expensive area as the western district – especially when he showed so little interest in his clientele and struggled to express even the smallest of civilities. But to Mr Taffin there was no mystery. He supposed – though he was loath to admit it – that he and Gene were fellow opportunists, and their common employers had ensured the war had been kind to both their businesses.

With the door locked, and the shop sign turned to 'Closed', Mr Taffin stepped up to the counter with a fresh smile. From the inside pocket of his suit jacket he produced an envelope, bulging with money, which he placed upon the countertop and slid towards Gene.

'For your efforts,' he said with a wink.

Gene looked at the envelope, but did not move.

'Count it, if you wish,' Mr Taffin chuckled. 'But I assure you, Master Gene, it is all there, as usual.'

Without a word, the apothecary took the envelope, stuffed it beneath his waistcoat, and then flipped back the hatch in the countertop. 'You remember the room?' he said, standing to one side.

'How could I forget?' Mr Taffin said, and stepped through. 'Thank you.'

Glad to leave the miserable old apothecary behind, Mr Taffin walked through a door behind the counter and entered a short hallway. The first door on his left opened on a stuffy and dim storage room, where boxes of ingredients and bottles of liquids decorated the shelves. It smelled as sickly-sweet as the shop. There he found the man waiting for him, a man sitting upon packing crates. He wore a long coat and a wide-brimmed hat that concealed his face so completely in shadows that Mr Taffin could not make out a single feature. But what was easy to see was the short rifle lying across the man's lap, power stone primed and glowing.

'A pleasure to meet with you again,' Mr Taffin volunteered, a little nervously. 'I trust you have been well?'

The man remained silent, and Mr Taffin's gaze moved on to where a flat and square package wrapped in brown paper rested upon a crate. Mr Taffin's eyes lingered upon it.

'Is that for me?' he asked, knowing full well that it was. 'It is, perhaps, a new consignment of the *merchant's poison of choice*?' He rocked back on his heels, chuckling at his witticism.

'Shut up, Taffin,' the man snapped, 'before I smack that smug look off your face.'

There had been many occasions on which Mr Taffin had met this man with the shadowed face. As always, his blunt manner convinced Mr Taffin to grip his cane tightly and look at the floor.

'Now,' said the man. 'You say you have new information, so let's hear it.'

'Ah – yes …'

Dealing with the agents of the Relic Guild was a dangerous business.

They were a tricky bunch, as humourless as they were merciless. No one knew their real identities, but every denizen of Labrys Town understood that you didn't mess with the Relic Guild, and you gave its agents a wide berth – if you could. Mr Taffin's business was not exactly legal, and not all his clients were wealthy merchants. He often dealt with seedier characters from the underworld, and, from time to time, he heard them speaking of interesting things. Of course, they would kill him in a second if they knew he was an informant, but the Relic Guild served the highest authority in Labrys Town, and they ensured Mr Taffin's risks were very well recompensed.

'I have a client,' he told the shrouded agent of the Relic Guild. 'He is an alchemist who has fallen upon hard times since the war began. He often comes to me for … *escape*. Yesterday, I overheard him speaking about a job that has come his way. You have, perhaps, heard of an infamous treasure hunter named Carrick?'

'Yes, I know him,' said the agent.

'It would seem this Carrick and his team of treasure hunters recently procured passage to an Aelfirian House, and—'

'Wait!' The Relic Guild agent sat forward, but still his face remained hidden in the shadows cast by the brim of his hat. 'They *left* the Labyrinth?'

'And returned, or so I'm told.'

'The portals are guarded, Taffin. No one's supposed to get out into the Great Labyrinth. How did they manage it?'

'I thought you might ask that,' Mr Taffin replied, 'but sadly I cannot say. My client did not seem to know.'

The man was quiet for a moment, and then sat back with a grunt of displeasure. 'Go on.'

'From what I can gather, when Carrick returned, it was with an Aelfirian artefact of some value. What it is, I do not know, but I can tell you that a buyer has already been found for it, and this buyer has employed my client, the alchemist, to validate the artefact's magical properties.'

'Details, Taffin,' the agent demanded. 'The transaction. When and where?'

'Ah, that I *do* know. Tomorrow night, during the first hour of Silver

Moon, the sale is due to take place at Chaney's Den, a tavern in the eastern district.'

Another quiet moment passed, and the agent tapped the barrel of his rifle against his thighs. 'I want names,' he said. 'Every denizen involved with Carrick's team.'

'Here again, I cannot be of much help,' Mr Taffin replied. He smiled. 'But it hardly matters – from what I've heard, Carrick was the only member of the treasure hunters to survive the excursion.'

The agent scoffed. 'And I suppose you don't know the name of the buyer, either?'

'I have told you everything I know,' Mr Taffin assured him. His eyes flickered to the brown paper package again.

'I doubt that,' the agent growled. He deactivated the rifle's power stone with his thumb and slid the weapon into a holster upon his back. 'But for your sake, I hope you've told me enough.' He then snatched up the package from the crate beside him and threw it at Taffin, who caught it clumsily. 'Now take your drugs and get out.'

'Much obliged,' Mr Taffin said, giving a quick bow. He turned to the door, relieved that he would soon be out of the Relic Guild agent's company, and he clutched the package to his chest, protectively, triumphantly.

'Oh,' he said from the doorway. 'Please relay my gratitude to the Resident, won't you?'

But the shadowed agent had disappeared.

CHAPTER FOUR

NIGHTSHADE

Inside the police building in the northern district of Labrys Town, Clara sat alone in an interrogation room. It was a cold room, intimidating – its floor, walls and ceiling all made of smooth grey stone. Clara faced a door that was closed and locked, and lacked windows. A single eye was fixed to the wall to her left. The milky fluid stirred gently inside it: a sure sign that the eye was active, watching Clara with a piercing stare.

She sat on an uncomfortable metal chair before a metal table. Her hands were in her lap, her wrists bound by thick cuffs, and rain water dripped from her ill-fitting clothes. On the opposite side of the table were two more chairs; these were made of wood with padded backs and seats. Deliberately set up like an unwanted guest, Clara kept her expression neutral for the eye on the wall, though she rubbed at the ache where the patrolwoman's baton had bruised her thigh.

She had only wanted to get her medicine, to change out of a dead man's clothes, and then to try and make sense of the last few nights' events. Instead, in the space of an hour, she had escaped the Great Labyrinth only to be caught by the police. Where was her mysterious guardian angel now?

Marney's kiss still tingled upon Clara's lips.

At least she had got as far as taking her medicine; at least she had some control over the inner monster … for a while.

The door opened. A man and woman entered the interrogation room. The woman was street patrol. Stocky and broad, she carried her receptor helmet under one arm. Her hair was shaved close to the scalp, her eyes were dark and humourless. Clara recognised her scent – she was the one who had accosted her outside the Lazy House. The baton hung at the officer's waist, but she carried no gun.

The man, however, had a pistol holstered at his hip. His receding hair was slicked back, and he wore round glasses, the lenses of which were tinted enough to hide the colour of his eyes. The skin of his angular face was as tight and smooth as the press of his pristine uniform. He carried an air of authority, and Clara knew who he was: Captain Jeter, the head of the Labrys Town Police Force.

Clara clamped her jaw and squeezed her hands into fists in her lap. She had endured plenty of run-ins with the police in her time, but never had she gained the attention of the captain.

Jeter slipped Clara's medicine tin from his pocket and rattled the tablets inside before placing it on the table with a crisp snap. He then took a seat while the policewoman remained standing beside him.

'Peppercorn Clara,' he said. His voice was low, soft almost. 'You have quite the reputation.'

'So I hear,' Clara said as casually as she could.

Jeter offered a small, cold smile. The policewoman simply stared at Clara, almost certainly contemptuous of her profession.

Jeter tapped the medicine tin with a finger. 'Would you mind telling me what these tablets are for?'

'My prescription,' she said. 'I have ... seizures.'

'Really?' His tone was dry, unconvinced.

Clara looked up at the policewoman, and then back at the captain. She had to be careful. It was obvious that Jeter didn't know she was a changeling; if he did, she would already be dead. But Charlie Hemlock had somehow discovered she was a magicker. It would probably only be a matter of time before Jeter did, too.

'The remains of a man were discovered,' the captain was saying, 'in a house on the east side of town. This man was a known associate of Charlie Hemlock, and he had been ... well, to say *brutally murdered* would be putting it mildly. And what remained of his body had been stripped naked, Clara.'

Jeter paused to make an obvious show of studying the over-sized clothes that Clara wore; the rips and tears and dark stains that decorated them. 'You wouldn't know anything about that, would you?'

'No,' she lied quickly, instinctively.

'Are you sure?' The captain's face was stony; his dark glasses like hollows in his face. 'You had no reason to run from the police?'

Clara shook her head and kept silent.

Jeter sighed. 'We know you were sold to Charlie Hemlock, and you've been missing for three days. But why sneak back to the Lazy House? Why not go straight to the nearest police station?'

There was no way Clara could answer that honestly. She stared down into her lap.

'Well?' Jeter snapped.

Clara flinched. 'I-I panicked, I suppose. I just wanted to be somewhere familiar.' It was mostly the truth, but even to her the words sounded unconvincing.

'I see.' Jeter looked up at the policewoman, who was still glaring at the prisoner.

'I'm easily bored, Clara,' Jeter continued. 'So let's try coming at this from a different angle. Fat Jacob sold you to Charlie Hemlock, but Hemlock has never been the brains behind any operation. So for whom was he buying you?'

'I don't know,' Clara said truthfully. 'He never told me who he was working for.'

'All right – I'll believe that for now. For what reason were you purchased?'

Clara opened her mouth, but no words came out.

Charlie Hemlock was a sick bastard. There was nothing he wouldn't dirty his hands with for money. But Jeter's question was a good one; Clara had never discovered the specific reason why he wanted her.

With a quick glance at the milky eye watching her from the grey wall, Clara shrugged at the police captain. 'Perhaps you should ask Fat Jacob.'

'I'll be sure to do that.' Jeter stared at her for a moment, and then he picked up the medicine tin, rattling it once more. 'So when did you last see Charlie Hemlock?' he asked.

Clara licked her lips. Her mouth began to work, but again she dared not answer.

'You whores should really learn when to help yourselves,' Jeter said with a sigh. 'I have a murder victim, Charlie Hemlock is as elusive as ever, and his mysterious employer has purchased a whore. You are the one link that connects them all, Clara, yet you really believe you can convince me that you know nothing?'

He leaned forwards and clenched his teeth. 'It's a ridiculous belief – especially as you were seen tonight, emerging from the Great Labyrinth.'

Clara's breath caught.

'I somehow doubt you managed to climb over the boundary wall, Clara. So it would seem that you have knowledge of these secret entranceways that are rumoured to exist. Tell me I'm wrong.'

What was she supposed to say? That Hemlock somehow got her inside the Great Labyrinth? That she left him there at the mercy of an empath; that she only escaped because of magic? Clara desperately willed Marney's box of secrets to edge open in her mind and show her the way out of this mess. It didn't happen. From all directions, it seemed, she was in deep trouble.

Clara recoiled as Jeter slammed his hand down on the table.

'How did you get into the Great Labyrinth?' he shouted.

'Hemlock took me there,' Clara blurted. 'I don't know how. I-I got away from him. He's still there as far as I know. That's the truth.'

'Is it? Because I have to wonder, Clara – are you in league with demons?'

'What?'

'Did you feed Hemlock's soul to the Retrospective?'

'No!'

Jeter sat back in his chair and clucked his tongue. 'You're in serious trouble, Clara, and if you insist on telling me lies, then I shall have to draw my own conclusions.'

'I'm not in league with demons,' she whispered.

'Perhaps that's the truth.' Jeter slipped the medicine tin into his pocket, and then checked the time on his pocket watch. 'I should warn you,' he said, rising from his chair, 'I'm not the only one to take a personal interest in this case.'

Clara's throat tightened as Jeter pointed to the eye on the wall.

'The Resident is watching you.'

Clara's heartbeat quickened, but she dared not look at the eye. The Resident … the governor of Labrys Town …

'Think on that for a while,' Jeter said. 'Perhaps the promise of being taken to the Nightshade will loosen your tongue.'

The police captain turned and headed for the door. 'Lock her up,' he told the policewoman as he stepped out of the room; the woman took obvious relish in grabbing Clara and yanking her to her feet.

In a small communal garden opposite the police station, Samuel hid in the shadow of a tree. The rain had lessened, and the smell of flowers and fresh cut grass was as thick as the drizzle that misted the air.

Though it was humid, Samuel kept his coat on. There were few townsfolk roaming the streets that time of night – most of those that did were enjoying themselves in the clubs and taverns down Green Glass Row – but a gun-wielding bounty hunter would still be easy to spot, and his coat provided good cover. But Samuel's mood was sour, and not just because of the stifling atmosphere of Ruby Moon.

The needle of the spirit compass pointed directly ahead at the police station across the street. Through the glass door, Samuel could see a duty sergeant sitting behind a desk, talking to two constables. The building wasn't particularly big, not like the police headquarters in the central district. Like so many official houses in Labrys Town, it looked almost bland, with so few windows in its grey stone walls.

A couple of hours ago a whore with a huge bounty on her head had been in Samuel's sights. Now she was safely protected from his guns, though in no less of a predicament. She had been arrested, and there was no way Samuel could just walk into the station and deal with her. Even Old Man Sam wasn't good enough to take on the Labrys Town Police Force.

She's a magicker, Marney had said, *did you know that, old man?* Of course he did. He just hadn't cared.

But he cared now.

Bounty hunters kept their ears to the ground, always listening for the next contract – the client didn't find you, you found them – that was how it worked. Samuel was good at hiding himself between jobs, but this time someone had tracked him down. His employer had remained anonymous, as was often the case in the Labyrinth; dirty deeds were always safer if the 'dirt' was on another's hands. Samuel's employer had sent an avatar, a ghostly presence of blue light. This avatar had discovered Samuel's hideout, and had come offering a generous contract for, as it turned out, killing a changeling.

If there were any practising magic-users left in Labrys Town, they would keep themselves well hidden through fear of discovery, arrest, execution. Samuel's employer had to be a magic-user; no one could conjure an avatar unless they were an adept. But things were no longer making sense to the old bounty hunter.

The girl was a changeling, and, as such, to any magic-user who had managed to stay hidden so far, she was worth much more alive than dead. The blood of a changeling was an efficient catalyst for creating powerful spells, yet Samuel had been employed to kill Clara, not harvest her blood. It just didn't add up.

From the shadows of the tree, Samuel watched as two patrolmen walked along the street towards the police station. The violet light from streetlamps gleamed off their black, bowl-like receptor helmets. They entered the station, removed their helmets, and conversed briefly with the duty sergeant before wandering off further into the building – probably ending their shifts for the night.

Samuel was caught by indecision, an unfamiliar state for him. He knew what he had to do next, but it was difficult for him to accept it. He struggled to believe what he had witnessed. Perhaps he was mistaken. He closed his eyes and once more replayed events in his head.

Marney was shot by an ice-bullet. Golems claimed her frozen body and dragged it through a portal. On the other side of the portal, in a chamber bathed in silver light, a man stood watching. There was some kind of plant or tree behind him. He wore a dark cassock. His hair was long and white; his skin almost as pale as an albino's. In Samuel's memory, his face was serious, but there was a smile on his lips, as slight as it was grim. He appeared ageless, looking exactly as he had when he had last been seen in Labrys Town. He was absolutely the man Samuel remembered from a long time ago. But it just couldn't be him. That man had died during the Genii War.

A snapping sound fizzed in the damp air, accompanied by the squeal of metal on metal. The old bounty hunter opened his eyes to see a tram pulling up outside the police building. It had a large square of dull silver riveted to its side. As Samuel looked at the symbol, he felt his resolve hardening.

The trams of Labrys Town were uniform, their bulky bodies painted a bland cream colour. But this tram was sleek and utterly black. Its windows were tinted so dark that it was impossible to see inside. The silver square on the side was the only decoration, and Samuel knew well what it represented.

A door slid open. A lone man disembarked and closed the door behind him. He stood before the police building. He was a small man, elderly, dressed in a smart suit and tie. He looked over in Samuel's general direction and gave a sardonic smile. Samuel swore and stepped further behind the tree. The elderly man then entered the police station, and the duty sergeant jumped to his feet as though he had been shocked.

Samuel looked at the spirit compass in his hand. With a calming breath, he screwed on the cap and slipped the device into his coat pocket. He no longer needed it to keep tabs on the girl.

He knew exactly where she was headed next.

Clara was hungry and her throat was parched. She had thought about asking for some food and water, but she doubted she could keep it in her stomach even if the guards obliged her. Still in handcuffs, she sat in a cell upon a thin mattress on a bunk. Her clothes were drying, but they smelt rank and musty.

The only light in the cell was the dull red glow of the moon coming through a small barred window, high on the wall. It looked as though the sky was clearing.

On the opposite wall was a second bunk. A large figure lay beneath the covers, difficult to make out in the cell's gloom and shadows. The reek of stale alcohol was strong. Clara didn't know if this person was a man or a woman, but whoever it was, they were good at snoring – and farting – in their sleep.

Clara wanted to wrap her arms around her body, but the cuffs prevented it. Anxiety clawed at her. Her palms were clammy. She would need to take her medicine again soon, but Captain Jeter had kept it with him. She cursed Fat Jacob; she cursed Charlie Hemlock; but most of all Clara cursed Marney for saving her life only to then leave her high and dry. Where was the empath now? What had she done to Clara?

At least she knew why Jeter had taken such an interest in her, though this knowledge brought no comfort. *The Resident is watching you …* Clara's hunger churned her stomach, and she fought the urge to gag. The promise of being taken to the Nightshade loomed over her like the threat of the Retrospective itself.

At that moment, her cellmate moaned, rolled over and noisily vomited onto the floor. Clara groaned and lay down on the bunk, clutching her knees to her chest, as her cellmate rolled over again with a creaking of springs, and the sound of snoring once more filled the air.

From somewhere outside, another inmate in another cell shouted some abuse at a guard, and was told to shut up. The argument grew louder and more intense. Clara covered her ears and squeezed her eyes shut, too exhausted to sob, too anxious to sleep.

The Nightshade was the home of the most powerful man in Labrys Town: the Resident. And the Resident was the law. He controlled every district, ruled over every denizen. His name was Van Bam, but few had ever seen him. It was said Van Bam's eyes were always watchful. Did he know she was a changeling? Did he, too, think she was in league with the wild demons of the Retrospective?

If Jeter's threat of sending Clara to the Resident was genuine, she would probably never see the sun again. Just as they did in the deep maze of the Great Labyrinth, people disappeared in the Nightshade.

The hunger, the humidity, the smell of vomit and stale alcohol, the pointless shouting raging outside – the entire situation swirled and slashed at Clara's senses and finally took its toll on her. Hurriedly, she moved to the edge of the bunk and gagged and retched, bringing up nothing more than bile. When she was done, she wiped it from her chin with the back of a shaking hand, and took several steadying breaths.

She stared at the thick chain that connected the metal cuffs around her wrists, wondering how strong it was.

If the effects of her medicine wore off and the metamorphosis occurred, here and now in this cell, if the magic in her veins activated and changed her into the wolf, could she escape? Could she break down the cell door and fight her way through unknown numbers of armed police? Did it matter? Clara blacked out when the wolf came. She never had any clear memory of being the monster – just flashes of images and sensations. She had no control over it. Chances were, if she changed, she would fight and slaughter until someone shot her dead. Clara almost welcomed the idea, wished it to happen: a clean end over a miserable alternative.

Was *that* what Marney wanted?

It was then she realised that the shouting between the inmate and the guard outside had stopped. And it wasn't due to a natural conclusion to an argument. It seemed to Clara as though something had interrupted, brought their exchanges to an abrupt halt. It was like a vague ringing had been left in the air, and the change in atmosphere was palpable to Clara's heightened senses.

Voices came from beyond the cell, muffled, whispered. The peep hole in the door slid open and then slid shut. The clunk of a key turning in the lock followed, and the door opened, spilling bright light into the cell.

Blinking, Clara moved further onto the bunk until her back was pressed up against the wall. A young police guard led a small, elderly man into the cell. The latter then waved the former away. As the guard left, the elderly man looked in disgust at Clara's cellmate and the puddle of vomit on the floor.

Clara had never seen him before. He was dressed in a smart three-piece-suit and tie. Grey, shoulder-length hair was swept back from his face, and a tuft of beard sprouted from the point of his chin. He smelled slightly of flowers. With a welcoming air, he offered Clara a sympathetic smile. He moved towards her with a small key in his hand, which he pointed at the cuffs about her wrists.

'Let's get you out of those,' he said kindly, 'and away from this disgusting cell, shall we?'

Clara hesitated, but she sensed nothing to fear about this man. He did not force the issue, did not demand anything of her, and waited patiently with the little key. Clara raised her hands to him. He unlocked the cuffs and threw them and the key onto the bunk.

'Thank you,' Clara mumbled, rubbing her wrists.

'You're most welcome,' said the man. 'Now, your chariot awaits, yes?'

Clara frowned up at him, and he smiled at her again with the kindest smile she had ever seen.

'The Nightshade is expecting you, Clara.'

She desperately wanted to object; she wanted to scream and claw and fight her way out of the building. But all she could manage was a quick choking sound before the elderly man placed a hand on her head and she immediately began slipping towards unconsciousness. From a distance, she heard him say 'Sleep,' and then there was nothing.

CHAPTER FIVE

THE RESIDENT

On the west side of Labrys Town, in a cemetery where grand mausoleums formed a cityscape of the dead, the white and grey stone glowed eerily beneath the hue of Ruby Moon. All was quiet among the statues and ornamentations crafted by the hands of master stonemasons. The lights of streetlamps and houses illuminated the near distance. Rain clouds were clearing from the night sky, and the wind had stiffened enough to flutter the cassock and long white hair of a solitary man standing before a moderately sized crypt.

He had been drawn to the cemetery by an alien signal, magic that did not originate in the Labyrinth. The source of the signal came from within the crypt, but it was weak, vague, barely detectable. It was almost as if the magic was fading, destined to be as dead as the corpses in the graves. It was not a favourable sign, and the man was not best pleased.

With gravel crunching beneath his boots, he stepped towards the crypt's entrance – tall double doors of stone set between white pillars that were cracked with age. Above the doors an ornate carving of the Timewatcher, supposedly watching over the soul inside, did not much impress him. With a grim expression on his pale face, he extended a hand. Energy rushed from his palm. The entrance shuddered inwards; shifting stone ground as if the crypt was drawing a ragged breath.

He stepped inside, ignoring the dust and cobwebs the wind swirled around him. The faded tapestry hanging on the back wall, the words of memorial engraved into the stone to his left and right, were wasted on him; he cared nothing for whose resting place he disturbed and wasted no time in descending the steep stairs that led to the crypt's vault.

There, a sarcophagus sat at the centre of the floor. Its lid was carved to resemble the man lying inside. The signal was a little stronger around it, but still not as strong as it should have been.

With his displeasure growing, the white-haired man barked a single word at the sarcophagus. The intricately carved lid cracked and broke into a thousand pieces which rose, slowly, hanging in the air for a moment, before he sent them flying away, like lethal projectiles, to shatter against the far wall.

He looked into the sarcophagus, feeling mild surprise that no skeletal remains lay inside; that there was no bottom upon which a skeleton might lie; that there was nothing to see except the deepest of shadows.

Jumping down through the hole, the man landed smoothly in a secret chamber beneath the vault.

The dark meant nothing to him; he could see perfectly well. The secret chamber was formed from hard-packed earth and was utterly empty. The only aspect of note was a crude hole dug in the floor. He crouched over it. It was a few feet deep and also empty. The source of the signal had at one time lain at the bottom of the hole, and the magic he could now sense was only the residue of its presence. He suspected some years had passed since the source had been removed.

The man leapt out of the secret chamber, up through the bottomless sarcophagus in a single bound, and ran up the stairs of the vault. Exiting the crypt, he stood in the cemetery and sniffed the air. He jumped up onto the crypt's roof. There he cast a spell, a simple incantation that altered his vision, allowing him to see the wind. Like fine grey smoke, it whipped around him.

The very foundations of Labrys Town were imbued with magic. A network of energy lines flowed beneath the ground and in the air, travelling like blood through veins. The network connected every district and every building. It provided homes with energy, kept trams running, and charged the little crystals that the denizens called power stones. If one were skilled enough, it was possible to feel the network, see it, use it, and to detect within it the presence of magic that did not belong to the Labyrinth.

White, luminescent lines crisscrossed through the misty wind, like an intricate spider web. But interwoven into these lines were four tendrils of dark purple: four signals from alien sources that snaked between the currents of the Labyrinth's energy. Three of the tendrils held a strong colour, vibrant and alive; but the fourth was undeniably weak, sickly. It rose from the crypt he stood on, struggling to exist as the wind threatened to scatter it in all directions. But it held its form, just, and weaved away into the distance, towards the lights of streetlamps and houses – and its source.

The man smiled grimly. Three signals were strong; they could wait, for the time being. The weakness of the fourth demanded attention before its time ran out and it disappeared completely.

He jumped down from the crypt's roof and began following the flagging purple tendril that twisted away deeper into the western district.

She was strong, unafraid, and Peppercorn Clara was a distant memory.

She was the wolf.

She ran through the dense forest, thorn and branch snagging her silver pelt. Leaf and dirt felt soft and damp beneath her calloused paws. The gleam of the moon was bright and fresh, glaring through the canopy to light the way as she weaved between trees and vaulted over roots. The scent of earth and mould filled her nostrils.

She was the wolf.

Her pack bayed loudly as it ran proudly with its leader. Hidden by foliage, the wolves kept a respectful distance as she led the hunt. A challenger had come to the forest, one who sought dominance over her territory. The challenge had to be met, defeated. The trees were alive with the voice of her family.

She was the wolf…

… A sweet aroma filled her nostrils. Her body lay upon a soft mattress. She gathered clean, silky sheets into fists as the dream faded to nothing. Other memories drifted up lazily to replace it …

A chase through the alleyways. A man in a cell. A kiss…

Clara jerked upright, confused and blinking against bright light.

She sat on a bed in a small room. Above, a prism shaped like a pyramid protruded from the ceiling, giving off clean and brilliant illumination. Her eyes struggled to gain focus. The walls were a bland cream colour, but decorated with a repetitive square pattern that looked like tiny mazes. There were hundreds of them, one after the other, in uniform lines.

There was no door.

Clara had no memory of leaving the police station or being brought to this room. But she remembered the elderly man in the three-piece-suit well enough. He had seemed so kindly, back in the cell. Clara knew he could not have been the Resident himself, but then who was he? *The Nightshade is expecting you*, he had said. Was she inside it now?

Swinging her legs over the side of the bed, Clara rubbed a hand through her short, greasy hair. A simple white gown had replaced the oversized rags she had been wearing and her feet had been carefully bandaged. She still stank like sewage.

Clara noticed a small scab on her forearm, no bigger than a pinprick, surrounded by the onset of a light bruise. She rubbed at it and smeared a tiny streak of blood across her skin.

This had to be the Nightshade.

Curiously, all Clara's anxiety and fear had gone. The silence in this doorless room was so total it was like being inside a sound-proofed cocoon, a safe bubble that calmed and soothed her senses. Was the Nightshade where Marney wanted her to be?

Clara's mouth watered at the sweet aroma in the air. It emanated from a table in the corner of the room, which had a thin cloth draped over its contents. Clara slipped off the bed, hobbled over on sore feet and peeled back the cloth to reveal a silver platter of various fruits and a glass jug of water.

Her stomach growled.

Three days had passed since she had last eaten – at least in her human form – and suddenly her location fell to the back of her mind, along with assassins and chases, kidnappers and empaths. She crammed a fig into her mouth greedily, washing it down with a glass of chilled water that she drained in one go. She ate a second fig, poured a second glass, and then picked up some sugar-coated lemon segments. Nothing had ever tasted better. She gorged herself.

Fresh fruit was hard to come by in Labrys Town; it was usually dried or preserved. Was this quality of food available to the Resident on a daily basis? Van Bam *was* the best-connected person in the Labyrinth.

Clara often heard the older denizens talking about Labrys Town and what it had been like before the Genii War, before the Retrospective came. They said there had been countless doorways out in the Great Labyrinth, each leading to realms and kingdoms beyond imagination. There, in these realms, the Aelfir had lived, and their Houses had co-existed in peace. The Aelfir were good friends to the denizens, and the Labyrinth was their common ground, the one House that connected all Houses, where they visited and traded, and life had been rich.

The Genii War ruined so much, it was said. At its conclusion, the doorways to the Houses of the Aelfir were sealed shut, and the endless shadows of the Retrospective began roaming the alleyways of the Great Labyrinth. No one had seen or heard from the Aelfir for forty years – no one save the Resident, of course. Only he still traded with the Houses. He procured all the materials and food stocks on which the denizens of Labrys Town survived.

Clara had to wonder, as she feasted on the fresh fruit, how many other privileges of his position Van Bam enjoyed; what luxuries that were denied the people he governed?

She checked herself. Here she was in the home of the most powerful man in Labrys Town, and she was worrying herself about food and history? All her life she had been taught to fear the Nightshade, but this didn't feel like a bad place. Even the wolf, that constant threat within her, felt sleepy in her breast, and it was not purely because of the effects of her medicine ...

Clara paused with a lemon segment halfway to her mouth. Her medicine! Did Jeter still have it?

At that moment a *click* startled her and she dropped the lemon segment to the floor. She backed away, both fearful and fascinated, as the outline of a door appeared on the wall opposite the bed. The door-shaped section swung inwards, and the small and elderly man stood on the threshold. His smile was as kindly as it had been at the police station.

'Ah, good, you are awake,' he said genially. 'I trust you have refreshed yourself?'

Words failing, Clara simply nodded.

The light was much brighter in this room than it had been in the cell, and she could see that his eyes were soft green, and that there was a patch of scarring at the centre of his forehead, starkly white against his olive skin.

'I'm Hamir, chief aide to the Resident. And you are possibly wondering what in the Timewatcher's name is going on, yes?'

Again, Clara didn't respond – she didn't know how to. She was no one, only a whore from the streets of Labrys Town, but this aide, this *Hamir* was welcoming her to the Nightshade as if she was a respected guest.

'Of course you're confused.' Hamir's tone was gentle, understanding. 'I apologise for accosting you so crudely at the police station. Sometimes explanations are best left until later, I'm sure you'll agree.'

Clara wondered for a moment if she was still in some bizarre dream. Why wasn't she scared? Perhaps the tiny scab on her arm was due to an injection of some strange, euphoria-inducing drug.

She pointed to the pinprick. 'What's this?'

'Nothing of concern,' Hamir answered quickly. 'Now, if you will follow me, the Resident is ready to receive you.'

Clara hadn't moved and was staring at Hamir. He chuckled lightly at her hesitation.

'Come,' he said. 'You've no cause for concern.'

He led Clara out of the room to a corridor. Though her bandaged feet were still sore, she hobbled after him without complaint. The door closed behind them; the outline disappeared leaving no sign that it had ever been there.

Clara said, 'I had a tin—'

'Don't worry,' Hamir said. 'Your medicine is quite safe,' and he set off at a brisk pace.

Clara followed. She noticed immediately that the cream walls of the corridor, like the room, were decorated with that same repetitive pattern – hundreds of tiny mazes, thousands. Hamir led her into a new corridor, and then another, and then another, each appearing much the same as the last. They ascended and descended various flights of stairs, some long, some short, and cut through antechambers into more corridors. At no time did they pass another person; at no time did Clara see a single visible door, and the pattern of tiny, square mazes never changed on the walls.

The types of people who usually came to the Nightshade fell into two categories: those who held high social positions, and those who were brought in for punishment. The former was not exactly the caste Clara mingled with; the latter were simply never seen again. Into what category had the Resident slotted her?

Van Bam was a mystery. He rarely left the Nightshade; he was almost never seen walking the streets he governed. He was the iron fist, the unseen watcher, and the denizens of the Labyrinth knew as much about their Resident as they did about the Retrospective. Every inch of Clara knew she should not be feeling so peaceful. She was struck suddenly by a sensation, a warm glow in her thoughts. Marney's kiss, the box of secrets in Clara's mind, somehow radiated satisfaction, as if letting Clara know she was supposed to be here.

Hamir led her out of the corridor into an antechamber, and Clara stopped and stifled a gasp. It was not the surprise of seeing someone other than Hamir that startled her; it was the nature of the person that stood in the antechamber.

It was dressed in a white gown, identical to hers, and it was hard to tell if this was man or woman. Clara doubted it was human. The dark brown skin of its hairless head was mottled with patches of grey. But the discolouration did not detract from its sense of grace and eerie beauty; it was almost as if this creature had been untouched by age or anxieties. Its ears, nose, and mouth – they were perfect features for a perfect head. However, its lack of eyes jarred against that perfection; smooth skin grew over the sockets, as if it had been born that way.

Clara kept her distance. The thing did not move, just stood before her, motionless. Its expression was impassive, but Clara knew that somehow it could see her, even though it had no eyes.

Hamir took her arm. 'Don't be frightened,' he said as he steered her around the creature.

'What is it?' she whispered.

'An aspect – one of the Resident's servants. It cannot harm you. Come.'

Hamir continued into the corridor beyond the antechamber, and

Clara looked over her shoulder as she followed. The servant had turned, as if to *watch* her leave. With a shiver, Clara kept pace with the elderly aide.

By the time they reached their destination, they had taken so many twists and turns it would have been impossible for Clara to retrace her steps back to the room she had woken up in. The Nightshade, it seemed, was every bit as complex as the deep maze of the Great Labyrinth itself. They reached a dead end, and Hamir pressed one of the mazes on the wall. It depressed with a click. Again the outline of a door materialised, and it swung inwards. Still gracious, still kindly, the old man led Clara into a room. The door closed and disappeared.

She took a few steps forward. Hamir stood close behind her.

If the Nightshade had thus far been a pleasant surprise for Clara, then this room revived her original concerns.

The only light source came from a glow lamp sitting on a desk where papers and books lay strewn. The edges of the room were steeped in darkness. Upon a long workbench sat implements for experimentation, strange looking things made of wires and tubes that passed fluids from one bell jar to another. There were magnifying glasses, and contraptions of sharp, twisted metal. Above the bench, shelves were filled with bottles and jars, the contents hidden in the gloomy light.

There was a smell in the room, a smell Clara did not care for.

She noticed her medicine tin sitting on the desk like a paperweight.

'This is my laboratory,' Hamir said. 'And there is someone here I believe you know.'

At the back of the room, a ceiling prism glared into life and shone down onto a square glass tank. It was no more than four-foot high, wide and deep, filled from top to bottom with murky water. The naked body of a man was trapped in the water. Twisted and contorted, his fat was pressed up against the walls of the tank. His face, unshaven and flabby, stared out at Clara, cross-eyed and vacant, his nose flattened against the glass. It was a face she knew all too well.

'Fat Jacob,' she whispered.

Hamir cleared his throat. 'If you have any lingering doubts as to who sold you to Charlie Hemlock, Clara, then you need not doubt any longer.'

Clara's hands began to tremble. 'Why are you showing me this?'

Hamir brushed past her to stand before the tank and spoke with his back to her.

'I have been trying to ascertain who Charlie Hemlock is working for,' he said. 'Who is it, Clara, that purchased you from your former employer?'

Clara swallowed, shook her head, but made no reply.

Hamir continued. 'Unfortunately, Jacob here also says he does not know who employed Charlie Hemlock. However, he has told me an interesting story about a spectre. Jacob claims he was recently visited by a ghost made of blue light, and this ghost told him that you were … *special*, shall we say?'

Special? Did Hamir know she was a changeling?

'Does that mean anything to you, Clara? Have you seen any ghosts lately?'

What was he talking about? 'No,' she said, but it sounded more like a grunt.

'Ah, then the mystery remains.'

In the tank, Fat Jacob suddenly flinched and his eyes gained focus. He looked at Clara, and the recognition in his eyes was full of panic, full of pain and hatred. His body shook, and pink, slug-like fat splayed as he tried in vain to escape his prison. Bubbles streamed from his mouth, but his scream was muffled by water and glass.

Hamir's chuckle was frightening in its amiability. 'Jacob feels quite ready to die, but until he decides to be more cooperative …' He clucked his tongue. 'Well, I can keep him on the brink of death for as long as I choose. I can keep filling his lungs with air, giving him false hope that he might just live yet, and then drown him again. A thousand times over, if I so choose.'

Fat Jacob's eyes rolled back and he shuddered as water again filled his lungs.

The owner of the Lazy House was a heartless bastard, but Clara could not have wished such torture on anyone.

The ceiling prism darkened, and the tank fell into shadows once more. Hamir turned to face Clara. Although his expression remained impassive, the bright green of his eyes swirled and darkened as if ink had been dripped into them. The scar on his forehead practically glowed in the dimness.

'Waste no sympathy on your former employer, Clara. However, I sincerely hope that you are feeling more cooperative than you were in Captain Jeter's interrogation room.'

Clara had heard stories about necromancy and the magic-users who liked to play with death. But the Resident, the governor of this town, practising death magic in his home? Allowing this *aide* to perform it? In that moment she feared for her life. The blood in her veins was the blood of a changeling; it was a priceless substance to magic-users, perhaps most especially to necromancers. She looked at the scab on her forearm. Evidently, Hamir had already taken some.

'Why have you brought me here?' Clara's voice was tight. 'What does the Resident want with me?'

Hamir bobbed his head in a quick bow. He backed away a few paces and his eyes returned to their bright green colour. He smiled at Clara as a new voice spoke from the room's shadows.

'A magicker is an illegal presence under the law of Labrys Town,' it said.

Clara swung around, but could not see anyone else in the room.

The voice continued, deep and resonant, confident and precise. 'For the time being, you have been allowed to enter the Nightshade under amnesty. This, you understand, is at the behest of a mutual friend. Yet I wonder – why should I trust you?'

The shadows wavered and an imposing figure stepped into the room, carrying a cane of deep green glass. Tall and broad, he was dressed in a loose shirt and trousers that shimmered and flowed as if reflecting the night sky. The dim light shone off the dark brown skin of his shaven head. On his strong face, two dull metal plates covered his eyes. Seemingly fused to the bone of the sockets, they glared with reflected light.

Somewhere deep inside her head, Clara felt Marney's lingering presence. But it gave no comfort as the dark, imposing man towered over her.

'Van-Van Bam?' she asked meekly.

He cocked his head to one side and held his green cane across his thighs. 'Welcome to my home, *Peppercorn* Clara.'

Halfway across the northern district of Labrys Town was the street known as Resident Approach. Wide and long, it ran southward in a straight line all the way to the central district. The southern region of Resident Approach accommodated shops and eateries, communal gardens and markets providing a place for work and pleasure alike – a source of life.

But the further north it stretched, the more desolate and lonely Resident Approach became. The gardens and buildings fell away. Tramlines ran along a section of the street which narrowed to half its original width and sloped downwards, cutting a gorge through the stone, creating a valley which flattened out some fifteen feet below street level, and the walls that loomed either side were smooth and grey.

Denizens did not linger here. There were no lamps, walkways or pavements, only lifeless statues lining the high walls. Eight feet tall and grim-faced, these statues were of past Residents, memorials to the former governors of Labrys Town that dated back a thousand years.

The clouds had cleared and the temperature was cooling as Samuel made his way along the northern reaches of Resident Approach. The night sky was on the cusp of changeover as Ruby Moon faded and Silver Moon began to rise. Samuel felt exposed, conscious of the taps and scratches of his footsteps, of the rasps and sighs of his breathing as he walked the deserted valley. The only cover offered him were shadows cast by the former Residents. He felt the gazes of those long deceased men and women upon him, as hard as the stone from which they were carved, judgemental, accusing. In the hands of each effigy was a milky eye device. There was nowhere to hide along Resident Approach.

Samuel's hand flexed, as if needing to hold something comforting in its grip; but the old bounty hunter resisted the urge to draw the revolver holstered to his leg.

As he neared the northernmost part of Resident Approach, he stopped and considered. The valley ended at a wall, as high as those flanking it, which would have formed a blind end had it not been for the fat tunnel burrowing into it. The tramlines converged into a single track that disappeared into the tunnel. Beyond it, a building was dimly highlighted under the fading glow of Ruby Moon. Constructed out of dark stone, the building rose high behind the wall, above the valley; its perfect square shape was shrouded slightly by the night's mist. It was a monumental building, by far the largest in Labrys Town: a giant cube that loomed, brooded, over Resident Approach.

The Nightshade.

Samuel didn't need to check the spirit compass in his pocket to know that the girl was inside. After all, he had seen Hamir, the Resident's aide, collect her from the police station.

Throughout the Labyrinth's history, the Nightshade had been home to the Residents, the governors of Labrys Town. Briefly Samuel looked back along the valley of Resident Approach, at the statues stretching off into the gloom. Each statue embodied a legend, had a story to tell.

Samuel turned back to the giant cube of the Nightshade. Another statue stood to the right of the tunnel cut into the wall. Samuel sighed, then made his way towards it.

Towering over the old bounty hunter, the statue's face was thin and angular with an expression as stern as the others. Samuel looked straight at the eye in its hands, and then down to read the name engraved into the plinth: GIDEON THE SELFLESS.

Samuel snorted.

Gideon had been the direct predecessor of the current Resident. He was called 'the Selfless' because he had given his life during the Genii War. Single-handedly, they said, he had battled Spiral's demons and saved the lives of every denizen in Labrys Town. And the denizens were eternally grateful for his sacrifice.

Allegedly.

The statue was a good likeness of the flesh. Samuel sneered his contempt up towards Gideon's face before walking into the tunnel.

The tram track ran right through to the other side. Dirty lamps fitted to the ceiling above the power line provided a sickly and dim light. Samuel felt his way along. The bricks of the walls were slick with moss. Water dripped. The tunnel ended at a set of iron gates that were already open, almost invitingly. Samuel hung back in the shadows.

Through the gates was a large forecourt where the sleek black bulk of the Resident's personal tram was parked. Beyond it, the wall of the Nightshade served as a vast backdrop. The dark stone was mostly smooth but engraved in places with square maze patterns. The Nightshade stood at the most northern edge, as if it were the head of Labrys Town; and behind it, beyond the mighty, hundred-foot-tall boundary wall, began the endless alleyways of the Great Labyrinth that completely surrounded the town and stretched away into the unknown.

The Nightshade had no doors or windows or obvious entranceways at all; you did not enter this building unless it wanted you inside. There was no checkpoint at the gates, no armed guards roaming the perimeter, for they were not required.

In the forecourt, upon pedestals rising from the ground like evenly-spaced stalagmites, sat eye devices. Unlike the eyes on the streets of Labrys Town, these eyes were full, head-sized spheres, seemingly dead in the dull, fading glow of Ruby Moon. But Samuel knew that these pedestals surrounded the Nightshade and he had only to step into the forecourt to activate the eyes; the milky fluid within them would flicker into illumination, and he would be seen.

Would he be welcomed?

For nearly forty years Samuel had been a bounty hunter. Violence and death had always been his trade, but there had been a time when he'd known a sense of loyalty and duty. Times had changed, and by reputation alone he was now a marked man. In Labrys Town good bounty hunters were always in competition for work, but these days a bounty hunter would hunt and kill his fellow kind simply for being competition. And no scalp came bigger than that of Old Man Sam.

Samuel's list of friends had dwindled over time; there weren't enough alive now to occupy the fingers of one hand, and those who were left he had spent long years avoiding. He belonged to a past generation, and was sick to the stomach of living his life with one eye looking over his shoulder. How long before someone younger and stronger caught up with him? It was only a matter of time.

Long ago, things had been very different. The Houses of the Aelfir had made life good, interesting – free. But with their departure, the Labyrinth had become isolated. The only things now waiting outside the boundary wall were the wild demons of the Retrospective. The denizens already had all they would ever get. And the man responsible for the change, the source of the nightmare, had returned tonight … and Samuel had let him take Marney.

The Nightshade and its law loomed before him like a gigantic puzzle box, bland but deceitful. Inside were secrets – secrets and monsters. Van Bam was the current Resident, and few denizens knew much about him at all. But Samuel knew, and he knew well.

Flexing fingers, his face grim, Samuel took a breath and stepped from the tunnel's shadows, through the gates, and into the Nightshade's forecourt. One by one, the eyes on the pedestals flickered and hummed and bathed Old Man Sam in bright light.

CHAPTER SIX

SECRETS & MONSTERS

'You recently killed a man?'

The bluntness of the question stung Clara and she could not meet the metal plates covering Van Bam's eyes. The light they reflected seemed to glare, as if the Resident could see directly into her thoughts. Her gaze flickered to the tin of medicine sitting on the desk, to the tank into which Fat Jacob was stuffed – dead but not dead – and she didn't dare speak. She looked to the floor and noted the Resident's feet were bare.

Hamir was no longer present. Van Bam had dismissed him from the laboratory; but before he left, the Resident had said that Fat Jacob was no longer of use, and that the aide was free to do with him as he pleased. Clara didn't know what that meant. She didn't want to know. She didn't even want to guess.

Van Bam tapped his green glass cane against the floor. 'Clara,' he said, 'I am not Captain Jeter. Silence will not buy you more time, and I will tolerate nothing but the truth here. Now – you recently killed a man, yes?'

'I had no choice,' Clara mumbled. Her throat felt dry. 'I was forced. I'm no murderer.'

'But you *are* a changeling,' Van Bam countered.

Clara was surprised to feel a flash of anger. She looked up and met the Resident's metal eyes. His dark brown face was inscrutable.

He said, 'I suspect you are an innocent party, Clara, or at least to some degree. If it were otherwise, Marney would have left you to Charlie Hemlock.'

Clara frowned.

The Resident continued. 'You are a victim of the dubious business conducted by Hemlock and the man you call Fat Jacob. But can you tell me who it is that Hemlock is working for?'

Clara shook her head.

'Then do you know why he wanted you? It was for your blood, perhaps?'

'I ... I thought that at first, too.' Clara rubbed the scab on her arm. 'But no, Hemlock wasn't interested in my blood at all.'

'Then what?'

'I don't know.' She shrugged. 'Fat Jacob hired me out for a home visit. It was just another night's work, or so I thought. But when I arrived at the address, Hemlock was waiting for me with an accomplice ...' She closed her eyes and relived distasteful memories.

'And then?'

'They tied me up,' she told Van Bam. 'They said they'd kill me if ... if I didn't change.'

'Change? Into the wolf?'

Clara nodded. 'They wanted to tire me out, they said, so I wouldn't be so much of a threat.'

'And they obviously succeeded.'

'I blacked out,' Clara continued, 'but I ... I can almost remember killing him—' *slaughtering him, ripping him apart, enjoying the taste of his blood ...*

Van Bam pursed his lips. 'But that was not Hemlock.'

'No – his accomplice. I never knew his name.'

'Go on.'

'There's a blank spot on my memory. When I woke up, I was in the Great Labyrinth. I don't remembering going there. I was wearing the dead man's clothes.

'Hemlock was nowhere to be seen at first. I-I tried to find my way out, but I was lost. When Hemlock caught up with me, he was with men dressed as priests. They had guns. I just ran. If Marney hadn't shown up, I-I don't know what would have happened.'

'Nothing good, one would presume.' Van Bam banged the tip of his green glass cane on the floor like a gavel striking a block. 'Clara, you should know that Marney and I were friends of old, but I have no real reason to trust her now. You will explain to me why she saved you. What instructions did she give you?'

Clara blinked several times. That glass box into which Fat Jacob's body was squashed seemed to be taunting her from the back of the room.

'I don't know,' she said. 'Marney didn't really say anything. She just let me go.'

This time, Van Bam's metal eyes followed Clara's gaze as she looked at her tin of medicine on the desk.

'Perhaps you are innocent, Clara. Perhaps you are not. Either way, if you want your medicine, I would be more forthcoming if I were you.'

Clara licked her lips, as if to sample the lingering taste of the empath's kiss. 'I don't know what to tell you. Marney did something to me. She ... she kissed me—'

The conversation was interrupted by a click, and the door to the laboratory opened. Hamir stood on the threshold. He bobbed his head respectfully.

'Excuse the intrusion, Van Bam, but I thought you should know that the security eyes have activated in the forecourt. Someone has approached the Nightshade.'

Still facing Clara, Van Bam cocked his head to one side. 'Marney?'

'No. It is another *old friend*.'

'Ah ...'

Van Bam was silent for a moment, and Clara looked from one man to the other.

'Then have the servants bring him inside, Hamir,' said the Resident. 'Show him to my study.'

'As you wish.'

Hamir smiled at Clara, and she shuddered. He continued smiling at her as Van Bam strode out of the room, saying over his shoulder, 'Come, Clara.'

Confused and disturbed, Clara struggled to keep up with Van Bam's long strides. Each of his steps was punctuated by a *tick* of his green glass cane on the floor. He walked with the confidence of one with full sight. The endless, repetitive corridors and stairwells of the Nightshade had an hypnotic effect on Clara; she almost walked into the back of Van Bam as he stopped suddenly and opened another hidden door in the wall.

He led her into his study, where it was immediately evident that the Resident of Labrys Town had little time for personal comforts.

The study was as brightly lit as the corridor. The walls were the same cream colour, but they were devoid of the ubiquitous maze pattern, and Clara's eyes relaxed slightly. There was an ornate wooden desk at one end, with two matching chairs on opposing sides. To the right of the desk a full-length mirror stood in the corner, set in a silver frame. And that was it; no cabinets or bookcases, no paintings or plants – nothing that indicated any kind of taste or pleasure.

Van Bam closed the door, and it became indistinguishable from the wall. Taking Clara's arm, he led her gently over to the mirror and positioned her with her back to it. He gripped Clara's shoulders, and once more she got the impression that the metal plates covering his eyes were searching her face. In the bright light of the study, Van Bam looked much older than he had appeared in the shadows of Hamir's laboratory.

'You are young,' he said, 'and there is much you claim not to know. Yet I wonder, Clara, how much does Marney trust you?'

'I don't know what you mean!' Was he angry with her? 'I never knew her before tonight, I still don't—'

'You have heard of the Relic Guild?'

Clara looked puzzled. 'Yes, of course.'

'But was Marney trusting enough to tell you the truth?'

'I don't understand.'

Van Bam cocked his head to one side, as if listening to something. 'A *friend* has come to see me,' he said. 'He must not know of your presence. You will stand here, before this mirror, Clara. Remain quite still and you will not be noticed. Understand?'

His tone left no room for refusal or further questions, and so Clara nodded.

As Van Bam stepped away, he tapped his cane against the floor and whispered a word Clara didn't catch. The cane's glass flashed green. There was a low hum and the air surrounding the mirror shimmered. The rest of the room wavered, as if veiled by water. The sound of Clara's own breathing was loud in her ears, as if she was trapped within a bubble.

Clara looked back at the mirror; she cast no reflection in its dull and faded surface.

Magic!

Van Bam had taken a seat at his desk. He sat facing the invisible door to his study, his glass cane lying on the desktop before him. The more Clara looked at this man, the more familiar he seemed: his smell, the sound of his voice, the way he cocked his head to one side ... but she had never seen him before in her life. Had she?

In that moment, Clara felt warmth inside her head and breast, as if Marney's box of secrets had cracked open a little. It reassured her that Van Bam meant her no harm, even if he was a magic-user, even if his aide had scared her half to death. Even if he did speak in riddles.

All her life Clara had heard the tales and legends of Labrys Town from before the Genii War. Back then, treasure hunters ran an illegal but booming trade. They snuck out into the Great Labyrinth and travelled through the doorways to the Houses of the Aelfir, searching for artefacts and magical relics which they could steal and smuggle back into Labrys Town. The black market had been a serious problem for the Resident and the Aelfir in the old days, as wealthy collectors would pay vast sums of money for stolen Aelfirian antiques.

There were still some denizens nowadays who liked to call themselves treasure hunters. Nobody took them seriously, not even the police; after all, even if they found a way past the boundary wall, the only place left to search for treasure was the Retrospective, from which no one returned. However, before the Genii War, treasure hunters had caused so much trouble for the Resident that a special organisation was created, a group of agents whose purpose was to counteract the illegal trade in Aelfirian artefacts, to recoup the stolen merchandise and deal harshly with those involved. These agents were the only humans permitted to use magic; their identities were kept secret, and they were known as the Relic Guild. But like so much else, the Relic Guild had disappeared after the war. No one had heard from them for decades.

Why had Van Bam mentioned it? What *truth*?

In his chair at the desk, the Resident shifted. 'Remember, Clara,' he said, his voice clear and insistent inside the mirror's bubble, 'make no sound. Do not move.'

With a faint click, the door appeared in the wall. It swung open, and a man stepped into the study. Through the bubble, Clara's view of him was distorted. Then the water effect shimmered and shifted, finally smoothing to allow Clara a clearer view of the room and Van Bam's visitor.

A little shorter than the Resident, the man had broad shoulders, and was dressed in simple black garb and a long brown coat. His face, though strong and not unhandsome, was heavily lined with age and sported a white goatee beard. His lips were drawn into a grim line.

Though Clara had never seen the man before, she found his face familiar. Just as with the Resident, it was almost as if she had dreamt of him.

Beneath his coat, the man had a heavy utility belt, and a handgun was strapped to his left thigh. Over his shoulder protruded the butt of a rifle that was holstered upon his back. Clara knew intuitively that this rifle had at one time been aimed at her.

'This is an unusual pleasure, Samuel,' Van Bam said, as the door closed and disappeared. 'Please, take a seat.'

Rubbing a hand through his white, close-cropped hair, the man took the chair opposite Van Bam. His expression as he stared across the desk gave nothing away.

'Can I offer you some refreshments?' Van Bam asked.

'No.' The reply was curt. Samuel looked over at the mirror, and his pale blue eyes seemed to bore straight into Clara's. 'You've had contact with Marney recently,' he said, looking back to his host. It was a statement.

'I will not deny that,' Van Bam replied.

'It concerned a girl. A whore.'

Van Bam sat back in his seat and a ghost of a smile danced on his lips. 'This girl means something to you?'

After a moment's silence, the newcomer responded. 'I was offered a bounty contract.'

'Oh?'

'For her death.'

Clara stifled a gasp. There was a bounty on her head?

'Yet your quarry eluded you?' Van Bam said.

'Marney stopped me.'

'I see. Then I suppose this girl can boast of being among the lucky few who have escaped the attentions of Old Man Sam.'

Old Man Sam …? Clara's insides froze. It was said that this bounty hunter had killed more people than anyone else alive. He was a legend, and many believed he had died years ago. But Clara was convinced she knew him from somewhere, somewhere other than his reputation.

'I am curious,' Van Bam said. 'I did not commission, or agree to, a standard bounty on this girl. Was your contract issued in the formal way, Samuel?'

Samuel shook his head. 'I'm pretty sure it was a bogus offer.'

'Then could you give me the name of the one who employed your services?'

'I was hoping you could tell me. The contract was offered by avatar.'

'Avatar?'

'Yes. It was just an image of blue light.'

Van Bam nodded slowly as if Samuel was making perfect sense.

What had Hamir told Clara? Something about Fat Jacob being visited by a blue ghost?

'I don't know how it found my hideout,' Samuel continued, 'but the avatar seemed to know all about me.'

Van Bam took a breath. 'Samuel, if you believe the avatar's bounty contract to be fake, then that begs the question of why your interest in this girl is continuing.'

'Because of promises we made.'

'Ah.' The Resident steepled his fingers and bounced them lightly upon his lips. 'Then we must speak openly. I received a message that Marney would steer a young girl in my direction. I have taken the girl in, but I have yet to discover for what reason Marney saved her.'

'She's a magicker, Van Bam. What other reason do you want?'

'What other reason indeed.'

Clara couldn't figure out if these two men liked or loathed each other, but it was obvious that neither was comfortable with this conversation.

'Tell me,' Van Bam continued. 'Where is our empathic friend now?'

'That's a good question, but it doesn't have a good answer.'

'She is in trouble?'

Samuel paused. 'The girl was bait. She was part of a trap.'

'For Marney?'

Samuel nodded.

Clara's chest fluttered. Her wolf stirred. Van Bam appeared calm and assured as he waited for his guest to reveal more. Clara held her breath.

Samuel seemed tired, weary to the bone. 'Marney was kidnapped, abducted by someone I prayed to the Timewatcher I'd never see again.' He lowered his pale eyes. 'Van Bam, it was Fabian Moor.'

Something unspoken passed between the two men. If it was fear, Clara didn't blame them. Fabian Moor was an infamous name, known throughout the town, a legend. He was a demon that had terrorised Labrys Town during the Genii War. But Fabian Moor had been killed by Gideon the Selfless, long before Clara was born. What was going on?

'You are certain it was Moor?' Van Bam said levelly.

'I couldn't be mistaken,' Samuel replied. 'I saw him with my own eyes. Marney … she didn't even try to defend herself, Van Bam.' He rubbed his face. 'Look, there's a chance I can find her, but I need to see the girl.'

'She knows where Marney was taken?'

'Not quite…' Old Man Sam's pale gaze turned pointedly to the mirror. 'But she knows a man who does – don't you, Clara?'

In the western district of Labrys Town, Briar's Boutique had long held a reputation as an esteemed seller of quality antiques. It was a reputation of which Briar was proud, and his pride never allowed his standards to slip. He was courteous and patient with his clients, but he was shrewd, with a keen understanding of business. The wealthier antique collectors of the western district were easy with their money when something old caught their fancy; and Briar's prices were always reassuringly high.

He was an elderly gentleman approaching his mid-seventies who appreciated the value of a good night's sleep. But in the cold early hours of Silver Moon, he was surprised to have his rest disturbed by the ringing of the bell which sat upon the counter in the boutique below his living quarters. He remembered full well that he had locked the shop door before retiring for the night.

Wrapping a floral design gown over his nightshirt, sliding his feet into velvet slippers, Briar took an antique pistol from his bedside cabinet, before creeping down the stairs as the bell rang for a second time.

The glow lamps had been switched on in the boutique, and a gentleman stood before the counter. He was pale of skin, almost an albino, but his dark eyes scoured the antiques tastefully displayed around the shop. Briar watched from the shadows of the doorway behind the counter. The gentleman did not look or act like a burglar, and he wore the black cassock of a priest. Although seeing this garb gave Briar a sense of relief, he found it a little strange that his visitor's hair was white and long, and not the customary short style worn by the priests of the Timewatcher.

'Do I have to ring this bell for a third time,' the priest said in calm, even tones, 'or will you finally stop hiding in the shadows?'

Holding the pistol behind his back, Briar stepped through the door and into the boutique. He smiled from behind the counter.

'Forgive me, Father, but I'm surprised to find one of the cloth here at this time of night. Perhaps you could explain?'

The priest narrowed his eyes. 'It is almost time for the Sermons of Silver Moon. I was on my way to my church when I noticed that your lights were on and your door was open.' He smiled wryly. 'Does that give you cause enough to shoot me?'

Briar paused for a moment, and then a chuckle escaped his lips. 'Please excuse me, Father,' he said. 'Old age must be catching up with me. I could have sworn I closed up properly for the night. I'm rather afraid I mistook you for a burglar.' He placed the antique pistol on the countertop. 'An empty threat, I assure you,' he explained. 'Even if the pistol was loaded, its power stone no longer holds a charge.'

'Ah,' said the priest.

'I must thank you for your concern, sir, and bid you a good night. Enjoy your sermons, and may the Timewatcher go with you.'

The priest's smile became decidedly thin. It did not reach his dark eyes. 'Before I go, perhaps you would indulge me. I am led to believe that you are selling an item that is of particular interest to me.'

'Oh?'

'Yes. It is a small jar, plain, made of terracotta.'

Briar thought for a moment, and then made a small noise of surprise. 'Yes, I believe know the piece you mean, but—'

'I do not see it on display.'

'No. It is stored in my backroom. I haven't had that jar on display for many years now. How did you come to hear of it, Father?

'Well now …' The priest paused and seemed amused. 'It is a long and interesting story. Would you like to hear it?'

Briar kept his professional smile in place. 'Most certainly, Father, but perhaps at a more sociable hour? If you would like to come back—'

'Please –' the priest held up a hand – 'I get so little time to indulge my fancies in my work. May I beg to see the jar now? You won't regret it – my story *is* fascinating.'

Briar was tired and wanted nothing more than to go back to bed, but the pride of his professionalism kicked in; he did not want his reputation tarnished by the news that he had turned away a priest of the Timewatcher after benefiting from his neighbourly deed.

'Of course,' he said with a well-practised smile. 'One moment, please.'

Briar left the boutique and entered his storeroom. The small terracotta jar sat at the back of a top shelf, long discarded and forgotten. With a grumble, Briar climbed a short stepladder and pulled it down. It was a small piece, about the size of the jars used to contain preserves. He blew away cobwebs and wiped clear a thick layer of dust to make it presentable. The terracotta was veined with many cracks upon its otherwise smooth and plain surface. It had no lid, and inside was a shallow layer of grey ash.

'I have to say, I'd completely forgotten I owned this piece,' he said as he took the jar into the boutique and placed it upon the counter. 'It gained so little interest from my customers that I stored it away years ago. I'm rather surprised to hear you enquire after it, Father.'

The priest stared at the jar for a long moment. 'May I ask how you came by it?'

'Let me see,' said Briar. 'Ah, yes. It is a strange tale. A wealthy merchant family, here in the western district, fell upon hard times after the war. But they claimed they were rescued from their monetary plight because of a visit from a ghost.'

Dark eyes fixed upon Briar with keen interest. 'A ghost?'

'Yes, of all things. It informed the family that beneath the crypt of a relative there was a hidden chamber full of riches. A dubious story,

I'm sure you'll agree. Personally, I suspect that they had concocted a convenient – although implausible – explanation for an illegal windfall. But the chamber was real enough, and *someone* had filled it with many relics and antiques. All of which I purchased from the family and sold on many years ago.'

'All except this jar,' said the priest.

'Quite correct, sir.' Briar sighed. 'I have always assumed it is the urn which holds the ashes of the dead relative. There is not much interest in such things among collectors, but it is of interest to you?'

'Yes.' The priest stepped forwards and picked up the jar. He studied the cracks on its surface, and then peered long and hard at the ashes inside.

'If I might ask, Father – how did you hear of it? You said you had a *fascinating* story to tell?'

The priest wasn't responding, and Briar frowned.

'I'm afraid I haven't thought of a price,' he began. 'Perhaps you would care to make an offer?'

'It doesn't matter,' the priest said. He looked up with a strange expression on his pale face. 'The magic is fading. The spell is all but dead.'

'Excuse me, sir?'

'It makes no difference, I suppose. The other signals are strong.'

The priest seemed to be talking to himself. Briar gave a nervous chuckle. 'My apologies, Father, but you're not making much sense.'

'This is not yours to sell,' the priest said, holding the terracotta jar aloft. 'It is not some trinket to decorate the shelves of your pathetic little shop.'

'I'm … I'm sorry?'

'You humans really need to learn your place.' The priest sneered at the boutique owner. 'I'm sick of the stench of you.'

He waved his hand. The light from every lamp in the room died. A snap filled the air as the shop door locked.

Nothing before in his long life had given Briar cause to scream as he did then.

From the study, Van Bam had taken Clara and Old Man Sam to a conference room within the Nightshade. Hamir the necromancer was absent, and the three of them sat at one end of a long conference table, with the Resident positioned in the head chair. Clara sat to his left and stared across the table's polished wood at Samuel. Samuel held her gaze evenly, and she felt her anger brewing.

The old bounty hunter had already explained what had occurred out in the Great Labyrinth after Clara had fled the courtyard; how Marney had summoned a wild demon to take Charlie Hemlock away, and how she herself had then been abducted. Van Bam had listened attentively, making very little comment. After Samuel had finished, no one had spoken for several moments. Both the old bounty hunter and the Resident confused Clara: in the study they had acted like enemies, but now they seemed less cagey with one another, as if they were comrades who had shared a long history. Their attitudes towards Clara had also changed. She no longer felt like an unwanted guest; less like a victim and more like a discovery, a catalyst for a situation she did not understand. And these changes in attitude had occurred with the mere mention of one name; a name that cast a long shadow from the Labyrinth's past.

Clara looked to the Resident. 'What's going on?' she asked, surprised by how calm her voice sounded. 'Marney can't have been taken by Fabian Moor.'

Van Bam turned his metallic eyes to Samuel. They looked at each other without speaking.

'The dead stay dead,' Clara stated.

'Clara,' replied Van Bam, 'I suspect that once you truly comprehend with whom you have become embroiled, then ignorance might just seem the preferable option.'

When Clara replied, her voice was resolute. 'I'll tell you what I understand. Marney saved my life tonight –' she looked pointedly at Samuel – 'twice, it appears. I don't doubt she had her own reasons, but people don't exactly stick their necks out for me very often. If she's in trouble, I want to help.'

Samuel and Van Bam shared another look, and then Samuel rose from his chair and bowed his head at Clara. He walked behind the Resident, around the conference table, and came to her side.

'You've suffered tonight, and you don't know why,' he said. 'You want answers, and that's only right. But if you want to help Marney, Clara, you need to trust us. Trust *me*.' He took a seat beside her. 'Give me your hand.'

Clara stiffened. 'What?'

Samuel unclipped a small kit bag from his utility belt and unzipped it. 'Tonight, out in the Great Labyrinth, you scratched Charlie Hemlock's face,' he produced a slim scalpel and a tiny glass phial from the bag, 'deep enough to draw blood. Let me see you hand, please.'

The only thing Clara offered the old bounty hunter was a glare.

'Clara,' Van Bam said coolly. 'If Charlie Hemlock was employed by Fabian Moor, then he has information that is of vital use to us. If there is any hope of helping Marney, Hemlock needs to be rescued from a demon. Time is a factor. Please, do as Samuel asks.'

'Fine,' she snapped.

Though grimy, her hand seemed small and delicate when placed in Samuel's worn and calloused palm.

'Now tell me,' she said, 'how can Fabian Moor still be alive? He was killed by Gideon the Selfless.'

'And that is true, in a manner of speaking,' Van Bam said. 'At least, that is what I believed until tonight.'

He sat back in his chair, holding his cane across his lap, his face thoughtful. 'Clara, do you know why the Genii War began?'

As Samuel inspected her fingernails with the scalpel, Clara answered with a shrug. 'Spiral rebelled against the Timewatcher. He tried to enslave the Aelfir.'

Van Bam nodded. 'That is the truth, more or less.' He sighed. 'There was a time when the Labyrinth was the one place throughout all the realms that connected every House of the Aelfir. Spiral saw Labrys Town and the Great Labyrinth as a seat of power from which he could invade the Aelfirian realms, conquer them, bend them to his rule and raise an army large enough to defeat the Timewatcher. He almost succeeded in this when he sent his assassin to our town.'

Clara watched as Van Bam's grip tightened on his glass cane. She kept quiet as he continued.

'There are not many left alive who actually knew Fabian Moor, Clara, but those of us who did remember him as a phantom, a lingering nightmare that reminds us of the frailty of existence within the Labyrinth.'

'He was bad news,' Clara said. 'I don't need a history lesson.'

'Yes, you do,' Samuel said as he dragged the scalpel along the underside of her fingernail. 'Myths and legends, Clara – they have a habit of diluting the truth.'

'Fabian Moor was a demon,' Clara said, as if there was nothing else to say. 'Spiral sent him here to spread a plague among the denizens.'

'Yes, Spiral did send him here during the war,' Samuel said, and Clara winced as he dug out some dark matter from beneath her nail – dried blood and skin that had once belonged to Charlie Hemlock's face, she hoped – and scraped it into the phial. 'But he was much more than some demon spreading disease.'

'Fabian Moor was Spiral's most trusted general,' said Van Bam. 'He was a Genii, Clara.'

Clara's mouth worked silently for a moment. What was this rubbish? She was no expert on the Genii War, but she knew about the great magickers who had fought alongside Spiral, and it was well known that the Timewatcher had protected the Labyrinth – town and maze – from the Genii and prevented them from invading it. In fact all the fighting, every battle, had taken place in the realms of the Aelfir, and the denizens had seen nothing of the war at all. That was why Spiral sent a demon to spread a plague. Such a low creature went unnoticed when it smuggled itself into Labrys Town, hiding in the stolen cargo of treasure hunters. Or so the story went.

She scoffed. 'But he can't have been,' she said, and then winced again as Samuel scraped more dark matter from under her fingernails. She pulled a sour expression. 'The Genii never entered the Labyrinth. The Timewatcher prevented it.'

'There is much that will confuse you at this time, Clara,' Van Bam said. 'For now, let us suppose that Fabian Moor was not the demon that legend has led you to believe, that he was a Genii who indeed found a way to enter Labrys Town, and that he most certainly did not come here solely for the purpose of spreading a plague.'

'Then why did he come?' Clara said, irritated.

'It gets complicated,' Samuel replied. 'We always supposed that Moor was trying to supplant the Resident and take control of the Nightshade for his master.' He shrugged. 'It was logical. Without control of the Nightshade Spiral couldn't hope to command the doorways of the Great Labyrinth, which he needed to subjugate the Aelfir.'

'But we never discovered the full extent of Moor's mission,' Van Bam said. 'We killed him before he could carry out his orders, or so we believed.'

'We?' Clara whispered. Something tingled inside her head, as if Marney's box of secrets was vibrating, encouraging her to see the obvious in this situation. '*You* killed him?'

'That's right, Clara,' Samuel said. 'Gideon wasn't the only one to fight Fabian Moor.' His voice became bitter. 'And he certainly wasn't the only one to die.'

Butterflies flittered in Clara's gut. The buzzing of Marney's lingering presence spread through her body. The notion that this was not the first time she had met these two men struck her with renewed force. She peered closely into Samuel's face as he finished filling the little phial with dried skin and blood and pressed a cork into the end.

'What's going on?' she said, feeling suddenly hot, clammy. 'I know you – both of you.' Her voice was feverish. 'Why am I here?'

Samuel frowned at Clara's intense, frustrated expression, and then looked to the Resident.

'Tell me,' Clara hissed. 'What am I to you?'

'It is your right to know the truth,' Van Bam told her. 'Though I suspect Marney has already given you some indication of the company you are presently keeping.'

'What?' Clara demanded. 'What has she told me?'

Van Bam's metallic eyes seemed to stare straight into her soul. 'You have heard stories of us, Clara, perhaps more, even, than the legends of the Genii War. Samuel, Marney and I, we are the last of a clandestine organisation. And forty years ago Fabian Moor ripped us apart ...'

THE RELIC GUILD

There had been a time, in the distant past, when the Houses of the Aelfir were feudal and war-torn. Their cultures, steeped in history, rich in resources, had been undermined by doubt and mistrust, scarred by battles that raged across the realms. None of them could remember the cause of the disharmony, none of them could answer why it was they continued to fight. Yet as generations passed the feuds grew ever more bitter, as each House fought for domination of its neighbours. So blinded had the Aelfir become by their nameless hatred, they refused to see there could never be a victor. For their lust for dominance had reached an impasse centuries ago.

Yet salvation was at hand.

In the far and ineffable realm of Mother Earth, the Timewatcher's all-seeing eye had been drawn to the stalemate. She found shame in the conduct of the Aelfir – that not one House among them could even consider so alien a concept as peace. So stuck were they in their ways, they did not recognise the bright future they could so easily fashion; the strong alliances they could form, the ancient cultures they could share, and the trade and immense riches they could enjoy together. So the Timewatcher, terrible in Her power, generous with Her kindness, journeyed from Mother Earth to show the Aelfir another way.

She brokered a fragile truce by creating for them a new realm that served as a neutral ground where all the Houses were welcome. She called this realm the Great Labyrinth, and to this place She summoned every House chief. For the first time in centuries, the Aelfir engaged in dialogue. Encouraged by the Timewatcher, they *listened* to each other, and started to understand the futility of their feuds. It was not an easy period, but the Houses slowly began extending hands of friendship.

Of all the Timewatcher's children, Her most beloved were the

Thaumaturgists, mighty and proud creatures of higher magic. The love and devotion the Thaumaturgists gave their Mother was without compromise, and never did they question Her word. She charged them with the duty of watching over the Aelfir, to protect them, to guide and nurture, but never to rule over and dominate them, for that was not the Timewatcher's plan. With gentle benevolence, She bade the Thaumaturgists to not interfere as the new friends built their bright future, and to never seek personal gain. There was to be no other benefit than ensuring harmony throughout all the realms.

Lastly, on each House of the Aelfir, the Timewatcher bestowed the gift of a doorway. Through these doorways, whenever they chose, each House might enter Labrys Town, the new common ground at the centre of Great Labyrinth – to meet and trade, to grow rich and strong. And the Timewatcher left them to make of themselves what they would.

For a thousand years the Aelfir met in peace at the Labyrinth.

But there came a day when one arose among the Thaumaturgists who dared to question the Timewatcher's directive. His name was Spiral, and he was revered among the creatures of higher magic. He could not accept that the Aelfir should be allowed to make their own laws and systems of government. Why should they reap all that they sowed, grow fat on their riches, while offering nothing back to the Timewatcher who had given them everything, who had saved them from such a miserable existence? The Timewatcher told Spiral, in no uncertain terms, that the love given by the Aelfir to Her, and Her Thaumaturgists, was reward enough. He was not to forget that. Or question Her again. The Aelfir and the Thaumaturgists were equals, She said.

Something changed in Spiral that day; his faith in his Mother waned, his love was compromised by resentment. And he turned his darkening thoughts to the Great Labyrinth.

The common ground, the meeting place, the realm that linked all realms – the Great Labyrinth was intrinsic to the status quo. But had the Timewatcher given custody of such a powerful House to creatures of higher magic? Or were the greatest and wisest Aelfirian politicians given rule of Labrys Town? No, She had given the House to *humans*, the lowest of all castes. Only Spiral seemed to recognise the deep insult of bestowing upon them this lofty position.

If the Great Labyrinth was ruled by the Thaumaturgists, they would be able to reach out with an iron fist, touch every House at once, and bend the Aelfir to their rule. They would punish ingratitude and greed by imposing servitude and taking the riches they were rightfully due by force. As for the humans … what part could they play in any plan?

The Timewatcher's eye was all-seeing, it was said, but She was blind to Spiral's growing hatred. She did not foresee that others among Her Thaumaturgists sympathised with him; She did not know there were Houses among the Aelfir harbouring anger and envy for their richer neighbours. Only when a great divide had split the Thaumaturgists in two did She see the truth; only when Spiral named his renegade followers the Genii did She feel the sting of betrayal; only when the Genii rose up against Her with an army of Aelfirian rebels a hundred thousand strong at their backs did She know despair.

And it was said that on the day Spiral declared war on his Mother, the sound of the Timewatcher's weeping could be heard across the skies of every realm …

Marney pulled her coat tighter around her body. Her breath frosted in the air. The night was fresh, and the sky was clear and bright now Silver Moon had outshone the humid red glow of Ruby Moon. She stood half way down a narrow and deserted side lane in the heart of the east side of town, facing a small and crooked tavern called Chaney's Den. It was squashed into a long line of terraced residential houses and, although a faint glow came from behind the grime-smeared windows, there was no sign of life inside. It was a sad and unwelcoming sort of place.

'Are you frightened?' asked Denton.

Marney looked at the tall and burly man standing beside her, and she shook her head.

'Good,' he said with a wink. 'Then neither am I.'

She managed a nervous smile.

Pushing eighty, standing well over six feet tall, Denton had the appearance of a gentleman giant. The waistcoat of his rumpled suit might have only just covered his large girth, his long overcoat might have been old and patched, and his wide-brimmed hat had definitely seen better days; but somehow Denton always managed to carry himself as though he belonged among the wealthy denizens on the west side of town. His round face carried a perpetually welcoming expression, and he had the energy of one thirty years younger. And he was wise, wiser than any teacher Marney had ever known. He was an empath, and her mentor.

He took out his fob watch and checked the time. 'What's keeping him?' he muttered.

As Denton slipped the watch back into his waistcoat pocket, Marney resumed staring at the sad little tavern.

Life had changed so much since this war had begun. Marney was only eighteen, had only been an agent of the Relic Guild for a little under six months, but it seemed like such a long time ago that she had been a simple student with aspirations of becoming a history teacher. She was part of a secret organisation now, for better or worse, and the Relic Guild was fighting its own war that the denizens knew little about.

'Ah,' said Denton. He smacked his lips as though tasting the air. 'Here he comes.'

Marney sensed it too, a moment later, a simmering presence that was heading their way. She switched her gaze to a slim, tunnel-like walkway on the left side of the tavern. A man in his late twenties emerged from the darkness and made his way towards the two empaths. He wore his long brown coat open and carried a short rifle in his hands, its power stone glowing. The swish of his coat revealed a revolver holstered to his thigh. His hair was close-cropped, dark brown; above pale eyes, his brow, as ever, was deeply furrowed.

'You took your time, Samuel,' Denton said jovially. 'I assume you found something that arrested your attention?'

'Not especially,' Samuel replied humourlessly. 'There's no backdoor, but I did find the entrance to the cellar. It's chained shut.'

'Did you see or hear anyone?'

'Nothing.'

Denton cast an appraising eye over the tavern. 'Samuel, this place obviously closed for business some hours ago. Are you sure your information was correct?'

'Chaney's Den,' Samuel said with a nod, 'the first hour of Silver Moon – this is definitely where it's happening.'

'Then perhaps the time was changed,' Denton said. 'Perhaps we are too late and our efforts are wasted here.'

Samuel huffed, and Marney could sense his irritation.

'Or maybe we should stop messing around and just go and wake up the landlord,' he said.

'An excellent suggestion, Samuel,' Denton replied cheerily. 'We'll take the back way, I think.'

Shaking his head, Samuel headed back towards the walkway, his rifle in hand.

Marney and Denton followed, and she smiled at the mischievous glint in her mentor's eye. Samuel wasn't the easiest person to get along with, and Denton enjoyed trying to lighten him up.

Despite Denton's joviality, Marney was struggling to quell a feeling of apprehension. True, she hadn't been a Relic Guild agent for very long, but she had gained experience enough to know that however deserted Chaney's Den appeared, when dealing with Aelfirian artefacts, nothing was ever as it seemed.

Behind the tavern was a small courtyard enclosed by a wall. Crates of empty bottles and old beer barrels lay discarded. The doors to the cellar were a pair of heavy wooden flaps set into the cobbled floor. A thick chain was looped around their handles, secured by a heavy padlock.

'I could freeze the lock and break it,' Samuel suggested, tapping the revolver at his thigh.

Denton gave him a disapproving look and shook his head. He produced a little phial from the inside pocket of his coat and, stepping past Samuel, crouched his impressive bulk before the cellar doors.

'Whenever applicable,' he said to Marney, 'the subtle approach is preferable to open aggression.' He nodded towards Samuel. 'Occasionally even the more established agents of the Relic Guild need reminding of this.'

'Just open the bloody doors,' Samuel growled.

Marney stifled a nervous chuckle.

Denton uncorked the phial and dripped several drops of liquid into the padlock. The metal hissed and steamed as the acid began eating through the locking mechanism. After a few moments, the padlock snapped open, and Denton removed the chain.

His expression now serious, the old empath nodded at Samuel who returned the gesture and aimed his rifle at the cellar doors. Denton then motioned to Marney. Together they grabbed a handle each and lifted the wooden flaps.

'It's clear,' Samuel said a moment later, and he led the way down a set of stone steps leading into the cellar.

Marney's stomach turned. In the light of wall-mounted glow lamps, beneath dusty cobwebs and surrounded by ale barrels and racks of wine bottles, were three dead bodies. Two were skeletons, sitting with alarming normality at a table by the far wall, their bones stripped clean and white as though bleached. The third was a man, still in possession of his flesh, lying face down upon the cellar floor. The back of his head was a pulped ruin. His blood pooled on the flagstones beneath him.

Samuel stepped up to the body and used his foot to roll it over. There was a neat bullet hole in the dead man's forehead. Scorch marks on his blood-drenched white shirt, indicated where he had been shot twice more in the chest. His face was craggy, grey and desiccated, as if the moisture had been sucked from it. Thin black lines streaked out from a ragged wound on his neck.

'This is him,' Samuel grunted. 'This is Carrick. He's the treasure hunter.'

'Ah,' said Denton. 'Then we have our seller –' he turned, pointing over to the skeletons at the table – 'and one of these must be our buyer.'

As Denton moved over to inspect the skeletons, Marney controlled her fear, just as Denton had taught her. Her mentor had already mastered his emotions and he gave off nothing that she could sense. She *could* sense Samuel's alertness, however, and it was strong, finely tuned, despite his stoic exterior.

'Look at this,' Denton whispered.

The skeleton he was inspecting appeared human enough, except for the face. The nasal cavities and jaw were small, but the eye sockets were large and round, much bigger than any human's, giving the face an oddly triangular shape.

'This skeleton belongs to an Aelf,' Denton said.

Samuel swore and moved for a closer look himself. 'Can you tell which House it comes from?'

'Could be any one of a hundred.' The old empath pursed his lips, clearly confused. 'An Aelf? I wonder what he was trying to buy.'

Samuel walked around the table to inspect the second skeleton. This one was definitely human, a denizen. Its claw-like hands were placed either side of a simple contraption comprising a square dish of metal and four metal rods that rose from each corner of the dish to meet and form the frame of a pyramid.

Marney knew this skeleton belonged to an alchemist, and alchemists were always present at the sale of magical artefacts. The contraption between its hands was a testing device, used to authenticate the merchandise. The artefact would be placed in the dish upon a bed of iron filings. The rods would siphon a little of the artefact's energy, and whatever substance it transformed the iron filings into indicated how powerful its magic was.

Samuel studied the contents of the dish. He puffed his cheeks and said, 'Whatever was on sale was powerful.' He looked at Denton, and Marney felt Samuel's deep surprise. 'The filings have turned to glass dust.'

And that, Marney also knew, was as strong as magic got.

Samuel's look went to the sprawled corpse of Carrick the treasure hunter, and then returned to the skeletons. 'What happened here, Denton?' he said. 'I've seen these kinds of deal go bad before, but nothing like this.'

Denton's brief pause betrayed a little of his uncertainty. 'Hard to fathom,' he said. 'I can detect some residual emotion, which only tells me these people were alive a few hours ago. It seems, unsurprisingly, that their last response was shock ... but it's strange. There's something else I can't quite put my finger on.'

Marney felt a little detached from the conversation. In the gloom of the cellar, she gravitated towards a flight of stairs against the left wall. She stared up them, at the door at the top that led to the tavern. She was nowhere near as skilled as Denton in empathic magic, and she could not feel the residual emotions as he could, but she could sense that elusive something he couldn't put his finger on. It was coming from above, but it was vague – there but not there – and it was almost human.

'I wonder where the merchandise is now,' Denton said.

'Maybe the landlord took it,' Samuel replied bitterly. 'He probably had one look at this mess, grabbed what he could, and ran for it.'

'No,' Marney said peering intently up the stairs. 'I think he's still here.'

She flinched as Denton placed a hand on her shoulder. He too looked at the closed door at the top of the stairs.

'Yes,' he said, nodding approval. 'Well detected, Marney.'

Led by Samuel and his rifle, the group left the carnage in the cellar and ascended the stairs. At the top, the door was locked. Denton used his phial of acid to open it, and they crept into the tavern.

Marney supposed that at any other time Chaney's Den might have been described as a homely place – in a rundown sort of way. The bar area was a rectangular shape, though not particularly wide or long. The carpet was worn and threadbare in places, its pattern eroded by years of passing feet. Time and tobacco smoke had not been kind to the paint on the walls; and the varnish on the small, round tables and their chairs was in need of revamping.

The wall-mounted glow lamps were on, but down low. There was an open fireplace, but it had not been cleaned, no fresh kindling and wood had been laid, and the fire had been left to burn to dead ashes. A few empty tankards lined the bar top, and the ashtrays on the tables had not been emptied. Chaney's Den appeared abandoned, but not to the senses of an empath.

There was a muffled thump from above. Marney worked to calm her anxiety as the group made its way through a door behind the bar, and then up more stairs to the tavern's living quarters. When they reached a landing, Samuel motioned for Marney and Denton to wait. He disappeared through an open doorway. A moment later the glow of the rifle's power stone signified his return, and Samuel beckoned his fellow agents in after him.

In a musty and cluttered living room, a middle-aged man sat in an armchair. At first Marney thought he was dead. But in the glow of Silver Moon that shone through a window, she could see his chest rising and falling in slow, sleeping breaths. His unshaven face was pale and coated with a sheen of sweat. His features twitched as though his dreams were bad. At his feet was a leather satchel. The flap was open and it was filled with Labyrinth pounds.

Marney and Denton kept a safe distance as Samuel passed the satchel back to them. Then he stood before the sleeping man, aiming his rifle at his face.

'Wake up,' he demanded, kicking the man's foot.

The man flinched and snorted, blinked open his eyes, and frowned at the barrel hovering before his face.

'Are you Chaney?' Samuel asked.

The man's gaze found the three people behind the rifle and he nodded vacantly.

Marney sensed emotions within the tavern landlord, but they were so vague it was almost as if they were fading in and out of existence. He smelt bad, too, with a hint of rotting vegetables.

She frowned at Denton beside her. Even though the old empath kept his troubled gaze firmly on Chaney, the sound of his voice filled her head.

Don't be alarmed, he said, *I can sense it, too.*

What does it mean, Denton?

I don't know yet, but while his emotions are phasing like this, we can't control him. Stay focused. Keep your distance.

'I know who you are,' Chaney said. His throat sounded dry. 'I suppose you had to come.'

Denton spoke next and his voice was kind. 'Tell us what happened here, Chaney.'

The landlord gave a hoarse chuckle that ended in a coughing fit. '*This* happened,' he said, tapping a terracotta jar that sat on a table beside the armchair.

He didn't try to prevent Denton stepping forwards and taking the jar. The old empath stepped back to Marney's side, and she leant in for a look as he studied the artefact.

It was a simple looking thing, around the same size and shape as those used for jams and marmalades. It was empty, though evidence of a wax seal remained around the lip. It was plain and undecorated, but Marney didn't get much more of a look before Denton slipped the terracotta jar into his coat pocket.

Chaney took a shuddering breath. 'I didn't ask any questions. Carrick said he had some big sale going on and he'd make it worth my while if he could use my cellar as a meeting place. I don't know what was in the jar, but it's put a curse on me. I'm sick.'

His words were slightly slurred and he fought to keep his eyes open. Marney felt his emotions pulsing weakly, like a heart struggling to beat.

'Tell us what you know and we'll do all we can to help you,' Denton said, but Marney knew it was a lie.

'Help from you lot?' Chaney tried to give a weary chuckle; he seemed all too aware that his number had been up from the moment the Relic Guild disturbed his slumber.

He wiped sweat from his pale face. 'I don't know what to tell you. There was screaming. Never heard men scream like that before. Then it was quiet. Took me a while to pluck up enough courage to go down and see what had happened. Wish I hadn't now … it was all so quiet …' His head nodded back towards sleep.

Samuel kicked his foot again. 'What happened down there?'

Chaney's head snapped upright. 'Two were already nothing but bones. But Carrick – he'd gone mad. Like a bloody animal, he was. Three times I shot him, and he didn't go down until I took off the back of his head. What else could I do?'

'You defended yourself, as you had the right to,' Denton said softly, but his tone carried a subtle inflection that caused Marney to shiver; it was the tone of one addressing a dead man.

'Old Carrick still managed to take a chunk of me with him, though …' With some effort, Chaney rolled up the sleeve of his shirt, exposing a crude wound on his arm from which dark lines spread out over his skin like black veins. 'Bit me like the animal he was.'

'Chaney, I need you to focus,' Denton said. 'Did Carrick tell you where the artefact came from?'

'Maybe.' Chaney shook his head, and Marney felt his emotions wane. 'It's hard to remember.'

'Did you see who was buying it?'

'I told you I can't remember,' Chaney hissed. 'Please help me. Whatever cursed Carrick is in me now. I can't control myself at times, I—'

A thump made the three Relic Guild agents tense. It came from the back of the room, behind a closed door. There was a second thump, and then silence resumed.

'Who else is here?' Samuel demanded.

'Oh,' Chaney said. 'That's Betsy – my bargirl. She was here when everything kicked off. I … I think I bit her. She locked herself in the bedroom. Hasn't come out since.'

Can you sense anyone in that room, Marney? Denton thought to her.

No, she replied.

Neither can I.

Chaney groaned and his eyes rolled back in his head.

Samuel looked at the empaths over his shoulder. 'Move,' he whispered.

At that moment Marney felt Chaney's every emotion fall flat, and even the vaguest of pulse of feeling disappeared. The black veins that splintered out from his bite wound had now snaked up his neck, creeping up the side of his face. The smell of rotting vegetables grew more pronounced.

Denton grabbed Marney's arm, and they backed further away from the landlord. Samuel remained standing over him, coolly aiming his rifle.

Chaney's breathing was shallow. He grinned, revealing long white teeth in receding gums. 'I know what's supposed to happen now,' he said, and to Marney's senses, his voice carried the undercurrent of a scream. 'But you won't take me to the Nightshade. I'll have your throats first!'

Chaney leapt up from the armchair with a roar of fury.

Samuel pulled the trigger. The power stone flashed and the rifle spat.

With a rumble like distant thunder, the fire-bullet took the landlord in the chest. A hot wind whipped around the room as the magic began incinerating his body from the inside out with the intensity of a furnace. Within seconds, blistering, orangey-red flames reduced Chaney to ashes, bones and all. Dry heat and the smell of burnt flesh filled Marney's nostrils. She felt Denton's empathy helping her to control her panic.

The armchair was covered in scorch marks and ash. A patch of carpet was burning. Samuel stamped it out and waved smoke from the air.

At the back of the room, the banging began again at the bedroom door, more violently this time, and it was accompanied by a bestial grunting.

Samuel turned to Marney with a sneer. 'Sometimes, open aggression is the *only* option. You should remember that, too.' He then strode across the living room towards the bedroom.

'Samuel, wait!' Denton snapped.

As the banging continued, Samuel paused at the locked door. He looked back at the old empath with a harsh expression. '*What*?'

'Chaney's illness has obviously spread,' Denton said firmly. 'Perhaps you should try to capture something for Hamir to study, something more substantial than a handful of ashes.'

Without a word, Samuel slid his rifle into its holster on his back and drew his revolver, thumbing the power stone. He leaned back and kicked the bedroom door open.

A second passed, which to Marney felt like an hour, and then a shadowy figure sprang from the room, lunging for Samuel with clawed fingers and long, gnashing teeth. With a flash of thaumaturgy and a low, hollow spitting sound, the revolver fired. A bitter wind moaned. The figure of a woman fell to the floor at Samuel's feet, frozen to ice.

Back at the Nightshade, Marney stood next to Denton in a corridor, and together they stared through a tinted window into a quarantine room. They watched as Hamir studied Betsy, the young bargirl from Chaney's Den, who was now thawed and struggling weakly against the thick straps that secured her to a metal gurney. Two other agents of the Relic Guild had been called in to assist Hamir: the apothecary Gene and the healer Angel. The three of them wore grey protective suits, though the hands of Angel and Gene were not covered by gloves.

Behind them, the back wall of the quarantine room was lined by five tall glass tanks. Three were filled with preservative fluid in which the remains of the dead floated. The skeletons of the Aelf and the alchemist were curled into the foetal position, slowly turning in the fluid. But the lifeless eyes of Carrick the treasure hunter seemed to stare out of the tank, across the room, through the tinted window, almost to glare accusingly at Marney. The bullet wounds in his chest and forehead were dark and ugly.

Next to Marney, Denton ran a hand through his silver hair. His expression was pensive and, although his emotions were shielded, she could tell he was troubled by the way he began crumpling his hat in his hands. Samuel was absent, having been summoned to see Gideon, the Resident. Marney felt tired, drained, but she had come to accept in recent months that sleep was often a luxury the Relic Guild could not afford. Besides, the events at Chaney's Den played heavy on her mind, and she was in no hurry to discover what dreams they might inspire.

On the gurney in the quarantine room, Betsy's skin, mottled with ice burns, had turned a sickly, clammy grey. There was a crude bite wound on her neck from the teeth of the tavern landlord. Black veins slithered out from the wound, snaking across her face and body and limbs. As the last of the effects from Samuel's ice-bullet thawed from her, she struggled against her restraints with increasing strength, gnashing her teeth at the agents around her; but the tight strap across her forehead ensured she could bite no one. Her eyes, a dirty yellow colour, rolled in their sockets as if she had no control over them.

Hamir watched impassively as Angel touched her hands to the bargirl's chest, and then felt down her torso. Angel was in her late forties, a doctor at Central District Hospital by day. Seen through the clear visor of her protective suit's hood, her face was lined with concentration. Wherever Angel touched the girl's body, her hands gave off a light flare, her skin tone brightening with the soft radiance of healing magic.

After a few moments, Angel said, 'As best I can tell, her internal organs have stopped working.' Angel's voice seeped through the walls of the quarantine room and sounded as clear as if she stood in the corridor next to Marney. 'How her body can still be functioning is a mystery,' she continued. 'It just doesn't make sense. Her heart's not beating. Her brain isn't conscious. She's not even using her lungs.'

Hamir looked at the other Relic Guild agent in the room. 'Gene?'

Gene was a slight, elderly man, around the same size as Hamir.

Not quite as old as Denton, but not far behind, the apothecary wore small, round, wire-framed glasses and a serious expression. He always presented a bedraggled and put upon appearance. He walked to the head of the gurney where he pressed his hands to the patient's neck. Slowly, carefully, he pushed both his index fingers through her skin as easily as if they were sharp needles.

Marney was disturbed by how young Betsy was; perhaps even younger than her. Marney looked to the dead bodies in the tanks at the back of the room. The terracotta jar they had found with Chaney was now with Gideon, and Marney found it hard to believe that such a simple looking artefact could be responsible for such terrible things.

'This *is* strange,' Gene said as he extracted his fingers from Betsy's neck. 'I'm pumping her full of antitoxins, but this virus is killing them before they can enter her system. I can't get a handle on what it is.'

Hamir nodded. 'She is petrifying.' The necromancer's normally unreadable expression became resigned. 'However, the process is incomplete. While the virus is still active, there is a slight chance we could reverse its effects.'

Hamir took off the gloves of his protective suit. 'Angel, if you would, please focus your magic around her heart and try to restart it. Gene, concentrate your efforts there also. I will try to hold the virus back and give the heart a chance to pump your antitoxins throughout what's left of her bloodstream.'

As Hamir and the two agents started to work, Betsy screamed, and the sound was amplified through the very walls of the Nightshade. It shredded Marney's nerves. She felt Denton's empathy encouraging calmer emotions within her. It felt like a comforting arm around her shoulders.

'I don't understand,' she said to her mentor. 'She's dead but still living?'

Denton nodded. 'The terracotta jar contained a spell, Marney, magic designed to turn a living person into a facile servant.'

'A golem, you said?'

'That's right ... eventually. At first, the spell acts like a virus that slowly destroys all humanity, driving its victim mad, giving them a hunger for blood—'

Betsy's scream pierced the corridor once again.

'– as you are now witnessing,' Denton added.

Marney shivered.

The old empath sighed. 'In the end, the spell will turn its victim's flesh and blood, hair and bone – all organic matter – into stone. It creates a slave, an abomination, neither alive nor dead, but stripped of all memory of who they once were, and incapable of thought or reason – a golem, Marney.'

Marney looked at the body of Carrick floating in the tank. 'And the virus passes from victim to victim through saliva?'

'Or blood, I suppose.'

'Have you seen this kind of magic before, Denton?'

'No, but Hamir has experience of it.' The old empath was thoughtful for a moment. 'A golem has no other reason to exist than to serve the one whose magic created it. And trust me, Marney, whoever contained that spell in the terracotta jar has a far greater understanding of magic than we of the Relic Guild.'

Marney's eyes darted to her mentor. 'Spiral?'

'Or one of his Genii, yes – it seems likely.'

Marney bit her lower lip. It was no secret that Spiral loathed the denizens, and if he took control of the Labyrinth there would be no mercy for any of them. A magical virus such as this would spread like a plague if it escaped into Labrys Town, not just eradicating every denizen, but also turning each of them into golems: a million servants, all loyal to Spiral. And it could so easily have happened had the Relic Guild not contained the virus at Chaney's Den.

Marney frowned. 'But if this jar carried magic so powerful, how did Carrick smuggle it into the Labyrinth unnoticed?' She shrugged, with a casual smile she didn't really feel. 'The Genii can't reach us here. We're protected.'

'Nothing is infallible, Marney,' Denton replied. 'True, the Time-watcher's barrier prevents creatures of a higher magic entering the Labyrinth, but this was a spell that was well concealed within a small artefact. As for how Carrick managed to bring it here … well, if I've learned anything it is that treasure hunters can be a resourceful lot, though I doubt Carrick ever really knew what he had found.' Denton sounded calm, but Marney could sense he was unconvinced when he added, 'The jar was probably a hopeful strike by the Genii.'

Marney stared through the window, past the gurney where Hamir, Gene and Angel were trying to save Betsy's humanity, to the tanks where the skeletons floated in preservative fluid.

'What about the Aelf and the alchemist?' she said. 'They weren't infected by this virus. Something else happened to them.'

'Hmm ...'

Denton twisted the fabric of his hat in his hands. Perplexed expressions were not often seen on the old empath's round face, and Marney was unsettled by the one that appeared there then.

Hamir's voice seeped through the wall of the quarantine room. 'We've failed,' he said. 'All we have done is encouraged the virus to take its full course.'

On the gurney, Betsy had ceased her struggles and screams, and now laid quite still and calm. She seemed to be staring up at the ceiling, though she no longer had eyes; just empty holes where they should have been. Her head was bald and lumpy, her face twisted into a grotesque mask. Even as Marney watched, the bargirl's limbs stretched and became painfully thin; her stomach shrank and her chest sank. The bite wound was gone, as were the black veins that snaked from it, and her skin was now the deep, clammy grey of soft stone.

She was a golem.

'What'll happen to her now?' Marney asked, but Denton didn't answer.

Gene removed his hood, took off his glasses, and pinched the bridge of his nose. His brow was beaded with sweat. Angel swore and also removed her hood. Her long black hair was streaked with moisture. Hamir, however, appeared as unaffected as ever. He looked at the two empaths standing in the corridor outside until the tint of the observation window darkened into a solid black rectangle in a cream wall decorated with tiny maze patterns.

'Poor Betsy,' Denton whispered in the following silence. 'I wonder if she had family.'

Marney tried not to think about that, but the idea was already in her head.

Thankfully, the moment was broken as the tall and broad figure of a young man strode down the corridor towards them. He was dressed in loose-fitting garb, his feet bare. His cane of green glass stabbed the floor with every step. Van Bam reached the empaths, his deep brown eyes showing concern.

'How is the girl?' he asked in deep, precise tones.

'Gone,' was all Denton said.

Van Bam nodded. His expression gave nothing away, and Marney refrained from reading his emotions.

'Gideon wants to see you,' he said to Denton, and then he looked at Marney with an apologetic expression. 'But not you.'

'Ah,' Denton said. He smiled lightly as he looked from Van Bam to his protégé. 'The Resident calls, and so I shall leave you two in each other's company.' He placed his crumpled hat on his head and set off down the corridor.

'Oh, Marney,' he called back. 'I'd not bother going to bed, if I were you. I suspect our day is only just beginning.'

Marney and Van Bam shared a long kiss. He towered over her and his embrace was strong and engulfing. She ran a hand over his smoothly-shaved head, down his neck, and felt the muscles of his shoulders and back. Van Bam placed one big hand gently upon Marney's cheek and with the other he pulled her tighter against his body. His passion was evident, but Marney was an empath, and she could sense that his mind was not fully focused on this stolen moment, the here and now, in her private room within the Nightshade.

She broke the kiss and frowned into Van Bam's brown eyes. 'What's wrong?' she said.

Van Bam sighed, and Marney allowed him to manoeuvre them to her bed, where they both sat.

'Is it the others?' she asked. 'Does someone know about us?'

Van Bam shook his head. 'If anyone does, they have not revealed it to me.'

'Then what, Van Bam?'

He took her hand into his. 'You have had a difficult time tonight,' he said. 'How are you feeling?'

Marney narrowed her eyes, feeling half-amused and half-irritated.

Van Bam's concern was genuine. Marney was an inexperienced agent of the Relic Guild, true enough, but he knew better than to try and mollycoddle her. He was deflecting, trying to circumnavigate something – a point he wished to make subtly, without upsetting her. But even an illusionist couldn't hide his emotions from an empath. She felt exactly what he was thinking now.

'You're not staying, are you?' she said disappointedly.

Van Bam chuckled and kissed her hand. 'No. Gideon has given Samuel and me a mission. He wants us to investigate the movements of Carrick prior to his death.'

'Now?'

Van Bam nodded. 'As soon as Samuel is ready to leave.'

'Why do *you* have to go? Samuel prefers his own company anyway.'

'There is truth to that, I suspect,' Van Bam said with a smile. 'But you know how Gideon is, Marney. His orders cannot be questioned, and duty always comes first.'

'Yeah, I know,' she said moodily.

And the truth was Marney really did understand how the Relic Guild operated, and she accepted it. But she was tired with controlling her emotions, of blocking what she felt. The night's work played heavily upon her, much heavier than she had allowed herself to yet acknowledge. She had hoped so deeply to be able to let her guard down while in Van Bam's arms – maybe to cry, maybe to laugh, or to just feel his body next to hers and know there was something other than the war against Spiral in her life.

Van Bam, apparently sensing how she felt, cupped her face. 'You saw what the contents of the jar did, Marney.'

She nodded.

'You know it was likely Genii magic.'

She pressed her forehead to his and squeezed her eyes shut. 'I know.'

'We have to know the identity of this Aelf that Carrick was dealing with,' Van Bam said warningly. 'There could be enemies of the Time-watcher within Labrys Town's walls.'

'Just go,' she whispered. 'I'll be all right.'

'Do not be so hasty.' He kissed her. 'You know, I had a surprise planned for you tonight.'

Marney felt his affection and managed a small chuckle. 'What surprise?'

'Ah, it is a secret that will now have to wait until we see each other next. For the meantime ...' He gave her a mischievous grin. 'I think Samuel will be a while yet.'

And he kissed her again, more soundly.

Marney could feel the rising heat of Van Bam's passion and she wanted nothing more than to share in it, to feel his skin against hers, and find the respite she craved from these dark days. But she could feel another presence now, standing outside the door to her chamber. Someone was eager to enter, but embarrassed to interrupt a private moment.

Marney broke the kiss. 'Too late,' she said.

Mentally, she thought to the loitering presence, *You can come in now, Denton.*

Immediately, there was a click, and the outline of a door appeared on the wall. Van Bam jumped to his feet and grabbed his green glass cane as the door swung inwards, and the big empath stepped into the room.

His voice entered Marney's mind. *Sorry for interrupting,* and then he addressed Van Bam aloud. 'Samuel's asking for you,' he said seriously. 'He's ready to leave.'

Van Bam nodded. He gave Marney a quick, disappointed look, and then strode from the room.

Marney pursed her lips at Denton. He was crushing his hat in his hands more than usual. Evidently, the meeting with Gideon had exposed extra cause for concern, and, just like Van Bam, he was struggling to find the right words to tell her. But unlike Van Bam, his emotions were cloaked and undecipherable.

'And what's wrong with *you*?' she asked with a sigh.

Denton pulled a face – a subtle approach to whatever he was withholding was impossible.

'Gideon has a mission for us,' he said. He shrugged, put his hat on and patted it down. 'Get your coat, Marney.' His grin was full-toothed. 'You're going to meet a Thaumaturgist.'

CHAPTER SEVEN

IN THE COLD LIGHT
OF SILVER MOON

In the Nightshade's spacious forecourt, Samuel stood beside the Resident's black tram. The rain had stopped and the clouds had cleared. Silver Moon hung in the sky among stars, its blue-grey light gleaming down, cold and clean. The atmosphere was refreshing, but the temperature would continue to drop, and soon Samuel's old bones would ache from the chill. Clara was still inside the Nightshade, but she would join him shortly, as soon as Van Bam had found her more fitting attire than a simple gown. For the time being, Samuel was glad for the moment of solitude.

The last time Fabian Moor was seen in Labrys Town, Samuel had been in his late twenties, Van Bam a little younger, and Marney scarcely older than Clara. They had been considered the rookies of the Relic Guild, the youngsters of the group. Gideon had been the Resident, of course, and the Resident always led the guild. Van Bam had not been blind back then, but Samuel struggled to remember what his eyes had looked like. Now, standing before the Nightshade, beneath the cold light of Silver Moon, Samuel could remember the agents who had died because of Fabian Moor, and it made him shiver. With stark clarity, he could see their faces and hear the sound of their voices.

Only he, Van Bam and Marney left now. This night was the first contact Samuel had had with either of them in almost forty years. The last three survivors of the Relic Guild ... were they really so old?

Shrugging off his reverie, Samuel fished the spirit compass from his coat pocket. He crouched and laid the compass upon the wet cobbles of the Nightshade's forecourt, and then produced the phial containing the dried blood and tiny pieces of skin that he had scraped from beneath Clara's fingernails.

As he was laying the phial down beside the compass, Clara appeared. Now dressed in black leggings, a thick, hooded jumper, and heavy, calf-length boots with silver buckles down the sides, she carried a cloth satchel that hung from her shoulder. She stopped beside Samuel, but didn't acknowledge him. Her expression was distant, lost to thought, as she stared down the tunnel that led out of the forecourt to Resident Approach.

Samuel said nothing to her at first. Still crouching, he watched as Clara produced a small and dented tin from which she took a little white tablet which she popped into her mouth. As she chewed, she ran a hand through her short, red-streaked hair. Then her attention was caught by a monument on the far side of the courtyard.

It was a large stone archway, standing fifteen feet high and twenty feet wide. It was situated several feet from the forecourt wall, a standalone structure, dull, lacking aesthetic character. Yet Clara was mesmerised by it.

'It's a portal,' Samuel told her. 'The last one standing in Labrys Town.'

As if realising for the first time she wasn't alone, Clara looked down at Samuel with a start.

'A portal to the Aelfir?' she said.

Samuel nodded. 'And our sole remaining link to them. They use that portal to send us rations and supplies. If it wasn't for their charity, Clara ...' Samuel didn't finish the sentence.

After a short pause, he stood, and motioned to the satchel hanging from her shoulder. 'Is that for me?'

She looked at the satchel as if she had never seen it before, and then shrugged it off into Samuel's hands.

'Van Bam said we'd need it,' she said.

He loosened the straps of the satchel, exposing several glass balls filled with liquid. He picked one out and shook it. The liquid glowed with faint green light.

'What are they?' Clara asked.

'Everything and nothing,' Samuel replied, replacing the glass ball back in the satchel. 'As the mirror in his study suggests, Van Bam is an adept illusionist.' He handed the satchel back to her. 'Those are spell spheres.'

'Of course they are,' Clara said sarcastically. The satchel clinked as she looped it over her shoulder again. Then she shook her head wistfully. 'You're the Relic Guild – or what's left of it. You're all magickers, and not as dead and buried as people believe you to be.'

Samuel didn't reply.

Clara rubbed her eyes. She seemed tired. 'I don't know how, but I remember you, Samuel. I remember Van Bam and Marney, too … There are others, but it's all so vague, I …'

'Clara,' said Samuel. 'About what Marney did to you tonight—'

'Van Bam has already asked me, Samuel!' she said, frustrated. 'I don't know what Marney did to me.'

'And I can't pretend to, either,' Samuel admitted. 'But that kiss is something to be grateful for. In part, I'm guessing Marney wanted to help you, to make the transition a little smoother.'

'You mean the transition into the Relic Guild,' Clara scoffed. 'So being a changeling automatically makes me an agent?'

'It certainly makes you dangerous enough to be a candidate.'

'But do I have a choice, Samuel? Can I say no?'

'I suppose you could. But then Van Bam would never allow you to leave the Nightshade.'

Clara's eyes flashed yellow, exhibiting some of her inner wolf's anger. 'What's that supposed to mean?'

Samuel sighed. 'Magickers are a danger to Labrys Town, Clara, and if you're not serving the Relic Guild then … well, you've met Hamir the necromancer, right?'

Clara shivered, her anger dissipating. She looked up at the moon and stars in the clear night sky.

'When I was a child,' she said, 'I was told so many stories about you – *us,* I suppose. The older denizens still reckon the streets were safer before you disappeared.' She looked down at Samuel. Her face was sad. 'Van Bam told me how everything changed after the war, after Fabian Moor. Not exactly catching the Relic Guild at its best, am I?'

'No,' Samuel said softly, 'you're not,' and he crouched again, returning his attentions to the compass on the floor.

Back in the old days, the duties of the Relic Guild had been straightforward. If a treasure hunter brought a magical artefact onto Labrys

Town's black market, the Relic Guild would hunt it down and deal with the seller and buyer. But now …

The Relic Guild had never been officially disbanded, but since the doorways to the Houses of the Aelfir had been closed, there had been nothing for them to do anymore. Samuel couldn't remember the last time a magical artefact had come onto the black market, and no new generation of magickers had been born to replace the agents who had died. But now there was Clara. Now Fabian Moor had returned. Now the Relic Guild had purpose again, even if most of its agents were dead.

'So,' Clara's voice startled Samuel. 'Charlie Hemlock is the only source of information we have.' She pointed at the compass and phial on the forecourt floor. 'And we're going to rescue him from a demon by using bits of his face and a fob watch?'

'This isn't a fob watch, Clara,' Samuel replied. 'It's a spirit compass.'

So saying, he took the compass and unscrewed its cap, revealing the face within.

Clara bent down for a closer look.

'It works with any organic material,' Samuel explained. 'Hair, skin, blood – anything – and it'll track the spirit of the donor.' Samuel pressed the compass face. It gave a click and sprang up on a hinge. 'It was how I was able to track you.'

Beneath the compass face was a hollow interior, like a tiny, flat-bottomed dish, and curled inside was a long, silver-grey hair, thick like twine. Samuel pulled the hair out and offered it to Clara. Tentatively, she took it and frowned.

'It's yours,' Samuel told her. 'A hair from the wolf. I found it on the remains of the man you killed.'

Her expression unreadable, Clara pulled the hair taut between her fingers and studied it. 'I've never seen it, you know,' she said, her tone strange. 'The wolf, I mean. I never remember … not clearly …' She released the hair and watched it fall away on the chilly breeze. Her lip trembled. 'I-I don't think I've ever killed anyone before, Samuel.'

Samuel said nothing, uncorked the phial, and began tapping its contents into the hollow interior of the compass.

'I have to ask,' Clara said, her voice small. 'Tonight, out in the Great Labyrinth, if Marney hadn't stopped you—'

'I would've shot you dead,' Samuel replied unhesitatingly.

He looked up at Clara. His blunt answer had obviously offended her. He felt a flush of shame, but saw no point in dressing things up for the young changeling.

'I'm two years away from my seventieth birthday,' he said, 'and I don't expect to reach that age. I've been a bounty hunter since the Genii War ended, Clara. It's how I get by, and I'll give you no apologies or excuses.'

She looked to the floor.

'Clara, you're an agent of the Relic Guild now. We may be shrouded in secrecy, but there's nothing but loyalty to our duties. From here on out, we trust each other.'

'What's done is done, eh?'

'Exactly.'

She nodded, looking like a scolded child. Samuel could see Clara was doing her best to shrug off lingering doubts. He didn't have the heart to tell her they never went away, and resumed filling the compass with dried blood and skin.

'So,' Clara said, 'the spirit compass will lead us to Hemlock.'

The phial empty now, Samuel clicked the compass face back into position, got to his feet and offered Clara a closer look.

'Sounds like magic to me,' she said. 'Where did you find it?'

'A good question. It doesn't exactly belong here, if you follow me.'

'It's a relic?'

Samuel nodded. 'A genuine artefact of the Aelfir.'

Clara's face flowed through a mixture of emotions, but finally she seemed to settle on awe.

Samuel continued. 'Usually, these relics were returned to their proper owners, but we never did discover which House this compass was stolen from.' Samuel allowed her a small smile. 'I like to think of it as a perk of the job.'

'A perk? What does Van Bam think of that?'

'Our Resident could hardly object,' he scoffed. 'Where do you think that cane of his came from?'

Clara laughed then, with genuine humour. It was good to see it on her young face.

'Tell me something,' she said. 'Van Bam is an illusionist, Marney an empath – and how magic touched me certainly isn't a secret anymore – but how did magic touch you, Samuel?'

Samuel didn't answer. The compass was vibrating in his hand.

The needle ticked around the face slowly, and then spun anti-clockwise in a full circle. It stopped, shivering, pointing directly south down Resident Approach. It was a strong reading.

'Got him,' Samuel said. He looked at the sleek black body of the Resident's personal tram sitting on its track in the forecourt. 'Let's go.'

The Resident of Labrys Town received few visitors. Most of those who came to the Nightshade did so on official business – the heads of the merchant and industry guilds, gambling and entertainment councils – and these visitors could never hide their discomfort when seeing the metal plates covering their governor's eyes. They wondered how one weakened by blindness could attain such a lofty position as the Residency. They did not realise that there was more than one way in which a man might see, and the Resident of Labrys Town saw everything.

Van Bam stood alone in his observatory, deep inside the Nightshade. The room was alive with wispy imagery and spectral visions that filled his inner sight with myriad shades of grey. On the streets of Labrys Town, the ubiquitous eye devices took in streams of information at all times. The police used the eyes to watch the hidden corners of town, but ultimately all audio and visual information was fed to the Nightshade for the attention of the Resident.

Van Bam observed Samuel and Clara, and it was almost as though he stood out in the forecourt beside them. But the young changeling and the old bounty hunter were unaware of the Resident's presence. He watched as they boarded the Nightshade's official tram and set off through the tunnel, heading south towards the central district. Van Bam followed them, jumping through the eyes held in the hands of the statues lining Resident Approach; and then he overtook the tram and travelled across the world he governed. Drifting, flying almost, he weaved through the streets and back alleys as a phantom, the unseen watcher.

Labrys Town held a population of close to a million denizens. It was divided into five districts and covered two and a half thousand square miles of ground. The town was boxed in by the sheer boundary walls, a hundred feet high on all four sides. Beyond the boundary lay the endless twists and turns of the Great Labyrinth, where the Retrospective roamed, where even Van Bam's vision could not see. There was no escaping this place, not anymore. Labrys Town was all the denizens had, all they would ever have, and they knew they were being watched.

The districts were all but deserted in the cold early hours of Silver Moon. The streets were wet and few people walked them. To Van Bam's inner sight, all was as it should be. He continued to follow the eyes southward until reaching the central district and a plaza known as Watchers' Gallery, located at the exact centre of town. Inside the plaza stood a square building that was the headquarters of the Labrys Town Police Force. Impressive in size, it was still much smaller than the Nightshade. Van Bam's vision entered the building, jumping through the eyes inside, until he reached the upper level and the office of Captain Jeter.

Jeter sat as his desk, working through a mountain of paperwork. He looked tired. Three empty cups before him were evidence of the coffee that was helping to keep him awake. The office now filled the observation room of the Nightshade as though Van Bam stood there before the desk, but it was only imagery, and he ensured that Jeter could not see him.

With a mental command, Van Bam activated the audio function. 'Working late, Captain?' he said.

Jeter started to his feet. He saluted his Resident, though in actuality the gesture was aimed at the eye device fixed to his office wall.

'Yes, sir,' the police captain said.

'It is good to see the denizens are in such dedicated hands. Please, be seated.'

'Thank you, sir.' Jeter took his chair again, but his body language remained stiff and formal and the dark lenses of his spectacles were concealing his eyes. Van Bam pursed his lips.

'I wish to speak with you, Captain, but first be so good as to remove your spectacles.'

Jeter did so hurriedly. Without their aid, his small, hazel eyes blinked and strained for focus.

Van Bam said, 'That's better.'

If one knew what signs to look for, the human face could give away much of what a person truly thought, of what they did not say – the eyes most especially. And who better to read those signs, to understand and detect the masking of what was real, than an illusionist?

'Do you have anything to report?' Van Bam continued.

'No, sir,' Jeter said. 'Our search for Charlie Hemlock is continuing, but we've hit nothing but dead ends so far.'

'That is hardly surprising, Captain. You may call off your efforts now. Charlie Hemlock is no longer your concern.'

Jeter frowned. 'And Fat Jacob, sir?'

'He will not be returning to the Lazy House.'

'Understood. I'll have the entertainment council terminate his license.'

'Thank you, Captain.'

'Sir, if I might, can I ask about the whore, Peppercorn Clara—'

'The matter is closed,' Van Bam responded sternly. 'Is that clear?'

'Yes, sir …'

Jeter was a model denizen, an excellent choice as head of the police; but whenever he was addressed by his Resident, his uncertainty displaced the confident arrogance he usually displayed before others. His frustration was evident now, though he dare not argue with Van Bam. How could a matter the Resident had deemed so important just a few scant hours ago be concluded so suddenly without explanation? Jeter's face was alive with micro-expressions, easily read by Van Bam.

The Resident said, 'You are wondering at the reasons for my decision, yes?'

Jeter lowered his eyes. 'It's not my place to question you, sir.'

'No, it is not. Put your frustration to one side, Captain. A matter has arisen of which we must speak.'

Jeter looked up, his expression professional once more. 'Of course, sir.'

Van Bam paused, choosing his words carefully. 'A wild demon has entered Labrys Town.'

Jeter's expression fell, almost imperceptibly. His Resident's revelation was clearly a problem he did not need in these early hours. 'Understood,' he said. 'I'll organise a search and destroy party immediately.'

This was standard procedure on the rare occurrence of a wild demon venturing from the Retrospective and managing to pass through the boundary wall into town; but Jeter did not appreciate that this time it was no ordinary demon his Resident was talking about.

'No,' Van Bam said. '*You* will double the street patrols, and police watchers will monitor the eyes at all times. *I* will coordinate the hunt personally.'

'Sir?'

'Captain, this demon is peculiarly gifted in magic. It will be hard to track and even harder to destroy. For that reason, I am reinstating the services of the Relic Guild.'

'The Relic Guild?' Jeter's surprise was obvious. Less apparent were the subtle shades of fear that opened his eyes fractionally wider.

'You heard me, Captain,' Van Bam said. 'You and your officers will pay every courtesy to my agents. You will not stand in the Relic Guild's way, but you will stand by as reinforcements should you be ordered. Do you understand?'

'Y-Yes, sir.'

'Good. You will watch and protect the denizens as always. Anything of the unusual is to be reported to me immediately. We must not underestimate the threat this demon poses.'

'Of course, sir.'

'Then you have your orders, Captain, and I bid you good night.'

Jeter jumped to his feet and saluted again. Van Bam said nothing further and withdrew his focus from the office, the police building and the plaza in which it stood. Once more his vision flowed through the eyes of Labrys Town.

Streets and buildings passed through his observation room, but Van Bam didn't know where he was heading and travelled in random directions across two and a half thousand square miles. Observing the town like this gave the Resident a sense of clarity and inner focus, and there was much on which he needed to meditate.

The dead stay dead, Clara had stated – if only that were true. The Relic Guild had stopped Fabian Moor once before, but things had been different back then, the organisation much stronger. Marney was missing, perhaps dead already; and that left two old men and an inexperienced young girl with the unenviable task of hunting Spiral's most dangerous general, the last of the Genii.

As he continued to travel across Labrys Town with this daunting thought in mind, a man's voice suddenly spoke inside Van Bam's head with cold, pernicious tones.

Are you feeling lucky, my idiot?

Van Bam sighed, but didn't reply, and the voice added: *Are you roaming the streets hoping you might catch Fabian Moor enjoying a night off? Doing his laundry, perhaps?*

Van Bam felt his direction veer to take a new route through the eyes. He was not in control of this change, and not from choice did his motion stop halfway down a wide street on the outskirts of the central district.

He stood outside a four storey hospital. Inside, a receptionist spoke with an orderly. The lights from windows shone down onto the wet cobbles. Van Bam felt a moment of sadness, remembering Angel. Many years ago, in this hospital, she had doubled as a doctor, using her gift of magical healing to help where she could.

The voice spoke again inside Van Bam's mind, and the cold tone was clearly amused: *Brings back memories, doesn't it?*

Why have you brought me here? Van Bam thought, but the voice didn't answer at first.

In the street before the Resident the figure of a man slowly materialised. His hair was short, and his gaunt face was shaded by stubble. He grinned lopsidedly, laconically, and his sunken eyes gleamed with menace.

This man did not truly stand in the street; he did not stand anywhere. He was the voice in Van Bam's head, the ghost that haunted the corridors of the Nightshade, the spirit who had at one time been the Resident of Labrys Town. He was forever remembered as Gideon the

Selfless, and he appeared to Van Bam exactly as he had the night he had been killed, forty years before.

'Why didn't you tell Captain Jeter the truth?' the ghost of Gideon demanded. 'Why not tell him that a Genii has returned?'

'You know why,' Van Bam replied. 'The very mention of Fabian Moor would send the denizens into a panic.'

'And rightly so.' Gideon watched as two nurses emerged from the hospital, ending their shifts for the night. They walked through Gideon, briefly disturbing his image, and he turned to watch them leave, unashamedly admiring their figures.

He turned back to Van Bam with lust in his eyes. 'But I think inducing panic will soon be the least of everyone's worries, don't you, my idiot?' He chuckled unkindly.

For forty years Van Bam had tolerated Gideon's voice in his head, and the ghost rarely made his point quickly. It was far easier to accept his incongruous manner than to battle against it.

He sighed and took a few steps closer to the former Resident. 'Gideon, there is something I do not understand.'

'Oh?'

'Fabian Moor is a Genii, a creature of higher magic – what possible use could he have for a magicker? Why did he abduct Marney instead of killing her?'

Gideon shrugged as if he didn't much care. 'Your guess, I suspect, is as useless as mine. Though we have always had our theories about Moor.'

Van Bam nodded. 'Let us hope that Charlie Hemlock will provide some definite answers.'

'If he's still alive.' A look of dark mirth came over Gideon's sharp features. 'Oh, by the way, I like Clara. She's a little ugly for my tastes, but when a whore earns the name of *Peppercorn* …' His grin was unfriendly.

Van Bam held in check a sudden and unexpected need to protect the changeling.

Gideon said, 'Do you think she is up to the task, my idiot?'

This gave Van Bam pause to consider. He exhaled heavily. 'Clara is strong, and we can be thankful that Marney has helped her to accept her predicament.'

'What, with a kiss?' Gideon snorted. 'Marney never did anything without reason – you know that, my idiot. Who can say *what* she did to the whore out in the Great Labyrinth tonight.'

'Regardless,' Van Bam said testily, 'Clara will have to learn fast, but at least she is in good hands.'

'Good hands?' Gideon's laughter was scornful. 'Are you really so sure?'

With that the ghost disappeared, and Van Bam felt a dizzying lurch as he was swept away from the hospital where an old friend had once worked, and his journey across Labrys Town was resumed.

Again, the streets and side lanes passed through the observation room. Faster and faster he travelled, the lights of streetlamps streaked and blurred, but Van Bam didn't try to stop Gideon leading him across the districts. Within seconds he reached the lower regions of Resident Approach, where a sleek and black tram was just heading into the central district from the north. Van Bam caught up with his personal tram, and then its interior filled the observation room.

He stared down the length of the carriage. Two bench seats lined either side. Samuel and Clara sat opposite each other. Samuel studied his spirit compass, and Clara looked down at the satchel of spell spheres in her lap. They did not speak; the atmosphere in the tram was clearly uncomfortable.

Gideon had materialised sitting next to Samuel. Van Bam ensured that he and the ghost could not be seen or heard, and pursed his lips as Gideon sneered into the old bounty hunter's face.

'Look at him,' he hissed. 'Always so proud. Always so ... *irritating*. You should have died years ago, Old Man Sam.'

Van Bam didn't comment. Gideon, even as a ghost, was a latent psychopath. When he was alive, his passion for confrontation was legendary among the agents of the Relic Guild. But he had been the Resident and his ways were tolerated. Except by Samuel. He and Gideon had shared a mutual hatred, which often boiled over, and on a few occasions they had needed to be separated. Van Bam had never discerned the specific reason why they loathed each other, but no one had ever dared suggest they reconcile their differences, not even old and wise Denton.

Gideon peered at Samuel's face. 'Oh, Samuel,' he said. 'I wonder, given your time again, would you still stand by your comrades in the Relic Guild? If you were the man you have become today, then I think not.'

Behind Gideon's caustic words, Van Bam could detect the point he was making, and it ran deeper than his hatred of an old bounty hunter. It was something that could be ignored no longer.

'Samuel concerns me,' the Resident said.

'And with good reason,' Gideon replied. He looked across the carriage at the young changeling sitting opposite. 'Clara is touched by magic,' he continued, 'the first to be born so for many years, as far as we know. She represents a new generation of Relic Guild agents. Marney knew it, and so did Samuel.'

'Yet he intended to kill Clara for the sake of a bounty,' Van Bam said, and he moved down the carriage to sit next to the changeling.

Samuel knew the duties of the Relic Guild, no matter how many years had passed. He should have been as keen as Marney to save Clara. The bounty contract was a mystery – undoubtedly bogus, perhaps a means to gain Samuel's attention – but what had it offered that could convince Old Man Sam to act so dishonourably, so foolishly?

Gideon passed a ghostly hand through Samuel's face and said, 'Who was it that offered this old fool a contract to end the life of a changeling whore?'

An avatar, Samuel had said; a ghost of blue light …

'You will have to watch him,' Gideon warned. 'Samuel is not the man you once knew, my idiot.'

'Perhaps,' Van Bam replied. 'But I do not believe Samuel to be a danger to me or Clara. Not now. He can be trusted. I can depend on him.'

'I certainly hope so.' To Van Bam's vision, Gideon's eyes flashed with sparkling colours. 'Because we all know what happened the last time Fabian Moor was around.'

With a sudden jolt, Van Bam found himself once again outside the black tram. He remained silent as Gideon steered him southward, deep into the southern district of Labrys Town. He passed recycling plants and water reservoirs, and then a landscape of storage warehouses shifted through the observation room. Van Bam floated through the yard of a metal-works and drifted down a lonely street, where nondescript houses lined either side in terraces. Down this street, all movement ceased, and Van Bam was left staring at damp cobbles reflecting the violet glow of streetlamps.

The ghost of Gideon once more materialised before the Resident. He pointed to the ground at his feet.

'I'm standing on the exact spot where I died.' His grin was broad. 'Did I ever tell you what it was like to die, my idiot? The pain and the emptiness I suffered?'

'Frequently,' Van Bam replied sourly.

'I've been thinking – since Fabian Moor has returned, my death seems a little in vain. Do you think they'll strip me of my "Selfless" title?'

'What is your point, Gideon?'

The tone of Gideon's reply suggested he was talking to an imbecile. 'What will you do if Charlie Hemlock is alive? If he can answer every one of your questions, how will that help you stop a Genii?' He sneered, and his tone returned to its cold and bitter state. 'These are not the old days, my idiot. There are no mighty friends watching over us anymore.'

Van Bam had to concede the truth of this, though it froze his soul to do so.

With a heavy sigh, he dispelled the spectral visions received through the eye devices. The imagery faded and swirled like fog caught in the wind until he stood in the dim glow of an inactive observatory within the Nightshade, surrounded by the dull walls, decorated with small maze patterns.

The ghost of Gideon remained in the room with him. His expression was as amused as it was expectant.

'You lead the Relic Guild now, my idiot, but your list of allies isn't exactly long anymore, is it?' He grinned. 'The denizens are all alone with a Genii in their midst.'

Van Bam remained silent.

'What to do, my idiot, what to do …' The lights of Gideon's ghostly eyes shone manically. 'The Timewatcher abandoned the Labyrinth forty years ago. Her Thaumaturgists haven't been seen since the war ended. Who will you call on for help this time?'

With that statement hanging in the air, Gideon's ghost faded and disappeared, leaving Van Bam in the observation room alone. But in his head, Gideon's voice whispered: *Does anyone out there remember us at all?*

CHAPTER EIGHT

WILD DEMONS

At the end of the Genii War there had been a mighty reckoning. No one knew why the Timewatcher abandoned the Labyrinth, but they said that, along with millions of Aelfir, the war had killed Her compassion. The retribution She vented upon Her enemies was as furious as it was merciless. For Spiral, the great and terrible instigator, She created a distant realm called Oldest Place, a prison of endless torment and suffering in which her gravest enemy was incarcerated for eternity. The Genii, those Thaumaturgists who had turned their backs upon their Mother to serve Spiral so loyally, were tossed screaming and writhing into the Nothing of Far and Deep, where their souls were lost forever to its primordial mists.

But it was reckoned the Timewatcher's greatest act of retribution was reserved for Spiral's armies, those Houses of the Aelfir who had joined the Genii in their malicious crusade.

The Timewatcher created a space, a gap between the fabric of existence and the emptiness of non-existence. Into this gap, She poured dead time, every second of every atrocity committed during the Genii War, and it became a vast realm of damnation, perversion, abomination. She called this place the Retrospective.

The renegade Aelfir were banished to the Retrospective, along with their lands. The decay of dead time corroded their realms into an uninhabitable wasteland. Their bodies were corrupted into the forms of hideous creatures, while their minds were torn and damaged beyond redemption. The hundreds of thousands of enemy Aelfir who had survived the war, whose Houses had once been great and wise, were reduced to nothing more than blood-thirsty animals, without a shadow of good or reason, left to scavenge upon each other in a landscape of poison and ashes.

There was no reprieve from the Retrospective, no chance of escape. Its doorway was set to drift aimlessly through the endless alleyways of the Great Labyrinth, as lost as the souls beyond it. It served as an example, a warning, an eternal deterrent for any denizen seeking passage to the Houses who had remained loyal to the Thaumaturgists and their Mother. The Labyrinth became a forbidden zone, and the cruelty and torture of the Retrospective bespoke a promise of what it meant to be an enemy of the Timewatcher.

Only the boundary wall kept the denizens safe from the Retrospective, and Clara shivered to recall the tales she had heard of the wild demons that dwelt within that damned House of dead time.

Under the bright glare of Silver Moon, the official tram of the Nightshade drove through the central district. It weaved through the main streets. The occasional purple spark of thaumaturgy snapped from the power line and flashed against its sleek black shell. Inside, Clara clutched the satchel of spell spheres in her lap with white-knuckled fingers. She fidgeted nervously beneath the violet light of a ceiling prism. Across from her, Samuel sat studying his spirit compass. He had not said a word since they had left the Nightshade's forecourt.

Clara had never seen a wild demon herself, but she had once had a client who claimed he had been attacked by one. His left leg was missing from just below the knee; three fingers on his right hand had been bitten off; and gouge marks and scars had decorated his body and face. Clara desperately tried not to think of what manner of monster could inflict such wounds.

Through the tram's tinted windows she watched the buildings and streetlamps passing by outside, along with a few denizens either making their way home or walking to work to begin an early morning shift. Mostly, the central district was quiet at this time.

Who drove the tram was a mystery. Clara had seen no driver, and the carriage ended at a smooth metal wall devoid of a door that might lead to a driver's compartment. But on that wall was an eye device. Public trams had no eyes fitted inside them, but the rheumy stare of the one fitted inside the Resident's tram made the hairs on the back of her neck stand up. Was someone watching them?

Judging by Samuel's composure, the tram was somehow in sync with his spirit compass, and they were headed in the right direction. But the right direction was leading them to Charlie Hemlock and a showdown with a wild demon of the Retrospective.

Deciding that breaking the silence was the best way to ease her nerves, she asked Samuel, 'Have you ever seen a Thaumaturgist?'

The old bounty hunter looked up from the compass and gave her a deep frown.

Clara added, 'I mean, back in the old days. They came to Labrys Town, didn't they?'

'Sometimes,' Samuel said. 'Other times denizens were taken to see them.'

'Like who? Relic Guild agents?'

Samuel paused for a moment. 'The Thaumaturgists are long gone, Clara, and I won't speak of them,' he said irritably. He returned his attention to the compass. 'Now let me concentrate.'

Clara didn't know why the compass demanded such attention, but she did know that Samuel was an easy man to dislike.

The old bounty hunter blew hot and cold, but always an air of arrogance surrounded him. It underlined his every word, his every action, as if his authority simply could not be challenged. But there was sadness too, something deep, something bitter. Clara suspected that Old Man Sam carried the weight of his experiences. She found him strange and uncomfortable company, and wished it was Van Bam travelling with her now.

Undeterred by Samuel's dismissive attitude, she said, 'Have you ever left the Labyrinth, Samuel? Did you ever travel to the Houses of the Aelfir?'

This time, when Samuel looked up, he did not glare at Clara or seem irritated. He stared past her, as if into some distance beyond the tram's window, beyond the central district and the Great Labyrinth itself.

'Yes,' he said. It was a simple statement.

'What about now?' said Clara. 'Aren't there any doorways still open? You know, secret ones that normal denizens don't know about?'

'Clara …' Samuel's voice was level as his eyes fixed onto hers. 'Just because we're agents of the Relic Guild, doesn't mean we have any special dispensation. The doorways of the Great Labyrinth are closed to all of us.'

'What about that portal outside the Nightshade?'

'It connects to the Aelfir directly and not to a doorway, Clara.' The hardness of his voice jolted her. 'The Timewatcher left it open so we didn't die. And it only goes one way. The Aelfir use that portal to send us provisions, but we can send nothing back, and no living thing can pass through. I doubt even Van Bam knows which House is on the other side. Be assured, no one gets into the Labyrinth, and no one gets out. Not *ever*.'

'Fabian Moor did.'

Samuel sucked air over his teeth, struggling to find patience. 'Marney has put all kinds of thoughts and questions into your head, child, but now is not the time for answers.'

There it was again – that odd mixture of arrogance and sadness. Clara sat back. Silence returned to the carriage, and the tram passed out of the central district and headed into the west side.

Clara had spent so long fearing her magic, scared of the day when the authorities would discover she was a magicker, or when the wolf freed itself of her control and … killed someone … Clara shook herself. Now the day she feared had arrived, she had been made to feel like her magic was to be celebrated, not condemned. She was no criminal, no out of control murderer, but part of some greater plan that she barely understood. Would she be required to kill again?

The effects of Marney's kiss still lingered inside her. It stripped away the fear, gave her courage and determination, and prepared her for the Relic Guild. She was beginning to feel that she had finally found a place where she might fit in. Samuel had been in Clara's position once; he too had learned there was a higher purpose for magickers in the Labyrinth. Why then was he being so intolerant of her?

As if pondering this very question himself, Samuel sighed and looked at her with a softer expression.

'Everything in its right place, Clara,' he said. 'I appreciate how confused you must be right now, but I think you understand what we're about to do, don't you?'

Clara felt a cold pang. 'Rescue Hemlock from a wild demon,' she whispered.

'Exactly. Focus on that. Save the questions for later. Take one step at a time.'

It wasn't long before the tram came to a stop. Samuel rose and slid open the door of the carriage. Clara followed him onto the street outside.

They had arrived at Web Street in the western district. The impressive buildings of Western University ran along the entire length of the street, on both sides. The school was four storeys high, and from a few of its tall windows light spilled onto the cobbles. Samuel set off without a word, following the compass in his hand. Clara adjusted the satchel strap on her shoulder and caught up with him. The black tram remained where it was.

'I take it you've done this kind of thing before?' she asked, struggling to keep up with him.

'Once or twice,' Samuel replied. 'Wild demons did exist prior to the Genii War, Clara. But they were much rarer. Before they found a better home in the Retrospective, they lurked in the Nothing of Far and Deep and, occasionally, they would sneak into Labrys Town. They liked to hide in the cargo imported from one House or another. The Relic Guild would hunt them down. Nowadays, it's a job for the police.'

'But we don't want the police involved this time,' Clara said.

'No. It is no ordinary wild demon that has Charlie Hemlock.'

'The Orphan,' Clara whispered. She stopped walking as nerves fluttered in her stomach again. Samuel disappeared into an alley that cut through the school building to the left. She hurried to catch up with him.

'Some demons are more intelligent than others,' he continued. 'The Orphan, though no less a monster, is a demon of habit and purpose. And this isn't its first visit to Labrys Town. This way ...'

He led Clara out of the alley and into a large square recreational courtyard, with benches around the outskirts and a pillar of eyes at the centre. As they headed towards a gate on the opposite side, Samuel explained further.

'Back in the old days, Marney and I encountered the Orphan at a house in the eastern district.'

Clara swore under her breath. The east side of Labrys Town was mostly a residential area, full of families – mothers, fathers, children – and she shuddered to think of a demon lurking among them.

'There were reports from the east side of missing people, random bouts of violent psychosis – all the signs of a wild demon's presence. The Resident sent us to investigate. We found the Orphan and the family it had stored for food.'

'Food?' Clara was repulsed.

'The Orphan feeds on blood, and it takes a long time harvesting what it likes to eat. But to Marney and me it was just a wayward demon that needed sending home.'

'Why didn't you just kill it?'

Samuel gave Clara a quick glance, before saying, 'I'm not even sure it's possible to kill a wild demon, Clara. Not really. Magic can affect them mentally, but not physically. The best you can hope for is to disrupt its connection to this realm, stamp on its fingers so it loses its grip, so to speak.' He gave her another quick look. 'But to do that, you have to get close, within touching distance. Point blank trauma to the head usually works.'

'*Usually* …?'

Samuel carried on through the gate, out of the courtyard, and into the school gardens. Clara stuck close to him.

The smell of flowers and freshly cut grass filled her nostrils. In the light of Silver Moon, she could see the silhouettes of trees, boughs full of leaves. She followed the old bounty hunter down a stone path that cut through the gardens.

'So how did you get rid of it last time?' she asked.

'Marney,' he replied. 'She wasn't very experienced back then, but she somehow managed to convince the Orphan to go back to whatever sanctuary it came from. And it … just did as it was told – a simplification, but that sums it up. As you've learnt, Clara, Marney can form an emotional bond with whomever she touches with her magic.'

Samuel stopped suddenly and looked up at the night sky. 'But I honestly never believed she could form such a strong connection with the Orphan as to actually summon it back from the Retrospective like she did tonight.'

'But she did,' Clara said, 'and now it has Hemlock.'

'Yes.'

'Then let me get this straight – we don't have an empath to control the Orphan, we can't kill it, and we have to be within touching distance to send it home. Please tell me you have a plan.'

'Of sorts,' Samuel replied. 'By summoning the Orphan, Marney has bought Hemlock – and us – some time … What's wrong?'

A scent on the breeze had jolted Clara away from the conversation. She sniffed the air and caught an aroma that carried a salty, rusty taste.

'I can smell blood,' she whispered.

Samuel checked the spirit compass, and then looked straight ahead.

At the end of the stone path was a Church of the Timewatcher. Warm light glowed through stained glass windows onto the grass of the gardens. It looked peaceful enough, but the building gave Clara a bad feeling. Unintelligible voices came from within, desperate, fearful, angry—

The doors to the church burst open and a small figure ran into the gardens, screaming. It was an altar boy. His white smock was stained with blood, black under the light of Silver Moon. His face was covered with small cuts and creased with panic. He ran, wailing, directly towards Clara and Samuel.

Clara made to help the boy, but Samuel gripped her arm and pulled her into the shadow of a tree.

'The boy isn't our concern,' he growled into her ear. 'Stay focused.'

Clara swallowed as the altar boy ran past them. She didn't know whether to feel disgusted at Samuel's resolve or terrified.

The old man headed doggedly towards the church, and Clara followed. They approached the door, and Samuel drew them to a halt. Someone was shouting – a man. Samuel opened the door a crack and took a peek into the church. Then he opened the door wide. He and Clara stood on the threshold, witnesses to a grim scene.

Another altar boy lay dead at their feet, his throat cut and his limbs twisted. On either side of him, a few denizens sat on rows of bench seats. Initially there to listen to the early morning sermons that gave thanks to Silver Moon, these denizens now rocked back and forth like simpletons, drooling and murmuring as though drugged.

'Demon sign,' Samuel whispered.

At the front of the church, a priest stood before the altar with his back to Clara and Samuel. His arms were outstretched, encompassing a stained glass window that depicted the Timewatcher – a purple cloud with a golden sun burning at its centre – as She banished Spiral, the Lord of the Genii – a shapeless mass of poison shadow – to the depths of Oldest Place. The priest's black cassock was dirty and torn.

'There is no afterlife,' he shouted. 'Our souls will never be delivered to the paradise of Mother Earth and the loving arms of the Timewatcher. For She has abandoned Her children in the Labyrinth!'

The priest turned to face Clara and Samuel revealing blood on his hands and more smeared over his face. Clara fought the urge to gag. It looked as though the priest had clawed his own eyes out.

Beside Clara, Samuel drew his revolver from his leg holster. The power stone whined as he thumbed it, and began to glow.

'We live in a festering shit-hole!' the priest screamed. 'We are mere crops, food to feed the hunger of demons.' He began stumbling towards the agents. 'Our souls are already condemned. The Retrospective awaits us—'

Samuel's pistol flashed. He shot the priest in the chest. There was a moaning like bitter wind, and the flames of candles on the altar fluttered and died to swirls of smoke. The priest dropped to his knees and his body hardened to ice.

Samuel walked further down the aisle.

Clara stepped over the dead altar boy, but was reluctant to go any further. The few denizens sitting on the rows of benches seemed unaware of what had occurred, and continued to rock and drool mindlessly. Clara watched them and struggled to catch her breath.

'Clara,' Samuel said. 'The police can clean up this mess, and they'll probably be here soon. Now come on!'

The strength in his voice gave her a little mettle. She skipped around the frozen priest and joined the old bounty hunter beside a door behind the altar. He opened the door to reveal a shadowed stairwell leading down.

'These stairs go to the catacombs,' he said. He was emptying his revolver of bullets that glowed with a faint blue light of magic within their glass casings. He put them into a pouch on his utility belt, and then produced eight regular slugs from a separate pouch. 'Can you sense anything down there, Clara?'

As Samuel reloaded his gun, Clara stuck her head out into the stairwell, trying to ignore the thud of her heart in her ears as she listened.

'I can hear ... it sounds like a child humming.' She sniffed the air, and then swallowed heavily. 'Someone's bleeding down there.'

'Give me the satchel,' Samuel said, holstering his revolver.

She passed him the satchel, and he took out two of the spell spheres, holding one in each hand as if weighing them.

'Keep still,' he said, and then broke a sphere against Clara's chest with a tinkle of glass.

She gasped as a shock ran through her body.

Samuel then broke the second sphere against his own chest. He then faded slowly and disappeared. Clara looked down, but could not see her hands or body or legs ...

'We're invisible,' she said in awe.

'Illusion,' Samuel's disembodied voice explained. 'It'll fool the Orphan, but not for long. We have to move quickly.'

Clara felt him take her hand, and he pulled her through the door. They crept down the darkened stairwell. It seemed to take a long time to reach the bottom, where they came to an archway that led into the catacombs.

Candles burned everywhere, at least a hundred of them, of varying thickness and length. They flickered in dark niches between tombs, upon mantels and statues, dripping hot wax down stony faces onto the dusty floor. On the far wall hung an old tapestry, once a monument to someone, now faded and torn.

At the centre of the room, side on to the archway, Charlie Hemlock was hanging by his wrists from a rope. The rope was threaded through a ceiling pulley and secured to a metal ring on the floor. It creaked as Hemlock's body swayed gently. His eyes were closed, his expression was vapid. His face was smeared with blood that also stained the front of his clothes. His lips were split and swollen; Clara's fingernail marks scored his cheek, and it looked as though a blade had been taken to his forehead.

A thin metal tube had been inserted into each of Hemlock's legs, just above the ankles. His blood dripped from them, slapping wetly into a small copper cauldron. And before the cauldron a child sat cross-legged, rocking back and forth as it hummed something akin to a nursery rhyme.

Samuel gave Clara's hand a reassuring squeeze before he released it.

She found it hard to believe that it was a wild demon from the Retrospective that had Hemlock at its mercy. The Orphan appeared to be a young boy of nine or ten years old; its limbs and body were thin, its belly slightly bloated, and golden curls crowned its head.

Samuel pressed the hilt of a knife into Clara's hand, and his lips brushed her ear as he whispered, 'I'll deal with the Orphan. As soon as it's distracted, you cut Hemlock free and get out as fast as you can. Don't wait for me. Don't look back.'

Clara nodded, though it was impossible for Samuel to see the gesture. She heard the faint chink of glass on glass and knew that Samuel was retrieving more spell spheres from the satchel.

The demon stopped its humming. For an agonising moment Clara thought it had heard the chink of glass too. But the Orphan only leaned forwards to pick at the end of one of the tubes that was inserted into Hemlock's leg. No doubt it was dislodging congealed blood. Satisfied, it sat back, sucking its finger clean. The humming resumed, as did the little slaps of blood slowly filling the cauldron.

'Get ready,' Samuel whispered.

Clara heard the light swish of material, and a spell sphere appeared in midair. It arced across the room and smashed on the floor close to the Orphan. Green mist swirled and spiralled up to form a perfect duplicate of Samuel aiming his revolver at the wild demon's head.

The Orphan rolled backwards and jumped to its feet. The façade of an innocent boy vanished. White eyes with thick red veins glared at the figure of Samuel. Long black nails sprang from its fingertips, and its mouth was filled with sharp, glass-like teeth. It hissed and flicked out a long, blood-red tongue. Muscles bunching, it made to lunge forward, but the image of Samuel pulled the trigger. The power stone flashed, and the Orphan jumped back, raising its clawed hands to protect itself.

But the weapon and the man that fired it were merely illusions that disappeared after the shot, and no bullet had hit the demon.

A second spell sphere arced through the air and smashed at the back of the catacombs. This time a joint of meat appeared, skinless, still on the bone and wet with blood. The Orphan pounced on it hungrily. The instant it sank its teeth into the bloody meat, the joint exploded into a cloud of angry insects that swarmed over the demon and sent it writhing and screaming to the floor.

'Go!' Samuel shouted.

Clara ran for Hemlock. She willed her hands to stop shaking as she sawed through the rope where it was connected to the floor ring. The rope parted with a dull twang, and Hemlock fell to the ground in a bone jarring heap. He stirred and groaned as Clara yanked the tubes from his legs.

'You don't deserve saving, you bastard!' she hissed into his ear. 'But if you want to live, *move*!'

Hemlock became more alert then. He struggled weakly to get to his feet. Clara helped him and put his arm over her shoulders. He stank. They stumbled towards the archway, knocking the cauldron of blood over in the process.

The insect swarm had now dispelled, and the Orphan was back on its feet. Its red-streaked eyes widened at the upturned cauldron and the red meal going to waste on the floor. It then glared at Clara and Hemlock.

With sudden alarm, Clara realised the illusion spell had worn off. She was no longer invisible.

The Orphan screeched at her. The voice of reason in her head told Clara to drop Hemlock and run, but her body would not react. She was frozen to the spot. The Orphan stepped forward. Clara whimpered.

Then Samuel materialised, holding his revolver an inch from the demon's temple. And this was no illusion.

With a low and hollow spitting sound, the power stone released a burst of thaumaturgy. The Orphan slammed sideways to the floor. Its blood, black as night, bubbled into a pool around its head. There was a hissing sound, and the demon's body began to steam. Slowly it dissolved, as though made of ice and melting. The Orphan became a puddle of shadow, which was drawn into the ground until it disappeared completely.

Its grip on this realm severed, the demon had returned to the Retrospective.

Clara dropped Hemlock, and collapsed heavily on the floor beside him, breathing hard. Samuel gave her no respite. With a grunt he grabbed Hemlock and hauled him up onto his shoulder. Hemlock murmured and passed out again.

Samuel offered a hand to Clara. She grabbed it and allowed him to pull her to her feet.

The old bounty hunter clapped her shoulder. 'Let's get out of here before the police arrive.'

CHAPTER NINE

HYPOCRISY

Down beneath the streets of Labrys Town, Fabian Moor walked through the sewers, guided by the dirty light of pale glow lamps. The stench of filth filled his nostrils, and the thick, oily atmosphere seemed to cling to his hair and cassock. But these minor discomforts mattered little to him; the thin line of purple magic that snaked and weaved through the foul air before him was vibrant and alive, and he followed to wherever it led, deep in the gloom ahead.

The sheer disappointment he had felt at the antiques boutique had faded away like an unimportant dream. Yes, it had stung at first to discover the magic in the terracotta jar dead after all these years, but the blood of the feeble old shop owner had given him more than adequate sustenance. Moor felt whole and strong again – for the time being, at least. It helped to put things back into perspective. Whatever disgust he felt towards his surroundings did not affect his impatience and drive, for the Genii's work was far from done.

Accompanying Moor was a doughy and round-shouldered man who struggled to keep pace on the walkway. He scuttled along, rubbing his hands together worriedly. His thinning hair hung in lank and greasy tendrils, and his unshaven face was parchment-dry and flaky. His mouth seemed perpetually agape, and his eyes never stopped watering. He blinked too much. He smelled of onions. And his very proximity irritated Moor to the point of murder.

'My real name's Clover,' said the man in his nasally voice. 'But ain't nobody calls me that anymore, sir.'

'Is that right,' Moor replied.

Clover nodded enthusiastically. 'They call me Dumb Boy.'

Which, Moor reasoned, was unsurprising; even an idiot would consider this man a simpleton.

Clover leant into him, and dropped his voice to a whisper. 'Are they all right, sir?' he said, jabbing a thumb over his shoulder. 'Only, I ain't never seen people like them before.'

He referred to the two golems following close behind. Spindly and withered within their black cassocks, submissive and unquestioning in their obedience, they carried pickaxes in their gnarled hands. All remnants of the humans they once had been were lost in their deformed faces. They were as 'all right' as they would ever be.

Moor sighed. 'Were you not told that keeping your mouth shut was a requirement for this job?' he said to his imbecilic companion.

'Oh, yeah – I remember.'

'Then kindly remain silent until I say otherwise.'

'Right you are, sir.'

In the gloomy light of the glow lamps, Moor continued following the line of purple magic that weaved through the air. He led his mismatched entourage down a short tunnel-way, and then out onto a path that ran alongside a river of rancid sewage water. The stone became slippery underfoot, the stench of filth grew stronger, but at least the silence endured.

Moor needed Clover more than the fool would ever realise. Not being the most intelligent specimen of humanity made him perfect for Moor's needs; and, like that cretin Charlie Hemlock, the fool had pounced at the chance to earn a fistful of Labyrinth pounds without question.

How like the denizens it was to place need before consideration. Even though they had been cast aside by the Timewatcher, these humans still worshipped Her as if She continued to watch over them; they still believed in their high social position among the Houses, even though every ally had long ago abandoned them. The denizens were in denial; they could not accept the pointlessness of their continued existence, or the hypocrisy by which they lived.

The personal use of magic had always been forbidden to humans. They simply could not be trusted with it. Before the war against the Timewatcher, magic-users had been punished with a petty prison sentence. But when the war had ended, the Resident decreed the crime punishable by death. With a straight face, the Resident told the denizens that the personal use of magic was a terrible thing, evil, that a powerful magic-user might destroy the boundary wall and set the Retrospective upon their precious town. While at the same time he knew that magic had always ensured his people's survival, that it was fundamental in keeping the Labyrinth's society functioning. And the denizens never questioned the hypocrisy.

Magic lit their streets, drove their trams, warmed their houses, and cooked their food. The little power stones they used absorbed ambient thaumaturgy from the atmosphere and energised their weapons and appliances. The Resident would keep them safe from magic abuse, he promised the humans, while utilising it to watch their every movement. Yes, under the Resident's law, the punishment for the personal use of magic was death ... unless it was being used by those rare humans who were born touched by magic, the agents who served that secret, rag-tag organisation called the Relic Guild ...

And they referred to themselves as *magickers*, as if a name could give them some authority equal to that of the Thaumaturgists. The agents of the Relic Guild were the epitome of the Labyrinth's double standards, just another bunch of hypocritical humans – filthy, pathetic humans.

Moor suppressed his angry thoughts as at long last the tendril of purple magic led him to where the river of putrid wastewater became shallower. The twisting thread disappeared beneath the surface of the water, as if stabbing down through the waste into the very stone of the river floor. He drew the ill-assorted group to a halt. The signal of magic was strong, healthy, and he felt a rush of triumph.

Moor turned to his golems. 'Do it,' he ordered them.

Without hesitation the golems splashed down into the river with their pickaxes. It was even shallower than Moor had first supposed, and the water barely covered the ankles of his servants. Without need of further instruction, the golems raised the pickaxes above their misshapen heads and began striking the river floor with muffled chinks, heedless of the human effluent their efforts splashed upon their cassocks.

Clover watched the golems work with some interest. He turned watery eyes to Moor. Rubbing his hands together, he hopped from foot to foot, and actually seemed pained by his new employer's prohibition on speaking.

Moor resisted the urge to snap the simpleton's neck and said, 'Your job is to supervise my servants. Ensure they remain undisturbed in their work. Understand?'

Clover blinked at him. 'You ... You're putting me in charge?'

'I suppose you could see it that way, yes.'

'Oh, sir!' Clover looked close to tears, though it was hard to be sure with his ever-watering eyes. 'Charlie said I could trust you, sir – said you'd do right by me.'

'Did he really?'

'And I'm obliged for the money, sir. It ain't easy for me to get a job in this town—'

'Clover, it is time to shut your mouth again.' Moor looked down at his golems working tirelessly, striking away with their pickaxes, over and over again. It would be some time before their work was finished.

'You will stay here,' he told Clover. 'When my servants find what I want, you will receive your reward. Serve me equally well, and perhaps there will be extra money in it for you – *no*! Don't speak. Merely nod if you understand.'

The idiot did, as if he was trying to work his head loose.

With a sudden desire to be far from this disgusting place, Fabian Moor turned and strode away.

Van Bam walked along the corridors of the Nightshade. Each of his steps was accompanied by a stamp of his cane, and each time the green glass struck the floor there was a sound like a distant chime, and the Resident's inner sight was filled with the corridor's layout in myriad shades of grey. His stride purposeful, his brow knitted with concern, he headed for Hamir's laboratory.

The necromancer was waiting where the corridor seemed to end at a wall, which like most in the Nightshade, was covered in tiny maze patterns. Hamir's body appeared to Van Bam's vision as a collective of sparkling colours: the iridescence of a magical being. Hamir's expression was as calm and unreadable as always.

'Your friends have returned unharmed,' he said, as Van Bam approached. 'Charlie Hemlock is alive.'

Van Bam nodded, and they faced each other in silence for a while.

'Hamir,' he said finally. 'When Clara was unconscious, did you happen to look into her mind?'

'No. Should I have?'

Van Bam thought for a moment. 'Clara said that Marney did something to her – *kissed* her. Samuel witnessed the event and claims there was a burst of energy between them. Does that mean anything to you?'

Hamir pursed his lips. 'It could have been a mental transference, I suppose,' he said. 'It's an old empath's trick. Transmit information and messages directly into a person's mind. It's quicker than using words, and it seems to me that Marney definitely had cause to hurry, yes?'

'Yes,' said Van Bam. 'Marney might have placed a message for the Relic Guild in Clara's mind? Something to do with Fabian Moor.'

'It is possible,' Hamir said. 'I assume you're talking to me about this because Clara has not yet remembered any such message?'

'That is correct,' Van Bam replied. 'But we need to pursue this matter, and soon, Hamir.' He inhaled and exhaled heavily. 'The situation is looking bleak. Gideon doubts our ability to deal with Fabian Moor.'

'Obviously,' said the necromancer. 'After all, Moor is a Genii.'

'Indeed. And we are alone, and maybe too few now. The Thaumaturgists can no longer be called upon.'

Hamir made no attempt to advance the conversation, or even nod in agreement.

Van Bam's brow knitted. 'When Moor was last in Labrys Town, we were made privy to certain secret arts that helped in his downfall.'

'Yes, I remember.'

'Could those arts be used again now, Hamir?'

The necromancer considered for a moment. 'It is not impossible.'

'Good,' Van Bam said with some relief. 'Then I want you to begin—'

'Van Bam...' Somehow, Hamir's interruption was both soft and biting. 'Using secret arts and uncovering hidden messages will take research and experimentation and time from a clock that is ticking for Marney, yes?'

The Resident stared at him.

'It might be wiser to focus on interrogating Charlie Hemlock first,' Hamir continued. 'Once we have all the facts to hand, we will be in a better position to judge our next course of action. Am I right?'

There was no disrespect in his words, only simple, clinical facts, as was the necromancer's way. But did he feel any fear or desperation at all for the situation?

Who could really tell what Hamir ever felt? He had been Van Bam's constant companion through his tenure as Resident – as he had been for Gideon and many of those who came before – yet Van Bam had learned so little about him. Never truly an agent of the Relic Guild, it often seemed that without the Nightshade, Hamir might not exist at all, as if he was a personification of the building itself, a manifestation of its secrets and magic.

The necromancer cleared his throat. 'Shall we join your friends?'

Van Bam nodded his permission. But Hamir, ever his own animal, was already opening the hidden door to his laboratory, and he led the way inside.

Clara turned as they entered. Though visibly shaken, she did not appear harmed by her experiences with the Orphan. Samuel looked none the worse for wear, as was to be expected. He stood further into the room, behind a terrified Charlie Hemlock.

Hemlock was too weak to stand, and needed Samuel's help to remain upright. To Van Bam the small and grubby man appeared as a dark grey shade, whose eyes were bright, round and confused. Hemlock's face and clothes were a mess of dried blood. He smelt like sewage. Hemlock looked towards Van Bam as if the Resident's arrival offered some kind of salvation. Sadly for Hemlock, there was little hope of sympathy to be found in the present company. Yet Van Bam knew that his quick mind was already working to turn the situation to his advantage. His face was alive with deceit.

All eyes were on the Resident. Van Bam allowed the silence in the laboratory to grow, and the voice of Gideon filled his head.

You realise that Hemlock cannot leave the Nightshade alive, my idiot.

Gideon was clearly amused by the situation, but he was also correct. If Hemlock had been working for Fabian Moor, he was now a bigger danger to society than he had ever been. He could not be allowed back among the denizens.

But don't give him to Hamir, Gideon said feverishly. *Let Clara have her way with him. I think she'd enjoy the thrill.*

After four decades suffering the ghost's voice in his head, Van Bam knew when to ignore his more provocative comments.

At that moment, Hemlock broke the silence in the laboratory.

'You saved me from a wild demon,' he said, with a well-practised measure of humbleness. 'I owe you my life.'

Directly behind him, Samuel snorted.

Clara stepped forward. She stood before Hemlock and locked gazes with him.

'I don't wish to sound ungrateful,' Hemlock said to her worriedly, 'but you can't blame me for being surprised.'

Clara slapped his face, hard. 'That's for making me kill your friend,' she hissed.

His legs buckling, Hemlock held a hand to his cheek. Clearly the blow had aggravated the earlier wounds. Samuel kept him upright and made him face the changeling again.

'He wasn't exactly my friend,' Hemlock told her sourly, 'but I hope that made you feel better all the same—'

He yelled as Clara kicked him between the legs. 'And that's for Marney!' she shouted.

Good girl, Gideon chuckled.

With a look of amusement, Samuel allowed Hemlock to fall to the floor. As Hemlock writhed and cupped his crotch, Clara loomed over him, her hands balled into fists. It was quite apparent she did not feel that he had received just punishment yet. The colours of her small, pointed face shone with some of the wolf's fury.

'Enough, Clara,' Van Bam said. 'I think your point has been well made.'

She seemed reluctant as she moved away.

Samuel grabbed Hemlock by the collar and hoisted him up into the chair at Hamir's desk. The smirk on his old features suggested he approved of Clara's actions as much as Gideon did.

'Prepare yourself, Charlie,' Samuel said, clamping both hands down on Hemlock's shoulders. 'It only gets worse from here.'

By this time, Hamir, aloof and silent, had made his way to the back of his laboratory, where he stood watching Hemlock. The necromancer's colours remained impassive to Van Bam's vision, but the lights of his eyes were darkening.

Holding Hemlock down, Samuel wheeled the chair towards Hamir. Hemlock's eyes were wide with pain and fear. Beside Hamir was a tall object, covered with a silk sheet. The necromancer pulled the sheet away, and there stood an obscene mannequin. The body and limbs were a wire frame of thin metal, but upon its neck was fixed a head of flesh, the head of Fat Jacob, the owner of the Lazy House.

Hemlock emitted a choking sound. 'Oh, Timewatcher! What is this?'

Atop the mannequin body, Jacob's milky eyes snapped open, and his expression was furious. 'Hemlock, you shit!' he screamed, his voice distorted and gurgling.

Hemlock squeezed his eyes shut.

'You said no one would know. You said it was easy business – just one of my whores. You bastard! You liar!'

Van Bam nodded to Hamir, and instantly he silenced the whore-house owner. Fat Jacob's eyes closed and his features dropped as if dead. Hamir did not cover him with the sheet again.

'Your business associate, Charlie,' said Samuel. 'You should be more careful who you get involved with.'

'I didn't do anything,' Hemlock shouted. He struggled in vain against Samuel's grip. 'You've got the wrong man!'

'Indeed,' Van Bam said. He moved to stand between the captive and Hamir's handiwork. 'Charlie, this is what I know for a fact. You were recently employed by Fabian Moor, and thus far you have performed questionable deeds in his name.'

Hemlock shook his head feverishly. 'Moor double-crossed me. I want nothing to do with him.'

'Too late,' Van Bam said. 'You know as well as we who and what Fabian Moor is, and you will tell us now where he has taken Marney.'

'And, Charlie,' Samuel added, 'if you lie, he'll know.'

'Lie?' Hemlock looked up at Samuel, and then at the Resident. 'You think I'd protect Moor after he left me high and dry? I don't care why you want him, but I hope it's as bad as it gets.'

'So start talking,' said Clara.

Hemlock's eyes flitted to the grisly sight of Fat Jacob's head atop the mannequin's wire body and he licked his lips. 'It's not that simple.'

He's stalling, Gideon said to Van Bam. He sounded almost bored. *He knows that information is the only thing keeping him alive.*

'Look,' Hemlock continued. 'Moor said a lot of things. He told me who you are – the Relic Guild, right? He said he could make Labrys Town a better place, only you want to prevent it.' His expression flashed the perfect degree of helplessness. 'He said that you're the real enemy.'

Clara scoffed. 'So you just went along with him, for a pocketful of money, no questions asked.'

'Oh, I know what you're thinking,' Hemlock said earnestly, 'typical me, right? But, for the first time in my life, Moor gave me something to hope for. He said he could reopen the doorways in the Great Labyrinth. He said we could see the Aelfir again.'

'Hemlock, you aren't even old enough to remember the Aelfir,' Samuel said scathingly.

'So what?' Hemlock replied. 'Moor said he could bring them back, and I believed in him.'

'Believing the word of a Genii is a dangerous thing to do,' Van Bam said, 'and a sure way to meet death, one could say.'

'Don't get me wrong,' Hemlock continued quickly. 'I see Moor for what he is now, but he convinced me that things could really change, started me dreaming. You must know what I mean – you live here too!'

Behind Hemlock, Samuel's face darkened and he looked to the floor, obviously suffering some inner turmoil. Again, Van Bam wondered what the mysterious avatar had offered his old comrade in exchange for Clara's life.

Hemlock is lying, Van Bam thought to Gideon. *He is saying all the things he thinks we wish to hear.*

Then play his game, my idiot, at least until his usefulness is diminished. Let him think compliance will keep him alive.

Van Bam took a step forward. 'Please understand,' he said to

Hemlock. 'You have been party to the schemes of a Genii, and I have many questions. If you refuse to answer them, Charlie, then you will never see the outside of the Nightshade again. Now, first of all, where is Fabian Moor hiding Marney?'

Hemlock licked his lips. 'Listen, he only employed me to set a trap for Marney. I don't know why he wants her. Moor never told me the details of his plans.'

'That is not what I asked you, Charlie.'

'I know, but ... but I can't tell you.'

'Not good enough,' Samuel growled. He drew his revolver, and pushed the barrel against the side of Hemlock's head. 'Tell us where she is or I'll shoot off your ear.'

'*Wait*!' Hemlock shouted, shying away from the weapon. 'I want to tell you, I really do, but I just *can't*! Something's stopping me.'

'Is that right?' Samuel said, and he primed the power stone.

'You have to believe me!' Hemlock was pleading now, on the verge of panic. His expression convinced even Van Bam. 'I know where he's taken Marney. I've seen the place. I could tell you how to get there, but ...' His breathing became laboured and he pressed a hand to his chest. 'Every time I try to put it into words, it ... it gets stuck.'

I think he's telling the truth, Gideon said. *Can't you see it, my idiot?*

Samuel reacted first. Abruptly he stepped away from Hemlock, aiming the revolver at the back of his head. 'Magic!' he hissed.

And he was right. Van Bam's vision detected a flare of colour inside Hemlock's chest.

'Keep clear,' he snapped. 'Everybody.'

'What is it?' Clara said.

The Resident addressed Hemlock. 'What are you feeling, Charlie?'

'I'm not—' Hemlock groaned, clutching his chest, and fell out of the chair to the floor. He screamed and then convulsed, entering some kind of fit.

Oh, this is interesting, Gideon chuckled.

'Hamir!' Van Bam shouted, and the necromancer quickly stepped over from the back of the room. He placed a hand on Hemlock's forehead and whispered a single word:

'Sleep.'

Instantly Hemlock ceased writhing and was still, though the magic in his chest continued to bloom to Van Bam's inner sight.

'What's wrong with him?' Samuel asked.

'He's been cursed,' Hamir replied. His eyes were closed as he lightly felt down Hemlock's body. 'There is magic wrapped around his heart. It's burning him from the inside out.'

'Is he dead?' Clara asked.

'No, not yet.' Hamir placed his hands on either side of Hemlock's head. 'Interesting,' he whispered. 'He didn't know he was cursed.'

Van Bam said, 'Can you dispel it, Hamir?'

The ageing necromancer shook his head. 'Not easily. This is the magic of a Genii.'

'There must be something we can do?' Clara said.

'Perhaps,' said Hamir. 'But he must be placed in stasis, and quickly.'

'Samuel,' Van Bam snapped, and together they lifted Hemlock and carried him from the laboratory.

THAUMATURGIST

Although dawn had broken and the sun had cleared the boundary wall, it was not yet high enough to banish the twilight that loitered over Labrys Town. Slowly, inexorably, its warm rays chased the shadows from the cold corners of town and evaporated the night's moisture. A light mist hung in the air, clinging to the last chill of Silver Moon, and Marney pulled her jacket tighter around her body.

Standing in the gloomy forecourt outside the Nightshade, she waited for Denton's arrival. She had projected a shield of empathic magic around her, like a cloak of emotions that hid her in plain sight by steering the perceptions of others away from her physical presence. For Marney was not the only person under the scrutiny of the security eyes in the forecourt, and it was important that she conceal herself from those who did not know the identities of the Relic Guild agents.

The forecourt gates were open and before the tunnel that led to Resident Approach was a large cargo tram. A team of warehousemen stood around the tram, waiting for delivery of the goods they would load into it. They chatted with a duo of armed police officers as they waited, entirely unaware of the young empath watching them.

To Marney's left stood a huge stone archway. The space within it was as black as a shroud of starless night. Its surface rippled like dark, glassy water, filling the morning air with a gentle humming as it prepared to receive cargo from somewhere far beyond the realm of the Labyrinth. Officially, this arched portal was the only one that connected directly to the Aelfir and was not a doorway of the Great Labyrinth. It was also the only portal currently permitted to function in town, and it did so for most of the hours in a day, every day. Since the war with Spiral had begun, trade with the Aelfir had been rationed to the importing of essential goods only. All export had ceased. All travel to and from the Labyrinth was prohibited.

Six months ago, when Marney had been a student at the Central District University, studying for a degree in history, she had been due to conduct a special project which would have allowed her to spend an entire term studying at a designated Aelfirian House. She could have learnt so much history, seen so much culture, while being guided by the Aelfir themselves. Of course, the war had put paid to such excursions – and Marney's student career had been cut short by her recruitment into the Relic Guild, anyway – but she always dreamed that one day she would get the chance to visit the realms outside the Labyrinth. Now that day had arrived, she did not feel so sure of herself.

She wished she and Van Bam could have spent more time together, but he and Samuel were already off following Gideon's orders, investigating the movements of Carrick the treasure hunter. Marney always felt more confident when Van Bam was around.

The humming of the arched portal dipped in pitch. The warehousemen and the police officers jumped to attention. From the portal, a floating platform was emerging, piled high with supplies. The glassy blackness clung to the cargo with fingers of viscous fluid that slowly raked over the crates and metal storage containers as more of the platform drifted into the forecourt. When it finally cleared the portal, two transport guards appeared, ushering it along, protecting the cargo stacked high and wide. Marney resisted the urge to step back from them, for these were no ordinary guards. They were automaton sentries.

Humanoid, the automatons stood eight feet tall at least. Their metal bodies were thin and skeletal, exposing their internal mechanisms like monstrous clockwork toys. Their faces were smoothly silver, lacking any kind of feature. The sounds of their feet clanged metallically against the hard stone of the forecourt floor, but there was something graceful about their movements as they pushed the loaded platform towards the cargo tram.

Beautiful, aren't they? Denton said in Marney's mind.

The old empath came to stand beside her. He was dressed in another rumpled three-piece-suit, his tatty coat and floppy hat, and he had shielded his presence to all but her.

Such a grand achievement in metallurgy, don't you think?

Marney nodded in agreement with 'grand', but she wasn't so sure the term 'beautiful' was strictly apt.

She had seen automatons before; they always acted as transport guards for these cargo deliveries, and they were the only things allowed to travel back out of the portal. Their impressive aesthetics were matched only by their intimidating size and incredible strength. They stood silent, their featureless faces moving slowly from side to side as if scanning the area, as the warehousemen began loading the tram with the crates and containers from the platform. The police supervised the transaction, while a smartly dressed official from the Merchants' Guild matched goods with his checklist. Every man worked in silence, clearly uncomfortable under the scrutiny of the automatons, and Marney did not blame them.

If so ordered, these intricate, 'beautiful' machines would become vicious warriors. Bullets would have no effect on them, and they were protected against magic. They were powered by a kind of energy the denizens of Labrys Town could barely understand. The automatons were the creations, the servants, of the Thaumaturgists.

Come, Denton thought to her. *We should be going.*

He led Marney away from the importing of cargo, and she gave one final glance back at the automatons before following her mentor along the towering south wall of the Nightshade. The old empath was in good cheer and he emoted a sense of joy to Marney, which she accepted gratefully – though, even with its help, she couldn't block her sense of nervousness entirely. Once they had walked beyond earshot of the warehousemen, Denton gave a flourish of his hand.

'The Great Labyrinth is larger than imagination, Marney.'

She nodded. 'I know.'

'And it sometimes seems that the doorways to the Houses of the Aelfir are too numerous to count.'

'I know.'

'However, identifying which Aelfirian House you wish to travel to is one thing, finding its doorway among the never ending alleyways of the Great Labyrinth is entirely another.'

Marney rolled her eyes. 'Yes, I *know*.'

But Denton wasn't deterred by the irritation in her voice.

'On foot, it could take days of wandering the alleyways – weeks, months, *years* – to find the doorway you seek. And that just won't do, will it? We're busy people, Marney, with little spare time on our hands.'

Marney sighed. 'Denton, I'm tired, I'm nervous, and you're not telling me anything I don't already know. Is there some point you're trying to make here?'

'Always!' Denton grinned and put a big arm around her shoulders. 'If I have taught you anything it is of the vast gulf between knowing a thing and experiencing it. And you, Marney, are about to experience what you have only read about in books.'

She gave her mentor a timid smile. 'I know.'

'That's my girl,' Denton beamed. 'Come on.'

Reaching the end of the south wall, they turned left and followed the Nightshade's eastern face all the way to its northern side. Halfway along the north wall, they came to a place where a slim column of light-coloured stone protruded from the ground, set back from the pedestals that held the security eyes. Between the column and the towering boundary wall, another arched portal was positioned, this one shorter and thinner than its counterpart on the south side.

Denton drew Marney up to the column. She looked into a square stone box fixed at the top of it. The box was filled with a thick, gelatinous substance that gave off a faint purple glow.

Denton said, 'To find the doorway to your desired destination, Marney, you need three things. The first is a portal.'

So saying, he pressed his hand into the gelatinous substance. When he withdrew, the perfect indent of his handprint glowed purple for a moment before sinking down deep into the substance. The stone archway before the column hummed and a rippling veil of glassy darkness appeared within it.

Denton raised a finger. 'Second, you need the correct House symbol for the House you wish to travel to,' and he used his finger to draw the shape of a diamond inside a circle into the gelatinous substance. It, too, glowed and sank.

'The third and final ingredient,' Denton said, 'is the means to connect the portal to the doorway of the House you are seeking – a shadow carriage.'

On the floor between the column and the portal, a large, black circle appeared, darker than the shadows cast by the Nightshade. Denton took Marney's hand and led her towards it. Together they stood upon the dark disc, and instantly Marney felt disorientated.

She gripped her mentor's hand tighter. Denton sent her a wave of confidence to dispel her uncertainty.

'Your trepidation is understandable,' he told her, 'but this trip is long overdue for you, Marney. You have nothing to fear.'

The edge of the dark circle began to ruffle and lift – folding upwards like a dying leaf. Tentacles of black matter stretched out and up over the empaths, thinning as they crisscrossed above them to form a mesh-like covering. The process continued until they stood inside a sphere made of thousands of wire-thin shadows that began to spin around them. The humming of the portal was drowned out by the high whine of gathering energy.

'Here it comes,' Denton said happily. 'Wait for it …'

As the lines of shadow spun faster and faster, Marney's stomach fluttered and gravity failed. She and Denton rose into the air within the sphere, floating as if they were in water. Marney's only thought was of escaping the cage.

'Don't panic!' Denton laughed, gripping her hand as she tried to wriggle free. 'It's quite normal.' With his free hand, he pointed through the lines of shadow at the portal outside. 'But brace yourself,' he warned. 'The trip can get a little rough.'

The dark lines were spinning so fast now that Marney felt sick to look at them. The high whining reached a crescendo, and then the sphere shot forwards with such a lurch, with such speed, she had no time to control her emotions.

She screamed as the shadow carriage shot into the portal.

Sudden darkness engulfed her. There was a *whomping* sound, as if someone had wobbled a thin sheet of wood, and then she was hurtling through the alleyways of the Great Labyrinth.

Black bricks flashed by with a steady stream of blurred motion. The sphere travelled the alleyways so fast it was impossible to tell if it took the twists and turns without slowing, or if it passed straight through the walls without hindrance.

Marney screamed again.

Denton's laugh was loud, full of joy, and his excited voice filled Marney's head.

When I first used a shadow carriage, I was sick all over my travelling companions! And he laughed again.

Marney found no joy in the experience. She still floated inside the sphere, quite gently, and felt no sense of movement beyond what her eyes perceived, not even the rush of wind upon her face. She felt dizzy, nauseated, as the alleyways sped by, and she desperately wanted something more solid than Denton's hand to cling to. She decided her mentor's arm, as free-floating as her own, would have to suffice. She clasped it tightly with both hands. She squeezed her eyes shut and buried her face in Denton's shoulder as the sphere flew deeper and deeper into the Great Labyrinth ...

Marney's feet touched ground.

A moment passed, and she found the courage to open her eyes. The shadow carriage was once again a dark, flat disc on the floor beneath her feet, and this time it was cast upon the cobbles of an alleyway. The journey had ended.

'Are you all right?' Denton asked.

Marney realised she was still gripping his arm and she released it. The moment she did, a wave of dizziness swamped her, and she had to steady herself against the alley wall.

Denton helped her to stay upright. 'Deep breaths,' he urged.

The dizziness passed, and Marney looked down the alleyway that stretched away into the gloom without turn. She could be anywhere in the Great Labyrinth, she realised, and she had no idea how far they had travelled from the Nightshade.

Turning around, she was surprised to be confronted by a wooden door set into the alley's end wall. Unassuming, it could have belonged to any house in Labrys Town. Above it, attached to the brickwork, was a plate of dulled metal into which was engraved a symbol depicting a diamond within a circle.

Denton said, 'When we again know a time of peace, Marney, you will learn the symbols that represent the Houses and realms beyond the

Labyrinth. And you can use these symbols to visit the Aelfir whenever you choose.' He grinned at her. 'Duties permitting, of course.'

When Marney replied, her voice was tight. 'But Gideon's not sending us to visit the Aelfir, is he?' She took a breath. 'We're going to see a Thaumaturgist.'

'Ah,' said Denton. 'Not just any Thaumaturgist, Marney. You're going to meet Lady Amilee – a Skywatcher.' He pointed at the diamond within a circle above the door. 'And that is her House symbol.'

The old empath moved his large bulk over to the door, which he opened to reveal a swirling whiteness on the other side.

Marney heard a low moaning like distant wind. The whiteness seemed almost fluid, as thick as churning glue, and she knew that it stretched back much further than the depth of the alley wall.

'The Nothing of Far and Deep,' Denton announced.

She swallowed and took a step away from it.

'The pathways to all Houses lead through its primordial mists, Marney, and you must not be afraid.' He offered her his hand. 'Shall we?'

Marney held back. She trusted her mentor as much as – if not more so – Van Bam, but something stopped her from reaching out and taking his hand.

Denton smiled kindly, patiently, and said, 'Gideon believes this trip will be good for you, Marney, and I concur wholeheartedly. It is high time you gained some experience, and it is not wise to keep a Thaumaturgist waiting.'

Marney's stomach swirled, but this time when Denton offered his hand she took it. He led her up to the doorway. She held her breath, gripped her mentor's hand tightly, and together they stepped into the heavy whiteness of the Nothing of Far and Deep.

The boundaries of the solid collapsed, bridging the distance between two different points in space. At first, Marney was utterly blind. She could still feel Denton's hand gripping hers, but there was no ground beneath her feet. She thought to feel wet or suffocated, but all that came to her was a curious sensation of falling slowly … so slowly. However, with sudden and brilliant streaks of silver-blue that crackled around her like lightning, she saw she travelled with forward motion, as if she was drifting along a tunnel that cut through storm clouds. Beyond the tunnel's ghostly walls, she could see their path continuing on, weaving through the Nothing of Far and Deep like a thread of black silk in a milky ocean.

Here it comes, Denton's thought warned her. *Don't fight against it.*

The streaks of lightning highlighted another portal up ahead. Like a stopper in the end of the tunnel, its glassy darkness swirled, devouring the wispy, cloud-like substance of the tunnel walls. Marney could not be certain if she travelled towards the portal, or if it was moving to her, but she was flying much faster than she realised. The portal and empath rushed to meet each other head on with a speed that showed no sign of slowing. Marney raised her hands to protect herself. The name of her lover tumbled from her lips, as if Van Bam could somehow materialise and save her from this madness ...

There was no bigger nocturnal haunt in Labrys Town than Green Glass Row. Many denizens considered it a scab on their town, beneath which all of society's immorality festered. Others worshipped its clubs and taverns, and abandoned themselves to the heady pleasures so readily available. Green Glass Row was the midnight creature that never slept, at least not while darkness shrouded the sky. Only sunshine could quieten the beast; only sunshine could send its worshippers scurrying like rats for their beds – sunshine and the shame that arrived with the cold light of day.

There was, however, one establishment that did not mourn the loss of night, a club that hid itself well along Green Glass Row: the Twilight Bar. It welcomed the morning sun, if less so the attentions of the Relic Guild.

Van Bam and Samuel stood in the main lounge of the Twilight Bar. The room was easily large enough to hold a dance floor and a stage for a band; but there was no stage or music playing, and where a dance floor might have been was a square expanse of carpet as thick as it was dark. Beneath the dull, blue glow of ceiling prisms, the stillness was broken only by occasional moans of pleasure, or sobs of despair, coming from a series of evenly spaced alcoves set into the walls. Behind diaphanous, backlit curtains, silhouettes writhed upon reclining chairs, lost to deep dreams. The bitter tang of narcotic smoke hung in the air.

Van Bam gazed at Samuel who was watching the silhouettes behind the curtains. He knew his fellow agent wore an expression of disgust, even though he could not see his face. Samuel's hat was made from enchanted material, and the shadows cast by its wide brim steeped his every feature in total darkness. As for Van Bam, he had cast an illusion upon himself that smeared his facial features into an unidentifiable blur.

He raised his green glass cane, now appearing as a plain walking stick made of wood, and he used it to tap Samuel lightly on the shoulder. He then nodded towards the small bar at the far end of the lounge, and they headed towards it.

The features of the serving girl appeared almost demonic in the blue glow that radiated up from the floor behind the bar. Her smooth, black hair fell about her shoulders like a mane of oil.

Samuel reached her first. 'Go and get Taffin,' he demanded in a growl.

She stared at Samuel for a long moment, quietly standing her ground, but her eyes became uncertain as they tried and failed to pierce the darkness shrouding his face. Finally, she turned her gaze to Van Bam's blurred features.

'I'll see if Mr Taffin is available,' she whispered.

'Of course,' Van Bam said.

The serving girl stepped from behind the bar and disappeared through a side door.

Van Bam shook his head at his fellow agent. 'Did it ever occur to you that you do not have to treat everyone like an enemy?'

Samuel snorted. 'I hate this place,' he said, gesturing to the alcoves. 'Look at them.'

Behind the curtains, the patrons of the Twilight Bar were attended by shadowy female forms. These women held long pipes to the lips of their clients; and after every inhalation, in every alcove around the room, so many mouths exhaled long plumes of smoke – smoke that had first been emptied of far and distant visions.

'They should learn to deal with things like the rest of us,' Samuel said bitterly. 'They're not the only ones to lose something in this war.'

Van Bam always found it a little disappointing when Samuel expressed his intolerant outlook on life; it was so hard to sympathise with his opinions. The Twilight Bar was an exclusive and discreet club that catered for the tastes of certain denizens who wished to maintain their good reputation in town. Many of the club's members were merchants who had enjoyed a lucrative import and export trade with the Houses of the Aelfir before the war. But in the two years since the use of the doorways of the Great Labyrinth had been forbidden, the wealth of these merchants had dwindled, with some of them now heading towards poverty. The Twilight Bar offered reprieve from reality and escape into dreams of what life had been like before the war began – if only for a short time – while the families of these struggling merchants believed them to be conducting business in the central district.

But where Van Bam saw fellow denizens on the brink of losing everything, Samuel saw greedy profiteers who had never deserved their privileged lifestyle in the first place.

'We do what we must to get by, Samuel,' Van Bam said. 'Not everything in life is as cut and dried as you see it. There is no point in causing trouble.'

'Me, cause trouble?' Samuel scoffed. 'I think you'd know more about that.'

'And what is that supposed to mean?'

'You know exactly what it means, Van Bam. And you and Marney are idiots if you think you're not making trouble for yourselves.'

Van Bam barely suppressed a glare. Evidently, his relationship with Marney was not as secret as they both would have liked.

He felt a sudden pang as he thought of his lover. Denton had taken her, along with the terracotta jar, to see Lady Amilee, the Skywatcher. He couldn't help but worry about how she would cope with meeting a member of the Thaumaturgists for the first time.

'Whatever Marney and I do is none of your business, Samuel.'

Samuel shrugged. 'I don't care either way.'

'Then why did you bring it up?'

Fortunately, before the conversation could go any further, the serving girl emerged through the side door and approached them.

'Mr Taffin is ready to see you now,' she whispered.

She led the Relic Guild agents out of the lounge of moaning silhouettes into a small stairwell, and then up a spiralling staircase of varnished wood.

Mr Taffin was the owner of the Twilight Bar. His clients paid him well to ensure they retained their anonymity and his employees asked no questions and saw nothing. The narcotic Taffin provided for his clients came from a fungus called cynobe. It grew in the forests of a few realms of the Aelfir, and was primarily used by oracles for revisiting dreams that might hold visions of the future. Officially cynobe was, and always had been, an illegal substance in Labrys Town, but Mr Taffin and the Twilight Bar were given special dispensation by the Resident.

Although it was impossible to import cynobe at present, Gideon had instructed Gene the apothecary to synthesise regular catchments of the narcotic so Mr Taffin could fulfil his clients' cravings. It was necessary to show the heads of important merchant families that they had a friend in their Resident, who was occasionally willing to turn a blind eye to his own laws for them. The Labyrinth needed to keep the Merchant Guild functioning, at least on some level, for they would be sorely needed to re-establish contact with the Aelfir when these troubled times ended.

As a result Mr Taffin, perhaps most of all, profited from the war between the Timewatcher and Spiral. And in return for his good fortunes, he had become an informant for the Relic Guild. Not all of his clients were merchants, and his ears were burrowed deep into Labrys Town's underworld. It was his information that had led them to the treasure hunter Carrick and the problems at Chaney's Den.

The spiralling staircase led to an open plan attic apartment, decorated with gaudy statues and brightly coloured artwork hanging on the walls. Mr Taffin sat on a long couch at the end of the room, under the bright dawn light shining in through a huge round window behind him.

Van Bam looked at the serving girl. 'You may leave us,' he said, quietly but firmly.

She didn't move at first, only looked to Mr Taffin for guidance. Not until he waved her away with his hand did she turn and head back down the stairs.

Once she was gone and out of earshot, Mr Taffin said, 'I wasn't expecting to see you again quite so soon, my friends.'

His words were met with stony silence.

Mr Taffin was a short, middle-aged fat man with a mop of grey hair and a perpetual smile that never quite reached his small eyes. He was dressed as garishly as always, in a suit of burgundy velvet with a matching cravat. Van Bam didn't need illusionist skills to see through his pomp and oily smile. The man was frightened; he'd never had the Relic Guild come into his home, and he knew the reason for this visit could not be good.

'Would you like to join me for breakfast?' he said, casually, motioning to the table before him where a carafe of coffee stood beside a large wicker basket filled with sugary pastries.

Van Bam shook his head.

He and Samuel approached the table.

Mr Taffin dabbed the corners of his mouth with a napkin and frowned up at the concealed faces of the agents. 'At least let me pour you some coffee.'

Further silence greeted the offer.

'You are sure?' he said, failing to hide the nervousness in his voice. 'It's ground from beans from Green Sky Forest. Expensive. Not easy to come by in the Labyrinth nowadays.'

'Shut up, Taffin,' Samuel said. 'We're not here for your bloody coffee.'

Mr Taffin struggled to keep his smile in place. 'I-I don't understand,' he said in a low voice. 'I sent no message to the Resident. I have nothing new to tell the Relic Guild. My stock of cynobe is full. I ...' Words failing, he looked at Van Bam as if seeking a more civil and understanding temperament.

'Do not look to me for sympathy,' Van Bam told him. 'Not after you chose to omit certain facts from the recent information you provided.'

'And by omitted,' Samuel said, 'he means you lied to us, Taffin.'

'Lied?' The club owner's expression was one of almost genuine bemusement – almost. 'Was my information not accurate?'

'In part,' said Samuel. 'Carrick did arrange the sale of an artefact at Chaney's Den, but the time of the meeting had been changed. When we got there everyone was dead.'

Unsuccessfully, Mr Taffin tried to blink away the fear in his small eyes. 'But you can't blame me for that,' he whispered. 'I pass on what I hear. I'm not responsible for what happens afterwards.'

'No,' said Van Bam, 'but you are obligated to divulge every fact of note.'

'Like Carrick's buyer being an Aelf,' Samuel added.

This time Mr Taffin's expression was genuinely bemused. 'I didn't know,' he said. 'I told you the truth. I never discovered the buyer's identity, or what Carrick was selling.'

'Yet there is something you are not telling us,' said Van Bam. 'It is apparent in your expression, Mr Taffin.'

Mr Taffin looked from the hidden face of one man to the other and shrugged his shoulders helplessly.

As an informant, Mr Taffin was very good at his job, but he was also sly, if not particularly clever about it. Van Bam knew as well as Samuel that he liked to hold back certain facts from the information he gave, as if he was collecting them as bargaining chips he could somehow use at a later date. Usually his information was sound enough, and whatever little secrets he kept were of no consequence. But not on this occasion; and the Relic Guild had no time to play his games.

Van Bam sighed. 'Mr Taffin, you have been helpful to us in the past, and we are always grateful for your service. But you should know that you are not the only denizen capable of running the Twilight Bar.'

'What?'

'He's right, Taffin,' Samuel added. 'One word to the entertainment council and a different name goes on this club's licence.'

These comments had the desired effect of drilling into Taffin's worst fears. During that moment of vulnerability, Van Bam read his micro-expressions and the answer to the secret he was keeping bloomed in the illusionist's mind.

'Ah,' he said. 'I believe there is something you forgot to tell us about Carrick, Mr Taffin. You are hiding a detail concerning his team of treasure hunters, yes?'

'Surely not?' Samuel said with mock disappointment. He then bent forwards over the table. 'Save yourself some trouble, you idiot, before I shoot you on principle.'

Mr Taffin threw his napkin onto his breakfast and sat back on the sofa. 'All right,' he said, his expression darkening. 'I didn't think it mattered.'

'Obviously it does,' Van Bam told him. 'So stop wasting our time.'

'Look,' he said, and all signs of the fop had disappeared from his manner. 'I told you that Carrick was the only member of his team to return to Labrys Town alive, right? Well ...' He blinked several times. 'I might've heard that one other treasure hunter survived the trip too.'

'Who?' Samuel demanded.

Taffin leant forwards again and dropped his voice to a whisper. 'His name's Llewellyn, a small time businessman who tried his hand at bigger things.' His small eyes darted from one agent to the other. 'Listen, you have to believe me – I really didn't think it mattered. See, from what I hear, he came back in a bad way and he hasn't got long to live.'

'Then get on with it,' Van Bam snapped. 'Where can this Llewellyn be found?'

Mr Taffin rubbed his fat chin. 'Last I heard he was holed up at the Anger Pitt. And that's all I know, I promise you.'

It was the truth, and Van Bam nodded that fact to Samuel.

After a short pause, Samuel pointed a finger at Mr Taffin. 'The next time you *forget* to mention something to the Relic Guild, we'll seize your assets and take you to the Nightshade. Got it?'

Mr Taffin averted his eyes.

Leaving him to his humility, Van Bam and Samuel strode away and headed down the spiralling staircase.

Halfway down, Samuel turned to Van Bam and said, 'The Anger Pitt?' He swore. 'That's going to be trouble.'

Van Bam agreed. 'We should give a report to Gideon.' He sucked air over his teeth. 'I think we need to call in Macy and Bryant on this one.'

Marney didn't know how long she had been unconscious but, as the warm and gentle emotions of Denton coaxed her awake, she suspected it had only been for moments. She opened her eyes to see Denton's round and ruddy face smiling down at her. As cheerful as ever, he helped her into a sitting position and she rubbed her eyes, feeling as though she could quite happily sleep for the rest of the day.

'I can't believe I fainted,' she said groggily.

Denton chuckled. 'I wouldn't let it bother you. When I first brought Samuel to this realm, he was light-headed for the entire visit. But don't tell him I told you.' He winked.

Marney rubbed her eyes again. 'I take it we reached the right place?'

'Oh yes. Are you feeling strong?'

Marney nodded, and Denton helped her to her feet.

They had arrived at a cave of some kind, dull and featureless and oddly unnatural in its domed formation. The stone of the walls, floor and ceiling was dark grey, smooth and polished almost to a metallic sheen. There was a little light shining in from the cave mouth, and it seemed to shift though varying shades and soft hues. On the back wall was a wooden door, which led to the Nothing of Far and Deep and the pathway that cut through it all the way back to the Labyrinth. There was something comforting about the door's innocuous appearance, as though it stood as reassurance that home was never far away.

'Come on,' said Denton. He seemed eager as he took Marney's arm and steered her towards the cave mouth. 'There's something I want you to see.'

Reaching the edge of the cave, Marney's ears were filled with a deep rumbling, and her breath caught.

'Don't block your emotions to this, Marney,' Denton said. 'Revel in what you see. Experience the moment.'

A little way ahead, a wide bridge arced over a mighty chasm. From above, falls of shimmering green water cascaded down into the depths from a high cliff wall that swept around in a great semi-circle. The air was misted with rainbow colours that glinted like jewels, and the roar of the falls was constant and powerful. In the near distance, where the bridge ended, a grand tower could be seen. Sleek and dark grey, it seemed to rise up from the chasm, reaching almost as high as the cliff top, and was capped by a dome of moonlight silver.

'The Tower of the Skywatcher,' Denton told her. He held his hat in his hands as if in a show of respect. 'Tell me how you feel, Marney?'

'Strange,' Marney replied in a small voice. She struggled to find the right words. 'I-I ...'

'Exactly,' Denton whispered. 'You don't see this kind of splendour in Labrys Town, do you?'

Taking her mentor's advice, Marney didn't try to block her emotions. She raised her hands to her mouth and laughed with the joy and wonder that filled her. So many times she had dreamed of what the realms outside the Labyrinth might look like, but no dream could ever compare to what she now saw.

She looked up. The cloud covering was luminous, brighter than Ruby Moon, but less so than the sun. The soft texture drifted like smoke, with colours shifting subtly through shades of purple and green, hues of red and gold, and more besides. Marney could see the deep darkness beyond the clouds, and the stars shining in a sky she most definitely did not recognise.

'A man could live to reach an exceptionally old age here, Marney. Time passes much slower in the realm of the Skywatcher than it does in the Labyrinth.' He patted his hat down onto his head. 'But there are no such luxuries for us, I'm afraid. We have work to do.'

At a brisk pace, he led Marney from the cave down to the bridge, which seemed to have little craftsmanship – it was just a smooth and polished path of dark grey stone that had no walls or guardrails. It was easily wide enough to safely walk two abreast, but Marney lagged behind Denton, marvelling at her surroundings. The rainbow-coloured mist didn't feel damp on her face, but caused a light and curious tingling sensation as if it was cleansing her skin. Her gaze travelled the full height of the emerald falls that enclosed the chasm in a semi-circle, and she wondered what kind of land might lie beyond the roaring waters.

Looking back over her shoulder, Marney was surprised to see the cave they had emerged from was set low in a great mountain even taller than the cliff wall. Just like the cave's interior, it appeared unnaturally smooth and metallic, and its peak disappeared into the shifting colours of the lazy clouds.

'Watch where you're walking, Marney,' Denton called above the noise of the falls. The old empath had stopped to peer over the edge of the bridge. 'No one knows how deep this chasm is, so it might be wise not to fall in.'

He grinned as Marney caught up with him. They continued on across the bridge, side by side, and he put an arm around her shoulders.

'Lady Amilee's function is now more pertinent than it has ever been,' he told her. 'Her duty is to monitor the Great Labyrinth. In many ways, she is our patron. More so than any other Thaumaturgist, she watches over the denizens, and has done so since the Labyrinth's creation.

'Spiral and the Genii might not be able to reach us through the Timewatcher's barrier, but it is Lady Amilee who guards the doorways to the Labyrinth, ensuring that Spiral's Aelfirian armies cannot invade us.'

'She guards *all* the doorways?'

'Every single one. And only she could have arranged our safe passage here today.'

Marney was suitably impressed.

Denton surveyed the tower ahead. 'It's disturbing enough that Carrick and his team of treasure hunters somehow managed to leave and re-enter the Labyrinth, but to do so without Lady Amilee noticing? It won't sit well with her, Marney. It won't sit well with her at all ...'

He drew Marney to a halt and gripped her shoulders so they stood face-to-face on the bridge. 'You must remember – Lady Amilee is always a creature of higher magic. She can appear aloof, arrogant – hostile even – but it is not our place to question the ways of a Thaumaturgist. This won't be like a meeting of the Relic Guild at the Nightshade. When you meet Lady Amilee, your opinions might mean little to her – and that's if she decides to let you speak at all – but it's important that you don't take offence. Understand?'

Marney nodded, wondering what in the realms she was heading toward.

'But then again,' Denton said, his grin returning, 'you might just find the Skywatcher in benevolent mood. I certainly hope so.'

Denton set off across the bridge again. Marney had to block out her nervousness as it rose, once more cutting through the awe she felt at her surroundings.

As far as she knew, she was the only one in the Relic Guild who had never met a Thaumaturgist; and, for whatever reason, her fellow agents had never been forthcoming about their experiences. This included Van Bam. Marney wondered if her lover had been to this realm, too, and met Lady Amilee, the patron of the denizens.

The pair reached the crest of the bridge and walked down the other side. Marney could see now that the Tower of the Skywatcher didn't rise from the depths of the chasm as she first supposed; its base, easily as wide and square as the Nightshade, was built upon a huge stone platform that grew from the end of the bridge like a gigantic disc shrouded in mist. She followed Denton onto the platform, and they headed towards the tower. With every step she took it seemed to grow taller; the more the mist thinned, the more she could see its looming surface glinting wetly under the light of the luminous clouds.

As the empaths approached the tower, a set of tall double doors swung outwards and a man emerged, seeming small between the two automaton sentries flanking him. The three figures strode out onto the platform, and, as they neared, Denton drew Marney to a halt.

Say nothing for the time being, he thought to her. *Let me do any talking.*

Absolutely, Marney replied nervously.

The automatons closed in, their silver faces featureless, their internal mechanisms exposed and intricate. Once they were within a few paces of the visitors they stood statuesque, and the man stepped before them.

His face was thin, his body limber. He was well groomed and clean. The fine cut of his suit indicated he was some kind of aide. His pointed ears identified him as an Aelf, as did his oddly triangular face and hazel eyes so much larger than any human's.

'The Lady Amilee welcomes you to her tower,' he said, but his tone and expression conveyed only disdain.

What's his problem? Marney thought to Denton.

The old empath didn't reply and, without regard for the automatons, he stepped forwards with his usual charm and humbleness, even though he stood at least a head and shoulders taller than the Aelf.

'I appreciate the irregularity of our presence in these times,' he said, smoothly and respectfully. 'But there is a matter on which the Skywatcher's guidance is urgently needed.'

From the deep pocket of his coat, Denton produced the small terracotta jar they had found at Chaney's Den. 'Her Ladyship will be most interested in this,' he said, holding it out to the aide.

Without response, the aide clicked his fingers and pointed at the jar. One of the automatons stepped forward. With surprisingly fluid and gentle motions, its big metal hands took the artefact from Denton. The aide then nodded towards the lofty tower. With clanging footsteps the automaton carried off the jar and disappeared through the tower doors.

The Aelf's expression was almost disgusted as he looked Marney up and down. Marney felt a flush of anger, but, as Denton had requested, she kept her silence.

'Lady Amilee is expecting you.' The aide sniffed and turned on his heel. 'Come with me,' he said, heading back towards the tower.

The remaining automaton moved behind Denton and Marney, encouraging them to follow the Aelf.

The heavy doors boomed shut behind them, cutting the roar of the falls dead. The silence was total. To Marney's surprise, the inside of the tower was hollow like a grand but plain hall. There was a ceiling high above, barely discernible in the dim light from glow lamps in sconces on the deep grey walls. Between the sconces, many alcoves at exactly the same distance apart were set into the walls. Inside each stood another automaton, motionless and inactive. There must have been at least fifty of them, Marney thought.

Lady Amilee's personal guard, Denton explained. *Even Spiral would think twice about attacking this place.*

The Aelfirian aide walked to the centre of the hall, where two glass elevator shafts rose up to disappear into the high ceiling. As the automaton waited behind Marney and Denton, the aide stopped before the right side elevator, whose door was open. He folded his arms across his chest and faced the Relic Guild agents.

He addressed Denton. '*You* will wait here,' and then, without so much as glancing at Marney, added, 'Lady Amilee wishes to see your *colleague* alone.'

Before Marney could express her surprise or raise any objections, the automaton began ushering her towards the elevator.

Denton? she thought desperately.

Don't concern yourself, Marney, he replied. Although there was a hint of surprise in his emotions, he was also clearly amused. And pleased. *I will be waiting when you return.*

As soon as the automaton had steered Marney into the elevator, it stepped back, and the clear glass doors slid closed. Marney's stomach tingled as she began to rise. She placed a hand against the glass, her wide eyes watching Denton's grin receding from her.

His gentle voice entered her head. *Experience, Marney. You should feel honoured.* And then she could no longer see him.

The elevator ascended the glass shaft, up into the shadows, up beyond the ceiling of the grand hall, higher into the Tower of the Skywatcher. A light prism flickered into life, bathing Marney in its pale glow. All remained dark outside the glass. The thump of her heart was loud in her ears. She steadied her breathing and marshalled her emotions.

The ascent didn't last long, and soon the doors slid open onto another hall. Cautiously, Marney stepped out of the elevator. Underfoot, the floor was made of clear glass, beneath which luminous purple mist drifted. The hall was circular, with a smooth wall that glowed with a dim, metallic grey. High above, the ceiling was domed, and Marney guessed this was as high as the tower went.

Marney flinched as she noticed a tall and lithe woman standing at the centre of the glass floor. The woman watched her for a moment more, and then advanced with graceful movements. She was smiling as she came. She wore a diaphanous white gown, but was clearly naked beneath it. Her scalp was as smoothly shaven as Van Bam's and a black diamond was tattooed onto her forehead. She came to stand within a few feet of Marney – close but not so close as to seem intimidating – and stared with unblinking eyes, round and tawny.

Marney knew that she stood before Lady Amilee. The black diamond tattoo on her forehead was the mark of the Thaumaturgist. It was the same mark the Genii had burned from their own skins with acid in a show of defiance towards the Timewatcher.

But this woman seemed so human-looking.

Marney skipped away as wings suddenly sprang from the Thaumaturgist's back and fanned out. They shimmered like polished metal, yet their movements were as soft and pliable as flesh and feather. They stretched as least twice Marney's arm-span.

Lady Amilee chuckled warmly at her surprise. 'This is my observatory,' she said, voice low and kind. 'And you are most welcome here, Marney.'

Marney found she had no voice.

'I apologise for my aide, Alexander,' Amilee continued. 'He has spent too long in isolation, I'm afraid, and he rarely takes kindly to visitors. But he serves me well.'

Still Marney could not speak. She had the sudden and daunting realisation that this woman standing so resplendent before her, this Thaumaturgist they called 'Skywatcher', had at some time gazed upon the very face of the Timewatcher Herself.

Amilee chuckled kindly. 'So, you are the Relic Guild's latest addition – and an empath, no less.'

Marney nodded, mutely, unable to avert her eyes from Amilee's tawny stare.

Amilee turned her back and took a few steps away. Her wings folded through slits in her diaphanous gown and nestled against her back, hanging down past the backs of her knees. Against her skin, the silver wings shimmered like liquid in the purple glow of the mists beneath the glass floor.

Still facing away from Marney, Amilee said, 'Denton is a fine teacher, don't you agree? And a gentleman to boot.'

Marney blinked. 'Yes. I-I owe him a lot.'

'He's always such a pleasant character to be around. Not a bad word to say about anyone.'

Amilee turned and gazed across the glass floor. 'You do not like to think about his advanced age, do you?' She moved forwards to stand close to the empath again. Marney resisted the urge to back away as Amilee reached out a hand and stroked her face almost lovingly. 'Denton will not always be with you, Marney, and you need to accept that.'

Amilee's words were not spoken unkindly, but she had hit a nerve. Marney worked hard to avoid thinking of the day when Denton would no longer be around, when she would have to face the world without his guidance.

The Skywatcher looked Marney up and down, studying her, and she seemed pleased with what she saw.

She said, 'It has long been my duty to meet each new member of the Relic Guild, to hear your promises that you will serve the Resident and protect the denizens of Labrys Town above all other things. But I suspect you have already been upholding that promise for some time now – and most adequately, I'm sure.'

Marney managed a small smile.

'Ordinarily, Marney, you would have been summoned to me before now, but the war with Spiral has changed many things. However, I am nonetheless happy to make your acquaintance.'

Marney nodded, but couldn't think how one was supposed to respond to such a greeting from a Thaumaturgist. She was acutely aware of Denton's absence.

'Don't be frightened, child,' Amilee said. 'All your friends have at one time stood before me. Samuel, Van Bam – and, yes, even your great and wise mentor.'

'They never mentioned it,' Marney said in a quiet voice.

'Nor would they.' The Skywatcher smiled again. 'Some experiences are personal and not for sharing. And what is learned at my tower is so very deeply personal, Marney. Would you like to see what is waiting for you?'

Marney frowned.

With surprising speed, Lady Amilee closed the remaining distance between them. She turned Marney around and wrapped her arms around her, crossing over Marney's chest. 'Hold tight,' Lady Amilee whispered into her ear.

Marney barely had time to take a breath before Amilee spread her silver wings and vaulted into the air. The glass floor of the observatory dissolved to nothing. Jets of luminous purple mist blasted upwards like steam from a vent. The acrid stench of magic filled Marney's nostrils and then she was flying, gliding on warm updrafts, spiralling higher and higher. Amilee ascended so fast that Marney thought they would crash into the domed ceiling. The rushing air whipped the yell from her mouth, and just as it seemed there was nowhere left to go, the observatory exploded into infinite light and colour ...

Van Bam and Samuel had to wait until twilight before the fight arena called the Anger Pitt opened its doors to the public. The humidity was already descending, and Ruby Moon was a faint red orb in a darkening sky where clouds had begun to gather. The two agents walked past a long queue of mostly grizzled warehouse workers, who chatted and joked while waiting in line to gamble their hard earned wages on the night's violence.

The Anger Pitt was situated deep in the southern district of Labrys Town, on the eastern side of a two square mile landscape of storage warehouses, close to the recycling plants. For longer than anyone alive could remember, it had provided a source of brutal entertainment. It was a popular venue both with the industrial workers who lived in the area, and many other denizens who flocked from every district to watch the fights held there three nights a week. The Anger Pitt was a vastly profitable business for the entertainment council and bookkeepers. It was also a good meeting place for the shady characters of the town's underworld.

The queue of denizens ended at a ticket kiosk, where, standing just outside the arena doors talking to one of the doormen, was the woman that Gideon had sent Van Bam and Samuel to meet. She was in her mid-thirties, tall and athletically built, dressed in black leggings and a roll-neck jumper. Her long blonde hair was tied into a tail, and her face verged on the masculine. She halted her conversation when she saw the Relic Guild agents heading her way. With a crooked smile, she came to meet them.

'Hello, boys,' she said. Her voice was strong and deep, and the look in her blue eyes carried an assured confidence.

'Macy,' Van Bam greeted, returning the smile.

She then nodded to Samuel, whose response was as direct and blunt as ever. 'What have you found?' he asked.

'Good to see you too, Samuel. Best not to talk here,' she told Van Bam, and then used her head to motion to the arena doors behind her. 'Come on, Bryant's waiting for us inside.'

Macy led them through the doors, past the scrutiny of the doormen, and ahead of the queue, much to the annoyance of some in the line. Weapons were not permitted in the Anger Pitt, and Samuel had left his rather obvious rifle and revolver behind. As for Van Bam's glass cane, he had again changed its appearance to that of a wooden walking stick. He leant against it, feigning a limp as he and Samuel followed their guide up a wide staircase.

At one time Macy had made a good living as a pit fighter, but that was long ago, before she became an agent of the Relic Guild. Along with her twin brother Bryant, magic had blessed Macy with inordinate strength and physical prowess. Even now, her movements as she climbed the stairs ahead of Van Bam were calculated, predatory – her mind was highly tuned to her body. Nowadays, when not protecting the denizens, the twins worked the doors of the clubs and taverns along Green Glass Row, making them well positioned for hearing anything of interest going on in the underworld. They were the Resident's secret moles. Whatever Macy had discovered regarding Mr Taffin's information, Van Bam found her presence reassuring, for at the Anger Pitt trouble was far too easy to start.

At the top of the stairs the group passed through a set of double doors out onto a gallery that looked down over rows upon rows of ascending seats, encircling the small square of the main fight pit. The pit had been laid with fresh sand, which two arena workers raked to a smooth and level surface. The buzz of voices filled the air as hundreds of spectators filed in and took their seats. The air smelt of sweat and stale bodies. The atmosphere was charged, eager for the first fight of the night to begin.

Macy grinned at Van Bam. 'Quickens the blood, doesn't it?' she said, and he could tell his fellow agent was invigorated to be back at her old hunting ground. 'This way – my brother's got us a box.'

Further along the gallery, she led them through a door on the outer wall and then up two short flights of stairs to a corridor that stretched away to the left and right, lined with archways covered with thin, cheap-looking curtains of some grey material. Macy turned right and walked down the corridor a little way, before holding a curtain to one side to allow Van Bam and Samuel into the private box beyond. Bryant was waiting there, sprawled lazily in his seat as he looked out over the arena.

He turned to greet his fellow agents. His features were almost identical to his sister's. His blond hair was cropped close to his scalp, and a deep, pale scar slashed down his cheek from the corner of his left eye.

'Glad you could make it,' he said, his voice laced with the same inflections as his twin's. 'How's Marney?' he asked Van Bam with a grin.

Van Bam shook his head as he and Samuel sat either side of Bryant. Macy took the chair directly behind him. Down below, more and more spectators were filling the arena, and the buzzing atmosphere continued to swell.

'We hear she's gone to see Lady Amilee,' Macy said.

'So I am told,' Van Bam replied levelly.

She placed her chin on his shoulder. 'Concerned?'

Van Bam ignored the question, and the amusement in Macy's voice. 'Perhaps you could tell us what you have discovered?' he said, shrugging her off.

Macy chuckled. 'Well, it looks like Taffin was telling the truth. We've been asking around about this Llewellyn. Interesting character. Bit of a chancer, by all accounts.'

'He's got a list of failed business schemes behind him as long as your arm,' Bryant continued. 'Seems as though he's been into just about everything at one time or another.'

'That's right,' Macy said. 'One of his schemes did come good for him, though. He was running messages for Aelfirian Ambassadors during their visits to Labrys Town, and making a good living out of it.'

Van Bam nodded. 'If he had dealings with Aelfirian Ambassadors, it would explain his connection to the Aelf who tried to buy the terracotta jar from Carrick.'

'Makes sense,' Macy said.

'Even more so when you consider Llewellyn's business collapsed when the war began,' Bryant added. 'He started borrowing money to fund other schemes that never panned out. He wound up broke and owing big debts to the wrong kinds of people. To solve his problems, he tried his hand at treasure hunting, and he was definitely part of Carrick's team.'

'But is he hiding here?' Van Bam asked.

'Oh yes,' said Macy. 'And that's where things get a little tricky.'

Bryant sucked air over his teeth. 'You see, at first, we thought he'd called in a favour, or managed to pay someone off, to get safely holed up at the Anger Pitt. But it turns out Llewellyn is being looked after by a relative.'

He gave a discreet point with his finger. Van Bam looked to a private box on the opposite side of the arena. There, a man in a sky blue suit held court to a group of other men just as smartly dressed. Each of them appeared to be in the company of a young woman. Van Bam didn't need to see the man in the blue suit up close to know who he was: Mr Pittman, the owner of the Anger Pitt. The men with him were undoubtedly business associates from the underworld. The young women were probably escorts from Green Glass Row.

'Pittman and Llewellyn are cousins,' Bryant continued. 'And, apparently, Pittman's big on looking out for family these days.'

'Especially when money's involved,' Macy added dryly. 'From what we've heard, whoever was trying to buy that jar was willing to pay Carrick through the nose for it. Llewellyn's cut was going to be fat and juicy, easily enough to pay off his debts – which, by the way, he mostly owes to his cousin over there.'

Samuel, who had remained quiet during the conversation thus far, decided it was time to give a derisory snort. 'Where's Llewellyn now?'

'Upstairs in Pittman's private apartment,' Bryant said. 'But it won't be easy getting to him. He's got his own security.'

'And by security,' Macy emphasised, 'my brother means Pittman's got a team of grunts protecting his asset with pistols and rifles and the Timewatcher only knows what else.'

'All you have to do is get me close to him,' Samuel said, as if it were a simple thing. He pulled up his trouser leg, reached into his boot, and produced a small snub-nosed pistol. 'Give me five minutes alone with Llewellyn – I'll get what we need. Pittman's a greedy bastard. Even he won't try anything while I've got a pistol to his money's head.'

Bryant rolled his eyes. 'Samuel, even if I was stupid enough to test Pittman's greed – which I'm definitely not, by the way – do you honestly think the four of us could walk away from any trouble we start here?'

Samuel didn't reply and slid the pistol back into his boot, moodily.

'Perhaps we should talk to Gideon,' Van Bam suggested, which didn't much improve Samuel's sour expression. 'He could arrange a raid on the Anger Pitt. While the police are keeping everyone busy, we can smuggle Llewellyn back to the Nightshade for questioning.'

'Don't think we haven't thought of that,' Macy said. 'But it's not an option. See, we've heard Llewellyn's in a bad way. Pittman's paying a doctor to stay with him at all times, just keeping him breathing until he gets his money. Llewellyn probably wouldn't survive a move to the Nightshade.'

Van Bam nodded slowly.

'So,' Bryant said, 'if we want to know where this artefact came from, and who was trying to buy it, we need to talk to Llewellyn here and now, while he's still breathing, and before word of Carrick's death gets out. And we need to do it the sneaky way.' He leant forwards and gave Van Bam's walking stick a light flick. The illusion of wood gave off a musical, distinctly glassy chime. 'The Relic Guild way, if you know what I mean?'

Macy rested her chin on Van Bam's shoulder again and grinned. 'Are you ready, boys?'

Samuel was on his feet before any of them. By his body language, he was eager to be doing something – anything – other than sitting around talking.

'Let's do this quick,' Bryant said, 'while Pittman's busy with his cronies.'

Van Bam took a final look across the arena. Pittman was looking over the balcony, down onto the cheap seats, where it seemed as though he would be enjoying the profits from yet another full house. Van Bam then followed Samuel and the twins out of the box to the corridor beyond the curtain.

Having first ensured that no denizen was around to view his actions, Van Bam dropped the illusion on the green glass cane and held it out, vertically. Once his fellow agents had each gripped the green glass with one hand, Van Bam stabbed it down against the floor, whispering to the illusionist magic in his veins as he did so. A dim chime was followed by a soft pulse of green light as the cane amplified his magic to surround the group. A moment passed, and then, one by one, each of them became invisible.

Van Bam knew that Samuel, Macy and Bryant could not see him or each other, but *he* could see them. His fellow agents appeared as lines of magic, like pale green skeletons. The illusion would last as long as his glass cane remained in his hand, and his companions remained in his immediate vicinity.

'Right,' said Macy. 'Bryant will lead us up to Pittman's apartment. Van Bam, you can see us well enough to follow. Samuel, hold my hand so you don't get lost – there's a good boy.'

Marney's eyes were pinched shut. She could feel Lady Amilee's arms crossed over her chest, holding her securely, and she knew they were flying, borne upon the Skywatcher's wings of fluid silver. A gentle breeze caressed Marney's face and her ears were filled with the distant moaning of a lonely wind. Her emotions were hardened like the wall of a dam, preventing her fear bursting to the fore, but she dared not open her eyes.

'Do not hold back from this,' Amilee whispered into her ear. Her voice was soothing, benevolent. 'You may never get the chance to experience it again.'

Marney opened her eyes and moaned.

The walls, floor and ceiling of the Skywatcher's observatory had disappeared, fallen away, expanded into an endless void of space.

'The sky above your realm,' Amilee told her.

Stars, millions of stars, more than Marney had ever seen from Labrys Town, in clusters and formations that she never had known existed. The sun, too, looked different, lighter in colour than when viewed from the ground, its edge jagged and alive with liquid fire. Silver Moon hid behind the sun, not so bright now in the glare of the great fiery orb, but Marney could see that the peaks and craters on its surface were monumental. And in the distance, loitering in the shadow of its silver sibling, Ruby Moon appeared small, smooth and blood red.

These visions might be majestic, but Marney's brain was struggling for understanding; she could not deny what she was seeing, but could not comprehend how she could be seeing it. Had Lady Amilee travelled far from her tower, or were they still in her observatory? Were the things she saw real or illusion?

'How ... how can this be happening?'

'Thaumaturgy,' Amilee explained, as if this word should give comfort and assurance and understanding. 'I am a Skywatcher and it has long been my duty to safeguard the Labyrinth from outside interference, to protect the denizens. I watch the sky, Marney. And I listen to it, decipher its language. For some time now, the sky has been speaking only of trouble and uncertainty. Still, it is beautiful to behold, yes?'

Marney clutched Amilee's arms. Such openness, such freedom – she felt like a child clinging to her mother. 'Yes,' she whispered.

'You are among the privileged. No denizen outside the Relic Guild has ever been permitted to my tower. But I have not brought you here merely to experience the grace of the sky. Observe ...'

Suddenly it felt as if Amilee had dived, and they were falling down into darkness. But Marney supposed they could have been heading in any direction. The effect was stomach wrenching nonetheless, and she fought back a wave of nausea. The star-studded darkness became a hazy blue, and when Amilee levelled out their flight she began circling high above a huge city.

It took Marney a moment to realise what she was looking at; but when she saw a cube-like building at the exact centre of the city, and followed the line of a road that led from it and headed directly north to a much, *much* bigger cube, it dawned on her that the road called Resident Approach connected the police headquarters building to the Nightshade, and she was gazing upon the town she called home.

'And now the Great Labyrinth,' Amilee said. Her body was pressed hard against Marney's back. 'The realm that connects all the Houses of the Aelfir.'

Beyond the town's boundary walls the alleyways of the Great Labyrinth went on and on, further than Marney could see, seemingly without end. She had been told so many times that no one but the Timewatcher knew how far the alleyways stretched, and to where they eventually led – if anywhere – but nothing could have prepared her for seeing the vastness of it all with her own eyes. Labrys Town was not only dwarfed by the endless maze that surrounded it, it was an inconsequential speck by comparison.

Amilee said, 'But for the creation of the Labyrinth, the Aelfir would have continued warring among themselves, existing within chaos and ignorance. Our Mother gave them a common ground in which to find order and peace. You, Marney, as an agent of the Relic Guild, play your part in preserving this state. Until now, your personal existence has been small, restricted, and it is high time you understood the full magnitude of Spiral's plan.'

The Great Labyrinth fell away as the Skywatcher gave a beat of her wings. Marney was carried upwards, fast, and soon the view of her home was obscured by thickening mist that quickly engulfed her in utter whiteness. Amilee gave another beat, and the mist thinned as she and her passenger rose out of it. With one final beat of those fluid silver wings, Marney's stomach was left behind as Amilee jaunted away at impossible speed; not stopping until the mist they had passed through seemed no more than a patch of fog at an unimaginable distance.

Then Marney saw it, hanging in a black void, like a vast, nebulous cloud of pale white. Bursts of luminous blue crackled along its surface, like brief but monstrous flashes of lightning.

'The Nothing of Far and Deep,' Amilee announced.

Marney could only stare in speechless awe. Her grip on her emotions slackened only slightly, but enough to let her know that if she lost her focus completely, she would be swamped, drowned, by what she saw.

'The Great Labyrinth sits at its core,' Amilee said. 'The pathways to the Aelfir lead through its primordial mist.'

From the body of the Nothing of Far and Deep, thin and wispy tendrils snaked out. Marney was too fearful to even guess at the distance each tendril covered before they halted at pinpricks of light – hundreds of them, it seemed – all glittering around the great white cloud like moths around a glow lamp.

'Every light you see is the sun of an Aelfirian House,' Amilee explained. 'Most, your people have had contact with. Some do not treat with the Labyrinth.'

'I …' Marney took a breath. 'I had no idea there were so many.' Her voice was hushed.

'Ah, but these are only those that you can see, Marney.'

Beneath Marney's emotive control, she realised she felt so small, so insignificant in the face of the Nothing of Far and Deep, she could have wept. Van Bam entered her thoughts; had he, at some time, been shown this awe-inspiring vision by the Skywatcher, too?

'At this very moment,' Amilee said, 'the war is raging, out among these lights. The Houses are divided, Marney. If Spiral succeeds in his quest to subjugate the Aelfir in their entirety, they will not revert to their warlike ways, squabbling among each other, harbouring petty hatreds. They will be united under Spiral's tyranny as a single, unimaginably huge army.'

The nebulous cloud flickered with blue lightning, and Marney struggled to comprehend the full significance of the Skywatcher's words. Each wispy tendril that connected the vast whiteness to a pinprick sun was a pathway from the Great Labyrinth to a House of the Aelfir. Countless realms divided, caught in a feud between creatures of higher magic; she could understand only that the scope of this war was too enormous for her mind to conceive. And to think, she had held to the ignorant belief that her role as a Relic Guild agent could really make a difference.

As if sensing her train of thought, Lady Amilee said, 'The protection of the Labyrinth, and the part of the Relic Guild is, without doubt, the most intrinsic element to this war, Marney. For without control of the Great Labyrinth and Labrys Town, there are too many Houses Spiral cannot reach, and without them he cannot hope to raise an army capable of defeating the Timewatcher.

'The Genii are greedy. They crave dominance and power, and – be assured – if this war ever went in their favour, if the Labyrinth fell under their control and all the Houses of the Aelfir stood with them, it would still not be enough for Spiral and his kind. His ambition has always looked beyond what you can now see …'

Once again, Amilee beat her silver wings, and Marney was speeding through the dark void of space. The Nothing of Far and Deep and its pinprick suns disappeared. For an instant, Marney felt pulled in all directions. She groaned as her emotive control slipped from her grasp a little more. The flight only lasted for a few heartbeats, and then she was motionless once more, clutching desperately to the arms of the Sky-watcher crossed over her chest.

She could see a new, vast cloud-like formation in the far, far distance. Unlike the nebulous whiteness of the Nothing of Far and Deep, it roiled almost angrily, churning with a deep purple luminescence in the darkness. It somehow seemed both violent and majestic, forbidding and welcoming. Of all the things the Skywatcher had shown Marney so far, the empath shied from this vision the most.

'What is it?' she whispered.

'We call it the Higher Thaumaturgic Cluster,' Amilee replied. 'There are many realms inside, Marney, but can you guess what world sits at its heart?'

Marney didn't reply; she didn't know how to. She both wanted and didn't want to know the answer. Even as Amilee's lips brushed against her ear, she could feel cracks beginning to splinter her last empathic defences, and she tried to bolster herself for the words that had to come.

'Mother Earth,' Amilee told her softly. 'The home of the Time-watcher.'

Marney's control shattered. With a moan her body fell limp, and if not for the Skywatcher's tight embrace she might have drifted off into the dark void, lost forever.

'This is where Spiral's ambition would lead him,' Amilee continued. 'And should he raise an army large enough to conquer the Higher Thaumaturgic Cluster, and the Timewatcher falls, then the Genii and their hordes would spread like a plague across distances and realms you could not comprehend, Marney. Nothing would be safe, and there would no longer be a Mother Earth waiting to welcome your soul when your end comes.'

Marney's mouth opened, but no words came forth. With fear and wonder, she watched the roiling mass of luminous purple within which the Timewatcher could see all things from Mother Earth.

'And so, I hope, you begin to appreciate the implications of Spiral's quest, Marney. When considering the full scale of the war, the Great Labyrinth might seem small, and you might feel smaller within Labrys Town, but if we allow your House's purpose to be perverted by Spiral, it would then become the catalyst for a time of darkness unlike anything we have seen before.'

It was more than she could fathom. With a daunting, sinking feeling, Marney suddenly wondered if the Timewatcher was watching now, staring out of this vast cloud to see an insignificant empath looking back at Her.

Again, Amilee's lips came close to Marney's ear. When she spoke, her voice was filled with such love and kindness that Marney found it hard to bear, so she closed her eyes to the Higher Thaumaturgic Cluster.

'Never underestimate the gratitude and respect that we Thaumaturgists hold for the Relic Guild, for your part in keeping the denizens safe. And have faith, always, that the Timewatcher most assuredly knows your name, Marney.'

She felt as though the Skywatcher had let go of her. She imagined floating away into space, curled into the foetal position. In actuality, Lady Amilee's embrace had tightened around her, and Marney's eyes squeezed shut even harder, spilling tears onto her cheeks as she wept deeply, unashamedly.

'To feel overwhelmed is no sin,' Amilee soothed, 'but I think, for now, you have seen enough.'

Marney's sobbing continued for some time. When it finally abated, she realised that she was no longer clinging to the Skywatcher, but kneeling upon solid ground, and her forehead was pressed against something smooth and cool. She opened her eyes to the soft glow of purple mist drifting beneath a glass floor. After another moment, Marney looked up; the circular, metallic grey wall of the domed observatory surrounded her once again.

Lady Amilee was nowhere to be seen. Had she just disappeared, or had she remained in the strange and far realms of space? But there was a man standing in the observatory, before the open doors to the elevator; an old and kindly gentleman in a rumpled suit, crushing a hat in his hands.

Denton smiled at Marney, sending her pulses of comforting emotions, but he seemed hesitant to move towards her, as though it was important for his protégé to make the first move.

Tears filled Marney's eyes again as she got to her feet.

Denton, she thought to him. *I saw … I saw …*

I know, Denton replied. *Something wonderful.*

Marney moved forward, half-stumbling, half-running to the sanctuary of her mentor's outstretched arms. He came to meet her, and his arms were as engulfing as his empathic embrace.

Invisible, the four agents of the Relic Guild made their way up to the topmost level of the Anger Pitt. Van Bam brought up the rear; ahead of him, his comrades appeared as faint green skeletons of illusionist magic. Bryant led the way. Behind him, Macy guided Samuel by the hand. Silently, the group entered a spiralling stairwell and began climbing the bare wood steps to Mr Pittman's private apartment.

Van Bam's thoughts turned to Marney.

Some things were too personal to share, even between lovers. The agents of the Relic Guild never talked about the details of their personal meetings with Lady Amilee. Only once had Denton alluded to it with Van Bam; he had said, for most, what was learnt at the Tower of the Skywatcher was a perception-altering experience, the moment when an agent finally understood the difference between promising to uphold a duty and believing in it. However, on very rare occasions an agent had found the experience too profound, too heavy for their minds to accept, and had fled from the duties, crushed by the staggering responsibility. Denton wouldn't say if he had known an agent who reacted adversely to what Lady Amilee had revealed to them, or what happened to them after, but Van Bam had to wonder how the experience would affect Marney … and their relationship.

He didn't realise that Bryant had brought the group to a halt until he almost walked into the back of Samuel. Up ahead, the stairs ended at a small landing and a set of closed double doors. Beside the doors, a thick-set man sat guard in a chair, reading a newspaper. The jacket of his crumpled suit was open, revealing the handgun holstered to the side of his meaty body, the power stone inactive and as clear as crystal. He seemed engrossed in the article he was reading.

Bryant's faint, green skeleton crept up the remaining stairs. A step creaked, but the guard didn't look up from his newspaper, and Bryant didn't pause until he stood directly in front of him. With two quick movements, the green skeleton first snatched the newspaper away, and then grabbed the man around the throat.

A shout of surprise was choked off by strong fingers as Bryant hoisted his heavy frame into the air with ease. Thick legs kicked and struggled but dangled limply as soon as the head met the ceiling with a dull crack. Bryant carefully lowered the guard back into the chair where he slumped, unconscious.

Bryant checked what lay behind the doors. He then whispered to the group that it was safe to continue after him.

Van Bam heard voices as the agents followed a short corridor. They came from a drawing room beyond an open archway. There, twelve of Pittman's henchmen lounged around on sofas, or sat at a long table, playing cards. Most of them looked bored. All of them were armed. There were two doors in the room, facing each other on the left and right walls. Both were closed, maybe locked. There was no way the group could sneak through the drawing room without attracting attention.

Van Bam took Samuel's arm and held him back in the archway while the skeletal forms of Macy and Bryant stepped into the room.

As the twins, unseen and predatory, moved among the guards, the sound of an amplified voice, muffled and unintelligible, rose up through the floor from the arena below. It was followed by a dampened roar from the crowd. Clearly, the first bout of the night had been announced.

One man playing cards at the table gave a groan and bemoaned the fact that he was missing out on the entertainment and gambling. As Macy moved up behind him, his proclamation was met by a few grunts of agreement, but the henchman sitting in the next chair along slapped his arm and said, 'Shut your moaning and make a bet. The boss said he'll see us right when Llewellyn comes through.'

'*If* he comes through,' sniffed the other, throwing a few chips onto the pile on the table. He shivered. 'You all saw the state he's in.'

'That's right,' said another, sitting on a sofa to the left of the card game. 'Gives me the creeps just looking at him. Don't know how the poor bastard's still breathing, but I'll tell you something—'

He didn't finish the sentence. Bryant punched him unconscious, hefted his limp body into the air, and threw him onto the table. Chips scattered and the card players jumped to their feet, staring with mute shock at their crumpled companion ruining their game.

Van Bam supposed that the stunned silence might have lasted a few moments more had Macy and Bryant not continued their assault. The twins set about the remaining henchmen with brutal precision.

Shouts of alarm and panic filled the room as Macy smashed two heads together with a sickening thud, and Bryant kicked a man so hard that his body cracked plaster when it hit the wall. Pittman's men tried to draw their weapons, but the twins swirled among them in a flurry of violence. They moved in synchronisation, as though one didn't need to see the other to know which head to crack next, and when. They kicked and punched and threw, speedily debilitating each man in turn. They were an unstoppable force.

However, one guard had managed to draw his pistol. He had dived for cover beneath the table when the trouble began. But now he had crawled out of hiding and was backed up against the wall watching the scene with frightened eyes. The pistol, its power stone primed and glowing, shook in his hands. He seemed unsure where exactly he should be aiming as the invisible entities whirled so violently through his friends. He was young, clearly inexperienced, and looked just about ready to start shooting blindly.

Beside Van Bam, Samuel had already sensed the danger. He drew the small, snub-nosed pistol from his boot, thumbed the power stone and took aim. He pulled the trigger and released the stone's charge. The spitting shot cracked into the young gunman's temple. He snapped sideways to the floor in a spray of red.

Of his companions, only one remained standing. Screaming, he ran for the archway, desperate to escape the mayhem. He headed straight for Van Bam, and the illusionist braced himself. But before the henchman got too close, Macy delivered a wicked punch to his temple. By the snapping sound that followed, it was obvious his neck had broken. He was dead before he hit the floor.

The fight had lasted less than a minute. In the sudden stillness of the aftermath, Macy spoke, not even sounding out of breath. 'Van Bam, you and Samuel go and find Llewellyn. Me and Bryant will stay here and watch your backs.'

'You are sure?' said Van Bam. 'Once I leave the room, my illusion will no longer conceal you.'

'Then you'd best be quick,' Bryant said. His green skeleton pointed to the closed door behind the body of the young henchman Samuel had shot. 'Van Bam, Llewellyn's through there, in Pittman's bedroom.'

Van Bam found the door unlocked. Samuel led the way out of the drawing room, and they left the twins and the carnage behind.

They ascended a short flight of stairs to a narrow corridor that ended at another closed door.

'Samuel, wait,' Van Bam whispered.

On the floor, stones had been placed at even spaces against the wall on either side of the corridor. They were the same size and shape as tin cans, and each was engraved with an identical rune symbol that glowed faint blue. The symbols faced each other across the floor, and Van Bam knew what they were, though it had been some time since he had last seen one. They were Aelfirian warning stones, made by the magic-users from a House called Web of Rock – a House that had sided with Spiral in the war. At one time, these stones had been cheap and popular security devices, readily available in Labrys Town. If the space between the rune symbols was broken then a warning signal would be sent to some kind of receiver device undoubtedly in the possession of Pittman, and he would be alerted to the intrusion.

Fortunately, although the stones were imbued with Aelfirian magic, they were simple devices, easily overcome. Once again whispering to his illusionist magic, Van Bam amplified its effects through the green glass cane. Silently, two mirrors appeared on either side of the corridor and stretched its length in front of the glowing runes. He and Samuel continued on between the mirrors and made it to the door at the other end without detection.

Samuel grabbed the handle. His skeletal form paused for a heartbeat before opening the door to Pittman's bedroom.

Inside, a doctor in a white coat stood before a four poster bed. By the way his pen hovered over the clipboard in his hand, the opening of the door had disturbed his note-taking. He blinked through thick spectacle lenses as the door closed again, clearly confused that no one had entered the room. He gave a quick grunt as Samuel stepped up behind him and smacked the butt of his pistol neatly across the back of his head. He crumpled to Samuel's feet and lay motionless.

'Watch the door,' Van Bam told his fellow agent. He then approached the bed to gaze down at the patient who lay there.

The henchmen had not exaggerated when they had spoken of the condition of Mr Pittman's cousin.

Llewellyn's right arm was missing from the shoulder, as was his right leg from the knee down. Both wounds had been cauterised. Bloodied bandages were wrapped around his torso. The left side of his face had been gouged; his teeth exposed through missing cheek flesh. His left eye had been ripped away, along with the socket, and parts of his skull could be seen through what remained of his hair. The pillow under his head was wet and red. If not for the slow rise and fall of his chest, no one would have supposed that Llewellyn still lived.

A number of needles had been inserted into his body and remaining limbs. A hair-thin copper wire ran from each needle to converge into the base of a small box that hung from a stand beside the bed. Like the warning stones outside, the box held a faint blue glow.

Van Bam had seen Angel use a medical device such as this before; the magic in the box would block pain, keep a patient coherent for a time, but it would not heal wounds. It was the only thing keeping Llewellyn's otherwise dead body functioning.

It was then that Van Bam noticed Llewellyn was awake. His remaining eye was open a crack and moving from side to side.

'Is someone there?' he said. Although his voice wheezed, he gave no indication that he felt pain, and his awareness seemed clear and bright. The box was doing its job. 'Carrick, is that you? Please tell me everything went as planned.'

Van Bam dropped the illusion of invisibility and he appeared standing at the foot of the bed.

'Oh!' Llewellyn's eye widened slightly, and then narrowed shrewdly. 'Well then … With magic like that, you must be the Resident's man.' He took a shuddering breath. It became clear that he was paralysed from the neck down. 'That can't be good for Carrick.'

'Your associate is dead,' Van Bam told him.

The man in the bed tried to laugh, but only managed a long wheeze. 'Of course he is.'

'Quicker, Van Bam,' Samuel hissed from over by the door. 'Get this over with before Pittman finds us.'

'Oh, there's two of you, is there?' said Llewellyn. 'Don't worry about Pittman – I'm useless to him with Carrick dead.' He gave another wheeze that might have been an attempt at a sigh. 'I never meant to get into the treasure hunting game,' he said. 'I'm a good denizen, really. I fell on hard times, but I knew the risks.'

'Llewellyn,' Van Bam said, 'the artefact you brought into Labrys Town contained a virus. It killed everyone involved in the sale, but could have easily spread to the streets. Is that what you and Carrick intended?'

Llewellyn made a noise that might have been a grunt of surprise. 'Well,' he said after a moment. 'I suppose it's too late to try and convince you I don't know anything about that. But it's the truth – it was just an old jar to me. And to Carrick, as far as I know.'

'Tell us everything you do know, and we will help you.'

'Oh, I doubt it.' Llewellyn's one eye rolled in its socket. 'I know the Relic Guild well enough. You don't let people like me see your faces unless you're taking them to the Nightshade. And people like me don't come out again, right?'

'We will not take you to the Nightshade, Llewellyn. But you will tell us what we wish to know.'

Llewellyn's discoloured and swollen tongue licked his cracked lips. 'Information, eh?'

'Concerning the artefact and its buyer – yes.'

'And what if I don't talk?' He tried and failed to laugh again. 'Sorry to be a disappointment, but there's really not a lot you boys can do to me now.'

Van Bam glared at him. 'You would be surprised.'

Llewellyn's eye sized him up. 'Look, you know as well as me I'm already done for – that's obvious – but when Pittman finds out I can't pay my debts, he'll keep me alive just to make me suffer, and I've suffered enough. So how about we make a deal?'

'State your terms,' Van Bam responded.

'I'll tell you what you want to know, and in return make it quick for me. Make it painless.'

'Done!' Samuel snapped. 'Now *come on*, Van Bam!'

But the illusionist remained compassionate and patient. The man in the bed should be dead already. With what little dignity remained to him, he was asking that his final end be without further suffering. Van Bam wouldn't deny him that.

'You have my word,' Van Bam promised.

Llewellyn paused. 'Then I suppose that'll have to be good enough,' he said. 'So, you want to know who Carrick's buyer was, right?'

'And where the artefact came from, yes.'

'Well, the first part is easy to answer. The buyer was an Aelf from House Mirage.'

'Mirage?'

'Yeah, there's a bunch of them living out in the western district – refugees who got stuck here when the war started.'

'Yes, I know who you mean.'

'I got to know one of them, a man called Ursa. We used to drown our sorrows together down Green Glass Row. I suppose we were friends ...'

He trailed off as if suddenly saddened by the realisation his drinking partner was now dead.

Van Bam said, 'And you told this Ursa of the artefact?'

'No – other way around.' Llewellyn coughed weakly. 'One day he asked me if I knew any good treasure hunters, said he knew where a priceless relic was hidden – some urn containing the ashes of some Aelfirian ancestor or other. He'd pay enough for it to solve everyone's money problems, he said. But he never mentioned anything about a virus.'

Interesting, thought Van Bam: until now he had supposed it was Carrick who had found the terracotta jar and then arranged a buyer. 'So *you* introduced Ursa to Carrick.'

'That's right,' said Llewellyn. 'Carrick has a lot of contacts. He knew who to bribe to gain passage out of town and into the Great Labyrinth. Don't ask me who. If he's dead, he took his contact list to the grave. But part of the deal was I went with Carrick's team. Insurance, Ursa said.'

'Where?' said Van Bam. 'In which House was the artefact found?'

Llewellyn coughed again, and this time blood spattered his lips and chin. He took a deep breath. 'The Icicle Forest, Ursa called it. I'd never heard of it before. Nor had Carrick.'

And nor had Van Bam. He looked at Samuel guarding the door, but his fellow agent shrugged, just as clueless.

'The Icicle Forest,' he echoed. 'You are sure this is the correct House, Llewellyn?'

'I'm not likely to forget it.' Llewellyn swallowed blood. 'Six of us went with Carrick. We found the relic all right, but ... by the Timewatcher, I've never known a place more savage. Evil. There are *things* there you wouldn't believe. Things I don't want to remember. I was the only one Carrick managed to bring back alive. Barely. Wish he hadn't bothered. I've been hooked up like this ever since.'

Van Bam followed the wires that connected the patient to the box of glowing light. 'Llewellyn, I need you to tell me the House symbol for the Icicle Forest.'

'I don't know it. Ursa was so secretive about that symbol. Protective, you know? He would only show it to Carrick. Even then Carrick wasn't allowed to write it down. He had to memorise it. And ... And that's all I know.'

'That's all we need,' Samuel said coldly. He used his pistol to point in the general direction of the bed. 'You want me to do this, Van Bam?'

Van Bam raised a disappointed eyebrow at his fellow agent and shook his head.

What was left of Llewellyn's face showed only unquestionable honesty, as it had throughout the interrogation. There really was nothing else he could help the Relic Guild with.

With a sigh, Van Bam moved around to the side of the bed to stand next to the box from which the copper wires ran to the needles puncturing the remains of Llewellyn. The blue glow of the magic within the medical device dulled almost imperceptibly, as if sensing its services were no longer required.

Van Bam looked down at the ruined man in the bed. 'Thank you,' he said.

Llewellyn gave a slow smile. 'Quick and painless, right?'

Van Bam reached out and grabbed the wires where they converged into the box.

'Wait!'

Van Bam paused, but did not relax his fist.

'I … I saw a Thaumaturgist once, from a distance,' Llewellyn told him. 'I really never meant anything bad to happen. I mean – the Thaumaturgists would know that, wouldn't they?'

'Perhaps.'

'Do you believe the Timewatcher can really see me from Mother Earth?'

Van Bam averted his eyes. 'Yes,' he whispered. 'I believe.'

'Then you believe the Thaumaturgists will guide my spirit to Her? That She'll forgive me?'

Van Bam nodded. Once. 'And I hope your journey is filled with some of the wonders I have seen. Goodbye, Llewellyn.'

He pulled every wire from the box with one yank. As the blue glow extinguished, a last, gurgling sigh came from Llewellyn's mouth.

'*Now* can we leave?' Samuel snapped.

Marney and Denton rode the elevator within the Tower of the Skywatcher. The descent was made in silence. She had no more tears to weep, she no longer felt overawed. Of course, Denton's empathy had been an immense help in stabilising Marney's emotions, but the calm that had settled on her now had little to do with magic. The truth was she didn't know how to feel. Perhaps her mind was unable to process the immensity of the things she had seen. Maybe she was in a state of denial. After such an intense experience, Marney just couldn't comprehend why she was feeling nothing but this eerie, all-encompassing apathy.

As if sensing her confusion, Denton gave her a smile that was at once understanding and contemplative.

'It's not unusual to feel strangely empty after spending time in Lady Amilee's observatory,' he said. 'Even for empaths. It can take time to

understand and accept the true magnitude of our duties. Seeing is
believing, Marney.'

She frowned at him. 'So the difference between knowing a thing and
experiencing it is, what – faith?'

'I like to think so – others might disagree. But you, Marney, now
have the space and freedom to come to terms with what you have seen.
To decide for yourself what it means to you.'

He gave a small chuckle. 'I've often wondered if we have all seen the
same visions, or if Lady Amilee has shown each of us something different.' His face became serious and he looked to the floor. 'Our colleagues
in the Relic Guild won't ask you of your experience, Marney, and it is
important that you never ask them of theirs. Understand?'

Marney wasn't sure she did understand, but she got the impression
that Denton had one particular agent in mind.

She didn't want to think about it anymore, and gave affirmation
with a silent nod.

'So what now?' she said. 'We go back to the Labyrinth?'

'In a while,' Denton replied. He tapped his rolled up hat against his
hand. 'The Skywatcher isn't quite done with us yet, Marney.'

The elevator stopped. Its doors swished open, and Marney followed
Denton out into a hall that surrounded the elevator's glass shaft. It was
smaller than the reception hall at the lowest level of the tower, but far
more welcoming. The floor was tiled with light brown marble, veined
with a rich golden colour; the walls were painted cream, soft beneath
the warm light of huge ceiling prisms. Three closed doors were set into
each wall, and beside them ornaments and flowers sat upon decorative
pedestals of dark grey stone.

Less welcoming, however, was the Aelfirian aide, Alexander, whose
overly large eyes glared at the Relic Guild agents. Once again, he was
flanked by two intimidating automaton sentries.

'This way,' he said curtly. He turned to head off for the centre door
on the far wall while the automatons waited for the visitors to follow.

As they did so, Marney's irritation rose. *You know, I'd really like to
pull that stick out of his—*

Now, now, Marney, Denton thought back with a hint of amusement.

I know you've been through an ordeal, but you should have learnt by now that not everyone you meet in life will be agreeable.

The Aelf led them to a chamber that was decorated by twists and folds of satin which gave the appearance of ice pillars in a frozen cave. Floor and ceiling, and every wall, the room was entirely draped in clean white. Lady Amilee waited for them as they entered, standing between two cloth pillars, her expression gentle.

'Thank you, Alexander,' she said to her aide. 'You may leave us now.'

With a quick bow, the small and smartly-dressed Aelf left the chamber with the automatons in tow and closed the door behind him. Marney was glad to see him leave, even more than she appreciated the automatons' departure.

Amilee's silver wings and diaphanous gown were now covered by robes of deep purple that were in stark contrast to the room's whiteness, as was the black diamond tattooed onto her forehead. She stood regally. Floating in the air beside her was the small terracotta jar the Relic Guild had found at Chaney's Den.

Amilee blinked her tawny eyes once, slowly. 'Master Denton, it is pleasing to see you again. You have been well, I trust?'

With his hat in hand, Denton gave an affectionate smile. 'Oh, I can't deny that I occasionally feel the long years creeping up on me, my Lady, but I always feel rejuvenated in your beautiful realm.'

'Ah, spoken like a true gentleman.'

Something Denton had said earlier suddenly dawned on Marney. She wasn't the first Relic Guild agent her mentor had brought to the Tower of the Skywatcher. Marney was the youngest agent of the guild, and Van Bam was the next in line. That meant the last time Denton was here it had probably been so her lover could be shown Lady Amilee's visions. What had he seen? Was it Van Bam whom the old empath was referring to when he said that Marney must not question her fellow agents?

Marney realised that Lady Amilee's gaze was upon her. Although she seemed pleased with what she saw, her expression had become a little more serious.

'I wish this meeting could be taking place in happier times, but as it is, we have matters to discuss.' She motioned to the terracotta jar hanging in the air beside her. 'It troubles me that this artefact could be smuggled into Labrys Town without my noticing. Tell me what you know of it?'

Amilee put the question directly to Marney, but because she was so used to everyone addressing Denton first and foremost, she was flummoxed for a moment.

'Ah … we … very little, my-my Lady.'

'Oh?'

'We are working to ascertain which House the artefact was stolen from,' Denton continued, much to Marney's relief, 'along with the identity of the Aelf who was trying to procure it.'

'I see.' Amilee turned her back and began pacing between the pillars of twisted satin. 'And what of the jar's contents?'

Denton gave Marney a meaningful look. When she pointed to herself, he gave a nod, and Marney said quickly, 'It was a spell, my Lady.' Her voice had grown in confidence. 'We believe it was Genii magic. It acted like a virus—'

'That turns a person into a golem?' Amilee stopped pacing and kept her back turned. 'But first, the victim acts like a bloodthirsty animal?' Something in her stance suggested she was bracing for the answer.

'Yes,' Marney said.

After a moment's pause, the Skywatcher walked back to the floating terracotta jar. Her face was creased by deep thought.

'Spiral's position in the war is not as strong as he would like his enemies to believe,' she said. 'Yet he remains well-hidden behind his Aelfirian armies, and what clandestine plans he creates are difficult to guess at. There have been rumours, however, snippets of information that have reached the Thaumaturgists. We have feared for a time now that a device like this artefact would reach the Labyrinth.'

'The virus was contained, my Lady,' Denton assured her. 'It did not reach the streets of Labrys Town.'

'You misunderstand me, Master Denton.' Her tawny eyes were troubled. 'Though it might have amused Spiral to do so, the design of this artefact was not intended to spread a plague among the denizens.'

Amilee stopped talking, long enough for Marney to send Denton a questioning pulse of emotions. Her mentor's voice entered her head, and it warned her to keep silent and not interrupt the Skywatcher's thoughts.

With a sigh, Amilee reached out to the terracotta jar and set it spinning slowly in the air. 'This artefact, such a small and simple looking thing, would have been easy to smuggle through the Timewatcher's barrier that protects the Great Labyrinth. But to contain such powerful magic within it would have been far more difficult to achieve.'

There was a distant edge to the Skywatcher's voice now, and it caused the hairs on the back of Marney's neck to stand on end. It was as though she spoke only to herself, thinking aloud, contemplating some affirmation that was too terrible to air.

'Forgive my ignorance, my Lady,' said Denton, frowning. 'If not to spread a virus, to eradicate the Labyrinth of humans, then what purpose does the artefact serve?'

Amilee's gaze travelled slowly from one Relic Guild agent to the other before she said, 'There is a high-ranking Genii among Spiral's followers – a former Thaumaturgist by the name of Fabian Moor – and his hatred of humans is perhaps second only to his master's. Moor is a vicious pragmatist. There is nothing he would not do to achieve Spiral's wishes. This little jar stands as testament to his devotion, for it contained his essence.'

Marney didn't know what that meant, but obviously Denton had some indication; his every emotion fell dead as he sealed them off from his protégé.

'It is a terrible art that we Thaumaturgists are forbidden to practise, and with good reason,' said Amilee. 'To hide his essence in the artefact, Fabian Moor would have subjected himself to tortures I will not speak of. Needless to say, such an act would take a horrifying toll on his physical form upon reanimation.'

'Reanimation?' Denton whispered.

'His body would be reduced to nothing more than ashes, waiting to be re-birthed into a half-life, where feeding on blood is the only way to ensure his survival. And his bite would carry the virus that you have already encountered.'

Amilee turned her gaze to Marney. It was angry. 'Given that, and the fact the jar is now empty, I think it safe to assume that Fabian Moor was successfully reanimated, and Labrys Town has a Genii on the loose.'

Some of Marney's emotions reawakened inside her then – they were mostly fearful.

'Surely not,' Denton said.

'The evidence speaks for itself, Master Denton. We must assume that Fabian Moor's mission is to discover a way to gain control of the Nightshade. Yet, as disturbing as this news is, it is, perhaps, not without an element of the fortuitous.'

'My Lady?'

'Moor is highly favoured among the Genii, Master Denton. He will have invaluable knowledge concerning Spiral's plans. The Relic Guild must capture him – and alive.'

Denton was once again twisting his hat in his hands. 'We cannot hope to stand against a creature of higher magic, my Lady. Not alone.'

'Nor would I expect you to,' Amilee said. 'We Thaumaturgists may not be able to pass through the Timewatcher's barrier, but that does not mean we cannot be of help. Before you return to the Labyrinth, I have something to give you – a gift for the Resident's necromancer. Come.'

The Skywatcher strode past the Relic Guild agents heading for the door. Marney shared a serious and puzzled look with her mentor before they turned and followed.

CHAPTER TEN

REANIMATION

Clara popped a little white pill into her mouth and chewed it to a bitter, chalky paste. Her tongue and gums tingled as she swallowed.

She stood in a corridor deep within the Nightshade, alongside Samuel and Van Bam. Together, in silence, the three agents looked through an observation window into an isolation room where Hamir laboured to keep Charlie Hemlock alive. The small necromancer had his work cut out for him as he tried to match his skills with a Genii's; to save his patient's life from the terminal magic Fabian Moor had cast upon him.

Despite the realities of what was undoubtedly the strangest and most frightening night of her life, Clara felt good. The aftermath of facing down the Orphan had left her exhilarated; venting her anger upon Hemlock in Hamir's laboratory had given her an overwhelming sense of control. It was the first time in her young life she had tasted such power over another human being. Yes, Clara felt good – better than she could ever remember feeling – but also free. Did she have Marney to thank for that? Was that what the empath had imparted to her with a kiss: control – over herself and others?

In the isolation room, Charlie Hemlock lay naked upon a gurney, surrounded by purple mist that drifted like thin smoke inside a confinement chamber of clear, cylindrical glass. Hamir was also in the chamber. There was a small metal table at his side, upon which sharp looking surgical implements were laid. The necromancer had taken off his suit jacket, and rolled the sleeves of his shirt to the elbows. He wore a leather apron, reminding Clara of a butcher. As he pressed his hands to various areas of Hemlock's body and head, his lips moved silently. Clara couldn't decide if Hamir was speaking to himself or to his unconscious patient.

At that moment, the three Relic Guild agents were disturbed by the approach of one of Van Bam's eyeless servants. With eerie grace, it moved towards them bearing a tray with three cups of coffee. As Clara took a cup, she was again struck by the near perfection of these creatures, their disconcerting beauty. Once Van Bam and Samuel had taken their drinks, the servant turned and walked away silently. Clara decided that it did not need thanking for the duty, and that it understood no other way than to serve.

She tried her coffee; it was hot and strong, though its flavour didn't mix well with the aftertaste of her medicine.

'I'll tell you what I don't understand,' Samuel said after sipping his own drink. 'What could Fabian Moor possibly gain by returning to the Labyrinth?'

'I have been wondering about that myself,' Van Bam replied.

Clara was suddenly aware that the intimidated young lady who had first met these two men was gone. She felt confident now, at ease in their presence, as though she had known them for years, not a handful of hours.

She said, 'Hemlock reckons Moor wants to reopen the doorways of the Great Labyrinth.'

Samuel snorted. 'Nothing Hemlock says and does can be trusted. You of all people should know that.'

Clara took another sip of coffee. 'Maybe he's telling the truth this time. Maybe Moor's trying to contact the Aelfir.'

'Unlikely, Clara,' Van Bam said. 'The doorways of the Great Labyrinth were not merely closed, they were removed entirely. All portals leading to the doorways from Labrys Town were destroyed, except for the portal outside the Nightshade – and *that* portal is unique, only going one way and connecting directly with … an *unknown location*. There are simply no channels left by which *anyone* could leave the Labyrinth. Yet, even if there were, contacting the Aelfir would not be a wise move on Fabian Moor's part. There are no Houses left with loyalties to the Genii.'

Clara thought of the Retrospective, of the hundreds of thousands of renegade Aelfir trapped there, and she hid a shudder behind her cup.

'That's what I don't understand,' said Samuel. 'Spiral is long gone, imprisoned to Oldest Place. The rest of the Genii are dead. Fabian

Moor is the last of his kind, with no way of making allies, Aelfirian or otherwise. He's as abandoned as the rest of us. There's nothing he can accomplish by returning to the Labyrinth.'

'Or so it would seem,' Van Bam said.

With the Resident's statement hanging in the air, the three agents fell quiet and continued watching Hamir work through the observation window.

The necromancer was now touching foreheads with Charlie Hemlock. The purple mist inside the glass chamber had darkened slightly, swirling as if a light breeze had been conjured.

Clara didn't want to guess at what kind of magic Hamir was performing. She drank more of her coffee, her thoughts dredging up some of the unsavoury characters she had met during her time at the Lazy House.

A few of her clients had been angry at the way life was. All of them were older men who remembered the Labyrinth before the Genii War. But their anger was as directionless as it was anarchic. It was as if all they wanted was to watch Labrys Town burn. There was no rhyme or reason for their anger, and they had long forgotten who it was they were angry at. It sometimes seemed to Clara they no longer had a motive for existence, and that the only solution for their inchoate state was the ending of life, theirs and everyone else's.

'Perhaps he wants revenge,' she found herself saying. The older agents looked at her, and she shrugged. 'If Moor really has nothing left to lose, maybe he has a death wish. And maybe he wants the satisfaction of taking the denizens with him.'

It was Van Bam who answered, and Clara was pleased to see by his expression that he had given her suggestion serious consideration.

'If Fabian Moor desires revenge for the outcome of the Genii War, he would certainly place the denizens high on his list, perhaps most especially the agents of the Relic Guild.' The tone of his voice matched his expression. 'But if it were so, the entire town would already be alerted to his wrath.'

Samuel nodded. 'There's a reason why he's sneaking around. If he was only interested in settling old scores, he would have killed Marney out in the Great Labyrinth last night, not captured her.' He looked down into his cup and swore softly, clearly frustrated. 'And right there is another question – what does Moor want with Marney?'

'If you remember, Samuel,' said Van Bam, 'the last time Fabian Moor was here he believed the agents of the Relic Guild could reveal secret ways to enter the Nightshade.'

'I remember all too well, Van Bam,' Samuel said darkly. 'But there isn't any truth to his belief. I mean – if he couldn't do it then, he can't do it now, can he?'

Van Bam was thoughtful for a moment. 'Let us hope we can rescue Marney before we find out.'

Startled by the sound of Hamir clearing his throat, Clara almost spilt her coffee. The necromancer had left the glass confinement chamber and was now standing on the other side of the observation window, his hands clasped behind his back.

'Excuse the interruption,' he said. 'I thought you might like to know I have managed to converse a little with Hemlock's consciousness.' His voice, as soft and genial as ever, came through the glass as clear as if he stood in the corridor.

'What has he told you, Hamir?' Van Bam said.

'Hemlock claims Fabian Moor is searching Labrys Town for something. It might be a specific item, but at this time, I am unable to discover much detail.'

'What about Marney?' Samuel asked. 'Could you get anything on her?'

'Nothing at all,' Hamir replied. 'To the best of my skills, I cannot force anything more from Hemlock in his current state. The Genii has placed a secrecy spell upon him. If I push for further information, the spell will kill him.'

'Clever,' mused Van Bam.

'And frustratingly simple,' Hamir replied. 'The spell only needs to be removed and Hemlock can divulge more than you already know. However, doing so will be complicated.'

The necromancer stopped speaking, and Van Bam tapped his green glass cane impatiently against the floor.

'But can it be done, Hamir?'

'I believe so. My initial assumption regarding Hemlock's condition was correct. The spell has indeed been cast around his heart, and, by interrogating him, we have activated it. The magic is incinerating him from the inside out. I have managed to dull the process, and so long as I don't push him too far my intervention will remain effective. But this only serves to slow the inevitable, Van Bam. Eventually, if nothing else is done, all that will remain of this man will be ashes.'

Hamir pursed his lips in thought. 'As far as I can tell, the only way to remove the spell is to also remove Hemlock's heart.'

'Undoubtedly killing him in the process,' Van Bam said.

'As you say.' On the other side of the glass, the necromancer made the slightest of movements that might have been a shrug. 'But his corpse will otherwise remain intact, and a corpse can still be questioned, yes?'

Clara's thoughts darkened as she remembered what Hamir had done to Fat Jacob.

'We don't have any choice,' Samuel said coldly. 'We need to learn everything Hemlock knows, and it's not as if anyone will mourn his passing.'

Clara looked to Van Bam, hoping that he might come up with some method to gain information other than ending a man's life, even if that man was a bastard like Charlie Hemlock. But the Resident's attention was elsewhere. He had his head cocked to one side, as Clara had often seen him do, as if he was listening to something that was beyond even a changeling's heightened hearing.

A few moments of silence passed.

'Van Bam?' she said softly.

The Resident straightened his head with a snappish movement as though suddenly remembering where he was. 'How long will it take, Hamir?'

Hamir looked back at his patient in the cylindrical chamber. 'Quite a while, I'm afraid,' he said, facing forwards again. 'We are dealing with the magic of a Genii and must approach with all caution. But, if I begin immediately, the heart can be removed from Hemlock before the spell consumes him wholly.'

'Then do it, Hamir,' Van Bam ordered, and something sank inside Clara. 'We will await your word.'

'As you wish,' the necromancer replied.

The observation window darkened to a black rectangle on the corridor wall.

Far to the east, on the very outskirts of Labrys Town, there was a place to which lost souls were banished – a house that tried to cure social blemishes, an asylum which kept mental sickness hidden away from the outside world. And in the bowels of this asylum, deep down in the vaults, were the cells inhabited by those souls perhaps most lost of all: the irrevocably mad, the criminally insane.

In one cold and damp cell, a nameless inmate sat upon the bare mattress of his bunk, secured by an old and stained straitjacket. He tapped his feet on the grey stone floor, grinning excitedly at the black square that had appeared on the wall opposite his bed. The square expanded, and the inmate began praying that it would continue growing until it was big enough to swallow Labrys Town entirely.

Fabian Moor saw and heard the madman before the portal grew wide and tall enough for him to step through. As it shrank and disappeared behind him, he gazed around the cell. Of course, this deep in the asylum there were no windows. The door was metal, with a small viewing hatch, and painted as grey as the stone of the walls. A caged ceiling prism gave off a low level light.

The inmate no longer seemed excited, but was frowning in thought. There were bruises on his face; his hair grew in patches on his scalp. Moor supposed the reason for the straitjacket was because this man was as much a danger to himself as he was to others. His madness was clear to see in his wandering eyes.

'Fitting,' Moor said.

The inmate licked his dry and cracked lips. 'Are you real?' he croaked.

'Mostly.'

The inmate leant forward, dropping his voice to a hushed tone. 'They say I'm dangerous, you know.'

'Perhaps *they* are right.'

The madman seemed pleased with this answer, and Moor turned his back on him.

The trail of magic that had led Moor to this cell in the asylum was as strong as that which had led him to the sewers. He crouched and laid his hand upon the hard cell floor, nodding satisfactorily as he felt the source of the magic warm and alive beneath the cold stone.

'If you release me, I promise I won't bother no one,' the inmate said, and his arms pulled uselessly against the straitjacket.

'I'm sure that's true.' Moor gave him a frosty smile. 'But wouldn't you like to learn my secrets first?'

Bloodshot eyes glinted. 'Will they set me free?'

'Undoubtedly. Observe ...'

With his hand still pressed to the floor, Moor whispered words not heard in Labrys Town for decades. His pale skin glowed with a reddish radiance, and the stone beneath his hand began to bubble and rise.

'Magic,' the inmate said. He chuckled and gave a madman's grin, revealing missing teeth. 'I know who you are. You're a Thaumaturgist, just like in the old stories.'

'Yes, I was once.' Molten stone rose, spewing and steaming to form a small circle around Moor's arm as he pushed his hand deeper into the floor. 'But I much prefer the term Genii,' he grunted.

The inmate began bouncing on his mattress as if he would be clapping his hands delightedly had they not been restrained by the jacket.

'Then tell me your secrets, *Genii*.'

His skin unharmed by the molten stone, Moor's arm sank until he was shoulder deep into the floor. Finally, his fingers closed around a small and smooth object and he pulled it out.

Holding the terracotta jar at arm's length, he waited for the last drops of molten stone to drip from it, steaming as they smacked on the floor.

Unlike the jar Moor had traced to the antiques shop, there were no cracks upon this artefact's surface, and its seal was intact, the contents undisturbed. The spell inside was as strong as it had been the day it was cast.

'Are you sure you want to know my secrets?'

The inmate grinned and nodded.

With a wave of his hands, and another whispered word, Moor released the straps on the straitjacket.

The inmate tore free of it. His body was naked, bruised and soiled. 'Tell me,' he hissed.

'All you need to know is hidden within this jar. Would you like to open it?'

The inmate held out clutching hands for the artefact. Moor passed it over to him, and then stepped back and watched as he stripped away the wax seal. The lid fell from the jar and shattered on the floor. The inmate looked inside. A sound like a distant shout of rage echoed around the cell.

'Freedom,' Moor whispered.

A sandstorm burst from the terracotta jar and hit the madman square in the face.

Without giving him time to scream or fight back, the sandstorm filled the inmate's mouth and nostrils. Fierce like a whirlwind, it engulfed his body, stripped his skin and absorbed his blood, swelling to a swarm of fiery locusts that devoured his muscles and organs, sucking the marrow from his bones.

Moor observed with grim satisfaction as the contents of the terracotta jar fed and grew thicker, fatter, stronger. A sinewy tendril snaked out like a fleshy bolt of lightning, reaching towards the Genii, as if eager to taste his flesh too.

Moor pulled a sour expression. 'Don't even think about it,' he snapped, and the tendril slithered away, back into the body of the storm, content to feed on the madman alone.

Within moments, every drop of the inmate's blood had been drained, every inch of his soft tissue had been devoured, and all that remained of him was his skeleton, sitting upon the bunk, still clutching the terracotta jar in claw-like hands.

The storm continued to grow thicker, more cohesive, swirling faster and faster as it bound itself into a solid shape – the shape of a person, crouching on the floor. The figure rose as the process completed, revealing a woman with long obsidian hair, as straight as a dark waterfall. She was naked and thin, painfully so. The expression on her porcelain face seemed dazed for a moment.

She looked at the skeleton on the bunk, and then up at the ceiling, as if seeing the upper levels of the asylum through the grey stone. The pale light from the prism shone on the patch of scarring on her forehead. She ran her tongue across her teeth.

Moor raised an eyebrow. 'Welcome back,' he said.

Mo Asajad looked at her fellow Genii and smacked her lips together. 'I'm hungry,' she whispered.

From the isolation room, Van Bam had led Clara to what she supposed was a common room. She sat in a high-backed leather armchair, staring around at the works of art on the walls. Van Bam sat in a matching chair on the other side of the room. Silent and lost to his thoughts, the Resident turned his cane in his hand almost absentmindedly. Samuel was not present, and Clara didn't know where he had gone or what he was up to.

On her lap, a slice of honey bread and a few grapes lay on a plate. In her hand, a fresh cup of coffee had grown cold.

Earlier she had felt so hungry, but now she could only summon appetite enough to worry one corner of the bread. The confidence she had experienced outside the isolation room had drained away during this period of inaction. Clara couldn't understand where it had gone. She had felt so strong – so assured and calm – but now, in the utter silence of the Nightshade, she felt anxious and irritable. Surely they should've been out doing something rather than just sitting around, waiting?

Rising from the armchair, she walked over to a tray of refreshments that Van Bam's servants had laid out on a table. She placed down the plate and cup, frowned at the food on display. There were all kinds of pastries and bread, and the fruit and meat were fresh, not dried. Once again, Clara wondered what other luxuries the Resident enjoyed while his people went without. Considering she and Van Bam were the only two present, the spread seemed a wasteful amount.

Clara's hunger just couldn't outweigh her anxiety, so she poured a glass of water and sipped at it as she began pacing the room.

The paintings on the walls were wonderfully realised; strange and alien landscapes that Clara presumed to be artistic impressions of Aelfirian Houses. But they could not hold her attention. A large bookcase was filled with novels and historical works, but she was uninterested in discovering what might lie between their covers. Was it purely this inaction that had swallowed her confidence? Perhaps, with nothing to do but wait for Hamir to finish his operation on Hemlock, Clara, in turn, had the time to fully realise what her life had become. And the lengths to which the Relic Guild was willing to go to achieve its objectives.

She noticed then that Van Bam had stopped turning the glass cane in his hands. He seemed frozen in the armchair, and once again his head was angled to one side. Clara watched him with growing irritation, until, after a few moments, he relaxed and began toying with the cane once more.

'Why do you do that?' she asked, unable to keep the irritability from her voice.

Van Bam raised an eyebrow. 'Excuse me?'

'*That*!' she snapped, and tilted her head to one side in an unflattering impression. 'You look ridiculous.'

Van Bam paused for a moment. 'Clara, have I offended you in some way?'

'*No.*'

'You are sure?'

'Of course I'm bloody sure!'

He stabbed his cane against the floor with a dull, discordant chime, and the soft rumble of his voice became decidedly spiky. 'Then you *will* address me in a more civil tone.'

Clara tried to glare at the metal plates covering Van Bam's eyes with as much defiance as she could muster, but the eerie chime of the green glass cane still hung in the air, and it seemed to drain all the boldness from her mood.

'Sorry,' she mumbled. 'I ... I just feel edgy.'

His metallic eyes bored into her. 'You are beginning to remember what Marney did to you? She gave you a message, perhaps?'

'No. I don't know. I ... don't remember.' Clara rubbed her lips and

sighed. 'To be honest, I'm finding this new life of mine a little complicated.'

'That is understandable.' Van Bam gave her a knowing smile. 'And in
answer to your question, I am listening to the Nightshade.'

Clara frowned. She could hear nothing. The room was calm and
silent. 'What?'

'You heard right. The Nightshade speaks to me.'

'It has a voice?'

'After a fashion.'

'It talks to you? Like we're talking?'

'It is not always that simple, Clara, but yes.'

She looked around the room, at the floor and ceiling, and that pattern on the walls. 'What's it saying?'

Van Bam chuckled lightly at the dubious tone in her voice. 'Right now,
it is letting me know that the police have dealt with the mess you and
Samuel left behind after rescuing Charlie Hemlock from the Orphan.'

'Oh …' Clara pulled an apologetic expression.

Van Bam chuckled again. 'In many ways the Nightshade is a sentient
building, and the Residents are attuned to it. The Nightshade *feeds* me
information, up here –' he tapped his temple '– in feelings and visions
that can say so much more than words. And it puts me in touch with
every aspect of this town.'

The deep tone of Van Bam's voice settled some of Clara's anxiety.
'You make it sound so peaceful,' she said. 'I was always taught to fear
this place.'

'And not without due reason,' Van Bam replied. Clearly warming
to the subject, he leant forwards in his chair and rested his hands upon
his cane. 'The Nightshade accepts and welcomes my presence, as it
does yours, but it can also recognise an enemy. It will defend itself to
prevent uninvited guests entering its walls. The Genii themselves would
find overpowering those defences a daunting task, for the magic of the
Nightshade is the magic of the Timewatcher.'

Clara was taken aback. 'The Timewatcher?'

'Yes. She created the Nightshade and all of the Labyrinth, Clara.'
He frowned. 'Surely you learned about the First and Greatest Spell at
school?'

She looked to her feet. 'I never went to school.'

'Ah ...' Van Bam was quiet for a moment. 'Then be assured, at this moment, you are standing in the safest house in Labrys Town, Clara. No one can enter the Nightshade unless the Nightshade allows you in.'

'Or unless Fabian Moor finds a secret way,' Clara said. She wrapped her arms around herself. 'Earlier, you and Samuel were talking about Marney. You said Moor believes she can show him how to enter the Nightshade.'

Van Bam nodded. 'The first time Moor came to the Labyrinth, he seemed to think that each agent of the Relic Guild held in their psyche information they were not aware of – an unconscious residue of the Nightshade's magic, a clue that would help Moor to bypass any defences.'

'But he was wrong?' Clara said.

'Well ... we certainly stopped him before he succeeded.' Van Bam's expression was uncertain. 'Though before his downfall, Moor refined his research to certain agents who were a particular type of magicker.'

'Empaths?' said Clara. 'That's why he trapped Marney.'

'Perhaps, Clara, but ...' Van Bam leaned back in his chair and became contemplative. 'I have often wondered exactly what the role of the Nightshade is within the Labyrinth. My home is not designed to be controlled or fully understood, not even by me. But by a creature of higher magic?' He sighed. 'I am the Resident, and the duty of the Resident is, perhaps, the only thing in Labrys Town that was simplified by the Genii War.'

Something tickled in Clara's mind then, something old. It was as if Marney's kiss had released a feeling of what it was like to travel to distant places, to meet the Aelfir, and to lay eyes on the Timewatcher's most loyal disciples, the Thaumaturgists. For a fleeting moment, Clara felt as though she was reliving genuine memories from a lost time, and she could almost remember the sights and sounds of things she had never experienced herself. But the sensation dulled, slipping from her mind like a fading dream, and Marney's box of secrets closed again.

Van Bam's metallic eyes were staring at her.

'Clara, there is something I am curious about,' he said. 'Now we are alone, perhaps you would tell me how is it that you managed to keep your magic secret for so long, especially given your profession?'

The question changed the atmosphere in the room to something decidedly chillier, and Clara felt her guard rising.

'There is no need to be defensive with me, Clara,' Van Bam assured her. 'I am only curious to know you a little better. Being a changeling could not have been an easy thing to hide from everyone you knew at the Lazy House.'

'You'd be surprised,' she said flatly.

'Truly?'

Clara shrugged. 'I had a friend – Willow. I'm pretty sure she knew there was something wrong with me, but we never spoke about it.'

'Then what about your childhood? Things must have been much harder back then.'

Clara stared at the Resident, speechless, and the walls seemed to close in on her. Didn't he realise this was none of his business? Nobody asked questions or gave a damn about her life, and that was just how she had always liked it. But when she looked at the Resident's expression of open, honest interest, the words of Samuel rattled in Clara's brain – *We trust each other* – and she relaxed her defences with a sigh.

'My mother was a whore,' she said. 'She died when I was very young. My father – he was just some trick she turned. I suppose he's still around in Labrys Town somewhere, but I never tried to find him. I don't even know where I'd begin if I wanted to.'

'There must have been those who knew your secrets?' Van Bam asked. 'Those who protected you?'

'Yes,' Clara said. 'A couple of the older women at the whorehouse brought me up. When I think back, I can remember times when I was sick for days on end. Gerdy and Brianne – my adoptive mothers – they always treated me well, loved me, and they were determined that I wouldn't become a whore myself. But sometimes they acted oddly around me, almost as if I frightened them.'

Clara snorted. 'Gerdy and Brianne were tough old birds, old enough to remember life before the war, when magickers were a little more common. They knew what was going on with me. As I got older, they explained why I was different.' She shook her head. 'Touched by magic, they said, and I could never tell anyone. But when I reached puberty that's when all my problems began. That's when I started blacking out.'

Van Bam nodded, and his expression was grave. 'It could not have been an easy time – for you or them.'

Was this genuine sympathy? Clara couldn't remember the last time she had experienced it, and she wasn't sure how to react.

'No, it wasn't easy,' she said, her voice trembling slightly. 'My mothers protected me. They'd learned enough tricks during the old times to teach me how to control my magic, and made sure no one ever discovered my secret.' Clara took a deep breath. 'But I …' Tears stung her eyes, and she felt too embarrassed by their presence to continue.

'Please, go on,' Van Bam encouraged.

'I lost Gerdy and Brianne on the same night,' she said bitterly. 'They were killed in a tavern brawl, and I was left to fend for myself. I moved to the Lazy House and …' She glared into the Resident's metallic eyes, daring him to judge her. 'I've been a whore since I was fourteen, Van Bam.'

'But not anymore,' he said softly. 'That life is behind you now.'

Clara nodded, and in doing so dislodged the tears from her eyes and sent them running down her cheeks.

'Although,' Van Bam continued with a hint of amusement in his voice, 'becoming an agent of the Relic Guild might be just as undesirable an alternative, yes?'

She laughed then, with genuine gratitude.

Van Bam bobbed his head to her. 'Thank you for your honesty, Clara. Your trust is not misplaced.'

With a *click*, the outline of a door appeared on the wall behind Clara. She quickly wiped the tears from her face as Samuel entered the room. He ignored her and Van Bam and moved straight to the table of refreshments. Selecting some meat, he crammed it into his mouth almost angrily and then poured himself a cup of coffee. He seemed agitated as he picked up a slice of bread and ripped off a chunk.

Samuel turned to Van Bam, the coffee cup in one hand, the bread in the other, his mouth still full. 'Any word from Hamir?'

'Not yet,' Van Bam replied, clearly amused by Samuel's restlessness. 'Where have you been?'

Samuel made a grumbling sound as he swallowed. 'Thinking.'

Van Bam's look of mock surprise forced Clara to stifle a laugh.

Samuel glared at her. 'I can't stand all this waiting around,' he said, biting into the bread again.

Van Bam shook his head and his amusement disappeared. 'We can do nothing until Hamir is finished with Hemlock, and that could be some time yet. Perhaps you should get some rest, Samuel, instead of walking the corridors like a caged animal. You too, Clara – your rooms are prepared.'

'I don't need to rest,' the old bounty hunter retorted. 'And since when did I have a room at the Nightshade ... Van Bam?'

The Resident had frozen in his chair again, and his head was tilted to one side.

'He's listening to the Nightshade,' Clara told Samuel with a smile. 'It speaks to him.'

Samuel ignored her and took a step towards the Resident. 'What is it?' he demanded.

'I have just received a police report,' Van Bam said seriously. 'There has been a disturbance in the western district.' He rose from the arm-chair. 'Come with me, both of you.'

Of all the rooms Clara had seen inside the Nightshade so far, the room to which Van Bam now led her and Samuel was the most astounding. When she entered, Clara thought at first she had stepped outside: the predawn streets of Labrys Town stretched before her, as real as if the damp cobbles were actually beneath her boots. But although she could hear the sound of the wind, the rumble of distant trams, she felt no chill in the air and no scents filled her nostrils. Most disconcerting of all, the imagery was moving, slowly, as if she was floating, drifting through the town. Clara found the effect disorientating and gripped Samuel's arm to steady herself.

He shrugged her off.

Van Bam called this room the Observatory, and he explained to

Clara that she was now looking through the eyes of Labrys Town.

'We are in the western district,' Van Bam said. 'Reports suggest that the disturbance was coming from this building here.'

The motion stopped in a plaza of quaint little shops, and the three Relic Guild agents stood before perhaps the quaintest of them all: a small and neat looking building called Briar's Boutique.

'It belongs to an antiques dealer,' Van Bam told them. 'One of the very few that remained in business after the war.'

'Looks quiet enough,' Samuel said.

Clara agreed. The door to Briar's Boutique was closed, and the lights inside were dead. The shop looked so homely and unassuming it almost appeared asleep. There were no signs of a disturbance, and if there had been one it was long over. And there was no one around in the plaza.

'Are you sure this is the right place?' Samuel added.

Van Bam gave a slow nod. 'The police received an emergency signal from a neighbour. Screams were heard coming from inside – along with the sound of things being smashed.'

'Perhaps the owner disturbed some burglars?' Clara suggested.

'I do not think so,' the Resident replied.

'Why don't we just go in and look around?'

'Because this is a private shop, Clara, and not an official building – it has no eye devices inside.'

Clara looked at the Resident. There had been a strange, distant quality to his voice as he stated the obvious, and he seemed troubled as he scrutinised the building.

Samuel seemed to notice this too, and said, 'What is it, Van Bam? What can you see?'

'Magic,' he replied.

Tentatively, Clara took a step closer to Briar's Boutique and peered through the window. The imagery inside was shadowy and vague.

'I can't see anything,' she said.

'And nor would you,' Van Bam told her. 'But the magic is there, nonetheless.'

'Moor?' Samuel asked.

'Perhaps a residue of his presence. It is weak, a barely detectable trace, but more than enough to be worthy of investigation, yes?'

Samuel's back straightened. 'I'll check it out,' he said eagerly.

'Take Clara with you,' Van Bam told him.

Clara bristled as she saw a look of irritation flit across Samuel's face.

'Fine,' he said. 'We'll get going.'

'Good.' Van Bam continued his intense perusal of the antiques shop. 'I will ensure the police keep clear for the time being, and monitor your progress from here.'

Samuel opened the observatory door and gave a curt gesture for Clara to follow him.

CHAPTER ELEVEN

IN THE SHADOW OF THE GENII

Shortly after the Resident's black tram headed off towards the western district, a long cream-coloured cargo tram pulled into the forecourt outside the Nightshade. A crew of six tired-looking warehousemen disembarked and grouped beneath the predawn sky. Closely following them was a blue and white striped police tram, which remained parked in the tunnel that led to Resident Approach. Two police officers emerged and headed over to the crew. Any conversation that occurred between them was short and half-hearted. They knew they were being watched.

Van Bam had remained in the observation room following Samuel and Clara's departure. He viewed the denizens through the security eyes outside the Nightshade, and he reasoned that even if they had been able to see their Resident's ghostly image hovering out beside them in the morning chill, their attention would remain preoccupied with the strange, stone archway on the left side of the forecourt: the last functioning portal in Labrys Town.

Soon, the portal would activate. The day's deliveries would begin. And the warehousemen, overseen by the police, would carry out the mundane service that was so vital to the survival of one million humans.

In the interim, Van Bam's unseen phantom looked up to the lightening sky and the fading image of Silver Moon. Was anyone up there watching *him*?

Something Samuel had said was tapping at the back of Van Bam's mind: *what could Fabian Moor possibly achieve by returning to the Labyrinth?* Petty revenge was highly unlikely, and it would be unwise to trust anything Charlie Hemlock had revealed of his own volition. But was Hemlock the only denizen Moor had employed? There were certainly plenty of other shady characters in Labrys Town whose thoughts didn't extend beyond filling their pockets with money. Was it only a matter of time before Moor began employing denizens who held higher, more official positions, too? From the councils and guilds, perhaps? The police? Yet even if he did, what ends did he hope to achieve? Fabian Moor was a creature of higher magic; he had no need – or love – for human servants. What was he seeking in Labrys Town?

Van Bam's thoughts were disturbed as the group assembled beside the cargo tram stirred.

The portal had activated.

Within the tall and wide archway of stone, a sheet of deepest black rippled slowly as it reflected light like liquid glass. The air was filled with a low, undulating hum, as though a mighty fan was powering up. As Van Bam watched, the blackness bulged outward and then prised apart, like a flower opening its petals, to reveal the head of a large floating platform.

While the police officers supervised, the crew of warehousemen moved forwards to help the platform's passage from the portal. These platforms were huge: fifteen feet wide and thirty feet long. The packing crates and metal containers on this one had been stacked six or more high and eight wide. A green cross painted upon the sides of the crates marked them as medical supplies.

For the past forty years these deliveries had come, seven days a week, eighteen hours a day, three or four platforms an hour. They brought ores and rolls of materials; sacks of grain, flour, sugar and salt; dried fruit and meat; powdered milk and egg; herbs, spices and medicines – all the rations that kept the denizens alive. Long ago, the Aelfir themselves had chaperoned these deliveries; had stayed in Labrys Town for pleasure and to conduct business with the merchant guild. Then, during the Genii War, the Aelfir had stopped coming. Only essential supplies were brought to the Labyrinth, and those deliveries were chaperoned by the Thaumaturgists' mighty automatons.

But no one had accompanied the imports since the Genii War had ended, and nothing could be exported in return. The platforms the goods arrived on were designed to be easily broken down and used at the lumberyards. The sacks, crates and metal containers were sent to the recycling plants, and the power stones that enabled the platforms to float were distributed among the weapons-smiths and appliance factories. Nothing was wasted in Labrys Town. Even the nightly rains mixed with the sewage beneath the streets and were filtered through sanitation plants and stored at the water reservoirs.

Trade with the Aelfir had died decades ago, and not one person in Labrys Town knew which House resided on the other side of this one-way portal, not even the Resident.

The delivery at last broke free of the liquid blackness, which then wobbled and became a flat sheet of glass again. The undulating hum lessened and fell silent. Deactivated, the portal waited for the next delivery, which would come in the next twenty minutes or so. The warehousemen steered the cargo over to the tram; when it had drifted close enough, one of the policemen pressed the power stone in the side of the platform and removed it from its casing. The platform settled down onto the forecourt floor. The crew, wasting no time and always under the supervision of the police officers, began loading the crates into the tram, ready for transporting to the storage warehouses on the south side of town.

Van Bam had lost count of the transactions he had witnessed down the years, enough, certainly, for them to seem a banal formality, the supervision of a conveyer belt. Beyond the Nightshade's forecourt, other cargo trams and police escorts would be lining up along Resident Approach, each ready to take the next delivery, and the next, and the next after that. Exactly as they had done every day for the past forty years.

As the warehousemen continued hefting crates, Van Bam began pacing the observation room.

Whatever Moor's motivation, if he sought to seize control of Labrys Town he would first need to have command of the Nightshade – and that he could not accomplish, not with the help of ordinary denizens. Decades back Moor had attempted to extract knowledge on how to enter the Nightshade from Relic Guild agents – secret knowledge, subliminal information that the agents themselves were unaware they carried, information that could help Moor bypass the Nightshade's defences. It had been reckoned that the probability of this unconscious knowledge being real was low to non-existent. But was it *possible*? Did the Nightshade have a blind spot that it had unwittingly imparted to the unsuspecting magickers of the Relic Guild? Was that the reason why Moor had taken Marney alive? Even if it was, the question remained: what did Fabian Moor want?

As Van Bam gave a snort of impatience, a warehouseman was approaching the Nightshade. He carried a wooden crate, which he placed down on the floor inside the line of security eyes before heading back quickly to rejoin his fellows. Van Bam stared at the shape of a square that had been burned into the crate's wood, the symbol of the Nightshade. This was a special delivery for the Resident, a gift from the Aelfir on the other side of the portal. Van Bam received these crates two – maybe three – times a week. They were always filled with fresh fruit or meat, or some other rare food that most of the denizens had never even seen let alone tasted.

In the beginning, Van Bam had felt some guilt for receiving these special deliveries – though never enough to share them with his people. Over time, he came to expect them, to look forward to them, to feel he deserved them. These delicacies were a privilege, reward for his tireless work, a perk of his position. And Van Bam had long ago forgotten how to feel guilty about enjoying them.

Gideon decided it was time to interrupt his musings.

I was listening to your conversation with Clara, earlier, my idiot. His voiced was laced with his usual spiteful amusement. *I don't think she appreciated your prying into her personal life.*

Van Bam sighed. *I disagree.*

Oh? Do tell.

Clara has been without true friendship for a long time – perhaps all her life. She needed assuring she is not alone anymore.

Friendship? Gideon paused for a heartbeat. *Is that really all you have in mind, my idiot?*

However Van Bam replied to that question he knew it would not be the right answer for Gideon, so he remained silent and resigned himself to whatever caustic remark was coming next.

You see, the ghost said, *I'm wondering if there is something about our young changeling that reminds you of someone else. Marney, perhaps?*

Van Bam's mood soured instantly, but again he said nothing as the voice in his head continued.

Marney did leave her mark upon the girl, after all. Do you have hopes that Clara will help you rekindle an old love affair?

That is enough, Gideon.

Gideon's chuckle was cruel. *Marney hasn't called you to her bed since the day you became Resident, my idiot. And you won't rediscover her warmth in an ugly whore. Whatever message she has left in Clara's head, I very much doubt it's a love letter to you.*

Van Bam quelled his rising anger. After forty years, he was well used to Gideon's malicious nature, but still the ghost could occasionally manage to make the Resident seethe.

Gideon, he thought softly, *if you do not have anything of use to say, please leave me to my thoughts.*

Oh, yes, I have been reading your thoughts. *And all they do is lead you in circles. I, on the other hand, have been pondering our predicament more constructively.*

Van Bam took a deep, calming breath as he watched the warehouse-men continue to load the cargo tram.

Go on, he thought.

So glad you asked, Gideon sneered. *Tell me – where do you suppose Fabian Moor has been hiding for the last four decades? Certainly not in Labrys Town, I think we can agree.*

Van Bam considered for a moment. He had been so wrapped up in Fabian Moor's return that he had not stopped to dwell on where he might have returned from.

Samuel said he summoned a portal to capture Marney.

Yes he did, didn't he …?

As usual, something in Gideon's tone suggested a hidden catch, something Van Bam had not yet grasped.

There was nothing surprising in what Samuel had told them. The Genii had at one time been Thaumaturgists, and it was well known that their magic could bridge two far-apart places, literally bring them within stepping distance of each other. It was by that same magic the doorways of the Great Labyrinth had led to the Houses of the Aelfir. But during the war, the Timewatcher had prevented the creatures of higher magic from using it to enter the Labyrinth by casting a defensive barrier.

Plucking this thought straight from the Resident's mind and latching onto it, Gideon said, *But the Timewatcher's barrier is no longer in place, my idiot. With Spiral defeated, the Genii dead, and their allies gone, there was simply no need for it. The Timewatcher abandoned us, and Her Thaumaturgists disappeared with Her, leaving the Labyrinth as a forbidden zone that no one could reach. After all, the Aelfir certainly aren't powerful enough to create portals. Fabian Moor, on the other hand, is. With no one watching over the Labyrinth, he is free to come and go as he pleases.*

Van Bam pursed his lips. *Free to go where?*

Ah, now you're thinking, my idiot. I suspect the Genii has a special little place to which he retires after a hard day's work.

You think he is travelling between realms?

I think he is a creature of higher magic and can do what he damn well wants. I think he can materialise in any part of this town at will.

Van Bam shook his head. *When Moor appeared to Samuel, he opened a portal out in the Great Labyrinth, where it would not be detected. If he is summoning portals within the boundary walls, I would know. The Nightshade would warn me.*

Like it warned you that Clara, a magicker, was hiding among your denizens? Gideon said bitterly. He made an angry noise. *The Nightshade cannot see everything, my idiot. You should have learned that by now.*

Van Bam had no answer to that, and he looked up at the sky again.

Consider this, Gideon continued. *We are yet to see evidence of Moor's feeding habits. There have been no signs of the virus he causes, and his golems remain as hidden as their creator. There are plenty of denizens in this town who wouldn't be missed if they disappeared. Perhaps Moor is smuggling his victims to and from a sanctuary beyond the realm of the Labyrinth.*

Van Bam tried to interject, *Nonetheless—*

No! Simply understand what I am telling you, my idiot. When Charlie Hemlock gives us the information we need, all he'll likely tell us is that Marney is a prisoner in a place the Relic Guild cannot reach.

Van Bam's grip tightened on his cane, and his gaze shifted to the black, glassy surface of the portal. An eruption of laughter came from the warehousemen as they shared some joke or another with the police officers. Such a happy sound seemed inappropriate as the Resident's mind raced.

So, Gideon purred, *instead of wasting time trying your hardest not to think about all those sweaty moments you and Marney once shared, perhaps you should focus your energies on something more productive than trying to save her. Accept the fact that unless Fabian Moor invites you through one of his portals, Marney is as lost as Spiral in Oldest Place.*

In the forecourt the warehousemen had finished unloading the platform. Before disembarking and allowing the next cargo tram through, the crew took a quick break. Each of them, including the police officers, sipped hot drinks poured from flasks. Two of them smoked pipes. These simple actions suddenly seemed unnervingly normal to Van Bam.

No, he told Gideon. *I will not accept that.*

And thus this conversation becomes boring, Gideon replied, returning to his spitefully amused tones. *Remain in denial if you wish, but please spare some time to remember your duties, especially as Captain Jeter needs to talk to you.*

Van Bam's attention was snapped away from the warehousemen and thoughts of Marney. *Jeter?*

Yes, he's waiting for you in his office, my idiot. Apparently, the lunatics have taken over the asylum.

By the time Samuel and Clara reached their destination in the western district the sky was light blue, and the morning sun was clearing the boundary wall. Shafts of light speared through gaps between buildings, and long shadows were cast upon the cobbled streets. Samuel disembarked from the Resident's tram, with Clara close behind him, and he took a deep breath. The nip of Silver Moon still lingered, but the air was clean and growing warm.

Leaving the tram on the street, Samuel led the way into the plaza of shops. Just as Van Bam had promised, the area was free of police presence, and no denizens were up and about at this time in the morning. He strode towards Briar's Boutique. Wedged between a bookshop and a jeweller's, the antiques store looked as sleepy and peaceful in the light of the dawning sun as it had from the observatory at the Nightshade.

His eyes alert, Samuel stopped before the shop's door. Clara stepped forwards and looked through the display window.

'Can you smell or hear anything?' he asked the changeling.

'No,' she said and pressed her forehead against the glass. 'But I think I can see someone lying on the floor inside. Whoever it is isn't moving.'

Samuel tried the door. It was locked. Kneeling before it, he took a lock-picking kit from his utility belt. The slim tools were tricky for his thick fingers to handle. He made an angry noise as he failed to open the lock, and the tools tumbled from his grasp.

Clara smiled down at him. 'I hope you're a better bounty hunter than you are a burglar,' she joked.

'Quiet,' Samuel snapped.

Clara bristled, but he ignored her, snatching up his tools and trying the lock again.

Almost immediately, he regretted his sharpness. Through so many years of living and working alone he had grown used to the isolation of his life. Was that part of the reason why Clara's youth and naivety irritated him so much? Had he grown intolerant of company of any kind? Or perhaps he was acknowledging a sense of guilt and shame from the strange circumstances that had brought them together. Maybe it was neither; maybe it was something else that was bothering the old bounty hunter.

I never remember the wolf, Clara had said.

She had no control over her magic ...

Samuel swore as he again failed with the lock. Just as he decided that kicking the door open was a much more preferable option, Clara reached down and took the lock-picking tools from his hands.

'Here,' she said softly. 'Let me try.'

Grudgingly, Samuel moved out of the way, and Clara crouched before the door.

'Maybe the only advantage of being a whore is that you meet people from all walks of life,' she said, toying with the lock. 'And it's a smart woman who takes the time to learn a new trick or two. Or so my mothers used to say.'

There was a small click, and Clara stood up to open the door into Briar's Boutique. A bell jingled lightly. Clara smiled at Samuel, clearly pleased with her lock-picking skills and anticipating some kind of praise. But he simply retrieved his tools, and then drew his revolver.

'Stay behind me,' he ordered as he walked through the doorway. He heard Clara mutter, 'You're welcome,' but paid her sarcasm no mind.

The antiques shop was a scene of devastation. Shelving and racks, along with the antiques they had once displayed, lay in pieces, strewn across a floor of thick carpet. Wall mounted glow lamps had been smashed. The air felt charged, as it did before a lightning storm, and it prickled upon Samuel's skin.

'*Whoa*,' Clara said. 'Do you feel that?'

'It's magic,' Samuel explained. 'It sometimes clings to the air. What you're feeling now is what Van Bam saw from the Nightshade.'

He stared down at the floor, where a pair of feet in expensive slippers protruded from beneath the smashed wood of some racking. Holstering his revolver, Samuel moved forwards and cleared away the debris until he revealed a figure wearing a nightshirt and gown, lying flat on its back.

Samuel stared at it for a moment, and his gut tightened.

'Well,' he said sourly, 'at least we can be sure Moor's been here.'

Clara stood beside him and gulped. 'Is that the shop owner?'

'What's left of him.'

In truth, it was impossible to tell if it was man or woman lying there. All flesh and bone had turned to dry and cracked grey stone. The head was bald and lumpy, and the disfigured face had no more than ragged holes for eyes, nostrils and its gaping mouth.

'Fabian Moor did this to him?' Clara asked, her voice barely above a whisper.

Samuel nodded. 'It's the end result of a virus he spreads when he feeds.'

'Feeds?' Clara's tone had risen in pitch.

'Fabian Moor did terrible things to himself to gain access to the Labyrinth, Clara. Feeding on the blood of denizens is the only way he can sustain his life.'

Clara licked her lips nervously. 'The old stories said that he tried to spread a plague. Is this how he did it – by drinking blood?'

Samuel shook his head. 'The virus is only a by-product of Moor's condition. But if allowed to take its full course, it will turn a person into stone, into a golem.'

Clara stared down at the ruins of the shop owner. 'Last night,' she said, 'out in the Great Labyrinth, I think things like this were with Hemlock, dressed as priests. Carrying guns.'

'Yes,' Samuel said. 'Golems are stupid but loyal to their creator. This shopkeeper must have been too weak to survive the process.'

He tapped the golem's head with the toe of his boot. It crumbled to fine powder.

Samuel looked around the wreckage on the floor. 'It doesn't make sense. Why would Moor come somewhere as public as a shop to feed? There are more secluded places in the Labrys Town.'

'Hemlock said that he was looking for something,' Clara said, and she gestured to the smashed wares around her. 'An antique, maybe?'

Before anything further could be said, Samuel heard someone calling his name. Looking through the boutique's open door, he saw a ghostly figure holding a cane of green glass.

'Is … is that Van Bam?' Clara asked in surprise.

Samuel didn't answer and walked outside with the changeling hot on his heels.

Van Bam gave a small smile as they approached. Samuel noted that Clara seemed perturbed by the Resident's presence, as though she wanted to reach out a hand to touch him, to see if he was real. Again, her naivety irritated him. Surely, after all she had witnessed already, Clara could fathom that this was nothing but an image projected from the Nightshade through the eyes in the plaza.

Van Bam turned his metal eyes to Samuel. 'What have you found?' he asked, his voice crackling slightly.

'Moor's definitely been here,' Samuel replied. 'One of his golems is inside. It's dead.'

'Any indication of why he came to this boutique?'

Samuel shook his head. 'He might've been looking for a relic, but even if so, there's no way of telling if he found it, or where he went to next.'

'Ah, but there is, Samuel,' said Van Bam. 'Captain Jeter has contacted the Nightshade. He reports another disturbance, at the asylum in the eastern district.'

'I know East Side Asylum,' Clara said. 'It's a grim place.'

'Reports so far have been vague,' Van Bam's image continued. 'Something has disrupted the asylum's eye devices and I cannot see inside it, but what I have managed to learn sounds suspiciously like the symptoms of Moor's virus. And the disturbance is continuing even as we speak.'

'We're on our way,' Samuel said.

'A word of caution, Samuel. The police have been advised that the Relic Guild is active once again, and will be present at the asylum. As far as they are concerned, we are tracking a wild demon.'

Samuel snorted. 'That sounds familiar.'

'Be mindful around them, Samuel.'

He sighed. 'Understood.'

'Good. There is a police tram outside the Nightshade. I will ride it to the asylum and meet you there.'

As Van Bam's image disappeared, Clara said, 'What did that mean? Be mindful of what?'

But Samuel was already heading for the Resident's black tram, which waited outside the plaza. 'It means you keep your face hidden and your mouth shut,' he called back. 'Now, come on!'

The old bounty hunter was his usual reticent self as the tram headed into the eastern district. Clara was glad of his silence now. She didn't want to hear any more answers to her questions. Samuel had pulled none of his punches when explaining exactly what they might be facing when they reached East Side Asylum. Clara fidgeted in her seat, wringing her hands as she tried not to think about it.

Animals, Samuel had called the victims of Fabian Moor's virus. The Genii's bite caused madness and a violent thirst for blood that rivalled that of the wild demons of the Retrospective. The infected lost all sense of reason, gave no regard to personal safety. There was no cure for their condition. Only a bullet to the head could end their insane lusts, unless the virus ran its full course and turned flesh and blood into the stone of a golem. But while Fabian Moor's victims remained bestial, they too could spread the virus with a single bite.

Clara watched the buildings of the eastern district passing the tram's windows. She recognised the area. East Side Asylum wasn't very far away.

Clara's skin itched. Finally she looked across the carriage into Samuel's pale blue eyes. 'I want a gun,' she said.

'Pardon me?'

'I won't get bitten, Samuel. I want something to protect myself with.'

'Clara, have you even held a gun before?'

'Well, no, but—'

'Then you have your answer.' Samuel stopped her before she could argue further. 'You don't need a gun while I'm with you. Put it from your mind.'

His arrogance needled her. 'Easy for you to say,' she grumbled, 'you've got two already,' and she turned back to the window.

Golems. In part, Clara could understand what it felt like to lose yourself, to forget who you were and everything you had done – she had experienced it herself, briefly, during her childhood, on those rare occasions when she had been unable to hold back the metamorphosis into the wolf – but to lose yourself forever? To become a mindless servant, unable to make even the simplest decisions, to be stripped of all conscience? Becoming a golem didn't bear thinking about.

'Now listen to me, Clara,' Samuel said as they neared the asylum. 'The police believe the Relic Guild is hunting down a wild demon. It's the same cover story we used the last time Fabian Moor was around. He and the Genii must not be mentioned to anyone, understand?'

Turning from the window, Clara gave him a miserable glare. 'I'm not an idiot.'

'All the same,' Samuel said in a slow, deliberate tone, 'it's best if you let me do the talking until Van Bam arrives. Agreed?'

Clara shrugged.

Samuel opened his coat and pulled from an inside pocket what Clara at first mistook for a roll of dark grey material. But when Samuel shook it out, it proved to be a rumpled, wide-brimmed hat.

'It's been forty years since the Relic Guild was last active,' he said. 'There'll be a lot of curious people at the asylum, but we always keep our true identities secret.'

Samuel put the hat on. The wide brim cast a shadow so dense it was as if his face had been shrouded in a thick, black cloth. No matter how Clara adjusted her position, or how close she peered, not one of his features was discernible.

'This hat's made from an Aelfirian material,' Samuel explained. 'It's charmed. Even Van Bam can't see through the effect. The hood of your jumper is made from the same stuff.'

'Really?' Clara pulled the hood over her head, but didn't feel any different beneath the charmed material. However, when she looked at Samuel he confirmed with a nod that the predicted effect had taken place.

Samuel looked out the window. 'We're here,' he said. 'Remember – let me do the talking.'

Outside, the wall surrounding East Side Asylum loomed broad and solid. The tram stopped, waiting as two street patrolmen opened a set of tall, black iron gates, and then it trundled forwards slowly along the tracks into the asylum's forecourt. A cluster of police officers parted as it went through. Clara could see many of them trying to peer through the tinted windows, undoubtedly hoping to catch a glimpse of the passengers inside, the agents of a guild only known from old stories.

The tram stopped behind a blue and white striped police tram already parked before the asylum.

Samuel stood up. Clara looked at his veiled face, her mind racing with thoughts of what they might find inside the building.

'I'm frightened,' she said, and then felt embarrassed by the admission.

To her surprise, Samuel didn't react with cold intolerance; instead he offered his hand and helped Clara to her feet. 'I never knew an agent who wasn't,' he said, and then opened the tram's door. 'Stay close and follow my lead.'

East Side Asylum was situated on the very outskirts of the eastern district: a grim building that sat in the shadow of the boundary wall. It rose three storeys high, and denizens could be seen milling around inside through tall windows. Activity within the asylum was agitated, much more than in the forecourt, where spectators generally displayed only calm curiosity. The police officers kept their distance as the two Relic Guild agents headed for the door. They stood in clusters, pointing and whispering. Although Clara knew her face was veiled by the charmed hood of her jumper she felt conspicuous and, for some reason, guilty.

'Where's Van Bam?' she whispered to Samuel.

He didn't reply.

As they climbed the stone steps that led up to the asylum's entrance, a young and clean-cut policeman emerged from the tall double doors and headed down the steps to meet them.

His face was lined with worry and, Clara could tell, he wasn't much impressed by who he was approaching.

'I'm Sergeant Ennis,' he said, less by way of introduction, than to affirm his authority. 'The Resident told us to expect you.' He frowned, more irritated than perturbed that he couldn't see the faces of the people he addressed. 'Come with me,' he ordered.

Clara sensed Samuel bristle as Ennis turned abruptly, and climbed the stone steps. The old bounty hunter followed him with the changeling in tow.

'No one's certain as to what actually occurred here,' the sergeant said stiffly as they entered the reception foyer. 'The trouble seems to be located below, in the sublevels. We've sealed them off, but we don't know if the demon's still down there.'

The foyer was a large open plan room. A reception desk sat at the centre, around which couches and chairs formed a square. In the plain walls, doors led to consultation rooms and offices, and at the far end a wide staircase led to the upper levels. Clara had been to East Side Asylum a few times in the past, to visit her friend Willow while she recuperated from a narcotics addiction. During those visits Clara had found the reception foyer a quiet place, peaceful almost, but now it was chaotic.

Doctors and orderlies tried to calm agitated patients; police officers took statements from therapists and tried to instil some order in the room. The atmosphere seemed close to hysteria, and no one paid much notice to the Relic Guild agents.

'Some staff and patients are trapped down in the sublevels,' Ennis said, and he gestured to the left side of the room and the closed doors of an elevator. 'I was told to wait for your arrival before attempting rescue.'

Samuel didn't appear to be listening, or to have picked up on the rancour in the sergeant's voice. He looked over the denizens in the room with an almost clinical gaze. 'Have any of these people been in contact with the demon?' he asked.

Ennis shrugged. 'I can't say,' he said, as if the question was as superfluous as the presence of the Relic Guild. 'Most of them were already here when we arrived.'

'Then maybe you can find me someone who *can* say,' Samuel said levelly.

'Why?' The tone was contemptuous. 'We've handled wild demons before.'

'Sergeant,' Samuel's voice was full of warning now. 'I have neither the time nor patience to wait while you try to piss on your territory.'

Ennis bridled. 'Excuse me?'

'You're embarrassing yourself.'

The policeman squared up to the old bounty hunter. 'What authority do you have here?'

'The Resident's authority,' Samuel replied, bringing his shadowed face within an inch of the sergeant's. 'Which is to say, the authority to shoot you dead if I thought for one second you were standing in the Relic Guild's way.'

Ennis flinched when he noticed the revolver that had magically appeared in Samuel's hand. Even Clara hadn't seen him draw it from his leg holster.

'Remember who you're talking to, Sergeant,' Samuel growled, his thumb hovering over the weapon's power stone. 'Find me someone who can answer my questions – *right now* – or maybe I'll spare you a bullet and just take you to the Nightshade.'

'Yes, sir,' Ennis said, rather more timidly, and he skipped over to a cluster of doctors.

'You certainly know how to make a point,' Clara said. 'I'm assuming you weren't the Relic Guild's diplomat in the old days?'

Samuel holstered his gun with a grunt. 'Focus, Clara,' he told her. 'Can you smell anything out of the ordinary?'

She could. She had noticed it when she first entered the foyer. It was like an underlying smell of rotten vegetables, and she told Samuel so.

'That's the virus,' he said. 'You'll never forget its stink.'

'I don't think it's coming from anyone here, though. It's too vague.'

'Well, let's be sure before we proceed.'

Clara's stomach flipped. 'Where's Van Bam?' she asked again, and once more Samuel didn't reply.

Sergeant Ennis returned with a woman in tow. She looked to be in her mid-fifties, and wore the white coat of a doctor. Her expression was pinched behind thick spectacles, and she did not seem pleased to have been diverted from her patients.

'This is Doctor Symes,' Ennis said respectfully. 'She's the chief of medicine here.'

Before Samuel could ask her any questions, Symes jumped in with a verbal attack.

'You say there's a wild demon in my asylum,' she snapped, 'and you're just leaving my staff and patients down there with it?'

'Doctor Symes,' Samuel said, and Clara could hear his teeth were already clenched. 'I need some information.'

'Information? What more information do you need? People have been reduced to animals. They're attacking each other!'

'And perhaps they're already dead.' Samuel's tone was quiet, but implied gathering storm clouds. 'Now tell me – do you know if any person who escaped the sublevels carries a bite wound? Because if they do—'

Symes interrupted with an impatient, angry sound. 'You need to act, not waste time asking stupid questions.'

'If they do—'

'Are you listening?

'*If they do*!' Samuel roared, and his voice brought a sudden hush in the foyer, along with many sudden stares, 'then Sergeant Ennis and his officers will need to isolate them,' he added with less volume.

To Clara's surprise, instead of cowering before the Relic Guild agent, the asylum chief drew herself up and got angrier. She stepped in close to the old bounty hunter, proudly, defiantly. Sergeant Ennis didn't know which way to turn.

'I'm old enough to remember the Relic Guild, and the people who disappeared because of you,' she said, voice low. 'But just because you hide your face, don't think that you can frighten me.'

Clara noticed Samuel's hand flex near his pistol.

'Now,' Symes added, 'what is the Resident going to do about my people?'

Acting on some instinct she didn't know she possessed, Clara stepped in before Samuel's brain followed through with what his gun-hand seemed to be thinking.

'Doctor Symes, listen to me,' she said, and the strength in her voice surprised her. 'You're angry and frightened, and we understand that. But if any person here was bitten by the demon, they'll be infected with a virus that has no cure. As a doctor, you must understand the severity of that.'

'Well, yes.' Symes's body language became somewhat less aggressive. 'But I have friends down in the sublevels, patients—'

'And we will do all we can to help them,' Clara promised with more confidence than she felt. 'But if this virus gets out onto the streets, we'll have an epidemic on our hands. We need to deal with this right here, right now, and we need your help.'

Symes gave Samuel a final glare, and then nodded. 'Of course,' she said.

'Thank you.' Clara turned to Ennis. 'Sergeant, please help Doctor Symes search for anyone who has been bitten. Isolate those you find. Keep them away from other people.'

'And you lock all the doors,' Samuel added menacingly. 'No one enters or leaves the asylum until we say so. Is that clear?'

'Yes, sir,' Ennis said, before he and Symes strode away to carry out their orders.

'I know you said to let you do the talking,' Clara whispered to Samuel, 'but I didn't think shooting a doctor was the best way forward.'

'Come on,' Samuel grumbled, and he started off across the foyer floor.

The brief but angry confrontation had drawn more attention to the Relic Guild agents, as they crossed the room. Clara kept her stride as confident as she could beside Samuel, reminding herself that her face was hidden as she did her best to ignore the stares and whispers.

Samuel steered her towards a door to the side of the elevator. To Clara's surprise the door opened by itself as they approached it, and then closed again after them with the sound of bolts sliding into place.

On the other side was the landing of a stairwell that led down into the sublevels of the asylum. The smell of rotting vegetables was much more pronounced here, but there was also another scent which was much more familiar.

Clara gave a sardonic smile. 'You can show yourself now, Van Bam.'

The Resident materialised, leaning back against the stairwell door. He had his green glass cane in one hand and a cloth satchel hung from his shoulder. Just his presence eased some of Clara's nerves.

'You did well with Doctor Symes, Clara,' he said.

'You were watching?'

'Always. And your diplomatic skills are, perhaps, a lesson to us all.' He turned his metallic eyes to Samuel.

With customary irascibility, Samuel ignored the comment and said, 'What have you found?'

'Not much more than you,' Van Bam replied. 'No one really seems to know what has occurred down in the sublevels. I am convinced, however, that Fabian Moor has been here, though it is likely he has already vanished again.'

Samuel sighed. 'Then we're clearing up after him, just like the old days.'

'So it would seem. However, I would be surprised if Moor came to the asylum simply to feed again. Like the antiques shop, it is conspicuous. Let us hope that somewhere below he has left a clue as to what his true purpose is.'

Samuel drew the rifle from the holster on his back, and checked its clip and power stone. 'Stay behind me,' he said, and then began descending the first flight of stairs.

Van Bam gave Clara a quick smile, and motioned after Samuel. 'Shall we?'

CHAPTER TWELVE

LUNACY

'Moor's presence has somehow disrupted the eye devices within the asylum,' Van Bam said as they descended the stairs. 'The Nightshade could show me nothing of the sublevels.'

Before him, he could see the colours in Clara's body were in turmoil as she followed immediately behind Samuel, her eyes concentrating on the steps.

'We should expect the worst,' he added.

After only four short flights, the stairs ended at the door to the first sublevel of East Side Asylum. Through a small, reinforced window, Van Bam caught a brief glimpse of a dimly lit corridor beyond, before Samuel pushed his face up against the glass and blocked his view.

'There are three sublevels to this asylum,' Van Bam said, 'and this first is mainly reserved for the treatment of those patients it is safer to keep segregated from the other inmates, as well as society.'

'Great,' Samuel grumbled without turning from the window, 'as if things weren't going to be dangerous enough.'

Beside Van Bam, Clara pulled her hood down.

'Keep your face concealed,' he told her. 'Encountering survivors is not impossible.'

Her troubled frown disappeared into impenetrable shadow as she pulled the hood back up.

Van Bam himself wore no hat or hood made from the charmed Aelfirian material, so he had cast an illusion upon his face that blurred his features.

'Are you sensing anything, Samuel?' he said.

Samuel turned from the window and rubbed his forehead as though he had a headache.

'Nothing much,' he said after a moment. 'But ... *something* is there.'

Van Bam nodded. 'Then we proceed with caution.'

He stepped past Samuel and laid a hand upon the door. The sound of bolts sliding free quickly followed as the magical energy that operated the asylum's inner mechanisms recognised the Resident's touch.

Van Bam stepped back and allowed Samuel to pull the door open. The stench of rotting vegetables became so strong that Clara raised a hand to her face, obviously fighting the urge to gag.

'Keep your distance,' Samuel said as he thumbed the rifle's power stone; it whined and began to glow as he stepped through the door. 'Don't get in front of me.'

With his rifle in hand, he walked to the left and disappeared from view.

Van Bam held Clara back a moment before they followed.

To the right, the dull metal doors of the elevator formed a dead end. Samuel was already several paces ahead, slowly making his way along a darkened corridor. He trod carefully, holding his rifle to his chest, the barrel pointing up to the ceiling. There were no other doors along the corridor, and the light prisms above glowed weakly. Van Bam and Clara followed Samuel at a distance.

'The asylum is in lockdown,' Van Bam mused. 'It has switched to emergency power.'

But Clara didn't appear to be listening, and Van Bam could see curiosity in the hues of her body. She was watching Samuel as he took careful steps along the corridor. The old bounty hunter's shadowed face was down-turned, as if he was relying on some inner instinct to steer his way.

Clara leaned into Van Bam. 'What's he doing?' she whispered.

'Waiting for a warning signal.' Van Bam replied, just as quietly. He didn't need to see the young changeling's face to know that it was questioning.

She said, 'When you asked him if he could sense anything, what did you mean?'

'Samuel was touched by magic in a peculiar way, Clara. It gave him a prescient awareness. He can sense the approach of danger moments before it arrives.'

Clara was quiet for a moment. 'That's a handy trick for a bounty hunter,' she said.

'And it has proved beneficial to the Relic Guild on more than a few occasions. However, not only does Samuel's gift alert him to danger, but it also feeds his baser instincts and, to some degree, controls his reactions. It gives him a preternatural survival mechanism that is as malevolent as it is prescient. When Samuel feels his magic stirring, Clara, it is better not to be too close to his guns.'

Up ahead, the corridor doglegged to the right, and Samuel slipped out of view.

When Van Bam reached the turn he saw another corridor stretching ahead, and this one was lined on both sides with doors to offices and therapy rooms. He and Clara inched forwards slowly as Samuel moved from door to door, finding each locked but pausing to peer through the windows. Evidently his prescient awareness did not detect any immediate danger, and he continued on. He didn't get far, however, before he stopped and signalled to his fellow agents to remain where they were.

As Van Bam drew Clara to a halt, he could tell by her body language that her own heightened senses had detected something.

'Van Bam, I—'

'Quiet,' Van Bam hissed, and his metal eyes remained on Samuel and the violet glow of the rifle's power stone.

He had made it halfway down the corridor, and now stood staring at something to the right. After a long moment he looked back up the corridor. 'You might want to see this,' Samuel said, his voice low and dispassionate.

Van Bam heard a shuffling sound as he led Clara to Samuel's position. The corridor broke to allow for some kind of common room. Tables and chairs had been overturned. A game of Hangman begun in chalk on a blackboard at the far end, had not been concluded. Van Bam reasoned that this room was where patients relearned how to interact on a social level. There were books and games strewn across the floor. Amongst the mess, a figure in the yellow uniform of an inmate lay shaking.

Apparently uninterested in the inmate, Samuel went off to check the few locked offices around the common room. Van Bam, however, stepped up to the convulsing figure. Clara joined him.

It was a victim of Fabian Moor's bite, entering the final stages of the viral infection. All skin had become grey stone, shining, soft and clammy. Features were disfigured, body twisted and limbs stretched thin.

Its movement stopped abruptly, and it lay still as a dead thing.

'The virus has run its course,' Van Bam said, and then moved Clara back as the golem stirred and clambered to its feet with stiff and awkward movements.

It made no move towards the Relic Guild agents, or to do anything at all. Seemingly devoid of comprehension, the golem simply stood and faced Van Bam with eyeless sockets as if waiting for him to issue an order.

'It … it won't hurt us?' Clara asked.

Van Bam shook his head. 'Not without orders.'

Samuel returned and stood before the golem. When it didn't react to his presence, he holstered his rifle and turned his back on it.

'Maybe we'll be lucky,' he said. 'Maybe the virus has already run its course everywhere, and we'll be facing nothing but golems.'

'That would be lucky indeed,' Van Bam said. But he and Samuel both knew that the incubation period of the virus was not the same for every victim.

'Either way,' said Samuel, 'we can't leave this thing behind us.'

So saying, he opened his coat and drew a mean-looking knife from a sheath strapped against his ribs. Turning, and without pause, he rammed the blade into the soft stone of the newly formed golem's face, and then stepped back.

There was a loud *pop* and Van Bam saw Clara flinch. The golem made a feeble attempt to remove the knife from its face, but then began convulsing, jerking and twisting, and a hissing sound filled the air. The smell of rotting vegetables vanished, replaced by a sour and acrid stench of dispelling magic which tingled upon Van Bam's skin. The golem's limbs bent to hideous angles, but not one sound of complaint came from its mouth. Within moments the damp stone of its head dried with a multitude of dull cracks. It shattered to grey rubble within its yellow uniform and fell to the floor in a heap.

In the following silence, Samuel remained staring down at the ruins of the golem. He kept his back to his comrades, and something about his shades unsettled Van Bam. More and more colour was blooming in the grey.

'Samuel?'

The old bounty hunter wheeled around, drawing his rifle and thumbing the power stone. He took aim straight at Clara's face.

'They're coming…'

Clara didn't seem to know which way to turn, but Van Bam grabbed her arm and dragged her to the back of the room until they stood by the blackboard.

She clutched to his arm tightly. 'I can hear them,' she whimpered.

And so could he: grunts, and shuffling footsteps heading towards them from somewhere unseen.

An age seemed to pass before the first animated victim of Fabian Moor's virus came into view. It staggered into the common area with a crippled gait. Pale and inhuman, it came forward. What remained of its hair was matted with blood, as was its face. More red stained its white doctor's coat. There was a vicious bite wound on its neck, from which a web of black veins spread out over its skin. Its expression was one of hatred, of a desire to destroy.

But Samuel didn't kill the monster as it shuffled towards him, exposing long, chattering teeth. With hardened nerve, he waited until three more infected victims appeared. They followed the first, clawing at each other in their eagerness to draw fresh blood from the Relic Guild agents. Two were in the earlier stages of the virus, their movements comparatively fluid. The third, caught in a state between flesh and stone, lagged behind as its fellows clawed ahead. Its legs seemed to become stiffer, faltering with each step it took. With voices caught somewhere between coughs and barks, hands reaching forwards hungrily, all four victims came for Samuel.

The lead monster tripped and fell to its knees, several paces from its intended prey. As it struggled to rise, the others caught up with it, and they became entangled in a bizarre, almost comical way.

Samuel's rifle released a burst of thaumaturgy.

The bullet slammed into the chest of the monster on its knees. Fire bloomed from within it, but not yellow flames that licked and danced; rather, a fierce storm of dull orange that consumed its victim from the inside out and spread to those within touching distance. Van Bam felt a sudden wave of heat, and smelt the reek of burning flesh mingled with the rotting stench of infection. The four virus victims screamed and writhed as the magic of Samuel's fire-bullet ate them greedily. Within seconds they had been reduced to piles of hot ash.

A few flames danced upon the carpet, but quickly died to leave dark, smouldering patches.

Samuel waved a hand to clear the smoke, and then, quite calmly, he holstered his rifle and drew his revolver. Clara looked at Van Bam, but the Resident raised a hand for continued silence. A chorus of shrieks was coming from the corridor now. Voice upon voice added to the terrible din; footstep after shuffling footstep grew louder and closer.

As the first of the new horde rounded the corner, Samuel began firing his revolver. This time he was using regular bullets. Cold and calculated, he fired shot after shot. Each time he pulled the trigger, the power stone flashed, the revolver made a low and hollow spitting sound, and, as soon as one of the infected appeared, it fell dead, its head ruined to a bloody pulp.

When eight victims in varying stages of infection lay motionless on the floor, Samuel opened the revolver's chamber and seemed unmoved as a new wave of the infected began emerging from the corridor, cough-barking and clambering over the dead bodies in their way.

'I need a moment to reload,' Samuel said calmly, as he began feeding grey metal slugs from his utility belt into the gun in an almost casual fashion.

Van Bam stepped in front of Clara, and dropped to one knee. Whispering to his magic, he stabbed his cane down onto the floor. The green glass flared with a sound like a distant chime. Streaks of light flew from it, then turned to wasps the size of rats in midair, which swarmed around the infected horde. Acting on some primal instinct, Fabian Moor's victims attacked the wasps, clawing and screeching manically as the oversized insects buzzed angrily among them, stinging, too fast to catch.

The illusion didn't last long. As the rat-sized wasps faded to wisps of light that quickly disappeared, Samuel snapped shut the chamber of his revolver. He began firing again.

Seven more infected inmates and asylum staff fell, their heads ruined by the cold accuracy of Samuel's marksmanship.

By the time he finished firing, the power stone's charge was low. Heavy use had dimmed its violet glow and left the rich scent of spent thaumaturgy in the air. Samuel twisted it loose and replaced it with another stone from his utility belt.

He gestured to the corpses. 'That's all of them,' he said. His voice was detached. 'For now.'

Van Bam nodded. Beside him, Clara released a breath. The Resident left her and moved up alongside Samuel. The floor before them was covered in ash and corpses. The stench of death was foul.

'They came as a group, more or less,' Van Bam said. 'It is as if we had distracted them.'

Samuel nodded as he again loaded fresh bullets into his revolver. 'But distracted them from what?'

Van Bam paused only for a moment. 'We must continue.'

'Wait,' Clara said before either man could move. 'What about them?' She gestured to the corpses lying across each other on the floor, and swallowed. 'Aren't they still infected? Shouldn't we burn the bodies or something?'

'I'm not wasting any more fire-bullets,' Samuel stated. 'I'll scout ahead.'

And with that he trampled over the corpses, showing not the slightest respect or concern. Revolver in hand, he turned to the right and disappeared into the corridor beyond.

Van Bam's metallic eyes remained on the dead. 'The virus is magical in nature, Clara. Death of the carrier is the surest way to extinguish it. These victims are no longer infected.' He held a hand out to her. 'Come.'

Clara stepped forwards and crouched to pick up Samuel's knife from the broken ruins of the golem. Van Bam said nothing to her as she tucked it into her boot. Her hand was hot and clammy when she placed it in his. Together they picked their way between the dead bodies as best they could, but treading on the odd hand or leg was unavoidable. They exited the common area and rejoined the corridor. The blood on the soles of Van Bam's bare feet left perfect prints on the carpet.

Up ahead, Samuel had resumed checking the locked doors that lined the corridor walls. As before, Van Bam ensured that he and Clara kept a suitable distance from him and his revolver. The corridor turned right and right again into the final stretch, where Samuel signalled a warning to his colleagues.

The corridor ended at another closed elevator. Beside it was the entrance to the stairwell that led down to sublevel two. Five bodies lying on the floor had been beaten and bitten, dead and no longer a threat. Samuel picked his way through them to the last door on the right hand wall. He stared at it for a long moment, his revolver hanging loose in his hand.

Finally he motioned for his colleagues to come forward. Van Bam saw light coming from the crack underneath the door.

'This is it,' Samuel whispered. 'Whatever's in here was attracting the infected. But I'm not getting any warning signals.'

'Can you sense anything beyond the door?' Van Bam whispered to Clara.

Clara listened for a moment. 'I can hear someone breathing,' she said. 'There're two of them.'

'Are they infected?'

She sniffed the air and then shrugged. 'It's hard to say. The whole place stinks of rotten vegetables.'

At the Resident's nod Samuel tried the door handle. Like all the other doors, it was locked. Samuel prepared to kick it open.

'Wait,' Van Bam said.

The crack of light under the door wavered, as if it was coming from a torch in someone's hand. And then it extinguished.

'Survivors?' said Clara.

Van Bam knocked on the door. 'Do not be afraid,' he called. 'We are here to help you.'

This was followed by agitated, argumentative whispers, and then silence. The door did not open.

Samuel thumped on it with the butt of his revolver. 'We're agents of the Resident,' he shouted. 'Now open up or I'll blow this damned door off its hinges.'

Footsteps approached the door. Van Bam and Clara stepped back as Samuel aimed his revolver. The door opened, and the anxious face of a young woman peeked out. Clearly exhausted, she flinched at the gun aimed at her face, and then frowned at the three agents with hidden faces standing out in the corridor.

'She's clean,' Clara said.

Samuel pushed past the woman and entered the room without a word. He smacked a wall switch, and the ceiling prism glowed with dull emergency light.

Van Bam, with more consideration, steered the woman back inside. Clara remained standing in the doorway.

There was no furniture in the room, and judging by the rectangular window set into the back wall, darkened and black, it seemed to be an observation chamber. The woman was accompanied by a man, portly and balding and somewhere around fifty. He held a torch in his hand. By their dress, he was an orderly and she a doctor.

'The agents of the Resident?' the man said, a sheen of sweat on his heavy face. 'I haven't heard that since I was a boy.' He gave the woman a meaningful look.

'Were either of you bitten?' Samuel growled.

The man shook his head quickly, the woman more slowly. It looked as though she had been crying.

Samuel grunted, and then moved to the back of the room to inspect the rectangular window.

'We are the Relic Guild,' Van Bam said reassuringly.

The orderly looked to the floor as if shying away from the confirmation of his suspicions. The woman frowned into Van Bam's blurred face. She seemed to know she had been told something important, but couldn't tell what.

'We are hunting a wild demon,' Van Bam continued. 'And you have encountered the virus it carries, yes?'

She nodded.

'It started with the inmates,' the orderly said, not looking up. 'They started attacking each other, like animals, tearing and biting and … and then the doctors …'

The orderly trailed off, and the woman laid a hand on his arm. 'It's all right, Karl,' she said, and turned to Van Bam. 'I'm Doctor Reeve. Karl was assisting me with a patient when the trouble began. You say there's a wild demon in the asylum?'

'Yes, it escaped the Retrospective late last night,' Van Bam lied.

Doctor Reeve nodded. 'That makes sense. The patients on sublevel three were talking about a monster just before the trouble began.'

'Did they speak with the demon? Does anyone know why it came to the asylum?'

'I honestly don't know,' Reeve said. 'Whatever virus it's carrying spread so fast. We managed to lock ourselves in here, but my patient ...' Her lip trembled and fresh tears came to her eyes.

'There's something in here,' Samuel interrupted. He was still standing by the rectangular window. He pressed a button on a wall mounted control panel, and the window's blackness cleared to reveal the padded cell beyond. Inside the cell a golem stood, naked, the full grotesqueness of its stone body on show.

'We put him in the cell for our own safety,' Reeve said. 'Thank the Timewatcher we did.'

'He started to turn,' Karl added. The orderly had found some composure, and his round face seemed angry. 'He went mad at first, like the others. Then he became this thing.'

Van Bam stared at the golem behind the glass. Its toothless mouth hung slack, and its thin neck looked too weak to hold the misshapen boulder of its head. He could only imagine what it must have been like for the doctor and the orderly, trapped inside this room with bloodthirsty creatures clawing at the door, tearing each other apart, and all the while having to watch the virus take its full course upon the patient.

'Can you help him?' Reeve asked, a little breathlessly. 'He was making such progress. Do you have a cure?'

No one replied.

Samuel moved to the door beside the window. 'Give me the key,' he ordered.

Karl took a bunch of keys from his belt, unclipped the correct one and passed it to Samuel.

'Can you help him?' Reeve said again, stronger this time. The question seemed to be aimed at all of the Relic Guild agents.

'We will do all we can,' Van Bam promised her. 'Come.'

He escorted the doctor and the orderly from the room. Out in the corridor they both paused, disconcerted by the dead bodies lying on the floor.

'Do not be frightened,' Van Bam said. 'The way behind us is clear. It is safe to use the stairs to the upper levels.'

'You-You're not escorting us out?' said Karl.

'No. We need to search for other survivors.'

'You can't be serious,' Doctor Reeves said. She pointed at the end of the corridor, at the elevator and stairwell door. 'Going to the lower levels is madness.'

Even as she said this, Van Bam heard the telltale spitting sound of a revolver. It was followed by a pop and hiss, and then the dull sound of cracking stone that told Van Bam Samuel had put an end to the golem in the padded cell.

'Please,' he told Reeve. 'Get yourselves to safety and let us do our jobs.'

'But don't you understand?' she said urgently. 'The demon was hiding all the way down in sublevel three.'

'Nonetheless,' Van Bam said, 'you will leave now.'

Karl the orderly seemed eager to do just that, but when he took the doctor's arm and tried to lead her away, she shook herself loose.

'Listen to me,' she said through clenched teeth. 'It found its way up to sublevel two, and that's where the patients sleep. Most of them were in their rooms when the virus spread. There could be up to fifty of those things down there. It's madness—'

'Doctor Reeve!' To Van Bam's surprise, the authoritative voice was Clara's. 'Get out. Right now.'

Reeve recoiled as if slapped. She stared at the young changeling for a moment, but when Samuel appeared from the room and she saw the revolver in his hand, she let Karl drag her away down the corridor. Soon they turned a corner and were gone.

Van Bam gave Clara an approving nod. Her shades and hues were alive with the wolf's courage. Nevertheless, when he turned to face the door to sublevel two, the dire warnings of Doctor Reeve remained in his mind.

'Samuel, if you would, please lead the way.'

CHAPTER THIRTEEN

DOWN THE SPIRAL

Samuel's world shifted when his magic activated. It was as if his consciousness and physical being switched places and his brain began following the orders his body gave it. He remained alert to his actions, but also detached from them. Surroundings became crystal clear, pressing on heightened instincts almost painfully. Every item of furniture, every locked or unlocked door, every twist and turn ahead and behind – he was acutely aware of them all; he felt even the tiniest shifts in the air. When danger approached Old Man Sam, his prescient awareness knew what to do, and his body knew how best to do it.

He felt each step of the stairs, firm beneath his feet, as he descended to the next floor of the asylum. The further and lower he went, the warmer his magic felt inside him. This time, when they reached the bottom of the stairs he led Van Bam and Clara into an isolated safe room where the atmosphere was eerily silent.

Samuel supposed that it was some kind of security station, where orderlies and security staff spent the bulk of their shifts and breaks. There were comfy chairs and a bookcase stuffed with novels. On one wall the door to a small toilet was open. On the opposite wall was a heavy security door that was closed and locked. Something about the security door made Samuel's magic pulse.

Two padded desk chairs were situated before a metal table, which sat beneath the black rectangle of another darkened observation window. Upon the desk was a control panel for the window, and a log book that lay open. Van Bam moved to the table and began flipping through the last few pages in the log book. Clara stayed behind both men, close to the stairwell door. Her fidgeting scratched upon Samuel's senses like nails down a blackboard.

'The last entry in this book states the inmates were restless,' Van Bam said. 'But the details are incomplete.'

'Probably didn't get the chance to write any more,' Samuel said. 'Let's see what we're dealing with.'

He pressed a button on the control panel, and the observation window cleared. He heard Clara catch her breath.

Outside the security station, sublevel two was revealed to be a huge hall around which two tiers of cells were cut into the walls. There, pandemonium reigned. The infected filled the hall, rushing around at frenetic speed, like savage animals. Doctor Reeves had said there could be up to fifty of them, and Samuel could well believe it. Staff and inmates alike – no one had been spared from Fabian Moor's virus. At least a third of them were already dead, lying upon the slick floor, bodies mutilated. Those still alive fought tirelessly and with no regard to defence; biting, clawing and feeding upon each other's flesh like addicts desperate for the drug of blood.

Samuel noted a fully-formed golem, impassive as it tried to keep its footing amidst the chaos that jostled and knocked it around. Made only of bloodless stone, it offered nothing for the hunger of the infected. Behind the golem, on the metal staircase that led to the upper level walkway, two victims bit at each other's faces like frenzied lovers. The fighting continued on the walkway above them, and a body fell over the balcony and smashed to the floor, scattering a group who were feeding on the dead. The group quickly began attacking each other, grappling and sinking long teeth into black-veined skin, tearing down until gouts of thick red coated them all.

Not one sound came through the observation window, and the eerie silence in the security room endured. It somehow made the images even more horrific.

'Well, I don't have enough ammunition to shoot them all,' Samuel said coldly.

'Maybe we should wait,' Clara said. She still stood by the door to the stairwell, and by the inflection in her voice, she was just about ready to flee back up to sublevel one. 'They'll kill each other eventually. Or turn into golems.'

'There is no time to wait, Clara,' Van Bam said. 'Our inaction gives

Fabian Moor time to move and plot unhindered. Our duty is to protect the denizens. We need an expedient method of clearing the asylum of the infected. The virus must be contained.'

Samuel looked at the Resident, and the satchel hanging from his shoulder. 'I'm assuming you brought one of Hamir's little toys with you.'

'Indeed.'

Van Bam put his cane on the metal desk, and then placed the satchel alongside it. From the satchel he produced a wooden box. He opened the lid and exposed a spell sphere held securely by the padded interior. Inside the sphere was a viscous liquid the colour of death. With care, Van Bam pulled the glass orb out.

'*This* should be handled with care,' he said, and then turned his metallic eyes to the right and the heavy security door that led to the hall. 'Your help, please, Samuel. I need only a second.'

Samuel followed the Resident over to the door. As they neared it, Clara said, 'What are you doing? You can't open it.'

'Silence, Clara,' Van Bam snapped.

Samuel placed his forehead against the security door and closed his eyes. Although his magic still pulsed with gentle warning, the infected did not detect their presence, and there was no immediate danger on the other side of the door. Even so, his prescient awareness was warning him not to go any further, that it was time to hide, not fight.

Ignoring the warning, he nodded to Van Bam, who then placed a hand against the door. As Samuel heard the locking bolts sliding free, he grabbed the door handle.

'Ready?' he whispered.

Van Bam dropped to one knee and held the sphere in both hands before him. Samuel opened the door, and the din of murder and rage filled the security station. Van Bam lobbed the sphere through the opening, and then silence returned as Samuel quickly closed the door.

Clara gasped, making both men wheel around. The young change-ling held a hand to her mouth, staring fearfully through the observation window. Samuel moved to see what she stared at, Van Bam beside him.

One of the infected – a woman, her face a mask of lustful fury – had smashed the head of a man against the window. She bit into the back of his neck, tearing free a chunk of wet flesh, and together they slid down to the floor, leaving a smear of blood on the glass.

As they disappeared from view, a column of grey mist could be seen drifting across the floor behind them. It spun slowly as it moved, like a lazy whirlwind. It reached the nearest pair of fighters and engulfed them. Almost instantly, the mist melted skin, flesh, bone – every inch of them – like the most powerful of acids. It reduced its victims to puddles of human matter. The misty column engulfed the golem next, devouring the magic that animated it, and crumbling it into a heap of broken stone.

As Hamir's magic moved on, its spinning increased, and it had grown a little fatter. It reached the next group of the infected, liquefied them and continued on, spinning faster and more hungry with each victim it devoured.

'Hamir is a master of death,' Van Bam muttered disappointedly. He pressed a button on the control panel to deactivate the observation window. He continued to stare at it, however, and Samuel knew he could still see through the blackened glass.

Folding his arms across his chest Samuel leant back against the desk. Still his magic warned him to go no further. He saw Clara glancing from one man to the other.

'So what now?' she asked.

'We wait until the way is clear,' Samuel replied, his tone suggesting the answer had been obvious.

Clara collapsed into one of the comfy chairs as if her legs had little strength left in them. She rubbed her shaking hands together as though doing so would take her mind off the events only Van Bam could see beyond the window.

'This situation is making less and less sense,' she blurted after a short while. 'If Moor wanted to create chaos in the Labyrinth, why do it at the asylum? Why not out in the open, where the whole town could be infected?'

'Clara,' Van Bam said with his back turned to her. 'You continue to presume Fabian Moor is a vindictive character whose actions are driven by spite and a desire for petty revenge. It is time you accepted that he is calculating, and does nothing without reason. Something drew him to the asylum.'

'Perhaps he wants to warn us,' Clara suggested. By the tone of her voice, Samuel knew she was talking more through a need to keep her mind occupied than any real desire to be helpful. 'Maybe this is his way of telling us to back off – that he knows the Relic Guild is on to him.'

'He doesn't care if we're on to him or not,' Samuel said derisively. 'That much should be obvious even to you by now.'

'Samuel is correct, Clara,' Van Bam said, though his tone was much more kindly. He turned from the window. 'But Charlie Hemlock claims Moor is looking for something. That fits with his excursion to the antiques boutique. It could easily have been some relic or artefact he searched for. But what could he possibly hope to find in this asylum?'

'Reeve said Moor first appeared on the third sublevel,' Samuel mused. 'Let's hope he left something down there to steer us in the right direction.'

Van Bam nodded and faced the darkened window again. 'Ah … it seems Hamir's necromancy has served its purpose.' He picked up his green glass cane. 'We can venture on.'

At these words Clara jumped to her feet, alert and tense.

Samuel moved over to the security door. Although his magic had dulled, it still pulsed with a gentle undercurrent. Danger remained in the asylum, but not in the immediate vicinity.

Samuel opened the security door fully and immediately bent double and retched. The wave of putrefaction hit Clara next, making her vomit what little contents her stomach held onto the security station floor. Van Bam seemed immune to the overpowering stench, and walked out into the hall. Clara followed, holding a hand to her face. Samuel drew his revolver and let the door close behind him.

The air had become so thick and heavy in the wake of the massacre that it seemed to coat the inside of Samuel's mouth with an oily film. Puddles of liquefied fat and muscle, hair and bone covered the floor. More dripped from the metal stairs and balcony above in greasy lumps that struck the ground with dull smacking sounds. There were a couple of piles of broken rubble, along with a stone leg or arm that had belonged to a victim entering the later stages of the virus; but for most,

Hamir's magic had reduced all organic matter to a human soup which was smeared across the detention hall like a coat of paint.

As he took careful steps across the slick and slippery floor, Samuel's disgust deepened when he remembered that Van Bam's feet were bare. Van Bam always said it was important for an illusionist to keep himself in physical contact with what was real. Even so, Samuel knew the Resident could feel every texture of the liquefied matter beneath the soles of his feet, and it made him shiver. But Van Bam seemed more concerned with steering Clara across the floor as she held tightly to his arm.

Samuel pushed ahead of his fellow agents.

He stopped beneath the balcony of the upper level, standing just out of reach of the human matter that dripped down and smacked on the floor. Directly ahead was a corridor, which seemed to be the only other exit point from the hall.

'There's no point checking the cells,' he said as Clara and Van Bam caught up with him. 'There's nothing left.'

'Agreed,' Van Bam said.

Dodging the viscous drops, Samuel led the way out of the hall. The other two followed several paces behind.

The corridor wasn't particularly long, and had no doors to offices or therapy rooms lining the walls. Soon it turned to the right, where the final stretch ended at yet another elevator and door to the next stairwell. Samuel stepped towards the door.

He froze as his magic flashed a warning.

He raised a hand for Van Bam and Clara to halt, scarcely aware of the Resident's voice asking what was wrong. Samuel could detect something: it felt, rather than sounded, like a shuffling or scratching. But coming from where?

And then, as though from a distance, he heard Clara ask, 'What's that noise?'

Samuel's prescient awareness went berserk.

It was as if time had slowed, and his surroundings pressed in on him from all directions, pointing him towards the danger. Samuel wheeled around and aimed his revolver back down the corridor at his colleagues.

'Down!' he roared.

But before Van Bam and Clara could move, a maintenance hatchway broke clear of the ceiling. Two infected jumped into the corridor.

The first died as soon as its feet touched ground. Samuel fired and it slammed sideways, head bursting, blood painting the wall. But the second fell directly upon Van Bam.

It sent the Resident crashing to the floor. The hatchway had fallen down with the monster, and the metal grille was now the only thing protecting Van Bam from the clawing fingers and snapping teeth and infection from Fabian Moor's virus.

'Clara, move!' Samuel shouted.

But the changeling didn't move out of aim. Instead, as if acting on some animal instinct, she ran at Van Bam's attacker. She leapt onto its back with a yell. In a fluid, almost graceful motion, she yanked the virus victim's head back with her left hand, while her right pulled a long knife with a serrated blade from her boot. With another yell of fury, she rammed the blade into the underside of the monster's chin with such force it sank to the hilt.

Gritting her teeth, the changeling pushed away the dead body before its blood could touch her. For one so small and scrawny, Clara radiated an aura of strength, of power, of something bestial.

Her eyes flashed yellow as she glared down the corridor at Samuel. He kept his revolver aimed in her direction. His magic had pulsed a new warning to him.

It was only for a second or two that they stood staring at each other, but to Samuel it felt a long, tense moment. Was Clara challenging him?

Thankfully she broke the standoff to look down at the Resident. Samuel's magic eased, and he lowered his gun with no small sense of relief.

Van Bam pushed the metal hatchway to one side and got to his feet. Apart from appearing a little shaken, he was unharmed.

Clara ducked down and picked up his green glass cane.

'Thank you, Clara,' he said as he took it from her. His breathing was a little shuddery.

Clara retrieved the knife from the dead body on the floor. She wiped blood from the blade on its clothes.

'I want that back when this is over,' Samuel told her.

In reply, she flashed him a yellow glare and slid the knife into her boot.

Samuel gave the Resident an inquisitive look. When Van Bam affirmed his well-being with a nod, Samuel turned and headed for the door to the last sublevel of the asylum.

Clara couldn't explain what had happened. She had experienced moments when the wolf had tried to control her reactions before – moments when blind anger and the need for violence had dominated her thoughts – but her medicine, or sheer force of will, had always kept those impulses in check. This time it had been different. This time, it felt as if she had tapped into the wolf's power, its grace and cunning, and used its strength to save Van Bam from the teeth of the infected. If Clara hadn't known better, she would swear *she* had controlled the monster.

Or perhaps she had been shown how to …

Clara was convinced she had felt Marney's influence during the incident. That illusive box of secrets buried deep inside her head had opened a crack, and the presence that slipped out had been full of panic, full of desperation. The catalyst had undoubtedly been the Resident and his plight. The moment Clara's instincts detected Van Bam was in trouble, she had been filled with a sudden and overwhelming desire to save him, and at any cost. But Clara knew intuitively that it had been Marney's desire that drove her instincts, put her in touch with the wolf and its courage. Why else would Clara have acted so rashly?

Whatever had prompted the recklessness, the incident had changed Clara. She was sure of it. A bond had grown between woman and wolf, and it seemed so … *natural*. It had given her a sixth sense, some animal intuition that put her fully in tune with her environment. Instinctively, she knew there was no danger ahead now; that the immediate trouble was over for the Relic Guild – even before Samuel said, 'We're in the clear,' and led them into sublevel three.

Another abandoned security station awaited the group. But unlike on the two previous levels, there was no sign of struggle. The security door, already wide open, led them to a short corridor of cells.

'This is where the most dangerous inmates are kept,' Van Bam said. His voice was like music to Clara, deep, familiar and comforting. She hadn't noticed before, but she was suddenly aware that he was a handsome man. He added, 'Evidently, Fabian Moor had no use for them,' and Clara shook herself.

The doors to the cells were heavy and secure. Clara peeked through the small reinforced window of one into the room beyond. An inmate sat on a bunk in his straitjacket, staring back at her. There was a madman's grin on his face.

'Wait here,' Samuel said.

He set off down the corridor. The door to the penultimate cell on the left was open. The old bounty hunter disappeared through it.

Clara flinched as a thump came from her right. She turned to see the inmate with the madman's grin had pressed his face up against the window. They locked eyes for a moment, and then he drew suddenly a deep breath.

'Monster!' he screamed.

Clara stepped away from the window, backing into Van Bam. His body felt strong and reassuring against her. The man screamed again. His voice was muffled but loud enough to be heard by the other inmates. More faces appeared at windows, and the cry of 'Monster' was taken up by them all.

In the cell opposite, a woman was watching the Relic Guild agents. Her eyes were watery and unfocused, and she laughed as if she had heard the funniest of jokes.

'Van Bam!' Samuel shouted from the open cell. The anxiety was easy to hear in his voice. 'Quickly!'

As the chorus of insane voices continued to swell and echo along the corridor, the two Relic Guild agents raced to him.

Clara was first to reach the cell. Samuel was clutching his revolver so tightly his knuckles had turned white. There was a grim look on his face as he stared down at the bunk. Upon the stained mattress sat a skeleton. In its claw-like hands was a small terracotta jar.

Van Bam entered the cell and stood alongside Samuel. He seemed to recoil at the sight of the jar in the skeleton's hands. Clara didn't need heightened senses to detect the fear radiating from both men.

Van Bam cocked his head to one side.

'Oh shit,' he whispered.

REFUGEE

Marney felt tired to the point of numbness. Only one spark of emotion survived within her, and that was a vague desire, a mindless need to share her body with an illusionist's. She wanted to be locked away with Van Bam inside a darkened room where the world outside could wait. She wanted to feel something familiar and passionate. And then, Marney wanted nothing more than the oblivion of dreamless sleep so her mind would have the chance to organise and understand the things she had seen.

But on returning to the Labyrinth, the young empath discovered that Gideon had other plans for her.

In the Nightshade's conference room, every agent of the Relic Guild had been summoned to an emergency meeting. It was late, and her colleagues looked as tired as Marney felt. The Resident sat in his customary position, at the head of the long conference table; Samuel sat at the bottom end, quiet and taciturn, with a few chairs' distance between him and his colleagues. Marney sat between Denton and Angel. On the opposite side of the table, Bryant sat next to his sister, and Van Bam sat between her and Gene. The only absentee was Hamir. The atmosphere was troubled.

Marney was surprised by the late hour; Ruby Moon was in the sky, and the day was long over. But it didn't feel as though she had spent that long at Lady Amilee's tower. She vaguely recalled Denton saying something about time passing slower in the Skywatcher's realm, but she didn't really care.

Across the table, Van Bam gave her a fleeting smile. She tried her best to return it.

He and Samuel had already told the group about their excursion to the Anger Pitt, and the information they had managed to extract from a dying treasure hunter called Llewellyn. But it was the news that Marney and Denton had brought back from Lady Amilee that had caused the moments to slip by, silent and fraught.

'Interesting times,' Gideon drawled. 'All Fabian Moor had to do to enter Labrys Town was climb inside a terracotta jar.' The Resident snorted, rose to his feet, and began pacing the floor behind his chair.

He seemed distracted as he paced. Marney knew he was speaking with Sophia, the ghost of the former Resident who now served as Gideon's spirit guide. Nobody around the table spoke or disturbed this private conversation.

Even while in contemplation, the Resident still managed to intimidate Marney. Tall and thin, his natural expression was a sullen scowl that hung on a gaunt face with a hooked nose and sunken eyes. His black hair was short, but always seemed to be in need of a cut. If not for the healthy olive tone to his skin, Gideon might have appeared terminally ill. Even for an empath, it was hard to gauge his mood, or anticipate his next reaction.

Van Bam caught Marney's eye again. He gave her a questioning frown. Distantly, she could feel his concern, but she couldn't summon enough energy to emote anything back to him.

'So,' Gideon said. He stopped pacing and gripped the back of his chair, looking at Van Bam. 'You say the Genii was discovered in a realm called the Icicle Forest?'

'So Llewellyn claimed,' Van Bam replied. 'He said it was a terrible place, but I have never heard of it.'

'Have any of us?' Although Gideon asked the question to all present, he looked pointedly at Denton. 'Do we even know its House symbol?'

Denton opened his arms in a helpless gesture. 'It's not a House I can recall being mentioned anywhere.'

'Perhaps Llewellyn lied to you,' Gideon said to Van Bam.

'There was no deceit in him,' Van Bam said quickly, almost defensively. Marney felt his remorse. 'He had no reason left to lie.'

'Says you. Maybe your skills were clouded by your obvious sympathy, you idiot.'

'I don't think so, Gideon,' said Denton before Van Bam could say anything further. 'Given that Lady Amilee was not alerted to Carrick and Llewellyn's movements, the Icicle Forest might just be a hidden realm that even a Skywatcher can't see. We've always been told there are such places out there.'

'Brilliant,' Gideon snapped. 'Then I shall have to send a message to Lady Amilee, begging for her guidance and apologising for our continued incompetence.' His face flushed with sudden anger. 'Not only was the Genii hiding in a House none of us can identify, but we also allowed simple-minded treasure hunters to fool us all and bring him to the Labyrinth. You might say I'm displeased.'

Just as it seemed that he would vent his full fury upon the group, he closed his eyes and gritted his teeth. Evidently, Sophia had something to say on the matter. Gideon's lips moved silently, as if arguing with the former Resident. Marney noted that all the agents around the table had averted their gaze.

Finally, Gideon took a deep breath and turned his sunken eyes to Denton. 'Lady Amilee believes Fabian Moor plans to infiltrate the Nightshade, is that right?'

'That would be the most logical reason for his mission, yes,' Denton replied. 'After all, he can't control the Labyrinth without it.'

'But could he do it?' Gene said. The small and elderly apothecary seemed more disturbed than any other present. 'I mean, he found a way through the Timewatcher's barrier. Maybe he knows how to bypass the Nightshade's magic too.'

'It's highly doubtful,' Denton assured him. 'This is likely still a hopeful strike by the Genii. I think if Fabian Moor knew of a way to enter the Nightshade, he'd already be here.'

'Unless he's too weak to act at the moment.' It was Angel who had spoken this time, and her face was thoughtful. 'We know he's fed at least once so far. Maybe he needs to do so again, to gather his strength.' She looked at the faces around the conference table. 'I have to tell you, if that virus hits the streets, the hospitals don't stand a chance. We'll be overrun in a matter of days.'

'And what's to say that's not what he wants?' Gene added. 'Should we warn the denizens?'

'Yes, and start widespread panic. Good idea, Gene.' Gideon sneered at the diminutive apothecary. 'You all heard what Denton had to say, so let's try and keep a little perspective, shall we? Even if Fabian Moor infected every denizen in Labrys Town, it still wouldn't grant him entrance into the Nightshade. He would have succeeded only in extinguishing his one source of sustenance. Without blood, he will die and achieve nothing.

'However, we should assume that he will find a way to invade the Nightshade, given time – and time is not something we will afford him. He must be stopped.'

'Easier said than done,' Bryant said. He rubbed at the scar on his cheek, as he so often did when he was troubled. 'Look, I'll stand against anything you put in front of me, but this is a creature of higher magic we're talking about. There's no telling what he's capable of.'

Beside him, his twin agreed. 'I don't see how the Thaumaturgists can expect us to kill a Genii, Gideon.'

'Oh, stop prattling, both of you,' Gideon sighed. With an unfriendly smile, he began pacing again. 'The Thaumaturgists don't want the Genii dead. Denton …?'

All eyes turned to the old empath.

Denton leant back in his chair and interlaced his fingers across his generous stomach. He had blocked his emotions, and his face was creased with thought. 'Lady Amilee has given us orders to capture Fabian Moor for questioning.'

So far, Marney had been happy to let the meeting wash over her, only vaguely aware of the details. But now her torpor was interrupted as her empathic senses were assaulted by the incredulity that had blossomed in the conference room. If killing a Genii was an impossible task for the Relic Guild, then Lady Amilee's orders had just made the impossible even harder.

Denton continued. 'I understand your reactions, my friends, but the Skywatcher was quite clear on this. Fabian Moor is a high-ranking Genii. He can provide valuable insight into the plans of Spiral. He is vastly important to the war effort. For both sides, it seems.'

Gideon, clearly enjoying the uncertainty of his agents, allowed an uncomfortable moment to pass by before snarling, 'Stop your childish fretting.'

Marney saw Gene flinch.

'The Thaumaturgists wouldn't leave us high and dry. Would they?' Gideon flashed a laconic grin. 'Quickly, Denton, tell them about the Skywatcher's *gift* before they soil themselves.'

Denton's pause suggested irritation at the Resident's abusive manner. He continued with a kind tone. 'Before we left her realm, Lady Amilee gave Marney and me two items – a box and a book.' He shrugged helplessly. 'I can't pretend to understand what she has given us, my friends, but she assured me they are apparatus for a secret art that will make Fabian Moor's capture possible. However, she also said no magicker of the Relic Guild could hope to comprehend their use—'

'The point being,' Gideon interrupted, 'the only one among us who can utilise Amilee's gift is Hamir. And he is learning how to do so even as we speak. Until he is ready, there isn't much we can do about our unwanted guest.'

The Resident seated himself. His eyes darted from side to side as he conversed with his spirit guide again. Whatever the ghost of Sophia had to say this time, Gideon seemed to be in agreement as he nodded slowly.

'Denton,' he said sternly, 'there are matters we need to discuss. You will remain here.'

The old empath nodded, and he flashed a message to Marney that she was to remain also.

'Bryant, Macy,' Gideon continued, 'talk to your contacts in the underworld. Find out if there's anyone new on the scene that might match this Fabian Moor. If you're lucky, you might learn something about his movements.'

The Resident turned a slow smile to Angel. 'You will monitor the hospitals and surgeries. Talk to the chiefs of medicines – *all* of them – and brief them on the virus. Anyone – and I mean *anyone* – who shows signs of infection will be handled with zero tolerance. And this goes for the rest of you, too.

'As far as the denizens are concerned, we will tell them a wild demon has found its way into Labrys Town. For now, that is our cover story. Fabian Moor and the Genii are not to be mentioned to anyone. Understood?'

As these words were greeted by nods, the Resident turned his attention to Van Bam. 'You're mostly useless now, so you might as well go and help Hamir. You'll find him in his laboratory.'

He then leant across the table to give Gene a close and cold glare. 'As for you, I believe there is a little task I've asked you to perform?'

Gene backed away from the glare. He was either reluctant or unable to meet Gideon's eyes, and he blinked rapidly behind his spectacles as he nodded.

'Then off you go.'

Five agents rose from their chairs and headed for the door. Van Bam gave Marney a furtive glance, and she felt his disappointment. There would be no sharing each other tonight.

At the bottom end of the conference table, Samuel also rose and made to leave with his colleagues. But he stopped as Gideon clucked his tongue.

'Samuel, I'm not entirely convinced I gave you permission to leave. Or did I?' He looked around at the group as if he was addressing schoolchildren. 'Did anyone hear me give him permission?'

Samuel's pale eyes burned as he stared along the length of the table at the Resident. The rest of the agents froze. Marney knew as well as any present that whenever Gideon and Samuel conversed it was never with much civility. She could feel that Bryant and Macy were tense, ready to jump between the two if need be. And it wouldn't the first time these exchanges had warranted such action.

But Samuel managed to keep his tongue civil this time. 'What do you want, Gideon?'

Gideon grinned at him. 'We need to talk. Go and wait for me in my study.' The grin disappeared and he glared at the other agents. 'Now get out.'

Needing no further prompting, they left the conference room. The door closed and disappeared behind them.

With their departure, Marney found the atmosphere decidedly less tense. Even Gideon seemed to relax slightly, sitting back in his chair, drumming his fingers upon the tabletop – though his sullen expression remained unreadable. Marney didn't know why she had been kept there; the Resident nearly always ignored her presence. Or ridiculed any suggestion she made. She sank back in her seat, wishing she could sleep.

'Llewellyn,' Gideon growled. 'Do you think we can trust his information?'

'I would say so,' Denton said. 'And I'm certainly confident in Van Bam's word.'

Gideon snorted. 'Llewellyn's Aelfirian contact – this man called *Ursa* – he is a refugee from House Mirage?'

Denton nodded. 'He must be a member of Ambassador Ebril's entourage.'

'We have always supposed that all the refugees were stranded here by the war. But what if some of them were planted as part of some plot?' Gideon's lips twisted into a half smile. 'I think I'll have to ask Ebril himself. It's been a while since the Ambassador of Mirage last came to the Nightshade. I'll be most interested to hear what he has to say about the actions of his *entourage*.'

'Wait a moment,' Denton said. 'I know what you're thinking, Gideon, but there's nothing to say that Ursa knew what he was bringing into the Labyrinth.'

'And there's nothing to say he didn't,' Gideon retorted. 'This is what we know – Ursa, an Aelf of Mirage, was in possession of a symbol for a mysterious House called the Icicle Forest. No one else has ever heard of this House, yet somehow Ursa knew an artefact was hidden there, an artefact that contained the essence of a Genii.' Gideon's expression was dark. 'I think we can agree, Denton, someone in House Mirage is harbouring loyalties to Spiral.'

Denton raised a finger. 'Nonetheless, we are not talking about some shady denizen you can haul in off the street. You have no evidence that Ursa was acting under Ebril's orders. We have grounds for suspicion, yes – but you can't just arrest an ambassador and accuse his House of smuggling Fabian Moor into the Labyrinth.'

Gideon gritted his teeth. 'Can't I?'

Denton sighed. 'All I'm suggesting is that you take the diplomatic route for now. Think of the future, Gideon. When this bloody war finally ends, we will need all our friends to rebuild what we once had. Blindly accusing House Mirage will not go down well with the rest of the Aelfir, and—'

'Denton—'

'And if you are wrong, Gideon, it will carry ramifications for us all. Please, let me talk to Ambassador Ebril.'

If any other member of the Relic Guild had spoken to the Resident so boldly, the retort would have been like verbal fire. As it was, even Gideon respected the honest and dependable wisdom of the old empath. Judging by the way Gideon's eyes were moving from side to side, Marney reasoned that so did Sophia.

'Perhaps you're right,' the Resident said, nodding. It was unclear whether he was talking to Denton or the ghost in his head. He drummed his fingers on the tabletop again. 'I'm going to send a message to Ebril – tonight – requesting an audience with him in the morning.' The unconvincing smile returned to his gaunt face. 'But I won't tell him the reason why, and I'll order the police to watch his house. Let's make him twitchy and see if he does anything suspicious during the night.'

Denton gave an approving nod.

'Come the morning,' Gideon continued, 'you will go to the ambassador's home and find out what you can.'

'How much should I tell him?' Denton asked. 'I'm not sure the wild demon story is strictly applicable in this instance.'

'Hmm, good point. Use your judgement.'

'I'll be discreet.'

Gideon gave a decisive nod. 'Then it's settled. And you might as well take your *pupil* with you.'

Marney wasn't offended by the 'pupil' tag; she supposed it made a nice change to be acknowledged at all.

'I'd like to take Van Bam, too,' Denton said. 'Aelfirian ambassadors are trained to hide what they are feeling and thinking. Van Bam's talent for reading expressions will come in handy.'

Marney liked the sound of that, but Gideon's next words drove away the smile she had been struggling to hide.

'No,' he said flatly. 'I want that maudlin idiot helping Hamir.' He seemed pleased with his decision as he rose from his chair. 'You have your orders. Now, if you'll excuse me, I have a meeting with our miserable sharpshooter. There's a loose end I want Samuel to kill.'

The dead of night often saw the dregs of Labrys Town riding the trams. Vagrants with nowhere else to sleep except the cold cobbles of back alleys used the last of the pennies scrounged from the day to pay for the warmth of a carriage. Denizens who should know better met to conduct dubious business away from the watchful eye devices on the streets. And someone with a troubled mind might ride the trams in the late hours, thinking of ways in which their burdens could be eased.

A man sat at the head of the carriage, behind the driver's compartment. He fidgeted nervously, as if impatient to reach his destination. Behind him, two vagrants were slumped in their seats, unconscious from cheap alcohol, filling the tram with the reek of rarely washed bodies. The man paid them no mind. Perhaps he was unconcerned by their presence, perhaps he was absorbed in his troubled thoughts. He was most definitely oblivious to the lone passenger in a long brown coat who sat in dim light at the back of the carriage, watching him.

Given the option, Samuel always preferred to travel on foot, under the cover of darkness where he could prowl in the shadows and no one would notice the rifle on his back. Never would he choose to travel via public transport. But if the Relic Guild had taught him anything, it was how to be a pragmatist. He didn't know his final destination, but he hoped the tram would reach it soon; the stink in the carriage was palpable, and he longed to be outside where Silver Moon promised fresher, cleaner air.

For now, he settled back in his seat, patient and thoughtful as he kept the man at the front under surveillance.

The private meeting with Gideon had been as acerbic and hostile as Samuel expected, but at least it had been brief. The other agents of the Relic Guild were well used to his and the Resident's mutual hatred. He supposed his colleagues must consider them both misanthropes in their own ways. But things hadn't always been like that for Samuel; he hadn't always been such a taciturn man.

There had been a time when he relished the perks of his job, and no perk had come bigger than the trips he took to the Houses of the Aelfir. He regarded the trips as reward for his hard work, escape from the stifling confines of this town. For the first time in his life, Samuel had discovered a genuine sense of joy and wonder amidst the Aelfir; he had found pleasure in their cultures for many years. But when the war stopped those trips, something was crushed inside him; and he recalled the day the portals were closed as the most grim of his many unpleasant memories.

Just over two years ago, during the early morning, Gideon had summoned his agents to an emergency meeting at the Nightshade. Everyone had thought it was just another day, another stolen artefact that needed recovering. But this time a message had been sent from Lady Amilee. Something terrible had happened.

One of the largest Aelfirian Houses was a realm called the Falls of Dust and Silver. It was a trading post that connected to five smaller Houses. A band of renegade Thaumaturgists had taken control of this House, and in the process they had murdered one of Amilee's fellow Skywatchers, a creature of higher magic called Lord Wolfe. It had been Spiral's first strike against the Timewatcher.

The royal family of the Falls of Dust and Silver openly supported Spiral and his act of murder, claiming that it was high time a new regime watched over the realms. Before anyone could intervene or retaliate, the five connecting Houses had been invaded. Thousands of Aelfir died, but most were subjugated. By the time word of the atrocities reached the Relic Guild, Spiral was already leading an army a hundred thousand strong. And many other Houses were declaring their loyalties to the Lord of the Genii. The Nightshade and the Labyrinth were ordered to cease communications with the Aelfir, and Samuel had not stepped beyond Labrys Town's boundary walls from that day to this.

The tram began to slow in the eastern district. The man Samuel was watching ceased fidgeting and was ready to disembark before the driver had brought them to a full stop. Samuel followed him onto the street outside.

The man had pulled his coat tightly around him and his face was down-turned as he headed up the street at a pace. To the untrained eye, he might have seemed like any other denizen hurrying to be somewhere warmer; but Samuel knew differently, and his magic stirred, warning him that the man was undoubtedly armed. The brightly lit shop signs and violet glow of streetlamps banished any shadows in which Samuel might conceal his presence. If the man glanced back, he would easily see the Relic Guild agent tracking him.

Samuel allowed some distance to grow between them before continuing to follow.

When the man reached a T-junction, he did indeed look back. But Samuel had pre-empted this. His instincts told him the man would turn left, so he crossed the street as if his direction lay down the right turn. He didn't need to look back to know his quarry had bought the deceit; and by the time he doubled-back and resumed the hunt, the man had entered a narrow lane where the shadows were dark and the shop doorways were deep.

After a short time, the man turned into another lane and disappeared from view. Guided by the gentle pulses of his prescient awareness, Samuel crept up to the corner and peeked around – he was just in time to see his quarry enter a small tavern.

With discretion, Samuel moved forwards and peered through the grimy window. The man had taken a seat at the bar. He ordered a drink from the landlady. There were a few other customers inside, but no one approached the newcomer. The landlady brought him a shot glass filled with a dark spirit. He downed it in one, and then ordered a second, which he sipped slowly.

This wasn't right. The tavern didn't feel like the man's destination. He was brooding over his second drink, and Samuel reasoned he had only stopped at this place to sip some courage before moving on.

Stepping away from the window, Samuel made his way back to the corner of the lane, content to wait until the man made his next move.

In over two years, the war with Spiral had never truly touched the Labyrinth. So little news filtered through, and, of course, none of the fighting was seen. If not for the isolation and rationing, there would have been no evidence to suggest the war was taking place at all; as if it were a myth, a lie or tall tale fed to the denizens. Fabian Moor's arrival was the stinging slap that dispelled any doubt.

Samuel fully understood just how daunting a task it would be to hunt down a Genii, to capture him alive. Yet he had faith that Lady Amilee's secret gift would see the Relic Guild through. Even so, he knew he should've felt afraid of Fabian Moor, angry at him at the very least. But he didn't. In truth, Samuel had no feelings about the Genii one way or the other. Oh, there was anger and fear inside him, sure enough; an ever deepening resentment at the way every spark of light in his life had been dampened to sour darkness. It surpassed even his loathing of Gideon. He had an irrational, visceral need to blame someone for the war. And that someone was a Skywatcher named Lord Wolfe. His death had been the crack that fractured a perfect equilibrium, and Samuel hated him for it.

The tavern door opened, and the man stepped out into the lane. Samuel ducked back. When he looked again the man had pulled up the collar of his coat and was walking away from him. Samuel stuck to the shadows as he tracked his steps.

The cramped side lanes soon led out into a park area, where a chapel of the Timewatcher sat beside a graveyard. On the other side of the graveyard was a small and rundown house. The man headed straight to it, casting a nervous glance around him before entering through the front door.

The house was dark as Samuel approached. It was clearly abandoned, and its door was open and hanging on one hinge. Through the doorway he could see a dim light shining from somewhere within. Samuel's quarry cast a silhouette as he followed a short hallway, and disappeared to the right. Samuel drew his revolver and stepped inside.

The musty smell of age and desertion assaulted his nostrils as he crept down the hallway. His prescient awareness ticked inside him, and when he reached the point where the man had turned, it flashed a warning that he must wait.

Taking a furtive glance around the corner, Samuel saw the man was standing in the doorway of a well-lit kitchen. Whatever the man was looking at had worried him enough to make him draw a pistol.

Samuel froze. Something moved in the shadows of a darkened doorway in the hallway. An instant later, a small figure emerged, stepped up behind the man and pressed fingers against his neck. The man gave a quick cry of surprise, dropped his pistol, and then crumpled to the floor.

Samuel's prescient awareness evaporated. With a frown, he holstered his revolver and stepped into the open.

'What are you doing here?' he demanded.

Startled, Gene turned and blinked rapidly through his round spectacle lenses. 'Samuel?'

'Gene, what's going on?'

Composing himself, the apothecary shook his head. 'We'll deal with that in a minute.' He gestured to the unconscious man on the floor. 'Help me move him, will you?'

They carried the man into the kitchen, where Samuel was surprised to discover a second unconscious person – a policewoman in uniform – sitting at a small dining table with her hands tied to the back of her chair. Once the man was placed into the chair opposite her, Samuel set about securing his hands. The kitchen light revealed a man much younger than Samuel had first thought, younger than himself. The policewoman looked to be in her middle years.

Gene stood to one side and took an empty phial from his coat pocket. 'I assume Gideon told you to follow this man?' he said, popping the cork from the phial. 'To see who he was meeting?'

Samuel grunted an affirmation. 'Gideon showed him to me through the eyes. But I've no idea who he is.'

Gene sighed. 'His name's Lansdale. She's Hope. They're both police constables of no particular note – not that I suppose it matters. Did Gideon at least tell you their crimes?'

Samuel nodded as he finished tying the policeman's hands to the back of the chair. He stood up, feeling irritated. 'But he didn't tell me you were on this one too.'

'No. Well … you know what our leader is like, Samuel. Why do things the easy way when he can have his fun? I have to say I'm glad you're here, nonetheless. I'm not really comfortable with this kind of work.'

Samuel swallowed his resentment. This was so typical of Gideon, to assign two of his agents to the same mission without informing one of the other's involvement. It was his haphazard and spiteful way of sending a message of admonishment. The Resident was telling Samuel to be less keen in his desire to work alone. And Gene was being warned that he could not always stand back while the other agents got blood on their hands.

But where Samuel was used to Gideon's little games, and could adapt to them, Gene found them hard. Never having been blessed with a brave heart, he had earned himself the reputation of a quiet coward. Not that Gene didn't serve the Relic Guild well; but even the thought of a situation like this would terrify him ... and amuse Gideon deeply.

Samuel was rarely troubled by compassion, but when he saw the lines of age and concern on Gene's face, the way his eyes avoided the unconscious police officers slumped at the dining table, he felt sorry for the old apothecary.

'Why don't you head off?' he told him. 'I can take things from here.'

'It's a thoughtful offer, Samuel, but no.' Gene attempted a smile. 'I might be old and weak, but I'm still a professional. I'll see this job through to the end.'

Despite Gene's defiant claim, Samuel thought it more likely that he was staying because he was afraid of Gideon; and Gideon had probably given him strict instructions to remain until the end, no matter what.

He mentioned nothing of this to Gene and watched as his colleague held the phial steady in one hand, while poising the index finger of his free hand above the uncorked opening.

The apothecary's face was now a mask of concentration. He squeezed his finger with a thumb. After a moment, clear fluid began to drip from his fingertip into the phial.

Gene's gift never failed to strike Samuel with its strangeness. From the chemicals and minerals in his own body it seemed Gene could manufacture every kind of poison, potion and remedy, and then excrete them through his skin. Samuel had often witnessed him use his fingers like hypodermic needles to administer help or harm to a person. But never once had he seen Gene act as if his magic was something he was proud of.

Gene replaced the cork. 'Here,' he said, handing the phial to Samuel. 'You'd better take charge of this.'

'What is it?'

'Antitoxin.' Gene shrugged. 'Gideon wants one of them left alive.'

Without further explanation, the apothecary took an ampoule from his coat pocket and cracked it open. He first held it under the nose of Lansdale, and then of Hope. As Gene stepped back, both police officers began to stir. Samuel took a seat at the dining table between them with the phial of antitoxin in hand.

Lansdale, his face unshaven, a sheen of sweat on his brow, was the first to reach full consciousness. He seemed confused as he stared across the table at Hope. Then he realised his hands were tied to the back of the chair, and – finally – noticed the two other people in the kitchen.

'What's going on here?' he slurred. He shook his head to clear the fog. 'What're you doing?'

Hope seemed less confused. She sized up the situation far quicker than her fellow constable. Her lips trembled, and her eyes were wide with fear.

Gene cleared his throat. 'The Nightshade has been watching you.'

'Shit,' Hope whimpered.

'You have both been poisoned,' Gene continued. Even though his voice was steady and devoid of emotion, Samuel noted he still could not meet the eyes of the captives. 'Should you doubt this, I would ask you to consider the slight burning sensation you are experiencing in your stomachs.'

Both constables froze and looked at each other across the table. Their expressions gave silent confirmation they were indeed feeling this.

'The poison is reacting with your stomach acid. The pain will continue to grow, slowly, until it becomes quite unbearable. The chemical reaction will burn a hole straight through you, and you will not survive. However, there is a cure.'

Taking his cue, Samuel leant forwards and placed the phial on the table between Lansdale and Hope. They both tried to reach for it, but struggled in vain against their bonds.

'We're police officers,' Lansdale shouted, his voice angry but laced with panic. 'You can't do this to us—'

'Shut up, you idiot,' Hope hissed. She glanced first at Gene and then at Samuel. 'They can do what they want. They're the Resident's men.'

Lansdale reacted as if he had been slapped. He licked his lips and cast furtive glances at the agents.

'She's quite right,' Gene told him. He hesitated, and gave Samuel an almost apologetic look. 'And you should know there is only enough antitoxin to save one person. Whichever of you is most helpful to our inquiries will live.'

Another tactic of Gideon's, Samuel knew. But as cruel as it was to force Gene into this position, he could see the clever trickery in the plan already at work. Lansdale and Hope stared at each other, their eyes alight with betrayal.

'Let's start with what we already know,' Samuel said with a nod to Gene. The apothecary seemed grateful to relinquish the lead. 'The two of you were recently assigned to sentry duty. You were supposed to be guarding a portal in the northern district. Your orders were to make sure that no one tried to use it. But instead of doing your job, you sold the use of that portal to a treasure hunter named Carrick.'

'Never heard of him,' Lansdale said quickly. Too quickly. 'Look, I don't know what you've been told, but you've got the wrong man. I swear, I'm loyal to the Resident.'

'Give it a rest,' Hope told her fellow officer. There were tears in her eyes and a crack in her voice. 'They obviously know everything.'

'No, not quite,' said Samuel. 'But let's make sure we have all the cards on the table. Not only did you allow Carrick to leave the Labyrinth, but also to return with a very dangerous artefact. You were due to meet him tonight in this house to collect your payment. For this reason, one of you is going to die. Now, which of you set up the deal?'

'She did,' Lansdale blurted. 'She made all the arrangements.'

'That's a lie,' Hope said, and two tears ran down her cheeks. 'He and Carrick were friends before I even met him—'

'Shut your mouth,' Lansdale shouted. 'You're the liar.'

'You have to believe me,' Hope pleaded to Samuel. 'I don't want to die—'

'And you think I do?' Lansdale said to Gene.

'Please listen to me. I—'

'No, don't listen to her—'

Lansdale fell silent as Samuel drew his revolver and held it to his head.

Samuel looked at Hope. 'You first.'

'Th-Thank you,' she said and sniffed. 'I won't try to convince you that I didn't go along with it for the money. I mean, that'd be stupid, right?'

'Just get on with it,' Samuel growled.

Hope stifled a sob. 'He introduced me to Carrick. He's always in the eastern district or along Green Glass Row, hanging around with *those* sorts.'

Samuel pressed the barrel of his gun harder against Lansdale's head as he made to object, and Hope continued.

'I knew what I was getting into. I knew it was wrong. But a constable's wage isn't much, and with the war going on, there aren't many ways left to make extra money. I didn't mean anything bad to happen.' She began to weep, and struggled with words as she addressed Lansdale. 'We knew that artefact was trouble the moment Carrick returned, didn't we?' She turned her liquid eyes to Samuel. 'Only one of his team came back with him—'

'Llewellyn,' Samuel said. 'Yes, I met him. He's dead now. So is Carrick.'

Hope closed her eyes, her weeping intensifying.

Samuel turned to Lansdale and removed the gun from his head, though he didn't holster it. 'What's your side?'

Lansdale's mouth was open slightly, and he stared at his colleague with undisguised disbelief.

'You bitch,' he spat.

'Be civil,' Samuel said. 'Your life depends on it.'

'Civil?' Lansdale looked at Samuel with a furious expression. 'When she's lying through her teeth? I've only ever been to Green Glass Row when on duty.'

'Is that right?'

'*Yes*! The first time I met Carrick was the night *she* brought him and his crew to the portal. I didn't have any choice but to go along with it. She said I was an accomplice whether I wanted to be or not. If I didn't take the money and keep my mouth shut, she said she'd set me up to take the blame. Just like she's doing now!'

Hope looked up and her face was tear-streaked. 'That's not true,' she whispered. 'We got into this together, Lansdale. Why—'

'Bitch!' Lansdale roared. He leant forward, straining against his bonds, as though desperate to reach across the table and throttle his accomplice.

Samuel shoved him back in his chair. He placed the revolver on the table, picked up the phial of antitoxin, and shared a quick look with Gene.

'I have one last question. Who else was involved? Was it just you two, or did Carrick pay off anyone else in the police force?'

'Ask her,' Lansdale snapped, still fuming. 'She arranged everything.'

Hope shook her head at her colleague. 'I don't know. He never mentioned anyone else. I don't suppose there was any need for help – it was only me and him guarding that portal, after all.'

'Well then …' Samuel sat back in his chair and studied the contents of the phial for a moment.

He looked at Lansdale. 'You know, I have a friend with a talent for spotting liars. I thought this would be hard without his help, but I think I can tell for myself who's not telling the truth here.'

'What?' Lansdale began to panic. 'No, I—'

He broke off as Samuel snatched up his revolver and swung it around to smash into the side of Hope's head. The policewoman slumped sideways in her seat, unconscious. A line of blood trickled down her face from a cut in her temple.

Lansdale made a choking sound, looking from one Relic Guild agent to the other with wide eyes. 'You … You believe me?'

Samuel didn't answer. He rose and grabbed Lansdale's hair, yanking his head back. With his free hand, he took the phial and popped the cork with his thumb. Lansdale could only utter a small noise of complaint before he was spluttering on the contents of the phial pouring down his throat. No sooner had he swallowed the antitoxin than he too slumped in his seat and fell unconscious.

Samuel gave Gene an enquiring look.

'I added a sedative to the mix,' Gene explained. The small apothecary looked at Hope and sighed. 'Do you really think she was lying?'

'Does it make a difference?'

'No, I suppose not,' Gene said miserably.

Samuel looked at Lansdale. 'Let's get him back to the Nightshade. There's an eye on the church outside. I'll go and call for the Resident's tram—'

'No.' Gene's tone was flat. 'Gideon wants him left here. By the time he wakes up, he'll be in police custody. Our Resident is concerned that other officers might decide to use the portals for a profitable sideline. The example made of Lansdale will serve as a deterrent.'

He removed his glasses and pinched the bridge of his nose. 'Samuel, would you mind leaving? The poison I've given this woman will …' He took a deep breath and rubbed his forehead. 'Gideon wants Hope's pain to be as bad as I can make it, but I don't want that on my conscience. I'd like to be alone with her. Before she wakes up, I'd like to … you see, I thought I could do it, but no one deserves to suffer that much, and—'

'It's all right, Gene,' Samuel said. 'I'll leave.'

'Thank you,' the apothecary whispered, and he put on his glasses.

There was really nothing else to say. The job was done, and if Gene needed to appease his conscience by giving this woman a painless death, then Samuel wouldn't stand in his way. With a nod to the apothecary, he turned and strode from the kitchen.

'Samuel,' Gene called after him.

'Don't worry,' Samuel called back. 'I won't say a word to anyone.'

Least of all to Gideon, he thought, as he left the house.

The next morning, Marney awoke with a clear mind and refreshed body. It was the best she had felt since becoming an agent of the Relic Guild. It was as though something had bloomed inside her during the hours of sleep, something good. It was everything she could have hoped for, but she couldn't fully explain it.

There was a war on, she reminded herself; there was a Genii on the loose in Labrys Town; Van Bam was absent from her bed, and there would be little or no chance in the coming days for the two of them to spend time together privately. All these grave facts Marney acknowledged with the full weight of understanding, yet still she could not deny the sense of fulfilment and acceptance she had awoken with. She felt … different.

Her mood buoyant, her mind focused, Marney readied herself and took a public tram to the central district where Denton had arranged to meet her. She enjoyed the journey, made in the bright morning sun, surrounded by fellow denizens: couples chatting and laughing, mothers trying to control their children, people just staring out the window in silent contemplation. This was life, Marney realised: people making the most of what they had. The Relic Guild always ensured there was nothing else for the denizens to worry about. For the most part. Until the war started.

Marney had always known there was so much more outside the Labyrinth, and she understood now the huge difference between believing Mother Earth was out there and experiencing the evidence first-hand. But still, she struggled to make sense of what Lady Amilee had shown her. What had she actually seen? The greater picture? Everything and nothing? Some strange and fantastic lightshow created within a Thaumaturgist's observatory?

And how *did* she feel about it? Certainly not overwhelmed anymore, but not euphoric either. Even had she wished to share her experiences with her fellow agents, Marney wouldn't have known where to begin. But she did know she felt more substantial, while the people around her seemed smaller – more in need of protecting than ever. Marney was no longer frightened: she welcomed the denizens of Labrys Town as a responsibility for whose safety she would sacrifice herself.

She was an agent of the Relic Guild. And she had faith in her duties.

Something tapped against Marney's foot. She reached down and picked up the ball that had knocked against her. A young girl, around ten years of age, came down from the front of the carriage to retrieve it. Marney smiled as she held the ball out to her.

'Be careful. You don't want to lose it.'

'Thanks.' The girl spoke with a lisp. Taking the ball she stared at Marney. 'You're very pretty,' she ventured.

Marney chuckled softly. 'You're not so bad yourself,' she replied, and mussed the girl's hair.

Delighted with this response, the youngster smiled, revealing a missing milk tooth. The smile quickly disappeared, however, when her mother arrived and took her by the hand.

Middle aged and care-worn, the woman began apologising for her daughter.

'It's not a problem,' Marney assured her, but the mother was already dragging the girl back to their seats.

Marney heard her say, 'What have I told you about talking to strangers?' as she settled her daughter into her seat.

'But she found my ball, mum,' the girl protested.

'I don't care. It's dangerous, especially now. So sit quietly and keep still.'

Marney frowned as the mother sat next to her daughter, but flashed a quick grin as the girl glanced back and gave her a furtive wave.

Yes, Marney thought as she gazed out of the window, *I have faith*. And the sense of validation that gave her was pleasant company for the remainder of the journey.

On the western edge of the central district, Marney found Denton in a quaint little eatery called Fibbers Tea Room. For many years now it had been the old empath's favourite place to eat, and when Marney arrived he was already tucking into a generous breakfast of scrambled eggs, sausages and fried potatoes, while reading a newspaper. He lowered the paper as his protégé approached, rose to his feet, removed the napkin tucked into his shirt, and gave a wide smile.

'Marney,' he said. She felt the wave of affection he sent her, and returned it. 'How are you feeling?'

'Good,' she said honestly. 'Ready to confront Ambassador Ebril.'

Denton placed a finger to his lips, nodded to the few other diners in the eatery, and his voice entered her head.

I'm glad you're filled with a sense of duty, Marney, but let's save the shop-talk until after breakfast, shall we? 'Come – sit down,' he said aloud. 'Order whatever you like. My treat.'

Marney didn't feel particularly hungry, but she knew this could be a long day, and it was best to keep up her strength. So when the waitress came over to the table, she ordered some bread and preserves, along with a pot of coffee.

'Food just isn't the same anymore,' Denton bemoaned as he cut into a fat sausage. 'Before all these damned embargos, food was fresher, tastier. Now it's all dried or powered or preserved, and the flavour of everything seems bland – not that I suppose you've noticed. You eat less than a mouse.'

Marney shrugged and bit into a slice of bread smeared with fruit jam.

Denton sipped his coffee and shook his head. 'A love of food is a love of life, Marney. When this war is over, I'll take you to a restaurant I know on the Island of Remember When. They serve a steak fried in a fungus butter that will invigorate even your taste buds.'

'I'd like that,' Marney said with a smile. 'I'd like that very much.'

Denton appraised her for a moment, seemed pleased, and then resumed devouring his breakfast.

The conversation remained on a fair-weather level until the morning meal was finished. Denton insisted on paying the bill, and then the two agents caught a tram into the western district. There were far fewer passengers than there had been on Marney's previous journey. They rode in silence for a while, and Marney gazed out of the window.

Have you seen the paper today? Denton thought to her.

Marney shook her head, and the old empath took his newspaper from the pocket of his coat and passed it to her.

It seems Gideon has decided to go public with our cover story.

Marney unrolled the newspaper and read the headline: WILD DEMON IN LABRYS TOWN – Denizens warned of infection …

Below the headline was an artist's impression of the demon: a lumbering, misshapen silhouette lurking in the shadows of a back alley.

Marney thought back to her earlier journey, and the concerned words the mother on the tram had addressed to her daughter.

I thought Gideon wanted to avoid panic. How does this help?

There's more method than madness to this, Marney, Denton thought to her as he took the newspaper back. *With the denizens on their toes, Fabian Moor will find it a little harder to move around town without drawing attention. That article also explains a little about the virus, but not everything. The denizens are ordered to isolate anyone who shows signs of infection and alert the authorities. But they are also assured the problem is being dealt with. Most will think this is happening to other people in some other part of town. The populace has been made aware, at least to some degree.*

Marney nodded. *Selective information. It could help to stop the virus spreading … you know, if it comes to that.*

Let's hope it doesn't. Denton turned his grim expression to her. *If*

*the denizens ever discover the wild demon is really a Genii, panic would
spread far quicker than any virus.*

Marney felt a chill.

But that's a problem for another day, Denton continued with a
cheerier delivery. *Right now, we have to remember our best manners,
Marney. An Aelfirian Ambassador and the western district await us.*

Marney nodded and gazed out of the window again, to watch her
small world going by.

The tram was already deep within the west side of town.

Like many of her fellow agents, Marney had been raised in an
orphanage. As a small girl, she held to a fantasy that one day her long-
lost parents would return to collect her. They would be rich, highly
respected, and they would take their daughter to live a life of luxury
in the western district. Of all the privileges in Labrys Town, that was
where the best could be found. At least, that was how it used to be, and
probably would be so again once the war ended.

It was easy to tell this was a wealthier part of town. The buildings
appeared better maintained; the streets were wider, freer, less cramped
and squashed than in the other districts. Even the air seemed fresher,
cleaner. Fewer denizens bustled through the streets, for fewer denizens
actually lived in the area. When Marney and Denton arrived at their
destination they were the only two occupants left in the tram.

'Is it just me,' said Denton as they walked along the street, 'or does
the sun shine a little brighter in this district?'

Marney smiled as the old empath removed his worn and patched
coat and slung it over his arm.

'Now then, Marney. Tell me what you know of House Mirage.'

Marney thought back to her lessons in Aelfirian history at university.
'Not a great deal,' she admitted. 'It's a desert realm. One of the few
remaining trading posts outside the Labyrinth, as far as we know, but
smaller than us.'

'Very good. And …?'

Marney pursed her lips. 'It's run by bureaucrats and politicians.
There's no royalty as such, though there is a line of succession that runs
through the family of the current High Governor.'

'High Governor Obanai, that's right,' Denton said. 'Anything else?'

She shrugged. 'They denounced Spiral and the Genii, but also abstained from fighting in the war. That's pretty much all I know.'

'Which is probably more than most of your fellow agents,' Denton beamed. 'High Governor Obanai claims to be a pacifist, but others would call him a bet-hedger or fence-sitter. Either way, House Mirage has never given anyone cause to doubt its loyalty to the Timewatcher.'

'Until now,' Marney replied.

'Perhaps, but don't be so quick with your judgement, Marney.'

They turned off the main street and headed down a wide and deserted road where the tramlines did not run. It was lined with lush gardens and grand houses, and Marney knew she had entered the merchants' quarter of the western district, the most expensive area in which to live in Labrys Town. The watchful eye devices sat atop evenly spaced pedestals, full spheres like those outside the Nightshade. Marney had never been to this area before; she looked at the size of the houses and realised the stories of its grandeur were in no way exaggerated.

'Caution and care must be taken on this mission,' Denton told her. 'We have reasonable cause to suspect Mirage's involvement with the artefact, but Ambassador Ebril and his entourage were by no means the only Aelfir to be stranded in the Labyrinth when the war began. Remember, we only have the word of a dying criminal to suggest that this Ursa belonged to House Mirage at all.

'Diplomacy and observation will be key here, Marney. But for now, let's hide ourselves, shall we?'

Up ahead, in the near distance, three police officers stood in a group outside the gates to a house. They chatted among themselves and looked bored. Marney felt Denton project his emotions to form a concealment shield around him, and she did the same. Denton continued the conversation mentally as they made their way towards the unsuspecting officers.

Although Mirage abstained from the fighting, it has not remained entirely neutral in the war. It might be a small House compared to the Labyrinth, but it is an important supply line for the Timewatcher's armies. Mirage remains connected to four other Houses – the Floating Stones of Up and Down, Green Sky Forest, the Burrows of Underneath and Ghost Mist Veldt. There used to be others, but they sided with Spiral.

However, the Burrows of Underneath and Ghost Mist Veldt are vast realms, Marney. There, the Aelfir have been fighting the Genii since the war began. Two years of hostilities, and the armies of both sides number in the millions. The Timewatcher only knows how many deaths those Houses have witnessed.

Denton paused to allow the gravity of his words to settle. Marney puffed her cheeks as she walked – millions of Aelfir fighting a brutal war against creatures of higher magic, and for two years solid, without respite. She couldn't imagine such hardship.

But with Mirage as a supply route, Denton continued, *Green Sky Forest can keep our troops fed, while the forges and laboratories of the Floating Stones of Up and Down can restock weaponry. Now consider – Mirage isn't guarded by the Timewatcher's barrier like us, Marney. If High Governor Obanai has switched allegiance, or if the enemy could fight through to the portals at any one of the connecting Houses, then Spiral could cut off a vital supply line, and four very important allies would fall.*

That Ursa had sympathies for Spiral, that he is most likely affiliated to House Mirage … well, you understand what kind of delicate situation we may or may not expose here.

The two agents approached the three police officers, slipped by them, unnoticed, and headed through the gates they were guarding.

A long and wide paved driveway stretched ahead, flanked by extravagant gardens. At the end of the driveway a huge, three-storey manor house stood. Marney was decidedly impressed as her mentor led her towards it.

Let me tell you something of the man you're about to meet, Denton said. *Ambassador Ebril is an old and experienced politician. You will find him charming, welcoming and, for the most part, very good company. However, like all Aelfirian ambassadors, he has been schooled in some form of magical art. And most assuredly, he will be prepared for this meeting.*

Every expression on Ebril's face may or may not be genuine. The emotions he projects might be visceral or misdirecting. The words he speaks can and cannot be believed. His every action will be calculated.

Denton grinned at his protégé. *Ebril will not trust you. He will not like you. But always he will smile for you, Marney. Now, I think it's time to announce our arrival. Drop your concealment.*

What? Marney stopped walking. *We're going to let him see our faces?*

Denton chuckled. *Ebril has seen my face a hundred times, Marney. He is not some denizen or blabbermouth. He is an Aelfirian Ambassador with every right to know the identities of the Resident's men. As does the merchant who owns this place. This household knows the importance of secrecy, so don't fret, and follow my lead …*

Evidently, the household was waiting for the Relic Guild agents. No sooner had they dropped their emotive cloaks then the ornate front doors opened and a smartly dressed servant stepped out to greet them. He was human, not Aelf; undoubtedly employed by the merchant who owned the house, and not one of Ebril's entourage. Marney felt naked and exposed with her face revealed to him, but if he was curious about her identity, or if he actually knew she was an agent of the Relic Guild, he gave no sign.

With a warm smile, he said, 'Welcome. The Ambassador is expecting you.' He bobbed his head humbly. 'If you would care to follow me …'

The interior of the house impressed Marney further. She and Denton entered a roomy hall, where a wide staircase of milky, black-veined stone led to the upper floors. Every door and ornament around the hall looked expensive and expertly crafted.

Like all the other Aelfirian refugees, the members of House Mirage had been lodged with the town merchants as respected and honoured guests. The Aelfir didn't mingle with the denizens, and were rarely spotted in the other districts, though they did, of course, have the free range of Labrys Town. The merchants pretended to be honoured to house them, but the refugees were a drain on resources as they had long ago depleted what finances they had brought with them, and had no means of gaining more. But the merchants grinned and bore the situation, focusing on the recompense that would undoubtedly come when peacetime arrived.

With another genial smile, the servant stopped and faced the two agents.

'Sir, miss, if you would be so kind as to wait here, I will announce your arrival.'

'Of course,' said Denton.

Opening a door, the servant slipped through, and closed it behind him. As soon as he was gone, Denton's voice entered Marney's head again.

Gideon and the police watched this house all night, but they monitored no unusual activity. Not that I really expected Ebril to do anything unusual. If he's involved with Fabian Moor at all, he certainly wouldn't meet him here. It's too conspicuous. Moor would find better places to hide within the town's underworld.

The door opened and the servant reappeared, once more wearing a humble smile. He stepped to one side and motioned to the doorway.

'The Ambassador is ready to receive you.'

With a nod of gratitude, Denton led the way to the room beyond.

Remember, Marney – question everything you see, hear and feel.

In a spacious drawing room, Ambassador Ebril welcomed his guests by opening his arms and beaming a smile. 'My friends – greetings.'

He stood mostly silhouetted before a tall window that gave a view of the gardens outside, and through which sunlight gleamed. He wore robes of a light material, perhaps better suited for desert conditions. His beard was long and grey, and his hair was covered by scarves. His Aelfirian features were lined with age, but his huge, round eyes were bright blue, clear and seemingly honest.

Before him was a low, square table, around which cushions were placed for sitting. Upon the table were baskets of pastries and breads, and two silver platters of fruits that weren't often seen in Labrys Town nowadays. There was also a tall teapot with a long spout, around which were placed six small, clay cups without handles. Marney got the impression that the usual decor of this drawing room had been altered to make the Ambassador feel more at home.

An Aelfirian girl was already seated on the cushions at the table beside Ebril. Clad similarly to the ambassador, but without head scarves, she had long hair dressed into a tight plait that hung over one shoulder like a dark snake. Her face was petite. The usual triangular features of the Aelfir were, on her, a more subtle heart shape; her pointed ears were small and delicate. Her huge eyes were soft green, unblinking and innocent, yet her expression was oddly noncommittal. She looked younger than Marney by a few years.

Without introducing the girl, Ebril said, 'Master Denton, it is good to see you again.' His tone was clear and confident. 'But I have not had the pleasure of meeting your delightful companion here.'

'Marney,' Marney said before Denton could introduce her. She moved forwards and offered her hand across the table. 'It's an honour, Ambassador.'

Ebril took her hand in both of his and gave it a gentle squeeze. 'The honour is all mine,' he said, his smile perfectly charming.

It was curious; Marney hadn't been able to sense the ambassador's emotions on entering the room; and now, even with the use of touch, he still felt closed and empty.

Nice try, Marney, Denton's voice chuckled in her mind. *But I did warn you. Ebril will reveal nothing that he does not wish us to know.*

'Come, sit, take some refreshments,' the ambassador said. He waited until his guests had settled themselves on the cushions – a feat which was by no means easy for a man of Denton's size and age – before seating himself beside the young Aelfirian girl.

'Can I offer you some pastries or fruit?' he asked Marney.

'Thank you, but I'm not hungry,' she replied with a grateful smile.

'Ah, then how about some tea? It is from the foothills of Green Sky Forest.'

Marney was about to decline again, but then Denton, who was already in the process of selecting a large pastry, answered with no small degree of desire in his voice.

'Tea from Green Sky Forest? I should think so.' He added a mental note to Marney: *Have a cup, Marney – it's both customary and polite.*

'Yes, please,' she said.

Ebril nodded at the girl beside him, who set about pouring four cups of dark green tea. She did so with a pleasant air, and only then did the ambassador introduce her.

'Master Denton, I don't believe you've met my daughter before.'

'Indeed not.'

'This is Namji. She is training to follow in the footsteps of her father.'

'And no doubt making her father proud,' Denton said. 'A pleasure, Miss Namji.'

'Likewise, Master Denton. And to you also, Mistress Marney.'

Her voice was as soft as her eye-colour.

Marney smiled at her in return. Although Namji's emotions were as closed as her father's, there was a quick, subtle movement of those innocent eyes that Van Bam had taught Marney indicated deceit.

I noticed it too, Denton thought to her as he accepted a cup of tea gratefully.

What's she hiding? Marney said.

Your guess is as good as mine. I didn't know Ebril even had a daughter.

Denton sipped his tea, and then smacked his lips. 'Perfect,' he said. 'Only this morning, Ambassador, I was bemoaning the recent decline in food quality.' He took a second sip. 'Absolutely perfect.'

Ebril chuckled. 'As part of her training, my daughter became an observer to my duties. Sadly, this trip to the Labyrinth was also her first time away from Mirage. It proved to be a much longer visit than anticipated – due to unforeseen circumstances, of course.'

'Of course,' replied Denton, and he then addressed Namji. 'Your exile from your homeland is most regrettable.'

'Thank you, Master Denton. Though, in truth, I have been told there are much worse places to be in exile than Labrys Town.'

Denton smiled at the reply. 'I see you've had a good teacher.'

'Indeed. The wisest.'

Ebril gave his daughter a look of pride. 'But now to business, my friends.' He cast a shrewd gaze over the two Relic Guild agents. His emotions remained blank. 'I have to tell you that Merchant Forester and her family do not appreciate having their home watched by the police – and nor do I.'

'My apologies, but the Resident thought it prudent,' Denton said. 'It was a precautionary measure only, I assure you.'

'I see.' The Ambassador looked disbelieving. 'I read this morning that a wild demon has found its way into Labrys Town. Is your visit here today merely coincidental to this news?'

Denton placed his empty cup down on the table. He paused for the perfect amount of time, giving the air of respectful consideration. 'Ambassador, we are investigating someone whom we believe belongs to your House.'

'Ah, then you must be talking about an Aelf by the name of Ursa?'

Openness? Denton thought to Marney. *That's an interesting tactic.*

She felt his mixture of surprise and suspicion, but he didn't elaborate further, and said aloud, 'Someone by that name is causing you trouble, Ambassador?'

'Not especially, but let's not be coy with each other, Master Denton. Ursa is my record keeper. He has been missing now for three days.'

'Three days?' said Denton.

Ebril nodded, and Marney said, 'Forgive me, Ambassador, but if your record keeper has been missing for so long, why didn't you report it to the police?'

'A fair question,' Ebril sighed. 'Ursa is an intelligent Aelf, but also sensitive. Our exile here was difficult for him to accept, and he frequently seeks escape by immersing himself in the seedier side of Labyrinth life so readily found along Green Glass Row. This is not the first time he has … taken the long way home.'

'I see,' Denton said. 'His exile has made him bitter, angry perhaps?'

'Sad is probably closer to the truth,' Ebril replied. 'I have always turned a blind eye to Ursa's nocturnal activities simply because he is discreet, and whatever release he finds along Green Glass Row seems to do him good. He has never given me a reason not to trust his judgement.'

'Really?'

The Ambassador sighed again and gave the approximation of an embarrassed smile. 'In truth, I have often wondered if it was a matter of time before Ursa landed himself in trouble. Given that this house is being guarded by police, I am willing to guess he has bitten off more than he can chew this time. Trouble has followed him home, as it were? In the form of a wild demon?'

Denton's expression suggested he was impressed by Ebril's deductive skills. 'That is a fair assessment, Ambassador.'

'Ah. Then can I also safely guess that because two agents of the Relic Guild have been sent to me, Ursa has also involved himself with characters of the treasure hunting persuasion?'

Denton's tight smile gave affirmation.

Interesting and *clever*, he thought to Marney. *To be so forthcoming with his suspicions, he is either honestly clueless to the situation, or he is trying to misdirect us.*

To Ebril he said, 'You know nothing of your record keeper's movements for the past few days?'

'Not a thing,' Ebril assured him firmly. 'So let us cut to the quick.' He seemed disappointed. 'Ursa is in some way responsible for the presence of this wild demon. He is being held at the Nightshade and the Resident requires my official approval for whatever punishment he is due?'

'Not exactly, Ambassador.'

'Oh? Then what, Master Denton?'

The old empath's expression became sad, and even Marney couldn't tell if it was genuine or not. 'You are quite correct in most of your suspicions. Treasure hunters recently smuggled an artefact into the Labyrinth. Your records keeper was trying to purchase this artefact.' He paused as if mustering his tact. 'I regret to inform you that he was found dead at the scene of the transaction.'

For a room that was already emotionally cold, the temperature dropped palpably. Ebril shared a long look with Namji, and Marney felt a fleeting sense of surprise and fear coming from her. Was it genuine?

'Dead?' Ebril said to Denton

'Killed by the demon hiding inside the artefact, yes,' Denton assured him. 'All that it left of Ursa was his skeleton.'

'By the Timewatcher,' Ebril whispered. 'What manner of demon is this?'

'Unfortunately, Ambassador, we are forbidden from revealing certain details at this time.'

'Forbidden?'

Denton bobbed his head apologetically. 'But I can tell you that Ursa's identity was revealed to us by his business associate. A man called Llewellyn.'

'Llewellyn?' Ebril seemed angry. 'The name means nothing to me.'

'You are sure?'

'Of course I am!'

The Ambassador glared across the table at Denton.

'I-I know of him.'

All eyes turned to Namji. The young Aelf seemed embarrassed to have interrupted the moment, uncertain in her body language. But

Marney noted her face didn't appear quite so innocent now.

'Llewellyn used to run messages between House Ambassadors and merchants,' she said. 'He and Ursa were friends, I believe –' to which she was quick to add – 'though I never spoke to him myself.'

'Who he was makes no difference,' Ebril said hotly, and he glared again at Denton. 'I want to know what kind of artefact could contain a wild demon. I've never heard of such a thing.'

'I have no wish to offend you, Ambassador,' Denton said calmly. 'But the Resident has tied my hands on this matter.'

The sudden emotional calm that settled on Ambassador Ebril frightened Marney with its gentleness. It was like still, glassy water, belying the dangers lurking in its depths.

'What nonsense is this?' His voice was a purr, his face a stony blank. 'You say the Resident has tied your hands, but even empaths cannot hide glaring facts.' His slow gaze moved to Marney and then back again. 'I recognise propaganda when I see it – as you damn well know, Master Denton – and what I read in the newspaper this morning is nothing more than a smoke screen. It would be embarrassing to continue this game, so I ask you, gentleman to gentleman, what has Ursa really done?'

Get ready, Denton thought to Marney. *This won't go down well.*

'Ambassador,' he said. 'I have no wish to insult your intelligence any further, so I will tell you this – Ursa has …' The old empath paused for effect and licked his lips. 'Forgive me, Ambassador, but the nature of the artefact, and the demon it contained, indicate that Ursa harboured loyalties to Spiral.'

Marney would've staked her life that the shocked silence both Ebril and his daughter lapsed into was genuine.

'Impossible,' Ebril snapped. 'The High Governor and the Aelfir of Mirage have ever been faithful to the Timewatcher.'

'Faiths can change,' Marney said before she could stop herself.

Ebril's expression became stony again, but Namji recoiled as if slapped.

Nicely done, Marney, Denton thought. *But don't push it too far. You've put them on the back foot, but it could be a deceit.*

'Let me tell you of something, young one,' Ebril said sternly, defensively. He pointed a gnarled finger at Marney. 'I am Mirage's longest serving Ambassador. High Governor Obanai and I are personal friends, and I can vouch that he and his people would *never* treat with Spiral.'

'But we're speaking of an individual, Ambassador, not a nation.' Denton's tone was resolute. 'The evidence against Ursa is very convincing.'

'Then show it to me,' Ebril demanded.

Denton remained silent, and for a moment Marney thought the Ambassador might explode with fury. But instead he decided to settle on quiet simmering. Marney gave up trying to decide if it was a visceral or calculated reaction.

'This accusation goes too far, Master Denton,' Ebril said. 'And I will not take the word of the Resident on it. Or yours.'

Again, Denton said nothing and matched the ambassador's even glare.

'What is your evidence?' Ebril shouted.

Denton did not flinch.

'Gentlemen ...'

It was Namji who had spoken. She seemed uncertain, perhaps embarrassed that she had somehow overstepped her position by twice interrupting her father's work. Her soft tone of voice and shy eyes had the effect of drawing Ebril's attention away from his apparent anger. Even Denton seemed grateful for her interruption.

It made Marney trust her less.

'Master Denton,' Namji continued, her eyes downcast, 'forgive me, but it is obvious to all present that in accusing Ursa of having loyalties to Spiral you are, by implication, raising doubts over the loyalties of House Mirage. Please understand that it has been two years since we last saw our homeland, and we have received very little news. Even so, it is most unlikely that Governor Obanai has switched his allegiance, and be assured that Ursa did not speak for those of us stranded in the Labyrinth with him. If he is as guilty as you say, that is.'

Throughout her dialogue, Namji's manner had remained respectful, humble, almost timid, but something in the way she had said the Governor of Mirage's name didn't sit right to Marney. She couldn't put her finger on it, but it was almost as if the name was awkward for Namji to say.

Denton sighed. 'Mistress Namji, Ambassador Ebril, make no mistake – the artefact was in every way connected to Spiral.' His voice was leaden. 'And Ursa was undoubtedly responsible for arranging its passage into the Labyrinth.'

Ebril, having exchanged a lengthy look with his daughter, rubbed his impressive beard as he turned to Denton. 'Am I to take it the Thaumaturgists have been made aware of your findings?'

'Naturally.'

Ebril leant across the table. 'And the evidence is irrefutable, you say?'

'Ambassador ...' Denton also leant forwards and brought their faces even closer. 'You said earlier that we were not to be coy with each other. Perhaps now is the time for genuine candour?'

They continued to stare at each other for a long moment, their expressions intensifying. At first, Marney was bemused by their postures, but then, by the way Ebril's old features twitched, it dawned on her that he and Denton were conversing mentally, and it was a conversation she was not to be a part of.

She realised Namji was staring at her.

'Troubling times,' the Aelf said, without exhibiting one inch of concern.

Marney nodded, disturbed by how naturally the Ambassador's daughter had slipped back into the appearance of an innocent young girl.

'You are not the first Relic Guild agent Master Denton has brought to see my father,' she said lightly.

'I'm sure I'm not,' Marney replied evenly.

'I observe all the meetings, you know – while hiding in the wings, as it were. There is no deceit in this, you understand. Watching and listening is part of my training. As it is yours, I suspect.' Her smile was perfectly friendly. 'I have to say, the other agents I've observed were never so open in their naivety as you, Mistress Marney. I really can't tell if you're being genuine or not.'

Marney frowned. 'I'm just doing my job.'

'Yes, as ordered by the Resident. It's a shame, I think, that Gideon didn't send Van Bam this time.'

'Excuse me?'

'Van Bam. He is strong yet kind. His voice is like music to the ears.'

For a brief instant, Marney felt a wave of girlish desire coming from Namji, and she had to put a lid on her rising jealousy.

Her voice remaining soft and friendly, Namji added, 'If he were here today, I would ask Van Bam to stay a while. I imagine he is such pleasant company.'

Marney stared at Namji's innocent expression, not knowing what to say and do except quash the impulse to lean across the table and slap her young Aelfirian face. They remained staring at each other until Denton and Ebril broke off their mental conversation.

'Thank you for your time, Ambassador,' Denton said, groaning as he struggled to his feet. 'I will speak with Gideon and do all I can to help you.'

'As always, you have my gratitude, Master Denton. We will await the Resident's word.'

With a nod to Marney, Denton indicated that it was time to leave. Marney rose from the cushions, scowled at Namji's smile, gave a nod to Ebril, and then followed the old empath out of the room.

The servant was waiting to escort them out of the house.

Well, that was different, Denton thought as he and Marney made their way up the long driveway.

You're telling me, Marney replied. *What in the Timewatcher's name just happened in there, Denton?*

Something encouraging, if not mysterious. Ursa was most certainly not acting under Ebril's orders. The Ambassador is genuinely clueless about the current situation in his homeland. In that, at least, Namji was telling the truth.

I really don't like her. Marney couldn't hide the anger in her thoughts.

I don't think she likes you much either. Denton replied. *Now hide yourself.*

The two empaths emoted cloaks of concealment. Passing through the gates and the police detachment, they headed back up the street beneath glorious sunshine.

'Ebril opened himself to me, Marney. It's the first time I've ever known him to do it. So I decided to trust him. I told him the truth about the terracotta jar and Fabian Moor, and of the Icicle Forest. Ebril says he wants to help, but …' Denton's face was creased by thought. 'Well, let's just say I hope my trust is not misplaced. We need to talk to Gideon.'

The old empath led Marney over to an eye sitting atop a pedestal that was partially concealed by the shadows of a tree with boughs full of leaves. Taking a deep breath, he laid his hand on the head-sized sphere of milky fluid.

If a denizen touched an eye, it would connect them to the police headquarters building in the central district, where they would be able to report any emergency. However, if a magicker of the Relic Guild touched an eye, it connected them directly with the Nightshade.

Almost instantly, a projection of the Resident appeared before the two agents. His image fizzed. He ignored Marney and looked straight to Denton.

'Well?' he said abruptly. His voice crackled.

'Ebril knows the truth,' Denton replied. 'He and the rest of his household are innocent, but he is convinced that Ursa could not have done this on his own.'

Gideon sneered cruelly. 'He believes Mirage is controlled by the Genii? That Ursa was planted in the Labrys Town before the war began?'

'Not exactly, but it's complicated, Gideon,' Denton raised his hands in a placating gesture, as if already sensing how the Resident would react to his next words. 'Ebril has asked to speak to you in person.'

'Why? If he's useless to our inquiry now, then he can stay under house arrest until the war is over.'

'Don't be so quick,' Denton said. 'He told me that Mirage was having some internal conflicts before the war began. A delicate political situation, he called it. He wouldn't tell me what exactly, but he's convinced Ursa's actions are connected. Ebril will reveal more, but only to you, and I think you should listen to him, Gideon.'

The Resident was quiet for a moment and his image fizzed again.

'Then you had better invite the Ambassador to the Nightshade,' he said in a low voice. 'I'll send my personal tram to collect you both. As for your *pupil*, I have an address for a surgery in the northern district. Send her to it. Angel needs her help.'

Deep in the southern district, amidst a two square mile landscape of storage warehouses, Van Bam sat upon a packing crate inside an old ore warehouse that most denizens believed to be disused and abandoned – if they even remembered it was there at all. Hamir had moved to this location a little before dawn. Van Bam had felt intrigued at first, fascinated, perhaps a little excited to act as Hamir's apprentice. But now the illusionist felt imperially bored.

It wasn't that Hamir was unpleasant company – though the necromancer could stand to use a few lessons on the art of conversation – but he needed no help. There was really nothing for Van Bam to do, except watch. Even then, there wasn't much for him to see.

With his jacket removed and his shirt sleeves rolled to the elbows, Hamir sat cross-legged in the middle of the dusty warehouse floor. He had three items with him. One was a sackcloth bag, the contents of which he had not revealed. The other two were the gifts from Lady Amilee: a large and sealed metal box around four-feet square, and the thin leather-bound book in Hamir's hands. His expression was perfectly focused as he read through the pages. It was as if he was altogether unaware of Van Bam's presence.

To amuse himself, Van Bam had taken to casting illusions. He created a miniature of the horse he had once learnt to ride during a visit to an Aelfirian House. The beast was cast with as much detail as he could remember: a grey mare with black stockings, tail and mane. The illusion snorted and shook its head as it ran on the floor before Van Bam, jumping over his green glass cane. He smiled as he watched it, recalling the exhilaration he had felt when man and beast had galloped across a landscape of open fields and freedom, the wind whipping at their faces. It seemed so long ago now. Would such a time ever come again? Would he and Marney ever get to travel the Aelfirian Houses together?

His thoughts lingering on his lover, Van Bam felt a pang of irritation. He so longed to spend some time with Marney, even just one private hour. He needed that to assure himself that she had adapted to her experiences with Lady Amilee. Instead, here he was, useless and bored, and all on the whim of the Resident.

It was pointless trying to question Gideon's orders, or fathom his reasoning. He enjoyed keeping his agents on edge – seemed to revel most especially in needling Samuel – but why order Van Bam to help Hamir when he so clearly required none? There were any number of useful duties the illusionist could have been performing at this time. If there really was nothing for him to do, he could have seized the opportunity to be alone with ... And there it was, the reason he'd been sent to this warehouse: Marney.

The illusion of the little horse shook its head and kicked out with its forelegs as Van Bam gritted his teeth.

Did Gideon know about him and Marney? Did he disapprove? Going out of his way to keep them apart was exactly the kind of tactic he would employ if that was the case. But was he doing it because he wanted them to understand that duty always came first, or did he plan to end their romantic involvement altogether?

The horse gave a shrill whinny and began running around wildly.

Hamir cleared his throat and Van Bam stared at him. The necromancer stared back with a raised eyebrow.

'As pleasing to the eye as your illusions are,' he said, 'might I suggest some other activity to occupy your time? A book from the library, perhaps?'

'Excuse me?'

'Your little horse, Van Bam. Beautiful, but very distracting.'

Van Bam gave Hamir a sour look. With a final whinny, the horse disappeared in a swirl of green mist. 'Better?'

'Ah, I have offended you.'

Van Bam sighed. 'No. I am just trying to decide why Gideon wanted me here at all.'

'So am I, to be frank,' Hamir replied. 'But the Resident's wish is our command, yes?' A strange expression came to his face then, something the illusionist couldn't decipher. 'And to think,' Hamir said, almost to himself, 'one day a new Resident will have to tolerate Gideon's voice in his head.'

Van Bam shivered. 'It does not bear thinking about.'

'No, it really doesn't, does it?'

Van Bam tried to chuckle, but the way the necromancer looked him up and down checked it in his throat.

Hamir was quiet, contemplative, for a moment. 'There might be something you can help me with – but until I think of what it could be, please let me concentrate.' And he returned to the book.

Frowning deeply, Van Bam reclined on the packing crate and leant his back against the warehouse wall. For some reason Hamir's words concerning Gideon disturbed him, and made him recall a conversation he had once had with Gene, some years before.

Van Bam had been curious to know what Gideon had been like before he became Resident, when he was just another agent of the Relic Guild. Back then, the Resident had been a telepath called Sophia. She had been a tough governor, by all accounts, harsh but fair in her rule of Labrys Town. But as tough as Sophia was, even she had difficulty controlling Gideon. He was, according to Gene, the most powerful magicker ever known to join the Relic Guild ... and the most unstable.

Magic had given Gideon a terrible gift that left a strain on his mental condition. It was reckoned that one of his relatives – probably a great-grandfather or grandmother – had belonged to a mysterious race known as the Nephilim. The Nephilim were unique among the Aelfir, nomadic giants with no House as such to call their own. They roamed wherever they would across the realms. Nobody knew where they came from. According to rumours, they had simply appeared around the time of the Labyrinth's creation. The other Aelfirian Houses left them well alone, and no one dared stand in their way. Although the Nephilim had no interest in commerce or sharing cultures, and they were not known for their aggression, they were greatly feared. For they were blood-magickers.

Gideon's physical appearance gave no sign of his heritage, but his magic was in every way connected with the Nephilim, or so Gene claimed. Van Bam had pressed the old apothecary for more details, but he had refused to relate what he had seen Gideon do with his magic. However, he had revealed that Gideon's body and limbs were covered with hundreds of scars; that he liked to cut himself – to use his own blood to do terrible things to criminals and treasure hunters. Sophia had been forced to watch him closely at all times.

Van Bam and Marney were the only two Relic Guild agents who hadn't served under Sophia. She had remained the Resident until the day she died of old age in her nineties. Gene told Van Bam that he would never understand why the magic of the Nightshade chose Gideon to replace her, especially when Denton would have been a much more logical choice. It had been hoped by all the agents that when Sophia became Gideon's spirit guide, her ghost would temper his sociopathic ways. But, if anything, the presence of Sophia's voice in his head had made Gideon more intolerant and hard to fathom.

The Resident orchestrated the movements of the Relic Guild, but was very rarely seen outside the Nightshade. Gene said that the only good thing to come from Gideon attaining the Residency was that it kept him off the streets. However, Van Bam *could* understand why the Nightshade had chosen him over someone like Denton to replace Sophia. Although Denton never shied from the grittier side of the Relic Guild's work, he was at heart a kind man whose strength lay in his wisdom. Van Bam was loath to admit it, but the old empath did not have the bite or harshness of character to be a good governor of Labrys Town. Perhaps Gideon had too much.

Either way, Hamir was right; the next Resident would have no easy time with their spirit guide.

His musings were disturbed as Hamir closed the thin leather-bound book with a thump. Holding it to his chest, the necromancer stared off into the middle distance for a while.

'Hmm,' he said eventually, and turned to Van Bam. 'Are you frightened?'

'Frightened?'

'Yes. Of Fabian Moor.'

Van Bam was taken aback by the question. 'Most certainly.' He gestured to the book and the metal box. 'But I trust we are in good hands.'

Hamir studied the book's blank cover for a moment and nodded slowly. 'Tell me something, Van Bam – do you know the key difference between thaumaturgy and magic?'

Van Bam couldn't stop a smile; it was most unlike the necromancer to be forthcoming with conversation. 'I have occasionally wondered, but ... please, enlighten me.'

Clutching the book to his chest again, Hamir got to his feet and began to pace. 'Let us push aside mundane magic-users, with their spells and tricks, and consider a magicker of the Relic Guild – an illusionist, for example. You are born with a gift, which gives you a prescribed ability. Oh, you can be as inventive as you like with your gift. You can alter perceptions. You can manipulate a person's belief so profoundly that your illusions can protect them, or cause harm to them. You can convince others that you are something you are not, but you can no more use your magic to change form than a changeling could cast an illusion. You are what you are, Van Bam.'

'Yes, I understand that.'

Hamir stopped and looked up at the rafters above. 'Thaumaturgy, on the other hand, is limited only by the imagination of its user. There are ethical codes, of course – rights and wrongs by which all societies must be divided – but, in reality, there are no limits to what a Thaumaturgist with a strong enough imagination can achieve.'

At first, Van Bam wasn't sure how to respond. Denton claimed that he had occasionally shared long and fascinating conversations with Hamir, but Van Bam had never heard of any other agent doing so. It was an odd experience.

'So … you are saying what, Hamir? The key difference between thaumaturgy and magic is creativity?'

'Yes,' said Hamir. 'Yes, that's it – or close enough, I suppose.'

Van Bam wasn't convinced. 'Forgive me, Hamir – I appreciate that thaumaturgy is a higher science beyond my understanding, but I do not see creative artistry in what Fabian Moor has done to himself.'

'Perceptions and opinions, Van Bam.' He began pacing again. 'Where you see a dark desire to cause pain at any cost, I see dedication to an art form.'

'A dedication that has turned a man into a ghoul,' Van Bam replied. 'Moor requires blood to sustain a life that will never be as full as it once was.'

The necromancer nodded. 'Vampire, some cultures would call him.'

'The word *monster* seems to serve better.'

The slightest of laughs escaped Hamir's lips. 'Please, don't misunderstand me. I'm not suggesting that the ends are anything less than terrible. But the means …? Fabian Moor could have survived in that terracotta jar for decades, maybe centuries, like powdered milk waiting to be hydrated.' He gave Van Bam a meaningful look. 'I am asking if you can appreciate the level of skill and imagination it takes to safely capture the essence of a life force within such a small and simple thing.'

'I—' Van Bam shrugged. 'I cannot. It is hard for me to comprehend, Hamir.'

'Your lack of comprehension in no way exposes a lesser mind, Van Bam. You are conditioned by a confined existence where all things have boundaries. Thaumaturgy is a great and wild science that has no shape or size or walls. And in the hands of the Genii …' He trailed off as he came to stand before the sealed metal box on the floor and stared down at it. 'Fortunately for us, one of the most creative thaumaturgic minds belongs to Lady Amilee. Come. See for yourself.'

Van Bam rose from the crate and approached the necromancer. As he came alongside him, Hamir laid a hand on the box. Immediately a lid sprang up on hinges, as though recognising his touch – like a door in the Nightshade. Hamir drew Van Bam back a couple of steps, and together they watched as an orb of dull grey slowly rose from inside.

The orb was easily three times the size of any man's head. To Van Bam it looked to be a metallic substance, at once appearing both solid and liquid. It continued to rise until it stopped to hover five feet from the floor. Hamir stepped closer to it. He reached out and touched it lightly. The surface rippled. For a moment, its dullness became smooth and clear like a mirror. The necromancer's reflection was bulbous.

'What is it?' Van Bam said with an awed whisper.

'Something I haven't seen for a very long time,' Hamir replied, and Van Bam detected the vaguest hint of excitement in his voice. 'My skills in metallurgy are found a little wanting, but with the help of this –' he held up the book – 'I should be able to muddle through.'

He turned to a random page and allowed Van Bam to see the script inside. It was unlike anything he had ever seen before. Sprawling symbols decorated the pages in such intricate designs and shapes that they looked more like artwork than words.

'The language of the Thaumaturgists,' Hamir said. 'Graceful, complicated … without boundaries.'

Not for the first time since joining the Relic Guild, Van Bam found himself staring at Hamir, wondering what mysteries lay in the necromancer's past.

'You … You can understand this language?'

In reply, Hamir closed the book and gave Van Bam what might have been the smallest of smiles. 'If you are willing,' he said, 'I've just thought of something you can help me with.'

A little under six months before, when Marney had been an agent of the Relic Guild for only a couple of weeks, Angel had decided that they should get to know each other better. At that time Marney's world had been turned upside down, and she grasped at Angel's easy offer of friendship, eager to fit in. Little did she know that Angel had actually planned to give her an initiation ceremony – of sorts – a proper induction into the Relic Guild. She treated Marney to a night out down Green Glass Row. The memory of it was blurred now, but the hangover had left Marney sick to the stomach for three days.

Denton hadn't been best pleased, of course. Ever protective of his protégé, he made sure Angel understood she wasn't to *treat* Marney to a night out like that again. And he cautioned Marney to be more wary around the healer. Angel might have mellowed somewhat with age but had not completely shrugged off the wildcat of her youth. Probably never would.

Even so, Marney remained fond of Angel. She wasn't like the other agents. Unlike Denton and Van Bam she didn't treat Marney as if she was delicate glass; she wasn't ignorant and unapproachable like Gideon and Samuel. Gene and the twins were always pleasant enough to her, but they rarely showed a real interest in her life. Angel was different; she treated Marney like an equal, for all the pros and cons that implied.

It was late morning by the time she reached the address for the doctor's surgery Gideon had given her. In the heart of the northern district, halfway along Carver's Road, she came to a small house that didn't look much like a surgery at all. She was happy to see Angel approaching from the opposite end of the road. She was dressed formally in a skirt suit and blouse. Her long black-and-grey hair was fixed into a neat bun, and she carried a black medicine bag.

She smiled as she approached the empath. She looked tired.

'Hello, Marney.' The slight sense of surprise she radiated was easy to detect. 'What are you doing here?'

'Gideon sent me.'

'Really?'

'He said you wanted my help.'

'Did he?'

'Well – yes. You didn't ask for me?'

'No.'

'Then why am I here?'

Angel snorted a laugh and shrugged her shoulders. 'You tell me. I've been up all night, warning the hospitals and surgeries about this virus – not that I needed to, by the way. Have you seen the bloody paper this morning?'

Marney nodded, and Angel shook her head, disgruntled.

'I was just about ready to crawl into bed,' she grumbled, 'but then Gideon tells me to come here.' She motioned to the small house. 'I wasn't going to bother with this place. I'm not even sure it qualifies as a surgery.'

'Oh …' Marney wasn't sure what else to say. 'I guess I'll get going then.'

With another smile, Angel patted Marney's shoulder. 'Why don't you stay? I'll introduce you to Doctor Wilf. He's a nice old boy, and his wife makes the best cakes. Come on – we'll say you're my nurse.'

The house fitted unpretentiously into the other residential homes along Carver's Road. Angel led the way through the garden gate, and then down a stone path that cut along a small patch of overgrown grass where no flowers grew. Halfway down the path, Angel looked back over her shoulder.

'So, what did Gideon do about House Mirage?'

'He sent me and Denton to see Ambassador Ebril this morning.'

'Oh really? How did that go?'

Marney's expression darkened. 'Long story,' she said.

'It usually is with Ebril. Tricky bastard, isn't he?'

'To be honest with you, Angel, I'm not really sure what happened. Denton spoke with Ebril privately, but he wouldn't tell me much of what was said.'

'That's empaths for you,' Angel quipped. 'They're a funny bunch, you know.'

They reached the house. A plaque on the wall announced that it was the abode of Doctor Wilfred West. Angel raised a fist to knock on the front door but paused to look at Marney.

'So, Van Bam didn't go with you?'

'No. He's helping Hamir,' Marney replied, adding pointedly, 'As you're fully aware.'

'Oh, that's right. You're here, and he's there.' She turned her head to one side and gave a full-toothed grin. 'I remember now.'

Marney sighed as she felt the amusement radiating from the healer. 'You know, Denton is just as smug and ham-fisted when he's trying to make a point, Angel. It's very annoying.'

Angel chuckled. 'Don't get uppity with me. I'm not the one keeping you away from your lover.'

'What? I-I don't—'

Angel rolled her eyes and knocked on the door. 'Give it a rest, Marney. You and Van Bam must be the worst kept secret I've ever known.' She rocked her head from side to side. 'Well, maybe not the worst, but certainly a contender.'

Marney was about to protest her innocence some more, but Angel cut her off.

'Seriously, woman, did you really think it was a secret?'

'Well . . .' Marney's shoulders sagged and she shook her head. 'I know Denton knows, but we've never talked about it.' She gave a resigned sigh. 'I suppose it must be obvious to the rest of you.'

'Oh, don't get me wrong,' Angel said quickly. 'I'm happy for you and Van Bam. And what you get up to is really nothing to do with any of us . . . except Gideon, maybe.'

'Gideon?'

'If *we* know, he knows, Marney. And, trust me, the Resident isn't keen on his agents having anything other than a professional relationship.'

Marney stared at Angel 'You think he's keeping me and Van Bam apart?' she said dubiously.

Angel knocked on the door a second time. 'Think about it. I didn't ask for help, I don't need help, yet here you are all the same, on the orders of Gideon. And I very much doubt Hamir needs Van Bam's help, either.'

Marney shook her head. 'No. If Gideon didn't like our relationship, he'd just tell us to stop seeing each other. It's not as if he's shy about confrontation.'

'Really? If you ask me, complicating your situation is exactly Gideon's style.' She knocked on the door for a third time. 'As for my unwitting part in this scenario, I'll just be glad to finish up here and get to bed – and I don't care whose bed it is, Marney. I need to sleep.'

With a fourth and final thump on the door, Angel stepped back and looked up at the house. 'Come on, Wilf,' she muttered. 'Open the bloody door.'

She noticed Marney's troubled expression and pursed her lips.

'Look,' she said, 'if you want my advice, don't let Gideon grind you down. Take whatever moments you can share with Van Bam and be grateful for them. But no matter what you do, don't ever put your relationship before the Relic Guild, and never bring your problems to work – and I say that for all our sakes, Marney, not just because of Gideon. Okay?'

Her tone was kind, not harsh, and Marney experienced a sudden, unexpected feeling of warmth from the healer. She knew that some of her fellow agents had careers outside the Relic Guild; Gene had his apothecary shop, Macy and Bryant worked as bouncers, and Angel was a doctor. But Marney had never seen the healer at work in her second career, and she realised in that moment that being a doctor, helping others, made Angel feel complete. It was easy to picture her using that same kindly tone of voice for her patients.

'I'm in love with him,' Marney blurted before she could stop herself.

Angel's eyes widened.

'Van Bam, I mean,' Marney added quickly. 'I'm in love with Van Bam.'

'Well, I didn't think you meant Gideon.'

Marney quashed a flustered feeling that threatened to turn her cheeks red.

'Have you told him?' Angel asked.

Marney shook her head.

'Maybe you should.' The healer gave a quirky smile. 'I hope it works out for you, Marney, I really do.'

'So do I.'

Angel squeezed her shoulder, and then looked at the house again with a sigh. 'He's probably taking a nap or just can't hear us,' she said. 'Let's check around the back.'

Angel led the way down the side of the house. Marney followed, feeling relieved and happy after her admission. She realised she had known for weeks her true feelings for Van Bam, but had pushed the emotion deep down inside her – hiding from it, perhaps. Now, Marney had been transformed, strengthened by her experiences at Lady Amilee's tower. It seemed pointless to continue hiding from something so true and pure. She loved him.

'Wilf's old and he doesn't go out much,' Angel was saying as they walked. 'He's supposed to be retired, but he and his wife still run this surgery from home. They don't have many patients, but it keeps them busy. Trouble is, they're both a bit deaf. They can't have a conversation without resorting to shouting.'

Marney chuckled as they came to a small, walled-in backyard that was paved with dark stone slabs and devoid of a single flower or blade of grass. The parasol was closed on the garden table, and no one sat in the chairs.

Angel tried the back door. It was unlocked. They stepped into a dingy and hot kitchen that carried the sickly sweet smell of baking. Two dirty cups and plates sat on the kitchen table.

'Wilf?' Angel shouted. 'It's me – Angel. Can I have a quick word?'

In reply, there was a crash of breaking glass from somewhere upstairs. Both agents flinched and stared at each other.

'Wilf?' Angel called again.

This time there came the sound of creaking floorboards and a muffled thump.

'Stay here,' Angel told Marney.

With a look of concern Angel made to investigate, but Marney stopped her.

'Angel, wait!' The empath stared up at the ceiling. The floorboards creaked again, and her gut froze.

'What is it, Marney?'

'Whoever's up there, I can't feel them.'

'What?'

'I can't feel any emotions. It's ... just like Chaney's Den.'

Angel paused for a moment and listened to the sound of shuffling from the rooms above.

'Marney,' she said in a whisper. 'Please tell me Denton lets you carry a weapon now.'

'No,' Marney replied. 'I mean – I'm having training, but—'

Angel swore.

She placed her black medicine bag on the kitchen table and opened it. 'Where's Samuel when you need him?' she muttered as she pulled out a wooden box. Inside was a small snub-nosed revolver. She opened the chamber and checked it was loaded, then thumbed the power stone into life. 'Stay behind me,' she said, and headed out of the kitchen.

Marney blocked her fear as she crept up the stairs behind the healer. They came to a corridor that dog-legged to the left. They passed two open doors: a bathroom and a spare bedroom that had been converted into a doctor's surgery. But, turning to the left, the corridor ended at the closed door to what must have been the master bedroom.

There came a muffled crunching as someone trod on broken glass.

Angel motioned for Marney to hang back a few feet as she approached the closed door. The empath could feel the healer's courage in the face of trepidation. When Angel reached the door, she bent down to peer through the keyhole.

A gun spat.

The bullet smashed through the door with a spray of splinters, passed through the space where Angel's head had been a moment before, and slammed into Marney's shoulder.

She couldn't remember falling onto her back, but she was suddenly looking up at the ceiling. It felt as if the breath had been punched from her lungs, but there was no pain. From somewhere distant, Angel was shouting. The healer crawled over to her. There were splinters of wood in her hair. The shooting continued, repeating flashes of power stones and a low and hollow spitting sound: two pistols, by the sound of things. Why did she feel so numb?

Angel grabbed the shoulders of Marney's jacket and dragged her around the turn in the corridor. That was when the pain hit her. She yelled and struggled in the healer's grip.

'Keep still,' Angel hissed. She pressed Marney down, opened her coat, ripped the button off her shirt, and inspected the bullet wound. Again, Marney yelled.

'Good, it's gone right through you.'

The guns continued to fire, and tears sprang to Marney's eyes.

'Come on, Marney,' Angel growled. 'Dampen the pain, like Denton showed you.'

'I-I can't.' Marney's breath came in short, sharp gasps. Her teeth chattered. 'It hurts too … it hurts too much.'

'Then brace yourself, woman.'

Angel pressed one hand against Marney's shoulder, and slid the other underneath her body to cover the exit wound. Marney looked up and saw blood – so much blood. Angel's skin began to glow with the pale radiance of magic. The pain that Marney had experienced so far was nothing compared to the white fire that spread through her then.

Her scream drowned out the noise of bullets cracking the wall. Bright light, wispy and fluid, filled her vision. The agonising fire seemed to burn for an eternity inside her, and Marney wasn't sure if she passed out or not. But when the pain finally receded, she became aware that although bullets no longer hit the corridor wall, the spitting of pistols had not stopped, and the scent of spent thaumaturgy reached her nostrils.

Marney looked down at her shoulder; lumpy scar tissue a shade of angry pink had formed over the bullet wound, though the blood surrounding it was still slick. The wound no longer hurt.

Her brow beaded with sweat, Angel wiped blood from her hands onto her clothes and picked up her revolver. She peered around the corner, and made an angry noise.

'Golems,' she said, looking back to Marney. 'Two of them.' The sound of spitting continued. 'They're so dumb they don't even know they've run out of bullets.'

Angel disappeared from view. Marney winced as she sat up, and then flinched as she heard the sound of hissing and cracking and something stony falling apart. The hollow noise of power stones releasing bursts of thaumaturgy had stopped.

Angel coughed. 'Marney, can you walk?'

Marney could feel the sense of sadness Angel emoted. Her shoulder stiff and aching, she got to her feet and took careful steps to join the healer in the bedroom.

Angel stood staring down at the wreckage. The pillows, blankets and mattress of a double bed had been shredded. Dressers had been upturned, ornaments smashed; and amidst the wreckage, the remains of two golems lay upon the floor, broken into stony pieces. The reek of magic hung in the air and prickled against Marney's skin.

'They just fell apart,' Angel said in a quiet voice. 'As soon as I shot them in the head.'

'Doctor Wilf and his wife?' Marney asked, rubbing her shoulder.

Angel didn't reply, as if it was too unbearable for her to imagine the torture inflicted upon two innocent, elderly denizens.

'What have we found here, Angel?' Marney asked fearfully. 'Is this Fabian Moor's hiding place?'

Angel's eyes narrowed, and Marney could feel her suspicion rising. Before she could air what she was thinking, a noise came from outside and she moved to the window.

'Oh, just what we need,' she whispered.

Marney looked for herself. On the road outside, several denizens had gathered. They talked hurriedly among themselves, and a few were pointing at the house. Obviously Marney's screams of pain had attracted their attentions.

'Can you focus enough to conceal us?' Angel asked Marney.

She felt a little disoriented and numb; her shoulder wound ached, but the pain was not distracting. 'I think so,' she said.

'Good. Let's sneak out before the police arrive.' Angel's face clouded angrily. 'I want to get back to the Nightshade and find out if Gideon knew what he was sending us into.'

CHAPTER FOURTEEN

HOPE

Clara thought that she would never be so relieved to see the light of day again. By the time Van Bam led her and Samuel out of East Side Asylum, the midmorning sun was high in a deep blue sky that was pillowed by clean white clouds. The air was warm but fresh, and at last Clara felt as though she could expunge the stench of infection that lingered in her nostrils, that clung to her hair and clothes and skin. The police and asylum staff were assigned to deal with the carnage left behind in the sublevels, while the Relic Guild boarded the black tram and headed out of the eastern district.

The mood in the carriage was sombre, and there was little discussion during the journey. Samuel remained silent throughout, brooding over the small terracotta jar they had found clutched in the hands of the skeleton. Van Bam had taken the time to explain to Clara the significance of the jar's presence: just as Fabian Moor had used such a device to smuggle himself into the Labyrinth during the Genii war, so it seemed he had used the same method to unleash another member of the Genii onto the town. Clara understood the gravity of the Resident's words, but she found it hard to fully comprehend. With the horror of the asylum now behind her, she felt mentally numb and physically drained.

To her mild surprise, the tram did not return its passengers to the Nightshade as she had expected, but instead stopped beside a lonely side lane in the central district. After the group disembarked, the tram pulled away, and once again Clara wondered with vague interest who or what drove it. Her weariness making everything around her seem unreal, Clara followed on tired legs as Samuel led the way down a narrow alley to the back of a tall apartment building, and then up the black frame of a metal fire escape to the roof. There, the group climbed down through a hatchway to reach its underwhelming destination.

Samuel referred to his home as a hideout, a place safe from the pit-falls and rivalries of the bounty hunting trade. It was a small and musty apartment whose living area was combined with a simple kitchen. There was a bathroom, one bedroom, and a single window with a thick curtain drawn across it. There wasn't much in the way of trappings and personal possessions, and it was sparsely furnished. There wasn't even a front door; the apartment was only accessible by climbing down the short ladder that led from the hatchway in the ceiling.

It was the closest place to rest up and regroup, Van Bam said; and there was no need to return to the Nightshade yet, as Hamir was still operating on Charlie Hemlock and he wouldn't be finished for a couple of hours. Clara didn't understand how the Resident could possibly know this without the necromancer being present to tell him, and nor did she care. Almost as soon as she entered Samuel's hideout, she spied a tatty but comfortable looking sofa, which she lay down upon, and was soon asleep …

… She was the wolf.

A challenger had dared to come to her forest and the trees were alive with the voice of her family. She led the hunt. The challenge would be met. The invader would be faced and destroyed. She would show her family how strong she was, how unafraid and ruthless, and no one would doubt her leadership again. This was her territory, her forest, and the baying of the pack filled her with lustful pride.

She was the wolf.

Beneath the silver glare of the moon, she bounded down an embank-ment to a clearing where the challenger waited for her. It was no ordinary wolf that lay there upon dead leaves and hard, root-veined earth. Its pelt was made of deep blue light that brightened and dimmed like the flexing of honed muscles. Its eyes were black holes from which dark tendrils leaked like tears of lazy smoke.

She wasn't afraid of it. She met its challenge with bared teeth and a low growl.

Its voice entered her head with deep male tones: I'm not your enemy, Clara.

*The name meant nothing to her, and she began circling the challenger,
slowly, gracefully, powerfully.*

It didn't move, but its dark eyes followed her and seemed amused. I
won't fight you.

She barked, once, loud and harsh, and her family howled from the trees.

The challenger's voice dared to chuckle inside her head. We weren't
supposed to meet just yet, Clara, *it said.* But we'll see each other again,
soon I think, when you'll be able to understand.

*She jumped at the challenger, teeth gnashing, nails sharp. It didn't rise
to defend itself, and when she crashed into it the challenger's body flared
and filled the clearing with blazing blue light.*

She was the wolf . . .

. . . The dream faded from memory as the sound of bickering voices
disturbed her sleep.

'. . . It's pointless,' Samuel was saying. 'It won't work.'

'We must try everything, Samuel,' Van Bam replied. 'Gideon also
believes that Moor can somehow access the Labyrinth from a remote
location. I, too, was dubious at first, but you said yourself that Moor
opened a portal to abduct Marney.'

'I never said I was dubious,' Samuel replied moodily. 'I said I don't
care what Gideon thinks.'

Gideon? Clara wondered. She didn't open her eyes and kept up the
pretence of being asleep.

'Nonetheless, we have few options,' Van Bam said sternly. 'Wherever
Marney is being held, Fabian Moor has been creating portals that lead
in and out of the Labyrinth. Think about it, Samuel – if we could find
one, we might be able to call for help. It is a reason for hope.'

'Hope?' Samuel snorted. 'Van Bam, stopping Moor was going to be
hard enough when we thought he was alone. But two Genii?' He gave a
bitter laugh. 'We were nine strong last time, and, even with the Thaumaturgist's help, Moor – on his own – still managed to kill half of us. This
fight has gone from difficult to impossible. I don't see any hope.'

'Samuel—'

'No,' he snapped. 'What you're suggesting just won't work, Van
Bam!'

'Still, I will try.'

'Do what you like.' Samuel's voice sounded old and tired. 'I'm not talking about this anymore. I need to think. I'm going to get some air.'

Clara heard the sound of Samuel climbing the ladder to the hatchway in the ceiling. The hatch was opened, and when it closed again a few moments of silence passed before Van Bam spoke.

'You can stop pretending to be asleep now, Clara.'

Clara opened her eyes and gave a coy smile.

Van Bam stood over her with his arms folded across his chest. He didn't return the smile. 'I trust you heard enough to understand the predicament we are in?'

She nodded and sat up on the sofa. The room was dim. The only light source was the weak glow of the sun filtering through the thick curtain over the window. She stretched her back and looked around the apartment. Stripped to the bare minimum in terms of living requirements, it seemed isolated and lonely in the shadows, and Clara was struck by a sudden, pitying notion that this apartment was a good representation of Samuel's life.

She looked up at the Resident. 'Who's Gideon?' she asked.

Van Bam tilted his head to one side. 'He was the former Resident of Labrys Town – my direct predecessor, in fact.'

Clara looked bemused. 'Gideon the Selfless?'

'As he is now known – yes.'

She wanted to laugh, believing Van Bam was making a joke, but the serious expression on his face stopped her. Neither did she feel inclined to make the obvious statement that Gideon the Selfless had died long before she was born.

Perhaps sensing her puzzlement, Van Bam explained further. 'Gideon is now a ghost that haunts the Nightshade. I hear his voice in my mind.'

'Oh,' was the only thing Clara could think of to say.

'It is the design of my position, Clara. When a Resident dies, he or she remains as a spirit guide of sorts to whoever next attains the governorship of the Labyrinth. Just as Gideon became my guide upon his death, so I will remain in spirit as an aide to whoever replaces me. But not, I think, if we fail to stop Fabian Moor and the new Genii he has brought to Labrys Town.'

His metallic eyes seemed to glare at her. 'Clara, if you have remembered anything of what Marney has placed inside your mind, now would be a very good time to tell me.'

She looked apologetic. 'She's there, up in my head. I can feel her, but ...' She shook her head. 'Sorry.'

It was then that Clara noticed the small and dented silver tin in Van Bam's hand. She checked the empty pockets of her hooded pullover even though she already knew it was her medicine tin he held.

Van Bam opened it and studied the little white tablets inside. 'Monkshood, if I am not mistaken,' he said. 'Usually a medicine prescribed to those denizens who suffer seizures during the hours of Silver Moon. But I suspect it is also efficient at keeping a wolf at bay, yes?'

She averted her eyes. It had been her adopted mothers, Gerdy and Brianne, who had discovered that monkshood worked on ailments other than moon-fever. Clara had lost count of how many years she had been taking it.

She looked back at Van Bam, hesitating before she spoke. 'It's the only way I can stop the change,' she said, hating the shame that rose in her voice. 'I have no control over the wolf.'

Van Bam's expression became slightly less serious and a little more sympathetic. 'Clara, being so afraid of your own shadow might just be the very cause of your troubles.' He closed the tin with a snap. 'Accept yourself first, and perhaps the wolf will follow your lead. But I do know this for certain – denying your magic will eventually drive you insane.'

He offered the tin, and Clara accepted it with no small amount of relief. Despite the Resident's comment, she took out a tablet, popped it into her mouth, and then slid the tin safely into her pocket.

'Now,' said Van Bam, 'I need to speak further with Samuel – if he is willing – so I suggest you refresh yourself, and take some food.'

At the mention of food, Clara's stomach growled. She noticed a small dining table, upon which sat a pot of fresh coffee and some bread and preserves. The terracotta jar also sat there, along with Van Bam's green glass cane.

The Resident picked up his cane and moved to the ladder beside the window that led up to the hatchway.

'Upon my return, Clara,' he said as he began to climb the ladder, 'there is a duty you and I must perform.'

Clara watched him with a questioning gaze.

Evidently sensing this, Van Bam added, 'Ready yourself, and you will see,' before disappearing through the hatchway.

'And you say Yves Harrow is dead?' Mo Asajad asked, without the slightest hint of surprise or remorse in her voice.

'Yes,' Moor replied. 'His containment device had been compromised long before I found it. Without flesh to reanimate his essence, Harrow died a slow death over many years, I suspect.'

Her lips drew into a thin line. 'So unfortunate.'

The sustenance Asajad had so gleefully hunted at the asylum seemed to agree with her. Gone was the fury and hunger that led a beast to rampage among madmen. A priest's black cassock now covered her pale and bony nakedness, and she was as stoic and calculating as Moor always remembered her.

'Tell me, Fabian,' she said. 'What of Viktor Gadreel and Hagi Tabet?'

'Our brother and sister will be with us soon enough,' he assured her.

'That is … pleasing, I suppose.'

The two Genii stood inside a square chamber with silver walls, floor and ceiling, which glowed with sterile radiance. Forty years this silver cube had served as Moor's only sanctuary, his tomb of isolation. From this place, it had taken decades of searching the Nothing of Far and Deep to find the pathway that led to the Labyrinth. It now felt strange to share the cube's confined space with another – although Asajad was not his only guest.

From the centre of the chamber grew a strange treelike creature. Its trunk was fat, and its bark was deep brown, shaded with green, with a texture more akin to the skin of a reptile. At its base, a mass of roots writhed like a nest of snakes, pointed tips digging down into the metallic substance of the floor. Bare branches, like slender, sinuous limbs, coiled and wavered in the air. They protruded from all over the leathery trunk, and reached high to probe the silver ceiling some fifteen feet above.

Asajad circled the tree, studying its strange form as she did so. Moor folded his arms across his chest and leant back against the silver wall as he watched her. She seemed impressed by the creature, though it was not in her character to say so.

She stopped to study the human that was being held securely in the tree's serpentine clutch. It was a woman. She was naked, suspended on thin and strong branches coiled around wrists and ankles. Another branch had punctured her lower back, spiralled up around her spine, and even now its tip was licking and probing at the base of her skull. The woman's chin was pressed to her chest, and auburn hair hung in damp tendrils, streaked with grey. Her skin was mottled with ice burns.

Asajad lifted her head by the hair to reveal a plain face, slack and unconscious. 'And this pathetic denizen harbours the secrets we need?' She let the woman's head drop, and looked up the length of the strange tree with a disappointed expression. 'Really, Fabian, I'm bored with waiting. Can't we just torture the information from her?'

Moor shook his head. 'We do nothing without Gadreel and Tabet. And that pathetic denizen is an empath of some skill. She would block any pain we inflict upon her both mentally and physically. She would gladly die before revealing her secrets.'

'Truly?'

'Trust me – I know these agents of the Relic Guild well.'

Asajad seemed amused. 'Then this human is one of those who thwarted you so long ago?'

'She is. Her name is Marney.'

Raising a hand to her mouth, Asajad tittered. 'Forgive me, Fabian, but I still find it strange that Lord Spiral's most merciless Genii would struggle against so lowly a magicker as an agent of the Relic Guild.'

Moor bit back an angry reply.

He could have told Asajad that the Relic Guild was not to be under-estimated. He could have explained that forty years ago this empath and all the Resident's agents had proved a force greater than even Lord Spiral had foreseen. But he saved his breath. In truth, Asajad had always been jealous that Spiral had chosen him over her as his favoured Genii. If she wasn't so ruthless, Moor might have considered her childish.

'Understand me,' he said levelly. 'I have been waiting for this day for four decades, and I will not risk everything we sacrificed simply because you are *bored*.'

She gave a pout, but her dark eyes glinted dangerously.

'Have faith,' Moor said, and he nodded towards the empath hanging so limp and wretched from the leathery branches. 'This tree is a design of my own. It will harvest the information we require from the human – slowly but assuredly. Hold to that and find some patience.'

'But all this inaction, Fabian!' Asajad reached out and stroked a coiling branch. 'Even the desire to feed has left me, and I grow restless.'

'Here in this chamber, we do not need to feed. Here, we are whole.'

'Funny,' she said distantly, 'but I find I miss it – the taste of blood, the fear and panic.' She turned from the tree to face him. 'Don't you?'

Moor paused for a moment, considering.

Asajad pressed her point. 'Surely we could use a few more golems about the place, Fabian?' She ran her tongue across her teeth. 'The denizens will learn to fear us soon enough, anyway. Am I right?'

Feeding needlessly seemed like a reckless thing to do, but then the days of hiding and waiting were over now. The chance to taste blood again, to drain that exquisite life-energy from a struggling human, was tempting, almost overpoweringly so. Perhaps it *was* time to return to Labrys Town. After all, it wouldn't be long before Viktor Gadreel and Hagi Tabet required their help. And, of course, there were still a few loose ends to tie up.

'What do you say, Fabian?'

'Come,' he replied.

He turned and pressed his hand against the cool, silver surface of the wall. The metal wavered, turning from solid to liquid. By the time it became shimmering air that gave a clear view into a shadowy alleyway, Asajad was already standing at Moor's shoulder. She grinned at him.

'Do try to temper your desire,' he told her.

Van Bam had no memory of his natural parents. They had died when he was an infant, and he had been taken in by a church orphanage. As a boy he had always felt alone, isolated from the other orphans. The priests mistook him for an introvert, a shy child who preferred his own company, but they were pleased with his great passion for studying scripture. Little did they know that Van Bam's devotion to the Timewatcher was born from a need for forgiveness. The shy and introverted boy kept a secret; there was magic in his veins, and he believed that only the Timewatcher could absolve him of this curse.

When he had grown into a young man, Van Bam became an acolyte, training to be a priest. Church life suited him well, and he considered himself an honest and faithful person learning from greater men. It was a simpler time, a good time, and he enjoyed tending the church gardens and reading scripture at services. He hid his magic well, but deep down he always knew that somebody would discover his secret one day.

He reached his late teens before an old man came to the church looking for him. His name was Denton, and he carried a summons from the Resident. Van Bam was to be taken to the Nightshade.

Of course, he hadn't appreciated at that moment that Denton was also a magicker; the empath's manner was kind and welcoming, and just being in his presence had a strange, calming effect. It hadn't even occurred to Van Bam that he might overpower the old man and run into hiding. Where in the Labyrinth could he have truly hidden, anyway? Curiously, Van Bam had felt somehow freed of burden. He remembered feeling relieved that there was no more need for lies and deception, and that his conscience would be clear when he faced whatever punishment awaited him at the hands of the Resident.

But when he had arrived at the Nightshade, there was no punishment. He learned the truth of the Relic Guild, and that being a magicker was no crime if you used your skills in service to the guild. Denton, that kind and generous old empath, had taught Van Bam that his magic was not a curse. It was a gift from the Timewatcher Herself.

So many years had passed since that day. Despite Van Bam's experiences as a Relic Guild agent, his duties as Resident had kept him too busy to acknowledge how much the Genii War had stolen from them all. Only now, with the Relic Guild so desperately needed, was he forced to fully appreciate what Labrys Town had lost. And with that recognition came a deeper sympathy for those he had once called friends, who had been abandoned by their Resident as well as the Timewatcher.

Van Bam found Samuel up on the roof of his hideout. The air was warm and the sun was bright, and he leaned against a guardrail, staring down onto a street in the central district below. He did not turn as the Resident approached, but Van Bam's vision could tell from Samuel's colours that he knew his old friend was approaching. The old bounty hunter was in turmoil, but his anger had vanished.

As he came alongside Samuel, Van Bam could feel Gideon's presence at the back of his mind. The ghost of the former Resident didn't speak, but it was clear his interest was piqued. Van Bam left him to play the voyeur and respected Samuel's silence, joining him in staring down into the street.

By day the central district was a hive of commerce, home to the merchant and industry guilds, the entertainment councils, the town bank, the main hospital and police headquarters. Below, the street teemed with people, and the sounds of their voices buzzed in the air along with the rumbling of trams.

Van Bam looked up towards the west, where the vague image of Ruby Moon hung in the clear sky. Invisible to normal eyes at this time of day, it was perceived by the Resident's as a red ghost. He enjoyed seeing its hue, even though it loitered within a sky that appeared to him as a dreary canvas the tone of slate. Magic and emotion Van Bam always saw in colour; but for too many years now all other things had appeared to him only in myriad shades of grey. And of all those things, he missed the colour of the sky the most.

'Do you ever think about it?' Samuel said. He didn't look up and continued watching the street below. 'About the night we thought we had killed Fabian Moor?'

Van Bam knew his answer instinctively. 'As his face was the last thing my eyes ever saw, it is occasionally difficult not to.'

Samuel nodded. 'Did we make a mistake, Van Bam? Did we do something wrong?'

'I have always reasoned we did enough.'

'But the way the Timewatcher abandoned us. The way the Thaumaturgists just left. We must have done something to make them angry.'

Van Bam frowned at his friend; he had never known him to sound so lost, so ... *ashamed*?

'Samuel, each of us thought Fabian Moor had died that night. We played our part in the Genii War to the best of our abilities. The decision to isolate the Labyrinth was not our fault. Why are you questioning this now?'

Samuel rubbed his face. His hands were shaking. 'I thought I'd grown too old and tired to really care about what the Relic Guild once stood for. But now Fabian Moor is back, everything we ever did feels so pointless. It's humiliating.'

Van Bam's metallic eyes scrutinised the hues of Samuel's emotions. At the back of his mind, he felt Gideon's amusement grow colder. Obviously he found joy in the old bounty hunter's uncustomary moment of vulnerability.

Van Bam took a deep breath of warm afternoon air. 'Samuel, even in light of Moor not being the sole surviving Genii, I have not lost hope for our situation – not while so much remains a mystery. For instance, I have been thinking about this avatar that offered you the bounty contract on Clara's life.'

At the mention of the contract Samuel stiffened – almost imperceptibly, but all too clearly to the Resident's inner vision. His shade flushed defensively.

'Avatars are conjurations,' Van Bam continued. 'And there is always a master controlling such things, yes?'

Samuel nodded, albeit reluctantly. 'I've been wondering about that, too,' he sighed. '*Someone* offered me that contract.'

'Indeed. But you are not the only one who was approached by the avatar. And that would include me.'

For the first time Samuel looked at Van Bam, his surprise evident. '*You* saw the avatar?'

'I did.'

'When?'

'The specifics are not important, Samuel. However, I am beginning to suspect that this avatar is more than a mere servant. I have been asking myself if it could be the manifestation of a portent.'

'A portent?' Samuel said. 'You mean a future guide? You think someone's using the avatar to *lead* us into the future?'

'To deliver us to a specific point in time after guiding us through a particular set of events – yes,' replied Van Bam. 'Such things have occurred before.'

'To the Aelfir, maybe, but not to us. Van Bam, who's left in the Labyrinth powerful enough to summon an avatar and use it as a future guide? Even Hamir couldn't do it.'

'But what is to say the avatar's master is even *in* the Labyrinth?"

Samuel shook his head. 'That's a giant leap of faith, Van Bam, even for you.'

Samuel's closed mind had obviously not opened with age. Van Bam sighed.

'Samuel, consider for a moment,' he said. 'What if the avatar used the owner of the Lazy House and Charlie Hemlock to bring Clara to Marney's attention?'

Samuel nodded.

'It then told me that Marney would send to the Nightshade the first magicker to be born for a generation.'

Samuel's shrug needled the Resident, but he pressed on.

'What if the avatar knew that offering you a bounty contract was the surest way to get you in the right place at the right time to see Fabian Moor return, but also knew that Marney would stop you killing Clara?'

Without even considering the exposition, Samuel shook his head. 'Van Bam, you're suggesting the avatar is a friend to us. I'm not ready to accept that.'

'No? If you ask me, the avatar had a mission to bring together what remained of the Relic Guild, and knew which events would need to occur for it to happen.'

The old bounty hunter stood his ground. 'What about Marney? Why didn't it warn her? Why did it allow Moor to take her?'

'If this avatar *is* being used as a portent, then it had no choice but to manipulate present events in a way that ensured they unfolded exactly as they had to so it could guide us to the future its master desires.'

'Then someone has a dangerous way of going about things,' Samuel said adamantly. 'You're talking about future knowledge, Van Bam.

That's the realm of the Thaumaturgists. For all we know, it's Fabian Moor who's controlling this thing, playing games with us.'

Van Bam's irritation finally boiled over, and he clenched his teeth. 'You were not so keen to distrust the avatar when it employed you to kill an innocent girl, Samuel!'

The older man reacted as if struck. Van Bam saw angry colours flare in his face, but before Samuel could reply the Resident took a step closer to him, ignoring the distant sound of Gideon's chuckles.

'What did the avatar offer you?' he demanded. 'I have to know, Samuel.'

The old bounty hunter's anger evaporated. His shades became regretful hues and he seemed to shrink, as though feeling the weight of his age.

He shifted his gaze back to the street below, and when he spoke, shame had returned to his voice.

'I've been thinking about Denton,' he said.

Van Bam balked at the swerve in topic. The statement was so unexpected that he couldn't prevent a laugh of surprise escaping his lips. 'Strange – I have been thinking of Denton myself.'

'We could really use his help right now, couldn't we?'

The unfamiliar hue of guilt now swirling in Samuel's body perturbed Van Bam. He said nothing as his old friend looked up at the sky and continued.

'When I joined the Relic Guild – before your arrival – Denton took me on my first trip to an Aelfirian House. The Aelfheim Archipelago – do you know of it?'

'I ... yes, though I never got the chance to visit it myself.'

'They have a sub-House there called Sunflower. It's a farming community.'

Van Bam nodded. 'So I have been told.'

'They keep livestock, you know – all kinds of different animals, running free and wild. There are greenhouses too, as big as the Nightshade, growing all manner of plants and food that we never see in Labrys Town anymore.'

Van Bam furrowed his brow. 'Samuel, perhaps you could tell me where this is leading?'

The old bounty hunter's voice became wistful. 'Over the years, I suppose I fell in love with the idea of returning to Sunflower. I still dream of it, sometimes – of being a farmer, keeping livestock, harvesting crops, walking among the trees in a forest.' He closed his eyes. '*Forests*, Van Bam! Can you remember those?'

Van Bam felt a sad sense of realisation. 'Am I to understand that the avatar offered you escape from the Labyrinth?'

Samuel's knuckles turned white as he gripped the guardrail tightly. 'The bounty was passage. Passage to any House of the Aelfir I chose. All I had to do was kill Clara and I'd be free. It didn't even occur to me to refuse.'

Inside Van Bam's head, he could feel Gideon relishing the moment.

'Samuel, you are not a naive man,' the Resident said, scorn entering his voice. 'Did you honestly believe the avatar could give you this reward? Such a bounty was a lie, a means to ensure your involvement—'

'I know that now,' Samuel snapped, and he glared. 'But for the first time in years I remembered what real hope felt like. It made me desperate.'

'I can sympathise, Samuel, but—'

'How long do you think I have left, Van Bam?' Although the anger remained in Samuel, his voice had softened somewhat. 'I'm old and tired, long forgotten by the people I served. I don't want to spend what time I have left slowly rotting away in a place where the sun barely shines. Do you?'

'We do not choose our life,' Van Bam retorted. 'There is only circumstance and duty. You know this, old friend.'

'Really?' Samuel swept an arm across the sky. 'Do you honestly believe the Timewatcher cares about what we do anymore? That the Thaumaturgists are still out there watching over us?'

'Yes, somewhere!' Van Bam said hotly. 'You and I are the last of a fading generation, Samuel. We have experienced every good and bad the worlds outside our realm have to offer. But ...'

He felt suddenly weary, as if the weight of his own years was pressing down on him. The weariness also crept into his voice. 'Think of Clara,' he said. 'That girl will never get the chance to see what we have seen.'

'Don't talk to me about Clara!' Samuel replied cruelly. 'Whatever information Marney has hidden in her head, you'd better get Hamir to extract it quickly, Van Bam. Clara won't remain a friend when she changes into the wolf. She has no training, no control over her magic. The chances are I'll have to put a bullet through her head. Forget Clara.'

'No.' Van Bam's tone was resolute, protective, and this seemed to amuse Gideon more than anything. 'Clara will have to become the wolf again, Samuel, you are right on that. But I will never believe she is a danger to us. Her emergence as a magicker is surely a sign that not everything has been forgotten in the Labyrinth.'

'Believe what you like,' Samuel said miserably. 'It makes no difference now, anyway.'

Van Bam accepted then that coming to the rooftop had been a mistake. There was no point in continuing this conversation.

'Clara and I have a job to do,' he said. 'We will be gone for a short time.'

Samuel did not respond. Van Bam turned away and walked to the hatchway in the roof. As he prepared to descend the ladder, Samuel's voice drifted back to him.

'Would you stop me?' he said as he continued to stare down onto the street. 'If Moor hadn't returned, if the bounty contract had been sound, would you stop me leaving the Labyrinth?'

Van Bam paused for a heartbeat. Without replying, he began climbing down into the apartment below, and Gideon's chuckles rattled in his head.

Oh, Samuel, the former Resident whispered. *I think you have your answer.*

CHAPTER FIFTEEN

NEW REGIME

It was generally believed that Hamir's emotions were so deadened that even an empath could not read him; that behind the inveterate shell of his genial manner he kept his true self hidden in a place where the machinations of a necromancer were preserved in dark dreams. Hamir felt in no way obligated to confirm or negate this supposition; though to claim he could feel no emotions whatsoever was not an entirely fair accusation. He was capable of feeling surprise, for example, if only on a mild level. And at that moment Hamir the necromancer most definitely felt mild surprise.

Surrounded by the purple, magical mists swirling within the glass confinement chamber, Hamir stared down at his patient. Charlie Hemlock lay naked upon a gurney. The skin of his chest had been sliced open, peeled back and clamped; his ribcage had been snapped and pulled away to expose the dark, gaping hole of his chest cavity. Hamir's brow was furrowed and his lips pursed as he gazed into the hole. The interior of the human body was well known to the necromancer, and things appeared generally as they should. However, Charlie Hemlock's heart was missing. In its place was a small terracotta jar, around the same size and shape as those used for storing preserves.

'Interesting,' Hamir muttered.

He turned his attention to the small metal trolley-table beside him. Upon the table lay bloodied surgical tools and pieces of ribcage. Hamir selected a long and sharp scalpel, and then turned to Hemlock again.

The terracotta jar appeared to be in symbiosis with his body, connected almost as a heart should have been. There were veins and arteries attached to it; and, although blackened and seemingly diseased, they obviously aided the transportation of blood somehow. In a rare moment of indecision, Hamir wondered if he could cut the jar free without disturbing the wax seal around its lid.

That slight sense of surprise deepened somewhat when Hamir noticed Charlie Hemlock's eyes were open and staring at him. He took a step back as Hemlock pushed his hands into his own chest cavity and began tugging at the terracotta heart. Before Hamir could react, he had pulled the jar free with a wet, slurping sound, and begun clawing at the seal.

Hamir's indecision vanished. He dropped the scalpel, turned, quickly stepped from the containment chamber into the isolation room beyond, and closed the door firmly behind him.

With thick, reinforced glass now separating him from his patient, Hamir watched as Charlie Hemlock made short work of the wax seal and removed the lid. The sound of a scream was muffled by the glass, and then a sandstorm rushed from the jar and filled the chamber.

It swirled and whipped violently, rattling against the glass like wind-blown rain. Not only did the storm strip the flesh from Hemlock's bones and absorb his blood, it also began devouring the purple mist that the Nightshade itself had created as defence against hostile magic.

'Curious,' Hamir remarked.

As the sandstorm continued to rage, the first cracks appeared in the containment chamber. With tight creaking and sharp snaps, they spread through the glass like jagged streaks of slow lightning. Hamir retreated further. He left the isolation room for the safety of the corridor outside. He sealed the door and activated the dark observation window on the wall. He was just in time to witness the containment chamber shattering into a thousand shards.

The sandstorm had coalesced to form a woman. Naked and pale-skinned, she stood with her back to Hamir, gently swaying on her feet, clearly orienting herself after the stresses of reanimation. After a moment, she inspected the fleshless skeleton of Charlie Hemlock on the gurney. She raised a fist, and then smashed it down to reduce the skull to dust. Picking through the remains, she plucked something out, and only then did she turn to face the necromancer through the window. She smiled at him triumphantly.

Hamir recognised her immediately: she was the Genii Hagi Tabet.

'Ingenious,' he whispered.

The Genii's hair grew in stubbly tufts. Her eyes had the vacant, distant lack of focus that Hamir had so often seen in the insane. She stepped closer to the observation window, untroubled by the broken glass that cut at her bare feet. She held between a thumb and forefinger a small egg-shaped object with a leathery shell of green-streaked brown. She smiled for Hamir one more time before pushing the egg into her mouth. Opening her arms wide, as though proud to expose her withered nakedness to the necromancer, she strained as she swallowed the egg whole.

Hagi Tabet's scream was silent in the corridor as she fell to her hands and knees.

The tips of tentacles broke through her pallid skin. A cross between vines and snakes, they slithered out of her back, twenty of them at least, coiling and writhing, whipping at the air. Hamir couldn't be sure if Tabet was in agony or rapture as she continued to scream silently. Her head was thrown back, her mouth opened wide, like a beast barking at the sky as her blood puddled on the floor beneath her.

The tentacles continued to grow as not even the confines of the isolation room could halt their progress. Splitting maze-patterned stone, they pierced the walls, the floor and ceiling, and burrowed deep into the Nightshade itself. The Genii was lifted from the floor, raised by the tentacles until she was suspended at the centre of the room like a spider sitting in its leathery web. Her head hung slack. Blood ran down her legs and dripped from the ends of her toes.

Around Hamir, the atmosphere shifted. The light darkened subtly. A static charge filled the air.

The Nightshade had changed..

'Troubling,' he mused.

Pausing for only a moment, the necromancer turned from the observation window and strode off down the corridor towards his laboratory.

The afternoon sun hung high, burning bright yellow through the vaguest wisps of white clouds, and seeming to banish every shadow on the streets. Voices buzzed beneath its heat as denizens milled through the central district. Trams rumbled by on their clean, silver tracks, and the thaumaturgic energy that drove them snapped along power lines with purple sparks. The air was laced with the smell of food cooking and freshly made coffee from eateries and street-side vendors. The scent of hot stone was dry and dusty.

Life in Labrys Town continued exactly as it always had; yet as Clara walked beside Van Bam through the heat of the afternoon she felt detached, distant from the people all around her.

The denizens seemed so normal, going about their mundane tasks, their day-to-day routines. Over the course of a single day, Clara's perception of the world had altered. There was nothing routine in what she saw. She pitied these people for the secrets that were being kept from them, yet envied them for their blissful ignorance. Old and young, not one of these denizens was aware of the shadow that had fallen across their town. Clara barely understood it herself.

She stopped outside the Central District Bank to watch a young boy shining shoes beside a food vendor's cart. He relished his work, labouring hard to earn his money, his expression entirely too serious for one so young. Clara had a sudden, horrifying vision of this innocent child as a slavering monster like those she had witnessed at the asylum.

With icy needles pricking her spine, she looked again at the denizens around her. Suddenly dizzied by their comings and goings, she was assailed by a burst of panic. Each of these denizens represented nothing more than fresh blood to the Genii. A single bite could start a virus that would destroy Labrys Town's entire population. And there were two of them now—

'Clara?'

She looked at Van Bam with a start – only it wasn't really him she saw.

The Resident had used his illusionist magic to disguise them both, and they now appeared as a middle-aged man and woman. There were no metal plates covering Van Bam's eyes; they were normal looking and soft hazel. His skin was no longer deep brown but an olive colour. His usually strong facial features were gaunt, drawn, and his smooth shaven head was now covered in short black hair etched with grey. The green glass cane appeared as a plain wooden walking stick.

'You seem distracted,' he said.

Clara looked back at the shoeshine boy, who smiled hopefully. 'Shine your shoes, missus?' he called.

Clara shook her head, her panic now a dull sadness.

'I'm fine,' she told Van Bam. 'Let's go.'

They continued on down the main street, just an ordinary couple out walking among fellow denizens on a day like any other in Labrys Town.

Van Bam still hadn't told her where they were going, or what they were about to do; and Clara hadn't asked. She was content for the time being simply to follow and not think.

She had caught her own image a few times, reflected in shop windows. It had been like looking at a vision of the future. She recognised herself – she still had the same gawky features and awkward body and limbs – but her hair was longer, devoid of red dye, and her face was older and plumper, sagging slightly. Under Van Bam's illusion, she might have been taken for her own mother.

At the end of the main street they came to a long and high wall with a single wide archway cut into it. On either side stood almost identical statues – over ten feet tall and carved from the same dark stone as the wall. Finely sculptured thick robes flowed from their broad masculine frames. Their heads were spherical, like the receptor helmets of the street patrols, and for faces each bore a single ovular eye, etched in white. The statues differed only in the symbols in their stone hands. Where one held an anvil, the other held a set of scales. Van Bam led Clara past the statues and through the archway, where they entered the great plaza known as Watchers' Gallery.

As in the streets, a high number of denizens were present, and Clara let the sounds of their lives wash over her. Some sat on the edge of the Gallery at tables outside an eatery, drinking and eating and laughing; others sat on benches beside colourful flowerbeds, chatting. Some stood clutching papers and dossiers, discussing and arguing over business with colleagues, their expressions serious. So wrapped up in their routines, so content with what they had, these denizens were interested only in what the day had brought them.

The high wall enclosed Watchers' Gallery in a circle. There were two ways in or out: one was the way Clara and Van Bam had come; the other was on the opposite side of the plaza, and that way led to the street that marked the beginning of Resident Approach, which ran in a straight line all the way to the Nightshade. Most of the buildings belonged to the various houses of the merchant guilds – though there was the usual presence of a Chapel of the Timewatcher, and a tavern called The Merchant's Ore, where the central district's businessmen and women met for a drink at the end of a hard day – but one building stood out from the others, and Clara viewed it with an ominous feeling.

The building stood at the plaza's centre. It was surrounded by a ring of grass, which was dissected into quarters by four narrow paths. Like the Nightshade, the building was an impressive size and a perfect cube in shape – though still much smaller than the Resident's home – and, unlike the Nightshade, its severity was mitigated by windows. Large wooden doors provided an entrance though which an unending stream of people entered and exited. This building was the heart of the law; it was the police headquarters, and its location not only marked the centre of Watchers' Gallery, but also the exact centre of Labrys Town.

With a worried frown, Clara followed Van Bam towards the police building.

She had been to Watchers' Gallery on a few occasions in the past, with her friend Willow, to see how the business class of Labrys Town lived. She had found the attitudes of the merchant guild types over-opinionated and judgemental. Now, Clara felt hemmed in, as if – even with her altered appearance – her every step was being scrutinised by the people around her, bound by their ignorance as they were.

She stuck close to Van Bam as he stopped at the beginning of a path that led across to the entrance of the police headquarters. He didn't speak as he faced the building.

Most people exiting or entering ignored the pathways and took short cuts directly over the grass, but a group of five denizens that emerged from the wooden doors headed directly towards the magickers. Clara stepped aside to let them pass, and then shied from two patrolmen who appeared from behind her and headed down the path to their place of work. But Van Bam stood his ground, unfazed by the slight objections of those who had to walk around him.

'What are we doing here?' she whispered.

'Secrets, Clara,' Van Bam replied. 'The Labyrinth has many of them. Come.'

He set off down the path and Clara followed him into the building, where they were met by a wall of sound.

The reception area was a hive of activity. A cluster of denizens had gathered around the reception desk, arguing and shouting and pushing one another. More denizens sat in chairs, clearly agitated, frustrated at being made to wait so long to be seen. A group of three men and two women were jabbing fingers angrily at each other. Even though Clara had never set foot in the police headquarters before, it was evident the level of activity was unusually high. Something was wrong.

'What's going on?' she asked Van Bam. 'Everybody's so angry.'

Without replying, the Resident set off across the reception floor. Clara kept pace with him.

The denizens paid no notice to the middle-aged couple that walked through them and headed for the stairs. As they ascended, Clara saw a fight break out amongst the three men and two women. Several police officers came charging down from the upper level, jostling Clara in their hurry to reach the disturbance. They drew their batons and started bringing the crowd to order.

'This way, Clara,' Van Bam said.

The disorder continued on the first floor of the police headquarters. In an open-plan office a host of police administrators sat at desks, questioning denizens and taking statements. Many of the denizens seemed distraught, agitated. The tumult of voices clashed together, and even Clara's heightened hearing could not decipher what the source of this agitation was. Still, no one noticed the magickers as they climbed another flight of stairs which led to the top floor.

There, the atmosphere was calmer. On either side of a long corridor groups of Police Watchers lay on reclining chairs in glass observation rooms. Their heads and faces were concealed within black, bowl-like receptor helmets. Clara knew that these Watchers were sifting through information received from the eyes on the streets of Labrys Town, and that they then transmitted orders to the street patrols.

Clara paused at a closed office door to read a plaque that said CAPTAIN JETER. With a shudder, she remembered her interrogation by the police captain and hurried after Van Bam, praying that the door didn't open.

The corridor came to a dead end, but to the right was a recess where a small square section of the wall was decorated with a pattern of tiny mazes, just like the walls at the Nightshade. Van Bam checked the corridor was clear, and then pressed his palm against one of the tiny mazes. The pattern glowed briefly beneath his hand, and was followed by a click. A door-shaped section of the wall slid to one side, revealing an elevator. Van Bam and Clara stepped in. As the door slid closed Van Bam halted his illusionist magic, and he and Clara reverted to their normal appearances.

Clara gave a weak smile as the elevator began to descend. 'Secrets, eh?'

'Clara,' said Van Bam, facing down at the floor, 'before the Timewatcher decreed the Labyrinth a forbidden zone, contacting the Thaumaturgists was relatively easy for the Resident.' He turned his metal eyes to her. 'But the Thaumaturgists disappeared long before you were born, yes?'

Clara nodded acknowledgement, and Van Bam continued.

'There is ... an emergency safeguard, I suppose you would call it, that was incorporated into the Labyrinth's design. Very few people know of this safeguard – not even every member of the Relic Guild was made aware of it – but, at least at one time, it formed a line of communication between us and certain guardians outside our realm.'

The elevator came to a stop and opened onto a narrow and gloomy corridor that must have run beneath the police headquarters. It was only wide enough to walk single file, and Clara once again followed the Resident. A low prickling of hope fluttered in her stomach.

'Wait,' she said. 'You know how to contact the Thaumaturgists?'

'No, I do not,' Van Bam replied. 'Understand, Clara, this emergency safeguard was designed for the unlikely event that the Resident and the agents of the Relic Guild were in some way incapacitated, and no longer able to protect the denizens. Should such an emergency occur, it would fall to certain individuals – the captain of the police force, for example – to send a distress signal to those who might be able to help.

'It is my prayer, Clara, that sending a distress signal now will at least alert someone out there who still knows how to reach the Thaumaturgists.'

Clara's sense of hope became a little brighter. 'So that's it? You flick a switch and we're saved?'

Her hope all but vanished as Van Bam stopped in front of her and looked back with a miserable expression.

He said, 'If Samuel were here, he would tell you my plan is foolhardy, an act of desperation that has no chance of success. He is adamant in his belief that no one is out there listening anymore.' He sighed. 'I cannot tell you he is wrong, Clara. But we will try. The distress signal takes two people to activate.'

He walked on.

The corridor turned to the left and ended at another wall decorated with tiny maze patterns. Van Bam pressed his hand to the patch of mazes. Another hidden door appeared, and the Resident led Clara into a chamber beyond. The door closed and disappeared behind them.

The air felt oppressive, unnaturally silent. The chamber was sparse and bland, and could easily have been a room in the Nightshade itself. It was lit by a ceiling prism, and that familiar maze pattern was repeated on each cream coloured wall. The only object of note was a slim pedestal that rose from the centre of the floor. Atop the pedestal was a clear glass sphere which contained wispy lights.

Clara moved forwards for a closer look. There was thick fluid inside the sphere, not quite milky like an eye, but alive with sparks and streaks as if a storm cloud had been charged with purple lightning. It was beautiful, and the effect was almost hypnotic. Clara noticed that on opposing sides of the sphere the glass was indented with two hand shapes. It was obvious to her that she and Van Bam were required to press their hands into these indents to activate the distress signal.

The idea of feeling the scintillating orb against her skin was suddenly so pleasing to Clara it was as if she had never wished to do anything else. Could everybody's troubles be over with a single touch?

Dazzled by the purple sparks, she reached out a hand—

'Do not touch it!' Van Bam snapped.

Clara withdrew her hand sharply.

The Resident was facing the wall through which they had entered. 'This is wrong,' he said. 'Someone else has been here, and recently.'

Clara looked around the sparse room with a frown. 'How can you tell?'

The light from the ceiling prism glared back from Van Bam's metal eyes as he turned to her and used his green cane to point at the glass sphere. 'There is a barrier of magic surrounding that device, and it should not be there.'

'What?' Clara took a step away.

'I can see it,' Van Bam said. 'One touch would mean death. Someone knew we planned to activate the distress signal, Clara, and they have used magic to stop us.'

Clara felt a sudden, chilled pang. In the stillness of the chamber, her heightened senses became so alert they were almost painful.

'Strange,' Van Bam said. 'There is only one place in this town from where the Labyrinth's magic could be used in this way.' He cocked his head to one side. After a second or two, his face fell. 'I . . . I can no longer hear Gideon's voice. I cannot feel the Nightshade—'

There was a sudden click. The outline of a door appeared on the wall. Clara looked at Van Bam for directions, but he gave none. The Resident whispered an unintelligible word and tapped his cane against the floor. There was a brief glow of soft green light, and then Van Bam disappeared as if he had blinked out of existence.

'No,' Clara implored.

Suddenly alone, she backed away as the door swung inwards and four police officers burst into the chamber, rifles aimed, power stones primed and glowing. Captain Jeter followed them, a sneer on his face and a pistol in his hand. The dark lenses of his spectacles glared at Clara with bitter satisfaction.

The magic of the Nightshade was as old as it was mysterious. Ever had it projected beings into existence, strange spectres that were not truly real. They were phantoms which represented some inner aspect of whoever held the position of Resident. They were servants who conducted those mundane chores that were clearly beneath Hamir's duties as chief aide.

Van Bam's servants had always been strange looking creatures – angelic, almost – but they carried the imperfection of eyeless faces. Knowing Van Bam as well as he did, Hamir found these phantoms a good representation of the Resident. Over the past forty years he had grown quite accustomed to their presence. However, now that the Genii had infiltrated the Nightshade, Van Bam's servants had disappeared, each and every one of them, as if even the smallest aspect of the Resident had been purged from the very stones of his home.

And now the new Resident's servants had begun to appear.

As Hamir tried to reach his laboratory, they dogged his path through the Nightshade's corridors. Their limbs were stick thin, and their bodies were withered. Puckered skin hung from them in folds, raw and pink. Their long necks lacked the strength to hold their spherical heads aloft properly. Their features seemed smeared across their faces, and their eyes were protruding, watery pink orbs that never blinked. They were gross representations of Hagi Tabet, who hung upon leathery tentacles back in the isolation room.

Hamir found himself intrigued. Although the servants of the Residents were never truly real, they were solid. Could they be killed? Hamir didn't know the answer because he had never had cause to find out before. The servants had been peaceful, docile creatures, but these new phantoms were far from that. It seemed that Tabet, in her quest to become the new Resident, had decided that Hamir's services as chief aide were no longer required. For her servants were certainly trying to kill him.

Hamir disliked doing two things at once. He preferred an orderly approach, where one task was dealt with at a time; but Tabet's aspects were sorely inconveniencing him. The necromancer needed to reach his laboratory to find some way of warning Van Bam and the other agents of the Relic Guild. Each corridor he turned into, however, held a new phantom waiting to pounce – though 'pounce' was perhaps too flattering a word for these creatures.

The aspects shambled with slow and dulled movements, heads lolloping on long necks. Mostly, Hamir found them easy to dodge and leave behind. Their hands were large, and their fat fingers were slow when they reached for the necromancer when he passed. But the merest touch from these slow fingers was like the hardest punch from the toughest brawler of the Anger Pitt. Hamir had only been struck once, and once was enough; his ribs were bruised and his face swollen from where the blow had sent him crashing against the maze-covered wall. It would not happen again.

As he hurried on, and dodged yet another phantom, a voice called to him.

'Hamir?' Hagi Tabet's tone was light, almost pleasant. Her voice came from the very stone of the Nightshade, from the walls and ceiling and floor. 'Where do you think you can run to?'

Staying silent, Hamir ignored the voice and continued on. But the new Resident was not to be deterred from her goading.

'I can see everything, Hamir,' her voice sighed. 'There is nowhere you can hide. Come back. Some friends of mine are on their way, and they so wish to see you again.'

Hamir turned into the corridor that led to his laboratory. Predictably, another of Tabet's aspects waited for him.

Enough was enough, the necromancer decided, and he took a scalpel from his pocket.

Side-stepping the grotesque phantom's lumbering reach, Hamir slashed the scalpel across its blubbery, pink throat as he skipped past. The phantom gave no cry of pain, spilled no blood, and fell to the floor where it faded out of existence.

'Hmm,' said Hamir.

'Now that was just rude,' Tabet whispered.

She chuckled with a curious hissing sound as Hamir continued on to the end of the corridor.

He placed his hand on the wall, feeling a mild sense of relief as the outline of his laboratory door appeared. At least the Nightshade still acknowledged his presence to a certain degree. But when he opened the door, he was not greeted by the usual gloom of his private chamber; a bright light shone from within, casting the corridor and the necromancer in a deep blue glow.

'Ah,' Hamir said with something close to a smile on his face. 'The mysterious avatar, I presume. I was wondering when you would visit me,' and he stepped into his laboratory, closing the door behind him.

Hagi Tabet screamed his name.

CHAPTER SIXTEEN

SECRET PLACES

All was quiet in Old Man Sam's hideout. Unlike most other agents of the Relic Guild, he had never taken rooms at the Nightshade. He preferred his own space, away from the utter lack of privacy offered at the Resident's home. Although he wasn't the first agent to live in his hideout, he had to wonder if he would be the last.

The apartment was situated in one of the few residential buildings in the central district. The front door had been bricked up years ago; and in the corridor outside, standing against the wall where the door used to be, was a janitor's locker. The sole entrance to the apartment was the hatchway in the ceiling – though it was not the only point of exit – which was only accessible from the fire escape that led to the roof. From the outside, to the unknowing eye, the hatchway appeared to be an air vent.

It was a peaceful building in which to live. The other tenants were mostly businessmen and women who liked to live close to their work-places. None of them appreciated that they had a secret neighbour; that they lived next door to the fabled hideout of Old Man Sam. So many of Samuel's rivals had tried to find this place – younger bounty hunters out with a point to prove – but not one of them had ever found success, and that was probably why they were still alive.

Samuel sat at a table in the bedroom – though there had never been a bed in the room, and he had always slept on the sofa in the lounge – and cleaned his guns. Pinned to the walls around him were a map of Labrys Town, old bounty notices, and handwritten notes of general information and routines concerning old marks, all of whom were long dead.

He had tried to sleep, but his thoughts refused to slow down or acknowledge the needs of his ageing body. Samuel's weapons were already in perfect working condition, but he conducted the cleaning process anyway, as a means to alleviate his growing restlessness. Until Van Bam and Clara returned from the police headquarters there wasn't much to do except wait.

With a sigh, Samuel laid his rifle upon the table, and then began checking his revolver.

He knew what Van Bam was going to attempt at the police station, and he was sure it would prove to be a waste of effort. There had been a time when the distress signal would have travelled far from the Labyrinth, through the never-ending mists of the Nothing of Far and Deep, all the way to the Tower of the Skywatcher. And there it would have alerted Lady Amilee, perhaps the greatest guardian the Labyrinth had ever known. But Lady Amilee, along with all her fellow Thaumaturgists, was long gone now. Even if the distress signal could still be activated, the chances were it would be lost in the Nothing of Far and Deep, unheard by anyone for eternity.

Placing his revolver down, he reached for a small wooden chest and opened it. Inside were stored empty magazines and ammunition – both magical and standard – along with a few spare power stones charged with ambient thaumaturgy absorbed from the air and ready for use. Samuel loaded his newly-cleaned revolver with eight regular metal slugs, and then placed some spare – fifteen or more rounds – into a pouch on his utility belt. He had seven ice-bullets left, which he also stored in the belt. His rifle was already fully loaded with his last four fire-bullets, and he loaded a spare magazine with four thumb-sized, regular slugs.

Over the years, he had always used his magical ammunition sparingly. But now, he reasoned, he could ask Hamir to replenish his dwindling stock. The thought gave him little comfort.

Clicking the last bullet into the magazine, Samuel's work was done. He sat back and rubbed his face.

Could he really think Van Bam a fool for attempting to activate the distress signal? Options were growing thin, the Relic Guild was in deep trouble, and the Timewatcher only knew how well Samuel understood that desperation could motivate actions. He had been blinded by the empty promise of a blue ghost. He had willed himself to believe the avatar, allowed its lies to manipulate him; and just at the point when he had acknowledged how desperately he needed some kind of hope, Van Bam had helped him to realise that he had never believed the avatar at all, and the shame he felt cut deep.

No, the Resident was not a fool, and Samuel hoped – prayed – that he himself was wrong, and that Van Bam would find success at the police headquarters.

A noise from the lounge disturbed his thoughts.

A brief hum was followed by a hissing, crackling sound.

In a second, Samuel was out of his chair and walking from the bedroom. The sound grew louder. It emanated from an innocuous looking cupboard fixed to the small space of wall between the bathroom and bedroom. Samuel opened its doors.

Inside the cupboard was an eye, like those on the streets of Labrys Town. It was covered in a thick layer of grime. Samuel wiped the grime away, and saw the milky fluid inside the hemisphere was agitated, as though it had been brought to the boil. Many years had passed since he had used this device; in the past, it had formed his direct line of communication to the Nightshade. He had built the cupboard around it to prevent Gideon from spying on him.

The eye buzzed and crackled with a sound like a distorted voice. One word came through, clear and intelligible: '*Samuel*'. It was the familiar voice of the necromancer.

'Hamir,' Samuel said. 'Can you hear me?'

When Hamir spoke, his words were gurgled and there were gaps in his sentences. '*Is ... Bam ... to speak ...*'

'Van Bam's at the police headquarters.' The necromancer's reply was nothing more than distorted static. 'Say again, Hamir.'

' *... Genii ... Nightshade. They know ... your hideout is ... you ... underground—*'

With a click, the eye device fell silent, and Samuel was dismayed to see the milky fluid inside become tinged with a shade of pink as it continued to boil. He slammed the cupboard doors shut and stepped back from it.

In that moment, time paused, and sharp needles speared through Samuel's veins as his prescient awareness awoke.

The apartment became Samuel's web and he the spider waiting for the feel of vibrations upon silky threads. He was starkly aware of every object around him; his hearing was acutely sensitive to all sound.

A scratch from above.

Someone was on the roof, at the hatchway.

It wasn't locked.

Quicker than he could think, Samuel drew his knife from the sheath strapped to his side. Steered by his magic, he moved to stand with his back to the wall below the ceiling hatch, the ladder before him. But his instincts told him not to climb up and lock the hatchway.

It was time to kill.

After a moment, the hatchway opened – just a crack at first, and then wider.

A hand holding a snub-nosed pistol descended into the apartment, followed by a man's shaven head. Leaning down from the ladder, and with his back to Samuel, the man scanned the apartment with his weapon. Samuel stepped forward, slapped a hand over the intruder's face and pulled his head back. In one smooth action, the old bounty hunter slit his throat.

The man gave a gurgled scream as Samuel pulled his body down onto the apartment floor, hard, and the hatchway slammed shut above him. Samuel kicked the snub-nosed pistol away and left the man to bleed and choke and writhe while he climbed the ladder, slid the bolt to lock the hatch, and jumped back down.

The dying man's eyes were wide with panic and he clawed with weak fingers as Samuel searched his clothes and found a letter. He unfolded it and read:

WANTED
BY ORDER OF THE RESIDENT

The bounty hunter known as Old Man Sam
is hereby proclaimed a demon-worshipper
and enemy of the Labyrinth. Wanted dead.
Proof of kill required.
No reward for live capture.

Samuel gritted his teeth as he screwed up the notice and let it drop onto the body of the dead bounty hunter. It bounced off his chest and settled in the blood that soaked the carpet beneath him.

Samuel strode into the bedroom, grabbed his rifle and revolver from the table and holstered them. Back in the living area, as he buckled up his utility belt, his prescient awareness flared, but more gently this time. More noise was coming from the roof. Someone was trying to open the hatchway again.

It was time to run.

Samuel bolted into the bathroom and locked the door behind him. As he did so, there was a dull thud from out in the lounge. The sound was followed by shattering glass, and Samuel knew that more bounty hunters had entered the apartment through the window. Without thinking, he dived to the hard, cold floor, just before a hail of bullets ripped through the bathroom door, cracking wall tiles, chipping the sink, and smashing the toilet cistern. A rush of cold water poured down onto Samuel's prone body.

It was impossible to count how many guns had spat their bullets at him … but his prescient awareness told Samuel there were four more assailants out there trying to kill him. He didn't hang around for the visual evidence.

Samuel dragged himself across the wet floor to the shower cubical. With a grunt, he hefted up the porcelain shower tray to expose a water-stained and slimy metal chute that was round enough to fit a full-grown man. A foul stench rose from the opening.

As a second hail of bullets smashed tiles around him, he threw the shower tray to one side. Without further pause, he slid headfirst down into the darkness of the foul smelling chute.

She was the wolf.

She howled and struggled, bit and clawed, with all her might, but she could not escape the challenger's embrace. Blinded by blue light, dizzied by the whirlwind that swept her up and spirited her away, she could no longer smell her forest, and the baying of her family faded to lonely wind.

When the light dulled, and all motion stopped, she found herself in a place of stone. A distant voice, long forgotten now, sang from the back of her mind. It told her that the huge cube of a building beside her was called the Nightshade, and the stone archway in the forecourt was a portal.

The challenger stood within the archway. No longer in the form of a wolf, it appeared now with an altogether different shape. It was surrounded by an aura of sky blue that licked out with wavering tendrils of light like strips of cloth drifting in water. At its core, the blueness deepened to the colour of twilight, and held a vaguely human shape. Its void-like eyes leaked tears of vaporous black.

Good to see you again, *its soft voice said in her mind.*

She growled in reply.

There is a long way to go from here, Clara, *it continued.* A long, long way.

She wanted to attack it, to force it to return her to her forest and her family. But the truth was, she felt right here, in this place of stone, as though she belonged, and the fight had all but left her – because, she realised, there was no fight to win.

I'd like to show you something, *the blue ghost said.* Something you must never forget.

She sat on the cold cobbles, attentive. She wanted to ask the challenger who it was, but the memory of speech was just beyond her grasp.

If I ask you to remember three things, Clara, will you do that for me?

She showed willing by bowing her head.

With tendrils of blue, wavering light licking at the stone archway surrounding it, the challenger said, The first is this portal. The second is the Resident. The third is the necromancer. The portal, the Resident, the necromancer – understand?

She did, and she knew that pleased the challenger. Something about its ghostly aura was giving her an enormous sense of inner peace.

These three things are connected, Clara. The Resident and the necromancer don't realise it, but I'm going to show you how, and you must not forget. When the time is right, it will be very important.

The challenger disappeared, its blue radiance nothing more than an afterglow in her eyes. She whined, immediately yearning for the light, but her senses became alert as a sheet of glassy darkness appeared within the stone archway.

Like thick water, it rippled. A low drone filled the air as it began swirling, faster and faster, until she felt a vacuum tugging at her silver pelt. She braced herself against the forecourt floor, but it was in vain. Sharp nails scraped over cobbles as the swirling darkness pulled her forward. She growled and barked, fearful and angry, but the voice of the challenger soothed her concerns.

Don't be frightened, Clara, *it said from somewhere distant.* You must remember.

She howled as the portal sucked her into its glassy whirlpool.

She was the wolf . . .

. . . Icy water splashed her face, and she gasped awake. Spluttering, disorientated, she looked up through bleary eyes and saw Captain Jeter standing over her with an empty cup in his hands and two patrolmen in dark receptor helmets standing either side of him. He dropped the cup and made fists as if ready and eager to strike her again.

Clara could feel swelling under her right eye, taste blood in her mouth. Her wrists and ankles were secured with heavy manacles, connected to the cell floor by a thick chain. Feeling sick and unsteady, she met the police captain's stare as evenly as she could.

'Let's try this again,' Jeter growled. 'Where is he?'

Clara made no reply. She wasn't frightened; she was angry. The wolf was stirring inside her, and she welcomed the feeling. It gave her courage.

Jeter pushed his dark glasses further up his nose. He had removed the jacket of his uniform, and on his white shirt were spots of Clara's blood.

'I know you brought Van Bam with you,' he said. 'Where is he now?'

Clara shrugged, and the chains rattled.

'Did he abandon you?' Jeter whispered cruelly. 'Is that it?'

'You have no idea of the trouble you're in, Jeter.'

A sneer came to his angular face.

'You should let me go,' she continued.

Jeter gave a lopsided smile and snorted. 'What I should have done was recognise you for what you are the first time I arrested you. I should've known that your aim was to get to the Nightshade and possess the Resident. I should never have let you go. But I won't make the same mistake twice.'

'You're an idiot.'

Jeter slapped her face.

Clara relished the sting.

The patrolmen flanking the police captain aimed short rifles at their captive. The violet glow of power stones set behind the barrels of the rifles reflected off the black glass of their receptor helmets. They hadn't spoken once during the interrogation and they gave off no scent. But their body language spoke volumes.

Earlier, when they had entered the grey security cell, they had stuck so close to their captain it suggested they were afraid to be in the room with Clara. They had done nothing but watch as Jeter beat her, and the cowardice of them all disgusted her.

'You've run out of options, demon-lover,' Jeter said. He tapped a square object in his breast pocket. Clara's tablets rattled inside her medicine tin. 'Your magic won't work on me.'

She looked down at her clenched fists, at her chains. Was she really so expendable? Would Van Bam really abandon her so easily, so quickly?

The whole situation seemed to have been turned upside down. Van Bam was the Resident, and Jeter had no choice but to remain subservient to him. But the police captain's belief that Clara had somehow possessed Van Bam and converted him to demon-worship, was gripping the man almost to the point of madness. What could have persuaded him of this?

'You think one of your followers will rescue you?' Jeter said. 'That Van Bam will return? Or are you hoping that Old Man Sam will storm the building to save you?'

Clara looked up sharply at Jeter, and he shook his head as if pitying her.

'I think you've outlived your usefulness, Miss Clara. As for Old Man Sam – well, I should think by now he's quite dead.'

Clara looked down at her hands again. She could feel Marney's presence in her head, but wasn't surprised that it offered no advice. Clara opened and closed her fingers. She felt so strong, but frustrated by the chains. If she could only get free … she wouldn't bother with her medicine.

'Look at me,' Jeter said.

When Clara didn't look up, the police captain grabbed her under the chin and forced her head back. His fingers dug into her skin painfully.

'Your plan to bring the Retrospective to Labrys Town will not succeed. So I ask you again – where is Van Bam, *whore*?'

Clara spat in his face.

To her surprise, Jeter didn't react with violence. Instead, he stepped back, took a handkerchief from his pocket, and calmly wiped the blood and spittle from his face and glasses. The two patrolmen, almost identical in their appearance, remained still, holding their rifles with cold, unwavering aims.

Jeter said, 'Your attempt to spread disease did not work at the asylum, and it won't work anywhere else.' He dropped the soiled handkerchief to the floor. 'You will never bring down the boundary wall and unleash the Retrospective. We have stopped you, demon-lover. You have failed.'

Clara laughed then, a dry, huffing sound that was full of scorn for this absurd change in events.

Jeter frowned at her. 'Feigning insanity won't save you.' His voice was low, loaded with menace. 'If it was up to me, I'd simply give you to the Retrospective, and then we'd see how far your love of demons gets you.' His teeth clenched as Clara's laughing deepened. 'But, unfortunately your fate isn't up to me. That's to be decided by the new Resident.'

Clara's laughing stopped abruptly. She looked at the two patrolmen, and then back at their captain. Anxiety stirred her blood as Jeter's strange pronouncements made less and less sense to her. 'The new Resident?'

Jeter raised a supercilious eyebrow, his smile triumphant. 'There's fear in your eyes, and rightly so. Hagi Tabet is stronger than that blind fool Van Bam, and she will ensure your end is as bad as it gets.'

'Jeter …' Clara's thoughts were suddenly dominated by the image of a terracotta jar clutched in the hands of a skeleton. 'What are you talking about? Who's Hagi Tabet?'

To Clara's surprise, it was the patrolman standing to Jeter's right who answered. 'It is no use, Clara,' he said, his voice low, clear, and strangely unmuffled by the receptor helmet. 'He will not listen to anything you say.'

Jeter looked at the patrolman with a frown, but then turned sharply to his left as there was an audible *pop* and the other patrolman turned to fine green smoke that swirled and faded and disappeared entirely.

Mouth hanging slack, Jeter turned back to his right. As he did so, the remaining patrolman rammed the butt of his rifle into his face. There was a light chime and a soft flash of green as the police captain fell to the floor. His nose was bloodied, his glasses broken in half, and he lay still and unconscious.

With no small amount of surprise, Clara watched as the patrolman's image shimmered. The heavy, thick uniform became loose fitting clothing made from a fine material so dark it was like the night sky; the black glass of the receptor helmet shrank and moulded into a smoothly-shaven head of dark brown skin and a strong face with metal plates covering the eyes. Lastly, the rifle morphed to a cane of green glass.

Clara cocked her head to one side. 'You know, for a minute there, I really thought you'd left me behind.'

'I am sorry, Clara,' Van Bam said. He found a key about Jeter's person and used it to unlock Clara's manacles. He reached out to her face and inspected the swelling under her eye. 'Are you all right?'

Clara nodded, and Van Bam helped her to her feet. His metallic eyes scrutinised her face. He seemed troubled by what he saw there.

'It is time to leave,' he said. He retrieved the small, dented tin from Jeter's shirt pocket and passed it to her. 'But perhaps you should take your medicine first.'

'Believe me, Clara,' Van Bam whispered, 'I had no wish to witness your mistreatment.'

His apology sounded hollow to Clara.

The security cells were situated in the lower levels of the police head-quarters. Taking Clara by the hand Van Bam led her up two flights of stairs, along a corridor, through a security door and into reception.

In spite of the high number of angry denizens and police officers congregated, they passed unnoticed as Van Bam had rendered them both invisible.

'I needed time to find out what could have provoked Jeter to act so incongruously,' Van Bam continued as they headed for the exit.

'He said we have a new Resident,' Clara replied.

'Indeed, Clara. I have been unable to contact Hamir. It would seem the Genii have infiltrated the Nightshade.'

'You told me that wasn't possible.'

'Obviously I was wrong.' His tone was frustrated, laced with confusion. 'This Hagi Tabet now controls every aspect of Labrys Town, including the police force. When Captain Jeter regains consciousness, I have no doubt he will deploy every officer at his disposal to hunt us down. Fabian Moor has made us the enemy.'

A denizen, complaining loudly that he had been made to wait in reception far too long, stepped in front of Clara, gesticulating wildly. With quick feet, she dodged around him, but had to fight a sudden urge to punch him in the back of the head. Taking her medicine had done little to check her anger, and she gritted her teeth as Van Bam led her across the reception area and out into Watchers' Gallery.

The plaza bustled with people, but Van Bam hauled Clara along at speed.

'What about Samuel?' Clara's tone was flat, and she realised her anger was lingering because of Van Bam and the way he had used her suffering to gain information. 'Jeter thinks he's dead already.'

'I am hoping not everything is as Jeter believes,' Van Bam replied. 'Old Man Sam has a bounty on his head, but Samuel has more than one trick up his sleeve, Clara. For now, let us focus on reaching a safer location.'

As she was pulled along through Watchers' Gallery, Clara glanced back at the police headquarters. When she faced forwards again, she shoulder-checked a businessman, and lost her grip on the Resident's hand. The businessman's folder of papers went fluttering into the air. He rubbed his shoulder and looked around, utterly bemused at being hit by apparently nothing.

Clara stepped away from him, and anxiety fluttered in her stomach.

'Van Bam?' she whispered hoarsely. Her head spun as she dodged the denizens passing by, searching frantically for her guide. But he was invisible ... and so was she—

A large, strong hand curled around Clara's, and Van Bam's low tones whispered in her ear. 'Do not worry, Clara. You cannot see me, but I can see you. Now quickly ...'

Having crossed the plaza, they ran through the archway, between the two statues and out onto the street beyond, where the press of denizens was thicker than ever. However, they hadn't got far before Van Bam slowed and drew Clara to a halt.

'I think Jeter has regained consciousness,' he said.

Up ahead, four patrolmen were cutting through the crowd towards them. Sunlight glinted from their black receptor helmets as they stopped in a line with their rifles drawn and aimed. Several denizens around Clara and Van Bam froze and put their hands in the air; others stopped and stared, intrigued by the aggressive posture of the police officers, wondering who it was they were about to arrest and why.

One of the patrolmen ordered the denizens to stand aside. The people with their hands in the air frowned and gave each other confused looks. More spectators began to gather. They appeared confused. Who were the police officers aiming their rifles at?

'Can they see us?' Clara whispered.

One of the patrolmen shouted, 'You are under arrest, demon-worshippers. On your knees! Put your hands behind your heads!'

Van Bam let go of Clara's hand. She heard a soft chime and a whispering as the Resident summoned his illusionist magic.

'Stop him!' the patrolman shouted.

But the crowd of denizens between the Relic Guild agents and the rifles had grown so large that no one dared fire a shot.

The crowd flinched as one as a loud crack sounded from behind Clara; it was followed by cries of alarm.

The statues guarding the entrance to Watchers' Gallery had come alive.

Their spherical heads turned left and right, their white eyes glowed as they broke free of their pedestals with the sound of ripping stone. One threw its anvil to the ground as if in a temper; the other did the same with its scales. Both objects shattered on impact. In unison, the statues stepped onto the street and came stamping towards the patrolmen, long arms raised, massive fists clenched and ready to smash.

The denizens panicked.

Screams filled the air, bodies fled in all directions, and the patrolmen were lost in a wave of chaos.

Van Bam took Clara's hand again. 'The illusion will not last long,' he said, and pulled her through the confusion.

The sound of rifles spitting out bullets came from behind the magickers as they ran from the main street, ducking down a deserted alley between a medical centre and an employment agency.

'We're invisible!' Clara said angrily. 'How could they see us?'

'The Genii are directing the street patrols via the Nightshade,' Van Bam replied. 'They must have tuned the receptor helmets to see magic. We must get off the streets.'

Reaching the end of the alley, they came to another busy street which slowed their pace as they picked their way carefully through unsuspecting denizens. Van Bam led Clara straight to a textiles merchant's shop. It was a small, unremarkable place with rolls of fabrics lining one wall. Behind a desk sat a middle-aged woman, who waited to take orders from haberdashers. The woman frowned at the door that had apparently come open by itself. As she rose and closed the door with a grumble of annoyance, Van Bam led Clara to the back of the shop and down to a cellar where packing crates and more rolls of fabric were stored.

Van Bam released Clara's hand and dropped the illusion of invisibility. He moved to the cellar's far wall and pushed aside some crates to reveal a patch of brickwork decorated with tiny maze patterns.

'More secrets?' Clara said levelly.

Van Bam didn't reply. He placed his hands against the patch, and yet another hidden door appeared. But this time, as it swung open, it revealed a space only as small as a closet, with a ladder that led down into a large hole in the floor.

A faint stench reached her nostrils, sour, stagnant.

'What's down there?' she asked.

'A place where the eyes of the Nightshade cannot see us,' Van Bam said, and he motioned to the ladder. 'After you.'

WATCHING THE WATCHERS

Van Bam had little idea of how much time had passed since he had last slept. At least twenty-four hours, he reasoned, but probably closer to forty-eight. Yet, at that moment, secreted away deep in the southern district, in an old and disused warehouse that was hidden amidst a landscape of other warehouses, sleeping was the last thing on the illusionist's mind.

He watched, stunned and amazed, as Hamir performed feats of thaumaturgy before his eyes. With the aid of the mysterious script on the pages of the leather-bound book, the small and elderly necromancer worked upon the sphere of dull grey metal that appeared at once solid and liquid, as it hovered five feet or so above the ground. Metallurgy, the necromancer called it, akin to the art used to create the impressive and imposing automatons; and with this art, he would turn the sphere into some kind of weapon that would aid the Relic Guild in their hunt for Fabian Moor.

Whispering all the while, Hamir manipulated the metallic substance like a sculptor moulding clay. He pinched at its dull surface, creating eight rough points that encircled the sphere as if it was a head wearing a crown of spikes. He stepped back to admire his handiwork, gave a soft 'Hmm,' and then continued to whisper the language of the Thaumaturgists. One by one, slowly but assuredly, each spike began to lengthen.

To Van Bam, it seemed he watched shoots growing from the giant, grey seed of some strange flower. He tried to listen and understand the words Hamir whispered, but in vain. The language of the Thaumaturgists was quick and breathy, fleeting, unintelligible, sighed like the eerie vocal accompaniment to unheard music. Van Bam resigned himself; of this greater science, there was clearly nothing he could hope to comprehend.

And for the hundredth time since entering this warehouse, he wondered what deeds and secrets lay in Hamir's past.

Each of the eight spikes grew to a thin and rigid limb, easily twice the length of a man's arm span, and the sphere diminished, shrank to the size of a watermelon. It reminded Van Bam of a metallic sun radiating shafts of silver light. Hamir continued to whisper and, with deft hands, work upon the stick-thin limbs in turn, fashioning knuckle joints halfway along their lengths. From these joints he bent the lower half of each limb, until they all pointed towards the floor.

Hamir stepped back and his breathy voice whispered to the construct as a whole. It ceased hovering. As the point of each limb touched the warehouse floor with a soft tick, the necromancer fell silent. The construct resembled a small-bodied spider; it rose and fell on its new legs with a gentle motion, as if breathing.

'A little crude,' Hamir said, 'but it will serve our purpose well enough.'

'It is impressive,' Van Bam replied. 'But a spider to catch a Genii?'

'Spiders are perhaps the most proficient hunters that ever lived, Van Bam. And they have been so for far longer than even the Timewatcher knows. However, your dubious tone isn't without some justification. This spider is not quite ready for the hunt – yet.'

So saying, the necromancer whispered more words of thaumaturgy. He waited until the construct had lowered its melon-sized body sufficiently for him to begin working upon it. He stepped closer, to stand between two of the construct's thin legs. The underside of the body he left as a hemisphere of dull grey; but the topside he flattened until it became a smooth surface. From the centre of this surface he pinched the metallic substance and fashioned a single spike, long and sharp.

'The problem you face with capturing Fabian Moor,' Hamir said, 'is that you have absolutely no idea what he looks like.' He turned his back on the spider and approached the sack-cloth bag, which so far had lain ignored by the warehouse wall. 'He is not a Skywatcher. There are no silver wings upon his back by which he might be identified. Fabian Moor, in most respects, will appear as any other denizen.'

Van Bam frowned as the necromancer opened the bag and pulled out a grotesque parody of a human head. The golem's clammy face looked like a clay model fashioned by a child's clumsy hands. Van Bam knew this head had once been flesh and blood, and had belonged to Betsy, the unfortunate barmaid that Denton, Samuel and Marney had found at Chaney's Den.

Hamir held the head up so he was face-to-face with it.

'The interesting thing about golems is that the magic which animates them always congregates within the cranium – like a brain, if you will. Even without its body and limbs, this golem is quite alive – or perhaps *active* is a better choice of word.'

Van Bam didn't doubt the necromancer, but he could detect no life. The golem appeared totally inanimate. There were no eyeballs in its sockets, no lids to blink. Its toothless maw hung agape, and not even a twitch moved its features.

Hamir carried the remains of the golem over to the metallic spider. Without pause, he pushed the soft stone down onto the spike protruding from the flattened body. The spike emerged from the top of the head and, with more whispered words from Hamir, the tip melted to form a rough cap that held the head in place. The golem's mouth moved, as if shocked into motion, and Van Bam half expected a scream of pain to come from it. But it remained silent and became still again.

Van Bam pursed his lips. 'You have killed it?' he asked.

'No, no – you misunderstand, Van Bam,' Hamir replied. 'The metal is absorbing the magic within the stone. The two are now in symbiosis.'

The necromancer came to stand beside the illusionist, and he studied his work with a slight expression of satisfaction. In truth, the thin-legged construct, with its small body and vaguely human head, appeared more an artist's surreal interpretation of a spider than a weapon capable of capturing a mighty Genii.

Hamir said, 'Fabian Moor created this golem, and golems are always loyal to their creators. You might say the spider now has eyes and ears with which to find its bearings and steer its course.'

'Ah,' said Van Bam. 'Then the magic in Fabian Moor's virus will work against him. It will lead the hunter to its prey, like Samuel's spirit compass?'

'Yes, the principles are not dissimilar. The golem will be keen to reunite itself with its master. The spider will be eager to capture him.'

'And bring him back here, to this warehouse?'

'Well, we can hardly invite a Genii inside the Nightshade, can we?'

'No, we cannot.' Van Bam stared at the spider. 'You make it sound so simple, Hamir. Success is assured?'

'There is always a chance of failure, Van Bam, even in thaumaturgy. However, my immediate concern is for the denizens. They will not react well to seeing this construct roaming their streets. And that is where you come in, my dear illusionist.' He gestured for Van Bam to step forward. 'As we discussed, if you would …'

Van Bam nodded and gave Hamir the green glass cane to hold for him.

As Van Bam approached the spider apprehensively, it lifted itself up on its legs, adjusting to his height, and he stood beneath it. Hemmed in by thin legs, the illusionist looked up at the lower hemisphere of the construct's body.

'Place your hand against the metal,' Hamir instructed. 'Ensure you do not touch the golem.'

Van Bam felt unsure. He was so used to the feel of the green glass cane in his hand that he scarcely remembered what it felt like to use magic without it.

'I do not understand,' he said. 'How can my magic affect a thing of thaumaturgy? Any illusion I cast upon it will wear off once it strays from my immediate vicinity.'

Hamir made a slight sound that might have been a chuckle. 'This metal is more intelligent than most humans,' he said. 'You will be teaching it, Van Bam, not casting upon it. All that is required is the touch of your skin. Now, if you please, lay your hand upon the construct's body.'

Gingerly, Van Bam reached up and cupped the dull grey hemisphere. At first it gave him a strange, tingling feeling. And then he gasped.

His thoughts were filled with an intense burst of colours and shapes. But it was not merely imagery that flooded his mind; the cool, grey metal was sending him a greeting, welcoming his presence. Its pulses travelled up and down Van Bam's arm, curious, searching for intents and meanings. It wanted to know the purpose for this union, and Van Bam let it know. Struggling against extreme sensations, he gave the spider directions, information, just as Hamir had instructed him to.

Sentient, intelligent, the metal accepted his knowledge, drank it from his mind even as he thought it. A soft configuration of shapes let him know that it understood; a blend of colours thanked him for his teaching, for his gift. A soft radiance rippled like water, asking him who he was.

'That is all, Van Bam. Stand clear, please.' The voice came from such a distant place that it seemed unimportant. 'Right now, Van Bam.'

'No,' he whispered.

The touch of the strange, conscious metallic substance was too alluring. The longer they remained connected, the more he would learn to understand it, just as it understood him. They were growing to know each other. A rush of desire filled him. Soon, he felt sure, he would come to gain an indelible insight into thaumaturgy and its use. He would rise above his colleagues in the Relic Guild, become so much more than a magicker—

'I said *stand clear*!'

Van Bam snapped his hand back. Momentarily weakened, he stumbled away from the spider, breathing hard.

Hamir gave him a knowing look. 'Addictive, isn't it?'

A little steadier on his feet now, Van Bam stood beside the necromancer and accepted his green glass cane. He looked at it as though he had never seen it before.

'In this instance,' Hamir said, 'the one advantage a magicker has over a Thaumaturgist is simplicity.' He took a step towards the spider. 'To teach this construct the art of illusion through the thaumaturgic language would be a lengthy process. But when instructed by one already adept in this simple, prescribed gift – well, observe ...'

Once again, Hamir spoke in fleeting, breathy whispers. Van Bam almost understood what the necromancer was saying this time, but the memory of the strange language was already slipping from his mind.

The spider shimmered as though a wave of energy had passed through it. Slowly, from the ground up, the construct faded until it disappeared entirely. Even Van Bam, who had always been able to see through his own illusions of invisibility, could not detect the spider in any form.

Hamir reached out until his hand found something solid in thin air. He rapped his knuckles upon it with a dull metallic ring.

'Even Fabian Moor will not see the spider coming,' he said.

Van Bam, still dazed by his experience, was filled with awe. To think that he, a simple magicker of the Relic Guild, had taught this incredible substance the art of invisibility.

At that moment, the security mechanisms in the warehouse door clicked and whirred. With a harsh rattling the shutter rose, and Angel ducked inside.

'Hello boys,' she said brightly. 'Having fun?'

Van Bam looked at her, but didn't know how to reply.

Hamir ignored her presence entirely. He picked up the book of thaumaturgy, sat cross-legged upon the floor, and began leafing through it again.

'Wh-What are you doing here?' Van Bam managed to ask.

'Gideon sent me.' With a frown, Angel looked around the warehouse, as though suspicious that something was hiding from her. 'Hamir, I need Van Bam.'

'Excellent timing,' Hamir replied without looking up from the book. 'I was just thinking the exact opposite.'

Angel smirked at the slight.

Van Bam stared at the necromancer for a moment. 'Thank you, Hamir,' he said. 'It has been an education.'

When the necromancer failed to acknowledge this statement of gratitude, Van Bam left the warehouse with Angel, leaving him to whatever acts of magical engineering he would perform next.

Outside, Van Bam was surprised to find it was late afternoon, and the sun was sinking towards the boundary wall. He rubbed his forehead and took several deep breaths.

'Are you all right?' Angel asked.

'Yes, yes I'm fine,' he replied, shaking himself. 'So, I'm assuming Gideon has assigned us a mission?'

'Yep.' She was grinning at him excitedly, but Van Bam could also read trepidation on Angel's face.

'Would you like to tell me what it is?'

'Well …' Angel pursed her lips. 'You'll definitely need to pack a bag first.'

'Why? Where are we going?'

She rocked her head from side to side. 'Look, if there's someone special in your life – and I'm guessing there is, Van Bam – you might want to take some time to say goodbye. Marney's had a rough enough day as it is.'

Small, slender throwing daggers slipped from Marney's hand – one, two, three, four – to whisper through the air before thudding into the torso of a well-padded mannequin. With grim satisfaction and gritted teeth Marney pulled the daggers free, returned to her original position, and threw them again. This time, each blade sank into the mannequin's face: one in each eye, one in the forehead, and the last was embedded into its mouth. Again, she retrieved her weapons; again, she threw them.

Marney had lost track of how much time she had spent practising in the training room within the Nightshade, but it was long enough to have reduced the mannequin to a wretched thing of shredded stuffing. Over and over she threw the daggers, always with a sense of anger.

The whole time, Denton had not said a word. The old empath sat in a tatty but comfortable armchair watching her efforts. Although he emoted nothing, Marney could feel his appraising gaze. She did her best to ignore him, but eventually his silence grated on her.

She threw the daggers one more time and left them stuck in her target as she turned to her mentor.

'How many times have I thrown?' she asked him.

Denton shrugged and pulled a face that suggested he had lost count.

'And how many times have I missed the mark?'

The old empath gave a wry smile. 'Marney, I know what you're going to say.'

'Then you know I won't be dissuaded. I'm carrying a weapon from now on, Denton. That's all there is to it.'

She worked her shoulder. It was stiff. The bullet wound had left a dull ache deep inside the joint, and Angel's healing had given her some crude and lumpy scarring.

'I need something to carry these daggers in,' she decided. 'A baldric. Do we have a baldric?'

'Marney, slow down,' Denton said. 'I can't fault your marksmanship, but you're aiming at a static dummy. It won't be so simple when your target is moving, when it is *living*.'

Marney shook her head. 'I don't care. There's no way I'm getting caught defenceless again, not like I did this morning.'

'You weren't defenceless. Angel was with you.'

'Angel was lucky,' Marney stormed. 'What would I have done if she had been killed?'

Denton pulled a face that suggested Marney's arguments carried little water. She swore and retrieved her daggers from the mannequin. One after the other they sank into their target again, and Marney was barely aware of the small, angry noises she made with each throw. Not until the mist of tears came to her eyes, and she missed the mannequin, sending a dagger clanging against the maze-patterned wall behind it, did she stop and face Denton again.

'Did he know?' she said angrily, breathing hard. 'Did Gideon send us to that house knowing what we would find?'

Denton pursed his lips. 'Marney, despite what you and the others might think of our Resident, Gideon would *not* send his agents into a life-threatening situation without warning them first.'

'No?' Marney gritted her teeth. 'Angel didn't ask for me to meet her, you know. Gideon was playing games with us, just like Angel said he would. We could've been killed, Denton. What if Fabian Moor had come back while we were there?'

'Believe me, Gideon did not know what he was sending you into. No doubt he suspected the house enough not to want Angel there alone. But knowing Fabian Moor was using the place as a hideout?' He shook his head.

'Well, we'll know soon enough,' Marney growled. 'Angel went to confront Gideon and find out the truth.'

'So you said.' Denton puffed his cheeks. 'If you ask me, it can't have gone well or she would've come back by now.'

'Well, I didn't ask you,' Marney snapped and she retrieved the daggers yet again. This time, at her first attempt, a sharp pain flared in her shoulder, and the blade missed its mark by a wide margin. She screamed a curse at the top of her lungs, and then rounded on her mentor.

'Those golems had guns, Denton! They shot me!'

For the first time, Marney felt Denton's empathy brush against her senses. He sent her sympathy filled with patience and kindness, but most of all she felt his deep sadness. She expected words of wisdom to follow, along with teachings and lessons that she was in no mind to hear; but then, to her surprise, he said, 'I got shot once.'

Marney's anger lessened immediately. 'When?'

Denton chuckled softly and crushed his hat between his hands. 'Such a long time ago now,' he said. 'Sophia hadn't long been Resident. Gene was a painfully young man – as young as you, if I recall.' He gave Marney a wink. 'And I was in the prime of my life. Two days away from my twenty-fifth birthday.' He looked rueful and his eyes became distant. 'Some things you tend to remember with clarity and detail.'

Marney stared at her mentor as silence followed. The very idea of this sweet, old man being shot suddenly disturbed her greatly.

'What happened?' she whispered.

'Well …' Denton sucked air over his teeth. 'Gene and I were on the trail of an Aelfirian artefact. It had been stolen from Hammer Light of Outside – a relatively small House with little to offer by way of trade, but a popular spiritual retreat among those searching for some inner peace and well-being.' He chuckled again. 'So much trouble that artefact caused us, and do you know what it was, Marney? A teapot. Pure and simple. It held no magic and posed no danger whatsoever – just a bloody old thing that did nothing but pour tea.'

Marney managed a smile.

'Priceless to the Aelfir, of course,' Denton continued. 'It once belonged to some religious teacher or philosopher – I don't remember which. Quite ancient.

'Anyway, there was another agent helping Gene and I, a changeling – a rare sort of magicker – by the name of Thomma. She was a good agent. Very headstrong, as changelings tend to be, and she never shied from a fight. A little like Gideon, you might say.'

'And Samuel,' Marney added.

'Yes. Yes, I suppose you're right.' Denton was quiet for a moment. 'We tracked the teapot to the black market trader who had bought it from some treasure hunters. Thomma was the older agent, and that put her in charge as far as she was concerned. Gene and I didn't argue with her.' His eyes glazed. 'Perhaps we should have …'

He shook himself. 'Needless to say, Thomma decided a full assault was required. She didn't even stop to think about the company she was keeping. Gene was never the warrior type, and I'm not far behind him. The black market trader had more men with him than any of us anticipated. I tried to defuse the situation, but back then my empathic skills were not as accomplished as they are today. There were simply too many of them. Thomma rushed in, nonetheless. She killed ruthlessly.'

Marney felt a wave of regret and anger coming from Denton, and she realised that he wanted her to know how he truly felt, to share a moment in his life that he had blocked for many years.

'The truth is, Marney, there were so many guns in the room I have no idea who actually shot me. But I can tell you it was someone with a very powerful weapon, something custom made, Aelfirian probably.' He patted his leg. 'The bullet lodged in my thigh muscle. I was lucky, you see. Thomma saved my life. Inadvertently.'

He sat forwards on the chair and twisted his hat tightly in his hands. 'The bullet passed straight through her on the way to my leg, Marney. It ripped away most of her body in the process. Gene and I did manage to get out of there, but … we had to leave Thomma behind. She was a good agent.'

Marney licked her lips. Just how many agents of the Relic Guild had the old empath outlived? 'I'm so sorry, Denton.'

'Oh, don't be,' Denton replied. 'I'm certain that Thomma's death would have been harder to get over than my leg injury, but I'm an empath. I never allowed myself to find out.'

He smiled. 'You were very lucky to have Angel with you today, Marney – that your wound was healed so quickly. Nonetheless, being shot is a traumatic experience. Anger is an understandable response, but so strong in its negativity. Even an empath can find it difficult to block. Am I right?'

Even as he said it, Marney realised that she couldn't stop feeling angry. No matter what she tried, the magic in her veins just couldn't block the emotion. It was as if she had lost that ability.

'We didn't have a healer back then,' Denton added. 'I got to spend a few weeks in a hospital bed to recuperate and come to terms with the trauma. The truth is, Marney, in an instance like this, I don't think it is healthy to block the anger. It's important to deal with it … and to let it go.'

Fresh tears came to Marney's eyes. 'I'm an empath,' she said. 'Angel expected me to deal with the pain. She thought I could block it. I think … I think she thought I'd be better trained by now. She's right, Denton. I should be. I could've got us both shot.'

'Utter nonsense,' Denton said softly.

It was as if the old empath had been waiting for Marney to show him a crack in her emotive barrier. And now that she had, his empathy wormed its way in and filled the gaps with reassurance, allowing her both to feel her anger and fright, and to recognise it as something that would heal and pass in time.

You are not to blame for what happened, his voice soothed her mind. *Nor is Angel or Gideon. Fabian Moor is the only culprit, and we'll make him take responsibility for that in time.*

Marney knew it was true. She wiped tears from her cheeks and nodded.

Denton beamed at her.

At that moment, the outline of the door appeared on the wall. When it swung inwards, Van Bam stepped into the training room, and pursed his lips at the mannequin that was now ripped to shreds.

'Busy?' he asked Marney.

Just to see the concern on his face made Marney's heart skip, and her emotional control threatened to shatter entirely. She checked an impulse to run into his arms, to tell him everything that had occurred that morning, and to have him soothe her with kisses. But Denton broke the moment.

'Aren't you supposed to be helping Hamir?' he asked.

'There has been a change of plan,' Van Bam replied.

Denton shared a quick look with Marney; they had both felt the anxiety radiating from the illusionist.

'Gideon has concluded his meeting with Ambassador Ebril,' Van Bam continued. 'He would like to see you, Denton. Alone.'

'Well then …' With a groan, Denton rose from the armchair. 'We all know how the Resident hates to be kept waiting. I'll see you later,' he said to Marney and, with a nod to Van Bam, left the training room.

Once they were alone, Marney and Van Bam stared at each other for a long moment.

'Angel tells me you have had a tough day,' he said softly. 'Are you all right?'

'No. No, not really, Van Bam.'

Marney ran to him then, and they embraced.

'Remember I said that I have a surprise for you?' he whispered into her ear. She held him tighter. 'I think it is high time you see what it is.'

Drums thumped a heavy beat. Bass rumbled like thunder. Guitars thrashed gutturally. And a voice wailed a demand for abandon and intoxication from a lawless cluster of sweating, writhing bodies on the dance floor. In return, the revellers screamed obeisance to the band, and the tempo picked up pace.

The Lazy House was in full swing.

Sheltering from the flashing lights and frenzied dancers, Samuel sat alone in a deep alcove. He wore his Aelfirian hat, his face hidden by the shadows it cast. Not that he made an unusual sight; he was by no means the only patron of the nightclub who wished to retain anonymity. Weaponless, Samuel kept alert by focusing on the warm, soft pulses of his magic. His ears might have been filled with the drone of music and shouting; his nostrils might have been filled with the smell of sweat, alcohol and smoke; but his prescient awareness mapped out his surroundings with stark clarity. In the Lazy House, potential danger was everywhere.

Two men argued at the bar. A woman sat alone at the opposite end to them. She gazed over at Samuel. In an alcove to the right, a narcotics trade took place. On the dance floor, a woman slapped a man for making improper advances. The woman at the bar looked at Samuel again. Another dancer, a man, tried to climb up on stage with the band, but two security guards pulled him down. He kicked and shouted as he was dragged to the exit. A fight broke out between the arguing men at the bar. Two more guards were quick to break it up. The woman's gaze lingered on Samuel and she smiled at him. Money and merchandise changed hands in the narcotics deal. Someone spilled a drink. A whore led a man towards the door that led to the bedrooms upstairs. A light prism fizzed and died. The drummer broke a drumstick. A barman smashed a glass ... The woman made her way over to the alcove.

'I've been watching you,' she said as she came to stand before Samuel. Her voice was raised against the music. 'Would you like some company?'

She was young, attractive, and dressed in a gown of loose material that clung to the shape of her body. Her hair was curly and wild, and the glaze in her eyes suggested intoxication. She was probably an employee of the Lazy House.

'No,' Samuel said. 'Earn your money somewhere else.'

The woman giggled into the back of her hand. 'I'm not a whore,' she said. 'You just caught my eye, is all.'

'I said no.'

Her expression was at once disappointed and playful. 'Well, if you change your mind ...' She shrugged and sauntered away.

As she left, the tall and broad figure of Bryant appeared at the alcove's entrance. He looked back after the woman, and then turned to Samuel.

'She was nice,' he said loudly. 'Tell me you didn't turn her down.'

'We have a job to do,' Samuel replied.

Bryant shook his head, bemused. He stepped into the alcove and pulled a curtain across the entrance. The enchanted material deadened the noise of the club, and his voice was easier to hear.

'You know, there're a lot of women in this place who just love a man of mystery, Samuel. You should look her up later – have some fun for a change.'

Samuel glowered at his fellow agent. 'We're in a whole world of trouble, and you want to talk about having fun?'

'Not so much. I'm just saying you must be the most tightly wrapped man I've ever met.' He sat beside his colleague and smiled. 'Please take that bloody thing off your head. I don't like talking to shadows.'

Samuel snorted and removed his Aelfirian hat, revealing his face. 'Better?'

'Not really,' Bryant replied. 'So, did you hear about Angel and Marney? They found Fabian Moor's hiding place today.'

'I know,' Samuel said, rolling his hat up. 'I went to check it out before I came here. The police are keeping an eye on the place, but Moor won't go back there now.'

'I think you're right.' Bryant looked reflective. 'I have to tell you, Samuel, the underworld's an unhappy playground at the moment. Lots of rumours flying around, lots of frightened criminals.'

'The wild demon story?' Samuel said. 'I heard Gideon made an official statement.'

'You didn't read the newspaper?'

'I didn't see the point.'

'Well, it's partly to do with that, I suppose. But word of Carrick's death is out – Llewellyn's too – and, apparently, two crooked police officers met the wrong end of the Relic Guild last night. I assume they were the topic of your private meeting with Gideon?'

Samuel nodded.

Bryant rubbed the scar on his cheek. 'Listen, the word is one of those officers was killed by poison. I took that to mean Gene was with you.'

Samuel's expression soured. 'I don't know why Gideon does it to him, Bryant. Gene's not cut out for that kind of work.'

'No, he's not.' Bryant sighed. 'And he hasn't taken it well, Samuel. I went to see him today – you know, to make sure he was all right – but he wasn't at home. His shop's not open for business. I guess he doesn't want to see anyone at the moment.'

'Well,' Samuel growled, 'I'm sure it'll amuse Gideon to drag him out of hiding soon enough.' He swallowed his anger and smacked his rolled up hat against his hand. 'So – what's going on, Bryant? I was ordered to come and meet you, and here I am.'

Even though the enchanted material of the curtain ensured no one could hear them, Bryant lowered the volume of his voice.

'There's someone new on the scene,' he said. 'He's wormed his way into the underworld and trod on more than a few toes. Could be Moor.'

'Could be?'

'It's likely, but we can't be sure. The trouble is, everyone's afraid of this newcomer. No one wants to talk about him, no one wants to say his name. Me and Macy, we've only found one person willing to open up. Actually, he came to us. But even then, he was too scared to tell us much.'

'Anyone I know?'

'Oh yeah. He's Gil, the owner of the Lazy House.' Bryant nodded as if agreeing with Samuel's look of surprise. 'Not exactly the type to scare easy, is he?'

Samuel agreed. 'So why did he come to you?'

'Well, Gil knows me and Macy are well connected. He told us something bad was going on, something bad enough that he asked if we could set up a meeting with the Resident. Of course, we had to tell him we weren't *that* well connected, but we could probably swing a meeting with someone from the Relic Guild. Which is where you come in.'

Bryant furrowed his brow. 'I've got to warn you, Samuel, whatever Gil has to say to you, he isn't happy about the Relic Guild being in his club. If anyone in the underworld found out, he could get his throat cut just for inviting you here.'

'I'll try to be careful,' Samuel said.

'Good. Let's go and find out what he knows.'

Samuel unrolled his hat, put it back on his head, and followed Bryant out of the alcove. Music and voices hit him in a wash of noise. They skirted around the dance floor to the opposite side of the club. Samuel's magic pulsed as a few patrons stared at him, undoubtedly wondering whose face lay within the shadows of his hat.

He was surprised by the identity of Bryant's contact. He knew all about the owner of the Lazy House, though he had never had a reason to deal with him personally in the past. Gil was something of an oddity in the Labyrinth; he was an Aelf, but not a refugee of the war. He had left his House and come to live in Labrys Town many years ago – some claimed he had actually been exiled for past crimes. Whatever the truth, Gil had made a comfortable life for himself by becoming a successful, if not entirely legal, businessman. In the underworld, he was a well-respected figure, and most definitely not easily frightened.

When Bryant had led the way to another curtained alcove, he stopped with his hand on the curtain, and whispered into Samuel's ear.

'Remember – you're the only Relic Guild agent here. And be careful with Gil. He's jumpy.'

He pulled the curtain aside, and held it open for Samuel to step into the alcove. The enchanted material fell back into place, leaving Bryant outside and reducing the noise of the nightclub to a muffled hum.

Gil sat to one side of a semi-circular bench seat upholstered with red leather. His hands were laid on the table that took up most of the alcove. Thick silver rings adorned each of his fingers and thumbs. His face carried a few scars, and his hair was shaved smooth to the scalp. He was a big Aelf, and looked as though he could handle himself, even though his years were advanced. He narrowed his large, Aelfirian eyes at Samuel's hidden face, but did not speak.

Beside him, Macy sat with her arms folded across her chest. Playing her part as a member of the underworld well, she glared at the Relic Guild agent with as much loathing as she could muster.

'Thank you for coming,' Gil said in a low and heavy voice, full of suspicion.

Samuel gave a curt nod. 'I hear you have something to tell me.'

Gil turned to Macy. 'Wait outside,' he told her.

'Are you sure you want to be alone with him?' Macy said, still glaring at Samuel. 'I'd never trust one of these bastards myself.'

'Oh, I don't trust him,' Gil said with a chilly smile, 'but I think I'll be safe enough.'

With seeming reluctance, Macy got to her feet, moved around the table, paused to sneer closely at Samuel, and then stepped through the curtain to join her brother.

Alone with Samuel now, Gil's demeanour relaxed slightly. 'Why don't you have a seat?' he said. 'We need to talk.'

Samuel sat on the other side of the bench seat, and looked across the table at the Aelf. 'So talk.'

Gil raised an eyebrow. 'I hear you boys and girls have been busy these past couple of days,' he said. 'You took care of Carrick, a couple of bent constables, and even squeezed in the time to raid the Anger Pitt. Pittman's still spitting fire over that one, by the way. You killed his cousin.'

'What's your point?'

'A lot of people are pissed off with the Relic Guild.'

Samuel shrugged. 'That's nothing new.'

Gil produced a newspaper and slapped it down on the table. 'But now, to top it all off, I read we have a wild demon on the loose. Having trouble catching it?'

The Aelf's self-satisfied expression irritated Samuel, but he knew Gil was testing the waters, seeing just how trustworthy this agent of the Relic Guild was.

He leant forward. 'If you're looking for assurance that you won't be exposed as an informant, then I give it to you. You have … amnesty. For now.'

Gil barked a laugh. 'I'm not your informant, and I never will be. But I supposed you could say my hand has been forced this time.'

'Then stop dancing around and get to the point. What do you want to talk about?'

The Aelf averted his large eyes and licked his lips. 'Wild demons are strange creatures, you know. Only the Timewatcher can say where they really come from. They're beasts. They have no social skills. The only form of communication they understand is violence.' He drummed his fingers upon the newspaper and his silver rings clinked together. 'But this demon running around Labrys Town, he can communicate quite civilly. He's very educated, in fact. Even given himself a name.'

'What name?' Samuel said quickly, demandingly.

'Don't play me for an idiot,' Gil retorted. 'You know damn well what name I'm talking about.'

'Humour me.' Samuel's voice was full of warning.

Gil clucked his tongue. 'We're not so different, you and I. We know a wild demon when we see one, right? We also know a magic-user. And I have to say, it's been a very long time since I met with a magic-user as powerful as Fabian Moor.'

Samuel's gut tightened. 'You met him?'

'A couple of times.' Gil's chilly smile returned. 'Oh, and I'm not the only one. He's introduced himself to quite a few people. But he came to me wanting a gunsmith, so I brought in a friend of mine, for a commission, of course – a commission I never received. My friend hasn't been seen since, and he's not the only one who's disappeared in the last couple of days—'

'I don't give a shit about your friends,' Samuel said through clenched

teeth. If security hadn't been so tight at the Lazy House, and Samuel
had been allowed to keep his weapons with him, he would have already
been holding his revolver to the big Aelf's head. 'You know how to find
Fabian Moor?'

'No,' Gil said flatly. 'He comes and goes as he pleases. You don't see
him unless he wants to be seen.'

'When was the last time *you* saw him?'

'Last night ... I think.'

'What do you mean, you *think*?' Samuel snapped. 'If you have any
sense of self-preservation—'

'Save your threats!' Gil shouted. He jabbed a meaty finger at the
Relic Guild agent. 'You don't understand.'

'Then explain it to me, Gil. Very quickly.'

For the first time, Samuel saw the fear that Bryant had mentioned on
the Lazy House owner's triangular face.

'Look,' he said, 'I'm not like my *peers* in the underworld. I'm not
human. I understand why the Relic Guild is necessary, but most others
can't see the bigger picture like me. I know – *really* know – what would
happen if Spiral ever reached Labrys Town.'

Beads of sweat had begun to appear on Gil's bald head. Samuel held
his tongue as the big Aelf paused to wipe them away.

'I'm Aelfir,' he continued. 'I recognise Fabian Moor for what he is,
and he's no wild demon. The underworld might be scared of him, but
no one's going to put a bounty on his head. In fact, most people are
rooting for him because ...' Gil shrugged helplessly. 'Because he wants
to take down the Relic Guild.'

Samuel sat back, missing his weapons more than ever.

'He makes no secret of it,' Gil added. 'He wants to take you out, one
by one, until he gets all the way to the Resident. He wants control of
this town, and he thinks the agents of the Relic Guild can tell him the
secret of how to enter the Nightshade.'

'The Nightshade looks after itself, Gil. We couldn't get Moor inside
even if we wanted to.'

'That's not what he thinks.' The Aelf seemed disturbed. 'As far as he's
concerned, the Nightshade has left its mark upon you magickers, some
residue of its magic, hidden in your heads that even you don't know

about. Moor reckons it'll expose a crack in the Nightshade's defences, let him slip inside.'

Was that possible? Samuel wondered.

'Moor has talked to just about every big boss in the underworld about it,' Gil continued. 'He's trying to find out who you are.'

Samuel leant forwards again, and his voice was low and menacing. 'But nobody knows our identities – do they, Gil?'

The Aelf wiped more sweat from his head. 'People have always talked about flushing out the agents of the Relic Guild, placing bounties on your heads. But nobody's ever been stupid enough to actually try – drunken boasts, mostly.'

'Mostly?'

Gil looked at his hands, and Samuel again saw fear in his inhumanly large eyes.

'I do a little digging from time to time, see what turns up,' he admitted. 'I thought a little knowledge on the Relic Guild might get me out of a tight spot some day.'

'Not the smartest thing to think,' Samuel said.

'I never learned anything definite – nothing beyond suspicions.'

Samuel's banged a fist upon the table. 'My patience is running out, Gil. What did you tell Fabian Moor?'

'That's just it, I can't remember.' The big Aelf chuckled sourly. 'Last night, he came to me asking about the Relic Guild. I told him I didn't know anything, but he called me a liar. He did something to me – used magic – and I blacked out.' He rubbed his face. 'I'm pretty sure he extracted information from me. Whatever I know, he knows.'

'And what do you know, Gil?' Samuel's voice was deadpan. 'What do you *suspect* about us?'

'Two things,' he said. 'One, there's a Relic Guild agent working as a doctor at the Central District Hospital.'

Samuel swallowed. 'And the other?'

'That pompous bastard from the Twilight Bar – Mr Taffin?'

'What about him?'

'I'm pretty sure he's your informant.'

Samuel was silent and his mind raced.

'I don't know if any of that is true,' Gil said. 'I don't want to know.

But I do know that I don't want the Labyrinth to fall.' His expression was almost desperate. 'I'm telling you now, Fabian Moor wants the Nightshade, and he's coming for you to get it.'

Samuel got to his feet.

Gil looked up at him and licked his lips. 'I have amnesty, right?'

'If I were you, I'd lay low for a while,' Samuel growled, and he left the alcove, closing the curtain behind him.

Bryant and Macy were waiting outside.

'We're in trouble,' he told them.

The twins shared a look. Macy said, 'Come on. We'll take you out the back way.'

Acting as though they were ejecting an unwanted guest from the club, the twins escorted Samuel across the Lazy House. The pounding music and flashing lights were distant things to him as his thoughts danced and swirled.

The Relic Guild knew that Fabian Moor would try to infiltrate the Nightshade and supplant the Resident. But could the agents of the Relic Guild really show him how to succeed? Had the Nightshade unwittingly placed the secrets of its weaknesses into their heads?

Gil's guesses were correct, but were they enough for the Genii to begin discovering identities of the Relic Guild? Angel and Marney had found Moor's hiding place. Or had they really stumbled into a trap?

Another, more daunting, thought flared in Samuel's mind.

The twins led him out of the main club through a side door to a hallway where stairs led to the upper levels. It was deserted. Muffled music came through the door.

'Well? What did you find out?' Macy asked.

Samuel tried to rest his hands against his revolver, forgetting it wasn't holstered to his leg.

'Fabian Moor's making his move,' he said. 'He's after the Relic Guild. He's trying to find out who we are. He thinks we can show him how to enter the Nightshade.' He held up a hand before either twin could question him further. 'Bryant, you said you couldn't find Gene today. Has anyone seen him since last night?'

Bryant shrugged. 'I don't think so. Why?'

'Moor knows Mr Taffin is our informant.'

'So what?' Macy said. 'Taffin doesn't know our identities.'

'Maybe not,' Samuel said, 'but I use the apothecary shop as our meeting place.' He cursed. 'If Moor got to Taffin, then he knows Gene is associated with the Relic Guild.'

Marney lay with her head upon Van Bam's chest. Thin, inexpensive sheets were twisted and tangled around her legs. The mattress was old and worn, but soft beneath her. In the hazy moments after sex, she felt relaxed and peaceful. It was an unexpected night, a stolen moment in amongst all the chaos, and there was nowhere Marney would have rather been than here in this small and dark attic apartment with the man she loved.

'How did you find this place?' she asked sleepily.

'It was not so hard,' Van Bam replied. 'I know it is not much, Marney, but at least we have some privacy here.'

She kissed his chest. 'It's perfect,' she told him, and she meant it.

The ceiling might have been water-stained and the wallpaper might have been faded and peeling; carpet on the rough and dusty floorboards would have added a nice touch, as would curtains over the solitary window or the presence of some furniture other than the rickety wooden bed; but the lack of aesthetics was more than made up for by the delicious smells of baking bread and cakes lingering from the bakery below. The apartment was perfect in every way to Marney; a space beyond the world and all its troubles, hidden from prying eyes – it was the very best surprise Van Bam could have given her.

'I tried to find a place in one of the other districts,' he explained, 'but I could only afford east side prices.'

Marney smiled. The Resident didn't pay his agents as much as their duties deserved, only enough to get by on. Yet it hadn't even occurred to Van Bam that they might share the cost of rent, and that was so typical of him.

'It doesn't matter where it is,' she said. 'We don't have to be agents of the Relic Guild while we're here. That's all I care about.'

'Yes. Yes, I suppose you are right.' He stared up at the dark stains on the ceiling, seemed about to say more, but decided to remain silent.

Marney frowned.

Earlier, she had clung to Van Bam almost desperately as she sobbed and told him the story of how she had been shot. He had comforted her, reassured her, but there had not been much talking. The love-making had been intense, and their clothes still lay strewn across the floor. Van Bam had shown affection – always that – but the lust and heat he had displayed were not something Marney had come to expect from a man usually so gentle and considerate. Not that she was complaining; the passion was exactly what she wanted, needed, and she had never known her lover to be so focused on the present, the here and now. Something had changed between them during that moment, as if their relationship had found a new, higher level on which to flourish and deepen.

And afterwards, while lying in her post-coital stupor, Marney knew it was the perfect time to tell Van Bam how she felt, that she loved him more than she had ever loved anyone. She had been on the cusp of projecting her emotions to him, so he could feel her love and know it was true. But now she held back. Van Bam was no longer in the moment. He stared at the ceiling in distant contemplation, and she could feel his emotions were oddly poised between confidence and insecurity.

'You know,' she said, raising herself up onto one elbow, 'Denton told me once he'd never known you to talk about your problems.'

Van Bam looked at her. 'Hmm?'

'Denton. He said you were the most internalised person he'd ever met.'

He chuckled. 'And Denton once told me that you were not quite as naive as you appeared.'

'Don't sidestep the point, Van Bam. There's something on your mind and you're keeping it to yourself. I didn't think you'd be like that with me.'

Van Bam's smile did not quite reach his deep brown eyes. 'Never try to hide your feelings from an empath, eh?' He looked back up at the ceiling. 'It is nothing personal, Marney. As you said, now is not the time to be agents of the Relic Guild. Let us not ruin the moment.'

'Too late,' Marney said. She made an angry noise as she kicked the sheets away from her legs and sat up. 'Talk to me, Van Bam. Is it Gideon? Angel thinks he knows about us.'

'I suspect Angel is right.' He ran his hand gently over the scarring on Marney's shoulder before placing it against her cheek. 'But no – that is not what is troubling me.'

He rose from the bed and walked to the window, staring out into the night. His naked figure was silhouetted by the violet light of streetlamps.

'The Nightshade received a message today,' he said. 'Gideon has been in contact with Lady Amilee.'

Marney sat up straighter. 'Was it about the Icicle Forest?' she said. 'Does Amilee know where it is?'

'If she does, I was not told.'

'Then what, Van Bam?'

He sighed. 'There have been some developments concerning Ambassador Ebril. Apparently, Mirage might be having problems that its High Governor is keeping secret. I was not given much detail, Marney, but Ebril claims the only way he can get to the truth of the matter is if he returns to his House. Lady Amilee has agreed with him.'

'Really?'

Van Bam turned from the window. His face was shaded, but Marney could tell by his emotions that his expression was grim.

'She has already arranged his passage home. Tomorrow morning, Angel and I will escort the Ambassador and his entourage back to Mirage.'

'You – *what*?'

'We have been ordered to help Ebril with his investigations.'

'You're leaving the Labyrinth?'

He nodded.

'But that's madness.' Marney felt suddenly cold and naked, and she wrapped her arms around herself. 'Mirage isn't protected by the Timewatcher's barrier, Van Bam. What if the Genii are waiting for you?'

'Do not think I have not thought of that myself,' he replied. 'But Lady Amilee would not send us blindly into trouble. And nor would Gideon.'

'Don't be so sure,' Marney said darkly. 'And come to that, why is Gideon sending you anyway? Denton's the diplomat.'

Van Bam nodded. 'Angel said she made the same point, but Gideon told her to shut up. I can only assume he has other duties for Denton.'

'Even so, it doesn't make sense, Van Bam. Why aren't the Thaumaturgists leading this investigation? Ursa was in league with the Genii—'

'Marney, stop!' The hard edge to his tone startled her. 'I have been given my orders, and nothing you say will change them. Your arguments are pointless.'

She recoiled from him then, locking down every emotion inside her.

He rubbed a hand over his bald head, and she could tell he regretted his harsh words. He turned to face the window again, staring out into the night.

'It has been a strange time for us both,' he said distantly. 'Something extraordinary happened to me today, Marney. I helped Hamir to …' He faltered. 'I do not know how to explain what I did. Something I will never fully comprehend, but will never forget.'

He peered closer to the window, looking up at the dark sky. 'Hamir and I talked, and it led me to thinking,' he continued. 'I have come to understand what a truly dangerous place the Labyrinth is.'

The emotions coming from him were alien and did not belong to the man Marney knew. She pulled the bed sheets around her to stave off a sudden chill.

'The Timewatcher protects us,' he said, his voice more distant than ever as he continued looking up at the stars. 'She does so because She wishes to. But if Fabian Moor paves a way for Spiral and the Genii to enter the Labyrinth … well, She cannot allow that to happen, Marney. *Cannot.*'

'What are you saying?' Marney asked in a timid voice.

'There are hundreds of realms out there.' His tone had become leaden, resigned, lost. 'Tens of millions of Aelfir, and the Genii are the greatest threat they have ever faced. If Spiral comes to control the Great Labyrinth, he could reach them all. *We* would be the greatest danger to every House in existence.' He snorted. 'What choice would the Timewatcher have but to destroy what She has tried so hard to protect? In the bigger picture, the sacrifice of one million humans is a small—'

'Stop it, Van Bam,' Marney hissed. 'You're frightening me.'

He turned from the window quickly, as if Marney had surprised him, as if he hadn't known she was in the room. He stared through the darkness at her for a moment, and then shook his head.

'Forgive me,' he whispered. 'I ... I—'

'Think too much?'

He flashed his teeth in a smile. 'Yes. Perhaps you are right.'

Tears came to Marney's eyes, and Van Bam walked back to the bed. He sat down beside her, wiped her face, and then took her hands in his.

'I *am* sorry,' he said softly. 'You might say this day has left me more inspired than ever to play my part in this war.'

'You're telling me,' Marney said. Van Bam's emotions had reverted to something more familiar, and she was warmed to recognise him again. 'I thought we were just having an argument.'

Van Bam chuckled and kissed her fingers. 'To answer your question, I do not know why the Thaumaturgists are not leading the investigation in Mirage. Perhaps none can be spared from the Timewatcher's armies. Whatever the reason, Marney, Gideon has ordered Angel and me to escort Ambassador Ebril home, and that is simple fact.'

He pulled her into an embrace.

'But the war, Van Bam,' she whispered. 'It's so dangerous to leave the Labyrinth.'

'It is not as if we are headed for the heart of the fighting, Marney. Mirage remains a safe zone, at least for now, but we must discover who Ursa was working for. It could be that the High Governor has an enemy hiding within his cabinet of ministers.'

He broke the embrace and held Marney's face in his hands. They felt strong and warm against her skin.

He smiled. 'You were right to say that in this place we can be lovers. But at all other times we are agents of the Relic Guild. It is vital we remember that.'

Marney nodded and closed her eyes as Van Bam kissed her forehead. He was right. He would always be right. And a part of her hated the reality. For all she had learnt, for everything she had been shown at Lady Amilee's tower, there would forever be a splinter in Marney's heart that resented the Relic Guild.

'When do you leave?' she asked.

'At dawn. Angel and I are to meet the ambassador and his entourage at the Nightshade.'

Marney pursed her lips. 'You'll have to watch out for Ebril's daughter.'

Van Bam looked surprised. 'I did not know he had a daughter.'

'Well, he does, and she knows all about the Relic Guild,' Marney said sourly.

'Really?'

'Her name's Namji. She's a slippery bitch, and I don't trust her, Van Bam. She's hiding something.' Marney raised an eyebrow. 'And she's got a *thing* for you. She was *admiring* you from the shadows when last you visited her father.'

'Oh … then I shall keep your warning in mind.' He grinned at her. 'Is this Namji attractive?'

Marney slapped Van Bam's chest, and he laughed.

'You could at least say you'll miss me,' she said moodily.

'Of course I will,' he replied with heartfelt honesty. 'I will be thinking of you every day we are apart.'

She bit her lower lip. 'How … how long will you be gone?'

'For as long as it takes, I'm afraid.'

Marney nodded, and then gave a smile that was as crooked as it was mischievous. 'Then I'd better give you something to remember me by.'

She pulled Van Bam down onto the bed and climbed on top of him.

As their lips met, Marney felt a sudden flash of emotion from him that frightened her at first; that the deeper part of her consciousness wanted to block. It wasn't the cold and hopeless alien reverie she had felt while he stood by the window; it was something warm and real that washed over her, passionate and strong. It trickled into her being like nothing she had experienced before, and she could not prevent a rush of happiness forcing a chuckle from her mouth as Van Bam revealed his true feelings for her.

'I love you too,' she breathed.

CHAPTER SEVENTEEN

UNDERGROUND

Considering that so much mystery surrounded the Nightshade, that its foundations were imbued with such ancient and powerful thaumaturgy, Fabian Moor felt surprisingly underwhelmed to be standing inside the Resident's fabled home. Its walls had been impossible to penetrate during the war. Even mighty Lord Spiral had not known of any way to breach its defences. But even with the war ended so long ago, and the Timewatcher having abandoned the Great Labyrinth and its town, the Nightshade should have been much harder to overcome than this. All it had taken was a simple trick. Moor considered himself almost disappointed. It was somewhat laughable.

Within a bland chamber that reeked of magic, he stood upon shards of broken glass which glittered like uncut jewels beneath the light of a ceiling prism. To one side, a skeleton lay upon a metal gurney, its ribcage missing and its skull smashed. Not one sliver of flesh remained on Charlie Hemlock's bones, and that was as it should be. The man had been a venal idiot in life, but he had served his purpose well enough. Moor supposed he should harbour a small if begrudging amount of gratitude for the way Hemlock had so easily smuggled the new Resident into the Nightshade.

Hagi Tabet hung in the centre of the chamber, dangling from a web of leathery tentacles that extended from her back to pierce the walls, floor and ceiling. They burrowed deep into the substance of the Nightshade, siphoning its magic. Considering Tabet was the recipient of such power, she seemed astoundingly relaxed; her eyes were closed, her expression slack as though sleeping, and she swayed gently in her web even as her blood dried upon the floor beneath her. Like a parasite that had wormed its way into the nerve-centre of a society, she now controlled a million humans. The Labyrinth was at last the domain of the Genii.

But there was so much further to go.

Tabet's face twitched. Her leg kicked out. She moaned softly. Moor found himself leaning forward, eager to hear the report he was waiting for. But Tabet didn't open her eyes or speak; she became still on her web once again, her expression one of dreamy contentment. With a frustrated snort, Moor dug deep to find the patience to continue waiting.

Always waiting, he thought with the same simmering anger that had been his only companion through the isolation of the past forty years. *Always waiting…*

Upon returning to the Labyrinth, Moor had been curious to discover what events had taken place at the end of the war against the Timewatcher. These humans did so like to write their histories. The libraries of Labrys Town contained any number of so-called *factual accounts,* written by supposedly learned men who compiled their *truths* with the arrogant air of actually having been witness to the events. Moor had been offended by almost every word he had read.

The Last Storm, human history called it; the day the armies of the Thaumaturgists conducted a synchronised attack on every last Genii stronghold. Spiral's forces were already weak, one historian claimed; another said the Genii had abandoned their posts and fled in fear. They made the Last Storm sound like an easy slaughter, a contest no harder to win than a child stamping on ants. In a single day, they alleged, the final denouement came, and the Timewatcher was victorious. And She Herself came out of hiding to serve *justice.*

Moor was intrigued to read of the creation of the Retrospective and of the Aelfir who had been banished to dwell in that place of dead time and corrosion. He had been unsurprised to learn the surviving Genii had been mercilessly executed, flung into the long death of the Nothing of Far and Deep. But what he could not stomach, what angered him the most, were the lies surrounding the final punishment of Lord Spiral.

These historians described Lord Spiral as a coward. They said he had begged the Timewatcher for forgiveness and mercy at the end. They said he had wept at Her feet and pleaded to reclaim his place at Her side on Mother Earth. But, disgraced and ridiculed, his pleas had fallen on deaf ears.

But the Timewatcher had not considered execution sufficient

punishment for Spiral. She had fashioned a timeless void in which, for always, Spiral would be forced to face and regret his every atrocity. She had created a prison realm, a terrible House of pain and suffering, which She called Oldest Place. And to Oldest Place, She exiled Spiral, thus chaining him to eternal torment.

Only the Timewatcher knew the true location of Oldest Place, the historians said. Some believed it was an unreachable realm, set to drift lost and aimless in the depths of space; others that it was buried deep beneath the wrath and nightmare of the Retrospective. But all agreed that as the sole prisoner of Oldest Place, Lord Spiral had been reduced to a slavering animal, an ignoble beast whose only desire was to feed upon the souls of the dead.

Not one of these learned *humans* had been capable of writing a logical historical account of the war. They had speculated with fairytales and ghost stories, myths and legends, guesses and lies. How little they knew of Spiral and Oldest Place. How little they suspected that a new storm was heading their way. The waiting was almost over.

'Hello, Fabian.'

Hagi Tabet's eyes were open. They were unfocused, directed vaguely in Moor's direction.

'Well?' he demanded of her.

'It's strange,' she said. 'So many eyes on the streets, so many ways in which to see this town, yet I cannot see the Relic Guild. They have disappeared from my sight.'

'You have people searching for them?'

'Oh yes.' She smiled dreamily. 'The denizens have taken to their new Resident quite favourably. Especially Captain Jeter. His police force continues to scour the town for the Relic Guild.'

Moor growled in irritation. 'What of the necromancer?'

'Ah, yes – Hamir …' Tabet swayed gently on her web of tentacles. 'He, too, has found a place to hide from my eyes, but he is still inside the Nightshade. Somewhere.'

'Ensure he cannot leave. I want him found.'

'Have patience, Fabian, my servants are hunting him down even as we speak.'

Moor had seen Tabet's *servants*, the monstrous aspects of the new

Resident that now roamed the corridors of the Nightshade. They clearly represented a damaged state of mind – the head injuries Tabet had sustained during the war with the Timewatcher must have been far worse than he realised.

'Good,' he said. 'Make sure they capture him alive.'

At that moment the door to the chamber opened, and Mo Asajad entered, dragging a struggling woman behind her by the hair. The woman sobbed and choked on grunted words, grabbing weakly at the hand that pulled her. Her eyes remained tightly closed until Asajad threw her beneath the dangling feet of Hagi Tabet.

On all fours, the woman looked up at the naked figure held aloft by leathery tentacles. She then turned to look at Moor. Her eyes were wide with terror, her face was tear-streaked, and blood coated her chin and the front of her clothes in a thick red line.

She grunted some unintelligible plea, and only then did Moor realise her tongue had been ripped out. He turned a questioning frown to his fellow Genii.

Asajad shrugged. 'She was *so* boring, Fabian.'

'Just get it done,' he told her.

Asajad turned her attention to the new Resident, who was gazing at the denizen almost lovingly. 'Hagi, I've brought you some supper.'

Up on her web, Tabet began shaking. Her eyes closed in ecstasy. Her mouth opened wide, releasing a low groan of pleasure towards the ceiling. Convulsions shook her body and set her swinging in her web.

Wailing like a panicked animal, the woman scrambled across the floor, cutting her hands and knees on shards of glass, desperate to reach the open door.

She didn't get far.

As Moor blocked her path, he noticed Tabet's stomach had distended as though she had completed the full cycle of pregnancy in a matter of seconds. Her navel protruded from the balloon of her body like the head of a snake. It turned this way and that, a tentacle wriggling to free its length. Slowly, more and more of the tentacle slid from Tabet's navel, lowering to the floor: a leathery length of rope coated in blood and pinkish jelly. It slithered through broken glass, and rose up behind the woman.

Still on her hands and knees, the woman looked up with pleading eyes at Moor, searching in the wrong place for mercy. She did not see that Tabet's appendage had opened its mouth behind her; that the toothless maw, stretching wider and wider, had risen above her. She didn't get time to grunt or scream as the tentacle struck, quick as a viper, and swallowed her head. Its greasy, thin lips sucked her wholly into a leathery sack that contracted and expanded with strong muscles, chewing, devouring.

Upon her web, Tabet's head was thrown back, her limbs splayed and rigid as though frozen. She made tight and violent jerking movements – sensitive, it seemed, to the flexes of the sack as it pushed nourishment up into her body.

Asajad sighed and shook her head. 'These denizens really aren't much sport,' she said, watching as the chewing sack grew steadily smaller.

'Now you've had your fun,' Moor said warningly, 'perhaps you might turn your attentions to more constructive pursuits?'

'Constructive pursuits?' Asajad looked dubious. 'Like searching for the Relic Guild? Really, Fabian, what's the point?'

Moor glared at her.

A lazy smile curled her lip. 'Surely it's a small matter. There's nothing those magickers can do to us.'

'Don't be so certain,' Moor said levelly.

Asajad clucked her tongue. 'Are you sure your desire for revenge is not clouding your judgement?'

She spoke with effortless confidence, and Moor's irritation deepened. He had not sacrificed his body, waited for so long in the shadows, to be drawn into a petty squabble over dominance. The misguided manner with which Asajad disregarded his leadership of this small band of Genii disturbed him. Her arrogance was growing, and, if it was left unchecked, mistakes would be made, something would get missed.

'I will not rest until the Relic Guild is destroyed,' he told her. 'And nor will you. Understood?'

She bobbed her head in a gesture of obeisance, but turned to face the feeding Resident. 'Then what *constructive pursuit* do you have in mind for me, my Lord Moor?'

'I want you to find Hamir,' he said, ignoring the mockery in her tone. 'He is here, somewhere, hiding.'

'Again, Fabian, what's the point?' There was a tired edge to Asajad's purr. 'Hamir is a minor nuisance, nothing more.'

'Ignorantly spoken,' Moor grumbled with a sneer. 'That necromancer knows as many of the Nightshade's secrets as the cursed Timewatcher. I, for one, would very much like to talk to him.'

Once more, open amusement decorated Asajad's gaunt face, and Moor rounded on her.

'Go and find Hamir!' he barked. 'Bring him to me for questioning.'

Asajad raised an eyebrow. 'He will not be compliant,' she said darkly.

'Then persuade him.'

'And if I cannot?'

'Kill him, of course!'

She seemed pleased, and gave another mock bow. 'As you wish, my Lord Moor.' She sauntered out of the room, but looked back over her shoulder to say, 'I'll see you for breakfast, Hagi.' Then she was gone.

On the floor, the bulbous sack of Tabet's appendage was now a limp mass, like a deflated balloon. It twitched and made a deep gurgling sound. Finally, its flaccid mouth opened and squeezed out a pile of sticky, pale bones. The skull was the last thing to emerge. Red jelly was impacted into both eye sockets. They shone like wet rubies.

Tabet sucked the appendage back into her body, leaving a fist-sized bud, raw and pink, in her navel. She stared down at Moor, once again surrounded by an air of serenity and contentment. Her arms and legs waved in the air with slow, graceful movements as if she was treading water, but her eyes vibrated, flickering from side to side as though trapped in the void between sanity and madness.

'Where is Viktor?' she asked. 'When will he be with us?'

'Do not concern yourself with Viktor Gadreel.' Moor replied. His lip curled and hatred entered his tone. 'Just find me the damned Relic Guild.'

In the gloom and stench of the sewers beneath the streets of Labrys Town, Samuel held the bounty hunter to his chest. With one hand covering his captive's nose and mouth, he used the other to crush his windpipe. Samuel's opponent was strong, but his struggles could not overpower Old Man Sam's iron grip. The depth of despair lacing his strangled pleas for mercy could not appeal to the magicker's sympathies. There would be no reprieve. The man hadn't seen Samuel coming, hadn't even heard him. Underestimating an old man would be the last thing he would ever do.

Samuel's fingers dug deeper into the man's throat, tightening like a vice. With a grunt, he leaned back, lifting his prey's feet off the floor. What would have been screams of pain were no more than choked sobs in the gloom. Samuel wrenched at the bounty hunter's throat – once, twice, again and again – mercilessly, desperate to cause pain, to strangle, to *break*. He ignored the wet and warm signals that his victim had soiled himself, and didn't stop wrenching until the bounty hunter's struggles had ceased and he fell limp.

Samuel let the dead body slide to the greasy floor.

He gritted his teeth, relishing the strength in his limbs. His prescient awareness felt warm inside him, but it did not flare or warn of imminent danger, and he took a few moments to steady his breathing, staring down at the dead man at his feet.

As a rule, bounty hunters didn't care for partnerships, as that meant sharing rewards. Evidently, the prize for scalping Old Man Sam was big enough to allow a temporary alliance. Samuel's prescient awareness had told him that four bounty hunters had followed him down into the sewers. His magic had also told him to let them come, to leave no enemy behind him, to allow the hunters to group in a place where they would become prey for Old Man Sam. Including the man Samuel had killed back at his hideout, that meant five assassins had picked up the contract. Three were still alive. Somewhere.

A chinking sound disturbed his thoughts.

It wasn't the first time he had heard it. It came from somewhere far off, echoing through the sewers like the distant clang of a hammer striking stone. After repeating several times, it fell silent again, the final echo ringing away to nothing. With a frown, Samuel left the dead bounty hunter behind, and moved off. The soft pulses of his magic steered his direction, and he trusted where they would lead him.

The term 'sewers' hardly did justice to the world beneath Labrys Town. They were more like the shadow of the town, a distorted mirror image, a reflection in a stagnant pond. Up above, trams ran along streets on their tracks; below, rivers of murky sewage water flowed beneath a series of grand arches. Where there were buildings, great support pillars of dark stone stretched from ground to ceiling; alleys and side lanes were mimicked by tunnels that led from one riverside walkway to another, as did the narrow bridges that curved over the flow of rancid waters; and where the sun or moons cast their light down upon the denizens, grimy glow lamps shed patches of pale illumination here and there to break the gloom.

The sewers had always provided the Relic Guild with a means to move undetected and unhindered. It was a secret place that no regular denizen was supposed to see. Samuel had shown his foes the entrance back in his bathroom, but at least they had been stupid enough to follow him.

Striding purposefully along a walkway, Samuel cut right into a tunnel. Every surface of the sewers was slick and damp. In dark corners, poisonous fungi sprouted from piles of filth. Glistening moss grew on the walls and paths, and the atmosphere was oddly clammy, as if a film of oil clung to the air. The stench of this place was more repulsive than Samuel remembered, but it was a familiar smell that reminded him of a better time, a bygone day when the Relic Guild had meant something.

Hamir's garbled warning rattled in his mind, and he thought of Van Bam.

That bounty notice had carried the official Labyrinth seal, which only the Resident could endorse. Had Labrys Town undergone a change of regime? Could the Genii have found a way to invade the Nightshade? He shook away the implications of that disturbing possibility. Now was not the time.

Approaching the end of the tunnel, he came to a halt. His magic was pressing on his senses, like an itch on the inside of his skull. Drawing his revolver and thumbing the power stone, he crept to the tunnel mouth and peered out, straining his ears for any sound of pursuit.

A river of sewage water ran before the tunnel. The opposite bank was well lit by a series of glow lamps that faded into the gloom. On Samuel's side, thirty or more paces down the walkway, a bridge crossed the river; a further ten paces on from where it ended on the opposite side was another tunnel.

This tunnel intrigued Samuel. A glow lamp was fixed to the wall directly above its opening, but he could see no signs of movement. Still, his prescient awareness was on the edge, just short of activating. His magic was warning him, moulding his instincts, telling him it was time to wait, not hunt.

Bounty hunters were too egocentric to hold together long as a collective. When the heat was on, loyalties vanished, and the greed and pride of the individual broke through. Samuel had already put two cracks in the team, and fear and a sense of self-preservation had opened those cracks to the final split. Samuel knew the value of patience. This ground was familiar territory for him, and he could wait as long as necessary until the final three assassins came to him, one at a time if necessary.

Revolver in hand, he hung back in the shadows of the tunnel mouth. Once again, his thoughts turned to Van Bam.

The last time Samuel had used the sewers had been forty years before, on the night the Relic Guild believed they had killed Fabian Moor. Moor had fought desperately, and his magic had been unlike anything Samuel had ever faced. And just before he met his end, Moor had destroyed Van Bam's eyes. Always such a calm and collected man, Van Bam had been reduced by his injuries to a hysterical wreck. He had thrashed and screamed, and complained of voices in his head. Marney had soothed his emotions and eased him into unconsciousness. Samuel had then carried him over his shoulder through the sewers all the way to the Nightshade.

It was thought that Hamir would take care of Van Bam; that the necromancer would be able to mend his eyes, fix him up so that he could return to the streets and his duties with the Relic Guild. No one had realised the voice in Van Bam's head was that of Gideon. Not one of them had guessed that Van Bam was to become the new Resident of Labrys Town.

So much time had passed since that night, and here he was, once again in the sewers, because of Fabian Moor. Samuel didn't know what had happened up in the town, whether Van Bam and Clara were alive or dead. Was Samuel now the only surviving member of the Relic Guild?

Movement caught his eye: a brief, shadowy blur ...

It came from the tunnel on the opposite side of the river. A figure bolted through the dim light and dived onto the bridge. Samuel's prescient awareness remained in check, and he understood that his would-be killer didn't know he was hiding nearby. The bounty hunter was now out of sight, using the wall of the bridge as cover, but Samuel lifted his revolver and took aim in that general direction. His hands were steady and true.

These petty assassins weren't worth wasting magic on, and there was no point using ice-bullets to capture them – interrogating them would only reveal what Samuel already knew. The fire-bullets in the rifle were also out of the question; they might ignite the gases and fumes in the sewers, and a fireball was the last thing he needed. A regular cold and grey metal slug was all the job required.

Samuel's magic prickled.

The bounty hunter's head appeared above the wall of the bridge, silhouetted against the pale light of glow lamps. Samuel's revolver spat out a single shot. The man's head snapped back. He barked a quick and piercing scream that sounded more of surprise than pain. For a moment he appeared to be feeling his way along the bridge, and then he rocked and stumbled and finally fell over the edge, splashing down into the river.

Face down in the rank waters, the dead body drifted past Samuel and continued on until it disappeared in the gloom. Samuel deactivated the power stone and holstered his revolver. He waited, listening to the silence. The only sound that reached his ears was the return of the distant chinking of hammer on stone, and it was closer this time. Whatever was making the noise, Samuel's prescient awareness was drawn towards it. His magic was egging him on. Two bounty hunters remained, and the source of the sound was where he would find them.

It was time to hunt.

Someone yelled. It was impossible to tell from which direction it came; a series of short screeches echoed through the sewers like a repeating death rattle, then faded into silence. Van Bam felt certain the voice did not belong to Samuel.

'He's definitely a bounty hunter,' Clara said, disturbing Van Bam's misery.

He looked down at the dead body the changeling crouched over, nodded in agreement, but said nothing.

In the pale green light of Van Bam's illuminated cane, the two agents stood in a slime-covered sewer tunnel. The dead man lay on his back, his eyes closed. There was no blood, but his tongue hung from the corner of his mouth, and his throat had been brutally disfigured. Van Bam almost pitied him.

Along with those screeches, the body was a sure sign that Samuel was still alive.

'How many do you think are after him?' Clara said.

'Impossible to say,' Van Bam replied. 'Unfortunately, Old Man Sam has many enemies among the bounty hunters of Labrys Town.'

'We have to help him.' Clara stated. 'Let's move.'

Van Bam remained where he was and stared at the young changeling. It wasn't just her cold, hard tone of voice that bothered him, it was her colours. Clara had been beaten and pulled in all directions, and Van Bam could detect hues of livid emotions blooming within her body. Her bruised and swollen face might have appeared impassive, but there was a magical yellow shine to her eyes. It suggested the wolf had fired up in her a need to find these bounty hunters and vent all her anger upon them.

'Clara, can you remember—'

'No, Van Bam!' she snapped. 'I still don't know what Marney did to me. Now, are we going to help Samuel or not?'

'There is no rush,' he told her.

Clara clenched her teeth. 'What?'

'We cannot help Samuel by chasing around in the shadows, Clara. In fact, we would only hinder him.'

Clara scoffed. 'You can't be serious. You've just said there's no telling how many bounty hunters are after him.'

Van Bam's metal eyes stared into the gloom beyond the tunnel. He felt no irritation at her scorn, only a deep sadness.

'Clara, if you could say you have learned one thing thus far, it should be that Samuel is a killer. You know he is exceedingly efficient at what he does.' Van Bam studied the dead body. 'Without doubt, the bounty hunters are the ones in need of help now.'

'Then what, Van Bam?' Her tone was accusing. 'We just hang back and let him fight his way out? Wait until he tells us the coast is clear?'

'After a fashion, yes.' He sighed. 'We will continue on, Clara, but at a careful pace. Your heightened senses will lead us to Samuel eventually.'

'Don't bet on it,' she snarled. 'All I can smell is shit!'

Van Bam faced her. He knew that Clara's protests were driven more by anger than a true desire to help Samuel, but they would never extricate themselves from this predicament unless she gathered herself.

'Your sense of smell led us to this dead body, Clara,' he said, 'and it will steer us to where we need to be. Please, point your aggression in the right direction and lead the way.'

She glowered at him. 'Fine,' she whispered and her nostrils flared. 'This way.'

With his cane held aloft like a torch, Van Bam followed Clara out of the tunnel to a walkway that ran alongside the river of flowing sewage. Although her colours had abated to something a little less hostile, Clara was clearly frustrated by their casual pace, and Van Bam had to ensure she did not stray too far ahead and exit the globe of light. The cane shed a strange illumination in which the agents cast no shadow; so long as they remained within its circle, they would not be seen or heard by any bounty hunter they happened upon.

As Clara led the way across a bridge that arched over the thick and rank river, Van Bam appreciated how the atmosphere of the sewers must have been cruel on her heightened senses. Stifling humidity ensured every surface was dank and slick, and the stench cloying the air was palpable as smoke. Breathing through the mouth was the preferable option, but Clara's nose was their best ally in this situation. Van Bam did not envy her.

He cocked his head to one side, searching for the voice of Gideon. The silence endured in his mind, and it was maddening. For the first time in forty years he missed the spiteful ghost's guidance. He hadn't felt so alone, so lost, since the day the Genii War had ended.

The Last Storm, they called it: the day the Timewatcher's armies vanquished the threat of Spiral and his hordes once and for all. It had been a time of celebration among the Houses of the Aelfir. But in the Labyrinth, the Last Storm had heralded a time of change.

Gideon the Selfless was dead, having sacrificed his life to save the denizens from Fabian Moor, and the Nightshade welcomed a new Resident: a mysterious blind man by the name of Van Bam. And Van Bam's first duty had been to inform his people that the Timewatcher and Her Thaumaturgists had abandoned them, and they would never see the Aelfir again.

Van Bam had always thought of that day as the saddest of his life. But now, he wasn't so sure.

The Nightshade had been taken from him, he no longer heard Gideon's voice in his head, and he had been forced to flee into the stinking sewers beneath the streets of the town he had once governed. He had never felt such a failure.

'Listen,' Clara whispered. She was staring down the tunnel she had been about to lead them into. 'Can you hear that?'

Van Bam could. A distant sound echoed through the sewers, the slow, rhythmic chinking of metal on stone.

'What is it?' Clara asked.

Van Bam didn't reply. He listened to the sound until it stopped and the last echo petered out.

He nodded to Clara to continue into the tunnel.

The Genii had gained control of the Nightshade. But why? What in the Timewatcher's name could they do with it? Spiral was long lost, the Thaumaturgists gone, and the Aelfir could not be reached from the Labyrinth. Was simple revenge upon the denizens Fabian Moor's driving reason for returning after all?

Van Bam's thoughts turned to the avatar, the mysterious blue ghost that had set so much in motion. Perhaps Samuel was right; perhaps it was no friend to the Relic Guild after all. Van Bam believed the avatar was a portent, that it was guiding them into a future that was for the good of the Labyrinth. But what good could come from the Genii controlling the Nightshade?

Frustrated, confused, Van Bam prayed that he would hear Gideon's voice again.

After navigating more slimy walkways and mould-coated tunnels, Clara paused to stare down at a spot in the river where the water bubbled and frothed. Bitter fumes filling the air dried the inside of Van Bam's mouth.

'Nice,' Clara said with disgust.

'Acid,' Van Bam explained. 'At certain spots the sewage water creates such high levels that it is potent enough to strip flesh from bone.'

'Stinks of eggs,' Clara muttered, unimpressed, and she led the way to another tunnel.

At the other end, she stopped again as they came to a spacious chamber where rats clambered over each other, and where mounds of filth had gathered here and there. The river continued flowing through the chamber, but it was covered by a rusty grille. From the darkness above, water and waste matter fell like foul rain, splashing and slapping upon the floor.

Clara pointed to a tunnel mouth on the other side of the chamber. 'We need to go that way.' She snorted. 'Should've brought an umbrella.'

As she made to step out into the falling filth, Van Bam gently took her arm and held her back. He whispered to his magic, and the light from his glass cane flared, sending rats scurrying and squealing to the edges of the chamber.

'My magic depends on belief to exist, Clara,' he said. 'It is easy for me to fool a mind so profoundly that it will *believe* my illusions into reality where they can cause real harm – or protection.' Van Bam lifted the cane higher. Its light cast a dome of tangible light around them both. '*Now* we have an umbrella,' he said.

Treading carefully, Van Bam led the way across. Water and waste matter fizzed and dissolved upon the enhanced light shining from the cane, and not one drop touched the magickers.

Once they had traversed the tunnel on the opposite side, they headed along a slippery walkway that was well lit by glow lamps, and Clara halted for a third time before yet another bridge.

She sniffed the air. 'I can smell blood,' she said and walked on.

Halfway across the bridge, she touched the dark stone of its wall. She showed Van Bam her hand. In the light of the cane, he saw her fingertips were wet.

She wiped her hand on her leggings and sniffed the air again. 'Samuel was here,' she growled. 'Not long ago.'

'Which way did he head, Clara?'

She waved in the vague direction of the opposite bank, and then turned a sour expression to Van Bam. The wolf's presence had returned to her yellow eyes.

'Should we catch up with him, or wait until he kills everyone?'

Van Bam could almost hear Gideon laughing as the changeling glared at him defiantly. The sound of metal striking stone echoed through the sewers once more.

CHAPTER EIGHTEEN

GHOSTS & MONSTERS

When Samuel had reached the source of the hammering sound, he hid in the shadows of a tunnel mouth and peered out onto the walkway furtively. On his right hand side, the river continued on and curved around to the right. He had a good view down into the murky water from his position. A little way ahead, the river widened and became shallow; and there, he saw a problem he hadn't anticipated: dressed in priest cassocks, ankle-deep in sewage, two of Fabian Moor's golems worked with slow and tireless automation, striking the river floor with pickaxes.

A man stood upon the walkway, watching proceedings. He wrung his hands nervously as the golems paused and knelt in the filth to remove pieces of loose stone. In the pale light of a glow lamp, Samuel could see that the man's face was careworn and unshaven; his hair was straggly and thinning. He wore old and tatty clothes, and stepped from foot to foot with anticipation. Samuel did not recognise this denizen, but knew he was no bounty hunter.

Movement caught the magicker's eye.

A little way ahead, someone was inching towards the man, creeping along the wall, stooped in the shadows beneath the glow lamps. The light caught the figure briefly, enabling Samuel to see that it was a woman. She carried a rifle in her hands. Her head was shaved smooth to the scalp, except for a shock of hair running down the middle. Although Samuel could not see her face, the uncommon hairstyle identified her immediately: her name was Aga, and she most definitely was a killer for hire.

It was an easy shot from Samuel's position. Once he'd killed Aga, the golems and the man would quickly follow. But even if his prescient awareness was not telling him to remain hidden, Samuel still wouldn't have taken the shot.

Aga never worked alone. She had a sister, a ruthless bitch called Nim. One never picked up a bounty contract without the other, and they had a bad reputation in Labrys Town. If Aga was out prowling in the open, then it was damn certain that Nim was hiding somewhere close by, covering her sister, waiting for Old Man Sam to make his move.

For the time being, with his magic pulsing warmly, sweat trickling down his back, Samuel remained concealed, letting events unfold however they would.

Aga approached the man watching the golems. He was oblivious to her presence and the rifle aimed at the back of his head. When she had stepped close enough to her target to make him out clearly, she paused and lowered her weapon.

'Dumb Boy?' she said in an incredulous tone.

The man wheeled around. Shocked and mute, he stared open-mouthed at the bounty hunter and the rifle in her hands.

The golems began striking stone again.

Aga looked back along the walkway. 'It's Dumb Boy Clover,' she called, her voice echoing softly among the *chinks*.

Although Nim didn't reply to her sister, she did reveal her position to Samuel. In the mouth of another tunnel several paces ahead, he saw shadowy movement. Nim was signalling to her sister with short, sharp hand gestures, clearly telling her to focus. From his location, Samuel could not get a clear shot at her.

As Aga rested her rifle upon her shoulder, the man – Dumb Boy – pressed his hands to his chest, and his voice drifted back to Samuel.

'Oh, it's you, Aga – you scared me to death.' He chuckled like a simpleton. 'You ain't got my money, have you?'

'What?'

'My money. The boss said someone would bring it to me. Have you got it?'

'*No.*' Aga looked around the sewers with a perplexed expression. 'Dumb Boy, what are you doing down here?'

He shrugged. 'Working.'

'Working? How can you stand the smell? It's making my eyes water.'

'Sewer gas,' Dumb Boy explained. 'It gets bad sometimes.' He pointed a finger at her. 'If you're here to help, I'm in charge, right? And—'

'Shut up,' Aga snapped. 'Who are you working for?'

'Don't know his name. I ain't allowed to talk to him, see? Charlie Hemlock got me the job.' He seemed surprised by the fact his finger was still in the air, and then used it to scratch his head. 'Has Charlie got my money?'

Again, Aga seemed utterly perplexed. 'Where have you been, Dumb Boy? No one's seen Hemlock for days, and he's not the only one who's disappeared.'

'Oh … who's got it then?'

'I don't care about your bloody money,' Aga hissed.

She pushed past Dumb Boy and peered over the walkway, down into the river. She saw the golems hefting their pickaxes and took a step back.

In a cold and flat tone, she said, 'What are they?'

Dumb Boy looked over the edge too. 'Not sure. Funny looking, ain't they?'

Laying their pickaxes aside, the golems began shifting more loose stone.

Aga looked back down the walkway. 'Nim, you really have to see this.'

Nim replied with another sharp wave of her hand, and her sister's gaze returned to the river.

One golem waited while the other remained kneeling in the filth. It submerged itself, clearly reaching down into the hole dug into the river floor.

Samuel's magic remained warm.

'When's the boss coming back?' Dumb Boy asked.

'I don't know,' Aga replied, her voice distant. 'What are they doing, Dumb Boy?'

'Don't know. They don't talk.'

The golem stood up, dripping waste water, and passed an object to its companion. By the time Samuel realised what the object was, it was already too late.

While one golem held the terracotta jar in its misshapen hands, the other scratched away the wax seal. In their ignorance, Aga and Dumb Boy bent forwards for a closer look as the lid came loose and splashed down into the river.

The smallest of moments passed, giving Samuel just enough time to wonder why his prescient awareness hadn't gone berserk, and then a scream echoed through the sewers. A hot sandstorm blasted from the terracotta jar.

Like a cloud of locusts the storm rose, whirling angrily. Aga jumped back, but Dumb Boy's reflexes were not so quick. The storm engulfed him and whipped so fast and fiery, he did not even get the chance to shout in surprise or pain. His clothes were shredded in a second; his skin disappeared in even less time. The storm blossomed to an angry shade of red as it drank Dumb Boy's blood and devoured his flesh.

In her surprise, Aga fell into a sitting position. Her rifle clattered along the walkway and joined the golems down in the river of waste. As she tried to scurry away from the storm like a crab, a tentacle of burning crimson lashed out and coiled around her legs, flipping her over. As she was dragged towards the body of the storm, Aga clawed at the walkway, calling desperately for her sister.

'Nim! Help me!'

Nim broke cover, marching forwards with a handgun raised and aimed. Her weapon spat two quick shots into the storm, but the bullets did nothing to disturb its hunger.

Aga reached out a hand. 'Please …' she whimpered.

Nim fired again, but could not prevent her sister being swallowed by the storm, stripped of flesh, drained of blood, devoured by its rage.

Nim screamed murderously as she unloaded her gun at the swirling mass. Unaffected, the storm tapered and began to coalesce into a humanoid shape. Hurriedly, Nim reloaded her weapon.

Samuel's revolver was heavy in his hand. He looked at the violet glow of its power stone. Frozen to inaction, he felt lost without his magic's guidance.

By the time Nim readied her weapon once more, the storm had gained the solid form of a man, obese and naked. His head was bald; his shoulders and arms were powerfully built. Two skeletons lay at his bare feet. Nim fired at him again, and continued to release bursts of thaumaturgy until the power stone was flashing on an empty chamber. The man recoiled as each bullet struck him, but he seemed more surprised than hurt, and not one wound appeared on his flabby, pale skin.

Nim's glowing gun dropped to her side. She flinched and skipped back as the man faced upward and bellowed at the sewer ceiling with all the fury of the storm that had birthed him. Nim turned and ran away down the tunnel she had emerged from.

Samuel swallowed as the reanimated Genii finished his bestial cry. He grinned and pointed a finger directly at him.

'I see you, little magicker,' he shouted. 'I am hungry!' and he came stamping forward.

Some part of Samuel's body remembered his hunting instincts. Holstering his revolver, he reached over his shoulder and drew his rifle. He primed the power stone and fired one single shot.

The fire-bullet struck the Genii's chest with a soft *whump*, and he staggered back. Red flame bloomed, hissing and intense. It caused the air to crackle and spark, finally igniting the sewer gas to a rich golden fire that engulfed the Genii.

Only when the fireball began spilling liquidly down the walkway did Samuel's prescient awareness activate. And it told him to most definitely run.

Followed by a blistering roar, Samuel fled down the tunnel. Searing light chased after him, heat upon heat caught up with him, fast. Flames burned at his back, licked about his shoulders, crackling his hair, singeing the flesh of his ears. And in that moment, Samuel knew he was too slow; he could not outrun the fireball, could not prevent the blaze overtaking him, roasting him to death. But his prescient awareness was urging his body to keep his ageing legs pumping as fast as they could go, onward – always onward – until they finally brought him to salvation.

His coat and hair smoking, Samuel reached the end of the tunnel and dived headfirst into the murky filth of a deep flood pool.

Cool waste dampened the heat and filled his mouth, bitter and foul. Somehow, Samuel resisted the urge to swallow or gag as he sank. He opened his eyes, fighting the sudden sharp stinging that wanted to close them again, and he looked up. Through the cloudy, thick water, he saw golden light illuminate the flood chamber. Fire roiled in a blistering storm that seemed without end.

Samuel was already fighting for breath. Clenching his teeth against the foul matter in his mouth, gripping his rifle hard, he obeyed the prescient awareness that forbade him to kick and rise and fill his desperate lungs with air. Fire continued to blossom above the pool, roll after roll of burning clouds, almost fluid and graceful to Samuel's stinging eyes. And then, thankfully, the golden glare diminished, the blaze receded, and Samuel was able to break for the surface.

He spat filth from his mouth and filled his lungs with gasping breaths. The air tasted of soot and ash. Smoke hung like thick fog.

A voice bellowed.

'Little magicker!'

It came from somewhere not too distant.

Gagging and spluttering, Samuel looked around the flood chamber frantically. On the wall opposite the mouth of the tunnel, a rusty metal ladder led up to a drain opening, easily wide enough for him to squeeze into. It was his only chance of escape.

But as Samuel holstered his rifle and made to swim towards the ladder, he felt his body gripped by something. It was as though the stagnant water was pressing in on him, becoming solid. He yelled in surprise as the waters lifted him, as though he were caught in a sudden wave. It rushed him across the pool, and threw him back out into the tunnel.

Samuel skidded to halt on his rump and raised a protective arm. But the wave didn't follow and crash down onto him. Instead, it hung in the entrance to the flood chamber, hovering across its width and height like a veil of filth. With a sudden snapping sound, it froze to a wall of dirty ice.

Samuel jumped to his feet and kicked at the barrier. But it was too thick and hard to break through.

A low chuckle came from behind him. He turned slowly.

Directly in front of him, the Genii materialised in the tunnel. This close, Samuel could see his true, imposing size. The Genii's pallid obesity made his nakedness seem all the more grotesque. The flab of his stomach hung over his genitals. His left eye was missing, and the socket was covered with smooth skin as pale as the rest of him. He had not a single wound or scorch mark.

Samuel's prescient awareness had deserted him yet again. But that was a small matter now. With cold resignation, with filth and water dripping from him, the old bounty hunter clenched his jaw and drew his rifle.

The Genii chuckled again at the small man aiming his insignificant weapon at him.

'Pray to your Timewatcher if you must, little magicker.' His voice was deep; his teeth were white and long. 'But your soul won't reach Her now.'

Hamir was on the move again. Of course, the moment he stepped from his laboratory Hagi Tabet had detected him, and the new Resident was quick to send her servants after the necromancer. But Hamir was not unprotected as he made his way through the never-ending corridors of the Nightshade. The time he had spent experimenting in his laboratory over the years easily amounted to the lifespan of several denizens, and he did so enjoy creating his little *toys*. The seriousness of the situation now demanded he travel with a bodyguard.

The thing that had once been called Fat Jacob stamped alongside Hamir. A perverse mannequin with a body of metal and a head of flesh, Jacob carried in one wire-frame hand a long and sharp surgical knife; in the other he held a cleaver. The first wave of servants came at them when they reached a crossroads in the corridors.

Stooped and leading with spherical heads on the ends of long necks, the aspects of Hagi Tabet glared at Hamir with protruding eyes, pink and watery. One headed down each of the corridors to the left, right and straight ahead. Looking over his shoulder Hamir saw that a fourth had materialised in the corridor behind him. Reaching out with meaty hands connected to stick-thin arms, the aspects sought to pen in the necromancer and his bodyguard.

'Kill them, Jacob.'

Hamir remained statue still as the mannequin danced around him. With a blur of razor-keen silver, Jacob set about the servants, slicing through folds of pink blubber, hacking at necks and heads, like a seasoned killer. In utter silence, the fight lasted seconds, and as each servant fell it slipped from existence. In the aftermath of the quick slaughter, Jacob awaited further orders.

Hamir allowed himself a tinge of satisfied pride. 'Come along,' he said, and his bodyguard followed him to a set of stairs that descended to the next level of the Nightshade.

Seeing the avatar in his laboratory had not surprised Hamir as much as what it had said to him. The secrets of the Nightshade were many, and the blue spectre seemed to know them all. It had told Hamir many things that he was inclined neither to believe nor disbelieve. However, being in the uncustomary position of having no choice, he had been forced to follow the avatar's instructions. The first of those instructions was to continue travelling down until he reached the deepest region of the Nightshade, and a room known as the Last and Lowest Chamber.

Curiously, the whispery voice of Hagi Tabet had ceased goading the necromancer as he journeyed downward. Undoubtedly, she must be watching him, but her silence endured even when he paused to allow Jacob to rid the way of three more of her servants. With everything considered, Hamir regarded the new Resident's silence with suspicion. She obviously knew something he did not.

The answer to his suspicions came just after he stepped through a narrow archway to the next set of descending stairs. There was a fizzing sound from behind him, followed by a wet slurp. Hamir turned and saw that Jacob had ceased following him. The flesh of his head had been melted and now dripped through his wire-frame body in greasy lumps. An instant later, Jacob's skull was reduced to dust, and the surgical implements fell from his grasp. As the mannequin toppled to the ground, a woman dressed in a priest's cassock was revealed standing behind it. Hamir recognised her long hair, dark and straight, and her small, porcelain face that would have been flawless if not for the patch of scarring on her forehead. All in all, her presence was unsurprising.

She walked towards him, stepping over Jacob's remains. Hamir raised a hand, whispered a word, and cast a barrier of wavering acid, transparent and sickly grey, to cover the archway. The woman smiled thinly.

'Hello, Hamir,' she said with only the barrier separating them. 'It has been such a long time. How are you faring?'

Hamir considered, and then rocked his head from side to side. 'Fair to middling. Yourself?'

'Never better.' Her smile grew thinner. 'Why are you running from us?'

He pursed his lips. 'From my perspective, that question sounds a little rhetorical, Lady Asajad.'

'Oh, Hamir.' She studied the barrier of acid magic. 'You are the Resident's aide. Hagi Tabet needs your help. Fabian and I need your help. And soon, Viktor Gadreel will need your help.'

'Doubtful.'

Asajad chuckled. 'Must you always be so mistrusting? The Relic Guild is no more. Your masters have gone. Service to the Nightshade is all that remains for you, and the Nightshade belongs to the Genii now.' Her attempt at a sympathetic expression could not hide the grim amusement lurking beneath. 'Time to choose a side, Hamir.'

'Yes. Yes, I suppose it is.'

She took a step closer to the barrier. 'We can give you what you want, you know,' she whispered. 'All the time and freedom to conduct your ... *experiments,* without question or restriction. You can go as far as you wish, and no one will stop you. What possible reason could you have not to share your secrets with us?'

Hamir raised an eyebrow. 'Another rhetorical question, or a genuine invitation to join the Genii?' He shook his head. 'You always were a difficult one to read, Lady Asajad.'

Her dark eyes glinted. 'You are either with us or against us, Hamir.' She peered through the barrier again 'But – come now – let us not be separated. Let us continue this conversation in a more personal manner.'

Asajad reached out and placed a hand against the acid barrier. She gritted her teeth as the skin of her palm hissed and smoked for but an instant, and then her thin smile returned as she began absorbing the deathly grey magic.

Hamir took a step back. The barrier was an improvisation, and he had known the instant he cast it that it would, at best, only serve to slow a Genii. However, the magic was strong enough to buy him the moments that might make the difference between success and failure. But success depended on the avatar being trustworthy.

'As considerate as your invitation is,' he told Asajad as she continued to absorb the barrier, 'I'm rather afraid I've had a better offer. Goodbye, my Lady.'

He turned and jogged down the stairs, Mo Asajad's screams of fury following him.

Without bodyguard or weapon, Hamir travelled down and down, twisting and turning through the maze of the Nightshade, mildly surprised and thankful that no more of Tabet's servants appeared to hinder his way. Still dogged by the shouts and screams of Lady Asajad, he quickened his pace along a lengthy corridor that led to an antechamber. Here two more corridors splintered off, one to the left and one directly ahead. Hamir continued on straight, and descended the final flight of stairs that would bring him to his destination.

Mo Asajad was not far behind.

As he exited into another small antechamber, he paused to cast an acid barrier over the stairwell entrance. Turning, he stepped up to the far wall and pressed a hand to its maze pattern. The outline of a door appeared instantly. But even as he made to push the door open, a voice spoke from behind him.

'You're a fool, Hamir.'

Lady Asajad had reached the bottom of the stairs. Her face was cold and calm as she pressed a hand to the barrier of acid. Already, the magic was diminishing.

'You could have had all that you crave,' she hissed. 'But now the side you have chosen is quite obvious, and –' she grinned with long white teeth – 'I suspect the blood of a necromancer will taste sweeter than any other.'

'Hmm.' Hamir pushed open the door, and the Genii could only snarl after him as he slipped into the Last and Lowest Chamber of the Nightshade.

Clara had never realised that such a grand but miserable place existed beneath the streets of her home. She supposed she should have felt astonished and repulsed in equal measures as she traipsed through this dank and slimy world. But the truth was, she felt nothing for her environment. Her mind could focus only on her simmering anger, which her every thought seemed to fuel. Not even her medicine could abate the heat inside her.

She stared at the two skeletons lying on the walkway beside the river. Stripped of flesh, the white bones were charred and blackened.

'Do you think one of them is Samuel?' she asked; her voice was neutral.

'Perhaps,' Van Bam replied.

The ex-Resident crouched at the edge of the walkway, facing down into the river. The ruins of two golems lay in the shallow water, raw sewage flowing around them. Atop one pile of grey and broken stone sat an empty terracotta jar.

'That's three of them,' Clara said. 'Well – three that we know of. How many more friends do you think Fabian Moor has?'

Van Bam didn't reply and continued to gaze at the golems as though lost in contemplation. But Clara knew that he was feeling lost; that he had run out of ideas and hopelessness had entered his soul. She could smell it on him, and the scent disgusted her more than that of the sewers.

It had been the sound of Samuel's fire-bullet that brought them to this area. The soft thunder of the impact had been quickly followed by a low roar that seemed to rock the stiff atmosphere and suck the moisture from the air. Van Bam said it was the sound of a fireball. Had Samuel died in the blast he had created? Did one of the blackened skeletons belong to the old bounty hunter? But a fireball wouldn't strip flesh from bone so completely. These skeletons must have been the food source the new Genii had devoured to reanimate itself once released from the terracotta jar.

'What do we do now, Van Bam?'

He didn't respond.

'Van Bam?' she pressed tersely.

He turned his metallic eyes to her. 'In all honesty, Clara, I do not know.'

Clara scoffed; the weakness in his voice offended her, and she was barely able to look at him.

Van Bam seemed to sense her disappointment, and his expression was almost apologetic as he rose to his feet. Standing with his back to the river, he looked left and right along the walkway.

Clara left him to his indecision and popped yet another tablet of monkshood into her mouth. As she chewed it to a bitter, chalky paste, she noted that there weren't many tablets left in her medicine tin. It would not be long before she needed to renew her supply – perhaps a day, two at the most if she rationed. But it wasn't as if she could just pop up into Labrys Town for a new prescription. Once her medicine ran out, the wolf wouldn't remain caged for long.

Clara wasn't sure she cared anymore.

'We should keep moving,' Van Bam announced.

'Where to?'

'Anywhere, Clara. Now the Genii is reanimated, he or she will soon have to feed, and—'

A scream echoed from somewhere not so very distant. Clara and Van Bam stared at each other for a quick, frozen moment.

'Can you tell from which direction it came?' Van Bam asked.

'I think so, it—' She flinched as a second scream came, full of rage. The voice carried an undercurrent, something not quite human, and Clara had heard it before, very recently, at East Side Asylum.

'There,' she said, pointing into the gloom. 'Not too far away.' A third scream shattered the air. 'And it's getting closer.'

Van Bam illuminated his cane. 'I have changed my mind,' he whispered. 'It is time to stay put and hide, Clara. Keep close.'

Under the concealing light of the green glass cane, the two agents stepped away from the river and backed up against the wall beside the mouth of a tunnel. Evidently the Genii had already fed, and whoever had been infected with the virus was heading their way, but a darker thought occurred to Clara. What if the skeletons on the walkway belonged to bounty hunters, and it was their flesh that had reanimated the Genii? What if Samuel had survived the fireball, but it was his blood that had provided the Genii with his first meal? What if Old Man Sam was now on his way to becoming a golem?

Clara cocked her ear as she heard someone coughing with a series of harsh barks. She saw Van Bam's face was tight, pensive. The sound was getting closer.

Clara's anger rose again. Wouldn't it be a kind of poetic justice if Samuel was infected? To be stripped of his arrogance as the virus ravaged his body; to be reduced to a slavering animal that cared for nothing save sating its bloodlust; to lose all knowledge of who he was and what he had done as he slowly changed into an indolent, servile golem – yes, Clara decided it would be.

She sniffed sharply. A smell reached her nostrils: the pungent, rotten stench of infection. A cruel smile curled her lips.

She'd have no problem putting Samuel out of his misery, ending his pathetic, bestial existence. After all, not so long ago, he had intended to kill *her* for the sake of a bounty contract. If it came to it, Clara would have to deal with Samuel anyway; Van Bam was in no fit state.

A moment later, she sensed Van Bam tensing as a figure emerged into the light of a glow lamp further ahead on the walkway. With hair shorn close to the scalp and wearing a long coat, the figure loped forwards, fingers claws and teeth bared.

It was a woman.

Clara's first reaction was a tinge of disappointment that the virus victim was not Samuel. But she experienced a rush of pleasure as the woman came closer, revealing a face belonging to someone else she knew: a bounty hunter called Nim.

Though Nim couldn't see the Relic Guild agents, she obviously knew that fresh blood was close by. Her red tongue darted from her mouth as if tasting the air like a snake. She stopped to look up and sniff. She screamed her frustration, and as her voice shattered the rancid atmosphere, Nim continued onwards, her pace now a stalking crawl. Clara's blood quickened.

Clara knew that Nim always worked with her sister, Aga – who was probably now one of those skeletons. Although an unpleasant bitch, Aga was much preferable to her sibling. A sociopath and a heavy drinker, Nim had been barred from every place along Green Glass Row – except for the Lazy House. Fat Jacob alone had welcomed Nim's money, turned a blind eye to the things she did to the whores. She had hired Clara once, and the bruises had been quicker to heal than the memories.

The stench of infection grew heavy as Nim crept closer. An empty gun holster was strapped to her leg. Black veins spread like cracks in glass from a bloody bite wound on her neck. She stopped several paces from Clara to turn full circle and lick the air once more. The mask of rage Nim wore on her pale face, the long white teeth, and her animalistic gait, all served to finally expose the brutal monster that had always lurked within her. It was a fitting look for the bounty hunter, a truer look, and it gave Clara an idea.

What reason did she have to let the beast live? Clara's anger was making her feel so strong; all she had to do was step from the circle of concealing light and she could simply snap Nim's neck with her bare hands. An excellent idea.

As she made to follow through with her reasoning, Van Bam grabbed her arm and his metallic eyes glared at her, desperate and questioning. Before Clara had time to think her actions through, she made a noise that might have been a bark, and then brought her knee sharply up into Van Bam's groin. With a gasp, he fell down onto all fours, gagging as his glass cane rolled away from his grasp. The sickly green light sputtered and died.

Nim exhibited not the slightest surprise at the noise. The moment the Relic Guild agents were revealed, she screamed and lunged towards them.

The changeling ran to meet her.

They crashed together, and Clara wrapped her hands around Nim's neck, holding the monster back as long teeth gnashed for her face and throat. Clara squeezed as hard as she could and throttled Nim as if trying to shake her head loose. The infected bounty hunter made no attempt to remove the hands around her neck but, with cold detachment in her dying eyes, her fists pounded viciously at Clara's body. She was concerned only with fresh blood.

Doubt suddenly blemished Clara's confidence.

And in that moment, she realised that she was nothing like as strong as she felt; that in her human form she could not use the power of the wolf, but the realisation came too late. Nim kicked her legs away, and together they tumbled to the hard and slimy floor.

Clara managed to keep hold of Nim's neck, but she knew deep down that she was no longer fighting to win, to conquer; this was now a desperate struggle for her own survival, to keep herself from being infected. It was not a fight she was likely to win. What had she been thinking?

She searched inside herself, looking for the wolf. For the first time in her life, she begged it to come forwards with its fiery heat and instigate the metamorphosis. She pleaded with it to bring the strength and fury that would allow her existence to continue. But the wolf was not to be found. Clara tried calling for Marney, begging her to intervene and save her, as Marney had out in the Great Labyrinth. But the box of secrets was locked tight and unresponsive in her mind, as if the empath had turned her back on Clara.

The infected bounty hunter was on top of her now, and the strength in Clara's arms was failing. A strangled scream broke from Nim's mouth, spilling the warmth of diseased breath over Clara's face. As Clara gritted her teeth against the urge to vomit, Nim grabbed her head, pulled it up, and smashed it down once, twice, against the stone floor.

Dark spots appeared before Clara's vision, winking like tiny holes opening and closing upon the pale and infected face nearing hers. Nim was pulling her victim's head towards her teeth. Dimly aware of the sound of Van Bam retching, Clara wondered with fleeting hope if he would recover in time to save her. But she knew he wouldn't. Her strength was all but spent, the world was growing dim, and Nim's hungry teeth were drawing closer and closer to her face.

Just when Clara was about to give up the fight, to succumb to the ravages of the Genii virus, there was a flash of violet and a low and hollow spitting sound. Nim's head snapped sideways with a spray of blood and the weight of her body slipped away. Clara's head thudded against the floor for a third time, and her mind spun into the void, where a ghostly blue light waited to engulf her.

Just as the pain receded to something less debilitating, and he was finally able to fill his lungs with a deep gulp of air, Van Bam heard the spitting sound of a handgun and instinctively lay flat. He looked up to see Samuel emerge from the tunnel. The old bounty hunter ignored him and stepped quickly over to Clara. He pulled her unconscious form away from Nim's dead body, and then crouched down to check her over.

Van Bam manoeuvred himself into a sitting position and took several steadying gulps of air.

'She's breathing,' Samuel said. 'There's a cut on the back of her head, but she hasn't been bitten. Lucky.' He growled in annoyance. 'What in the Timewatcher's name was she thinking of, Van Bam?'

'Clara is experiencing a lapse in reason,' Van Bam replied. He wiped vomit from his chin and recovered his green glass cane. As he got gingerly to his feet, he realised it had been a very long time since he had felt this relieved. A grin came to his face. 'Quite the day,' he remarked. 'It is good to see you alive, old friend.'

'Likewise,' Samuel replied gruffly.

His clothes were damp, but the back of his coat was covered in scorch marks and his short, matted hair had been well and truly singed. Judging by his appearance, the slick grime on his face and clothes, Van Bam reasoned that Samuel had only avoided being burned to death in the fireball by taking a dip into sewage.

Still crouching beside the unconscious changeling, Samuel looked back at Van Bam. 'Why didn't you stop her?'

'I tried, but …' He sighed. 'Samuel, Clara's medicine no longer seems to be tempering her magic.'

'You think she's going to change?'

'I do not know. She has become difficult to read. Unpredictable. It could be the wolf, or it might be connected to whatever Marney placed in her mind.'

Samuel was quiet for a moment, his shades calculating. 'We'll have to deal with that when the time comes,' he said before walking to where Nim lay dead.

With his foot he rolled her body off the walkway and sent it splashing down into the river of wastewater.

Van Bam came alongside him. In the stillness of the sewers, with only the rush of water to break the silence, the two agents stared down at the remains of the golems, and the empty terracotta jar.

'I saw him,' Samuel said solemnly. 'The Genii came after me. He had me cornered, Van Bam. I was a dead man.'

Van Bam frowned. 'Yet here you are, alive and well.'

Samuel snorted and gestured to where the dead bounty hunter was sprawled face down in the filth beside the golem ruins. 'Nim saved me, inadvertently. She watched her sister die, and, I suppose, went mad. She came back looking for revenge and attacked the Genii. Of course there was no real contest. While he fed on Nim's blood, I made a run for it, and … and …'

He rubbed his forehead. 'The Genii didn't come after me again. I don't think he's down here anymore.'

Van Bam nodded. 'He has probably gone to join his colleagues at the Nightshade.' His gut tightened and his teeth clenched. 'We have a new Resident. Her name is Hagi Tabet—'

'I was scared, Van Bam,' Samuel snapped. It was an angry confession, and his voice carried an uncustomary degree of uncertainty.

To Van Bam's inner vision, Samuel's colour became the dull hue of shame.

'My awareness couldn't detect the Genii,' he continued. 'I felt no danger in his presence. It wasn't until I started a fireball that my magic reacted. I've never felt that lost before.'

'I can empathise,' Van Bam admitted. 'Gideon no longer speaks to me. I cannot feel my home. The Genii most assuredly control the Nightshade.'

Samuel was quiet for a moment. 'Do you know how they did it?'

Van Bam's stony expression masked his sorrow. 'Perhaps. If I were to guess, I would say Moor has just confirmed his reason for capturing Marney alive.'

Samuel swore under his breath. 'What about Hamir?'

'In all likelihood, he is dead.'

The two agents faced each other, and Van Bam clutched his cane tightly. His old friend was looking to him for leadership, guidance, some way out of this mess, but all he could do was avert his metallic eyes. A long moment passed before Van Bam could voice what they both already knew.

'I am sorry, Samuel. Without the Nightshade, without Hamir's help, there is nothing we can do. The Labyrinth is lost.'

'That's not true,' a voice said dreamily.

Both men turned to face Clara. The young changeling stirred on the walkway. She yawned and stretched, as though coming out of a particularly satisfying nap.

'Surely you remember, Van Bam?' she murmured.

Van Bam shared a quick look with Samuel, and then moved to Clara's side. He crouched and took her hand in his.

'What, Clara?' he said gently. 'What should I remember?'

She sighed softly, but didn't reply, and her eyes remained closed. Her colours swirled with hues far more peaceful than her earlier anger. But there was something else there, a subtle shade Van Bam hadn't seen in the changeling before.

'Clara, can you hear me?'

'Of course I can hear you.' Still, her eyes did not open. 'Umm ... you and Hamir. You did a thing, didn't you?'

Again, Van Bam shared a quick look with Samuel. 'What did we do, Clara? Tell me.'

'No, it's not about *what* you did!' Clara huffed impatiently. 'It's where you did it that's important.'

The old bounty hunter joined the illusionist at Clara's side, utterly bemused.

'What's she talking about?' Samuel said.

'I am not sure,' Van Bam replied. 'She is not really awake, Samuel, but not asleep either.'

'Concussion? She does have a head injury.'

'Perhaps, though—'

'There's nothing wrong with my bloody head,' Clara told them sternly. Her eyes moved rapidly beneath her lids. 'Look – it was a long time ago. Before you were Resident. Hamir went to the south side. You had to go with him.'

'The south side?' Van Bam pursed his lips as something distant jogged his memory. 'Please, Clara, I need a little more than that.'

'Oh, all right. At first you didn't want to go with him, but then you were glad you did. You learned a ... a *key difference*. Remember now?'

'I think I do,' Van Bam whispered. He looked at Samuel sharply. 'She's talking about the abandoned ore warehouse in the southern district. Do you remember, Samuel – when Fabian Moor was last here? Lady Amilee's gift—'

'Oh, I recall it very well, Van Bam,' Samuel replied. 'The question is, how could *she* know about it?' He frowned heavily. 'Marney knew, didn't she?'

'That's the dumbest thing I've heard you say,' Clara chuckled. 'The avatar told me, of course.' Her chuckles died, her eyes snapped open, and she sat bolt upright. 'I-I saw the avatar— *shit!*' Wincing, Clara held the back of her head and swooned.

Van Bam was quick to help her maintain a sitting position. 'Easy,' he soothed. 'Deep breaths.'

Clara blinked heavily several times as if to help the dizziness to pass. Her eyes wide with surprise and confusion, she looked up at the old bounty hunter looming over her.

'Samuel. I thought you were dead.'

'You're not the only one,' he said with a raised eyebrow.

She pulled a face. 'You stink.'

'When did you see the avatar, Clara?'

She winced in pain again. 'Wait, wait, wait.' She screwed her face up in thought. 'No … yes … in a dream. I think.'

'A dream?' Samuel looked doubtfully at Van Bam. 'I don't want to start another argument, Van Bam, but do you still believe the avatar's a portent? That it's on our side?' He gestured to their grim surroundings. 'Events haven't exactly unfolded in our favour, have they?'

'True, but … hold on a moment, Samuel.' Van Bam checked the shades of Clara's face. She was shaken, a little disorientated, but definitely alert and conscious. 'What else did the avatar tell you, Clara?'

'You and Hamir, you went to a warehouse on the south side, and did –' she waggled her hands in the air – 'a *thing*.'

'That is correct,' Van Bam said patiently. 'But you said it was the location that was special, not what we did.'

'It's confusing, Van Bam. I can't, I can't …' She made a noise of frustration. 'There's something hidden underneath that warehouse. In the cellar. Something the avatar wants you to see.'

'Could be a weapon,' Samuel said, a spark of hope in his voice. 'Maybe Hamir hid it there after last time.'

'No. No, that's not it,' Clara said. 'It's something to do with the Nightshade – no, that's not right, either. Is it?' She swore and buried her face in her hands.

Van Bam could feel Samuel's impatience, as if he was on the verge of shaking out the information from the changeling. Van Bam wasn't far behind him. Clara had knowledge of things that she could not possibly know; her dealings with the avatar had to be real, however muddled her recollections. Whether the avatar could be trusted or not, the changeling had lit an ember of optimism at the end of a darkly pessimistic tunnel.

Van Bam remained calm and gently pulled Clara's hands away from her face. 'Compose yourself,' he said softly. 'Take your time and think carefully. What is hidden beneath the warehouse?'

'That's just it – I can't be sure,' she said apologetically. 'My dreams – they're strange to remember, Van Bam. I could see the avatar. It was floating beside the portal outside the Nightshade.' She looked from one man to the other, her eyes earnest. 'I don't know what it means, but you *have* to see what's in that warehouse. Everything depends on it.'

Van Bam paused for a heartbeat. 'Are you strong enough to walk?'

Clara nodded, and he helped her to her feet.

Samuel had opened the chamber of his revolver and was in the process of replacing spent bullets. He gave Van Bam a wry smile that turned one corner of his mouth. 'You know this might be a trap.'

'And what if it is?' Van Bam returned the smile. 'How could it possibly worsen our situation?'

'My thoughts exactly,' Samuel said and he slapped the chamber shut.

CHAPTER NINETEEN

BACKDOORS

If everything the avatar had said was to be believed, even the Resident was not aware that the Last and Lowest Chamber was hidden inside the Nightshade. Hamir reasoned there was truth to this as, until this day, he himself had not been privy to the chamber's existence, and he had had the advantage of several lifetimes to learn every hidden corner of the Nightshade. The avatar had also said that the Genii would not be able to penetrate this room. Seeing as the door remained closed and Hamir was not fighting to keep the teeth of Lady Asajad from his throat, he considered that to be the truth as well.

The size of the Last and Lowest Chamber was large enough, though hardly impressive – a plain and rough square shape, thirty feet by thirty feet – but at the centre of the room, a fat column of energy fizzed and spat with a light that hummed and assaulted both Hamir and the dark stone walls with flashes of purple lightning. The column stretched from floor to ceiling, but its lower half was encircled by a series of evenly spaced monoliths: great black tablets, shiny and smooth, not quite stone, not quite metal, not quite glass.

Hamir studied the configuration of solid matter and energy, and felt his imperturbability invaded by a twinge of something that might have been awe.

'Astonishing,' he whispered.

There was a plethora of history books in Labrys Town. Historians had been writing them since the Labyrinth had been created; and there were plenty of academics who spent their days studying these books, debating their contents, and arguing with each other to such a degree of complexity they could no longer separate fact from fiction. Petty squabbles had twisted the truth, smothered the fire that made the smoke. Over the long years, Hamir had watched with mild amusement as 'history' had become irretrievably confused with 'mythology' without the denizens ever realising it.

Had he even a few of those academics standing beside him right now, he would have asked the learned minds to identify the column of energy within the Last and Lowest Chamber of the Nightshade. Hamir was willing to bet that not one of them would have been able to reach a correct answer; that this column was named the First and Greatest Spell; that it had been cast by the Timewatcher Herself a thousand years ago; and that it was the thaumaturgy upon which the entire creation of the Labyrinth was founded.

Yes, Hamir decided, he was awed to be standing in its presence, but not so much that he could waste time gawking at it.

He approached the First and Greatest Spell. He stepped between two of the black and glassy tablets that surrounded it, and looked up and down the length of the humming, spitting column. The spell danced upon a dome of dull, grey metal on the floor, and rose to meet a second dome on the ceiling, thirty feet above. Beyond that, the magic suffused the entire Nightshade and turned it into a power station of sorts, from which energy flowed to every corner of Labrys Town. Outside this room, the power of the First and Greatest Spell had been harnessed, manipulated, perverted, by the Genii; but inside, it remained as pure as the day the Timewatcher had cast it.

The Last and Lowest Chamber of the Nightshade, and the secrets it kept, was the final shadow in the Labyrinth, which the fire of the Genii could not illuminate.

Or so the avatar had said.

Turning his back on the great column of energy, Hamir faced the smooth and glassy surfaces of the tall tablets enclosing the area. Moving to one side, he studied each one carefully, but found each surface unmarked. With limitless patience, he began again, and then again, until he found what he sought. From the corner of his eye, he spotted a small engraving high on one tablet, briefly caught in flickering light of the First and Greatest Spell. At the right angle, Hamir could see it was the engraving of a little diamond shape, just as the avatar had said it would be.

He reached up and felt the grooves of the symbol beneath his fingertip.

'Encouraging,' he murmured.

The necromancer dipped his hand into the inside pocket of his suit jacket, pulling out two corked phials. He lifted them up against the flashes of purple light and shook the thick liquid within.

Changeling blood: it was a precarious substance. Once removed from the vein, it would congeal far quicker than ordinary blood, and only one skilled in the art of necromancy had sufficient expertise to stabilise it. A strange fluid whose magical properties many magic-users found hard to understand. Unique and potent, it served as a catalyst that could fuel the most mundane spell of the lowest magic-user with the might of a Thaumaturgist. Yes, the blood of a changeling was potent and difficult to use, but oh so very dangerous, especially in the wrong hands.

Two days ago, before Fabian Moor had announced his return, the blue spectre had visited Van Bam and given him a very particular set of instructions. Before Hamir was sent to collect Clara from the police station, Van Bam had asked him to procure two phials of her blood, which Hamir had done while she lay unconscious. Why this was to be done had not been revealed at the time. Hamir supposed that if Van Bam still lived, then he still did not know, and had probably not even thought of these phials again. But Hamir had not forgotten them; he had sensed at the time that his task had been important.

Hamir slipped one of the phials back into his jacket pocket, whilst keeping the other in his hand. With a light frown, he studied the diamond symbol on the pillar. He gave a sigh, uncorked the phial, lifted it to his lips, and drank the contents in one go.

This was not the first time Hamir had tasted another's blood, though he had never particularly enjoyed the flavour. However, he only had to endure the salty, rusty tang for a moment, and then the energy began to swell inside him. It started as a warm wave of nausea that spread through his body and limbs with increasing heat. Hamir felt hotter and hotter, and sweat began beading on his skin. His ears were filled with a drone that was in tune with the humming of the First and Greatest Spell. Not until he looked at his shaking hands did the necromancer realise his entire body was vibrating.

The things he could accomplish with the power of changeling blood … Hamir could not remember the last time his magic had felt this strong. The feeling might have overwhelmed him with joy, but, with a surge of will honed over centuries, he focused on the instructions of the avatar.

Whispering words that felt at once alien and familiar on his tongue, fighting an urge to bellow them proudly, boastfully, Hamir gritted his teeth as molten heat seeped through his pores, causing his skin to glow with pale radiance. He reached out a hand and touched the diamond symbol again. This time it glowed, and a *crack* of energy splintered from the column and danced upon the black tablet upon which the symbol was engraved.

The tablet seemed to lurch before the necromancer, as if it had been momentarily displaced, jumped to one side and back again. Hamir watched with fascination as its glassy length stretched upward and arched over him, widening to cover him like a shroud. Its surface rippled as though it had turned to liquid, and Hamir felt the pull of a vortex. A hollow wind moaned.

If there was any trickery in the avatar's instructions, if there was any reason why Hamir should be afraid, it was no longer a concern to the necromancer. He closed his eyes as rippling obsidian descended on him, swallowed him, and sent him spinning into somewhere else.

The faint light of grimy lamps illuminated the walkways. Their sickly glow barely assisted the slow progress of a ragtag group of magickers heading southward through the sewers. A dark-skinned man led the group on bare feet; his eyes were plates of metal fused to the sockets, and he carried a cane of green glass. A pale-skinned young woman, small and gangly, her face bruised, the back of her head bloody, followed him with plodding steps, as if sleepwalking. A broad-shouldered and predatory-looking older man brought up the rear, a rifle in his hands, a shrewd and piercing gaze scanning the shadows, ever vigilant for signs of danger.

Van Bam didn't believe that anyone was tracking them now, but he was glad to have Samuel back, to know they had his unerring aim covering their journey to the southern district. The ex-Resident was glad to have a goal. He felt drive and purpose in his steps once more.

To lose all connection to the Nightshade, to have the voice of Gideon so suddenly severed from his mind – Van Bam could not have conceived a worse scenario. He had spent so much of his life relying on the magic of his home and on the acerbic advice grudgingly given by his spirit guide – he had often wondered if he could think for himself anymore. But now his mind was fully his own for the first time in decades, Van Bam was surprised to find his logic well-ordered, his thoughts clear, and his determination strong.

Clara's revelation concerning the avatar had given the Relic Guild a glimmer of hope when all hope seemed to have disappeared. Not everything was lost just yet. In an abandoned warehouse, where, so long ago, Van Bam had watched Hamir perform acts of thaumaturgy, a mystery was hidden, a mystery that everything depended on, or so the avatar said. Whether the strange blue ghost could be trusted or not was academic now. Perhaps the Relic Guild had found the one path that might lead to redemption.

No longer hindered by bounty hunters and Genii, the Relic Guild made good progress. After an hour of journeying in silence, Van Bam judged the group had passed out of the central district and had entered the south side. It had been a long time since he had last traversed the sewers, but he remembered the geography well. Unconcerned by the warm and fetid atmosphere, he led the way. Within an hour they would be beneath a landscape of storage warehouses. And then the Relic Guild would have to go above ground and face an unfamiliar problem: avoiding the eyes of the Nightshade.

As Van Bam made it to the end of a bridge, Samuel called him. Van Bam turned and saw Clara had stopped halfway across. Her brow was furrowed and her lips were pursed. Her shades pulsed with deep thought. Van Bam walked back to her.

'Clara?' he whispered. 'Are you all right?'

'Yes, I'm fine,' she replied, her eyes darting from side to side. 'Tell me something – that portal outside the Nightshade, it's not the only one, is it?'

'What do you mean?'

'There's a second portal, at the rear of the Nightshade.'

'There was once.'

'The Relic Guild used it to get to the doorways out in the Great Labyrinth. That's how you travelled to the Aelfirian Houses – wasn't it?'

Van Bam shared a quick look with Samuel. This was more information that Clara could not have known. But had the avatar told her, or was she remembering a time when Marney had used the portal?

'Clara,' Van Bam said. 'That portal was destroyed at the end of the Genii War, along with all the others.'

'That's right,' she said, nodding. 'The portal at the front of the Nightshade is the only one left.' She fell into silent contemplation again.

Samuel was unsettled. 'Why do you ask?'

Clara seemed to notice him for the first time. 'Hmm?'

'Are you remembering something the avatar told you?'

'Maybe. It could be one of Marney's memories.' She looked up. 'It's funny … I thought I was onto something. But it's fading, I …' She sighed. 'It's gone.'

Her shades swirled a mixture of frustration and disappointment.

'It will come to you, I am sure,' Van Bam said reassuringly. 'Let us continue.'

Van Bam turned and led the way once more.

The dismal aesthetics of the sewers never altered; the group traversed slime-covered walkways and tunnels, crossed rough and slick bridges, always heading south. The silence among the three agents endured, and Van Bam's thoughts turned to the town above, and the new regime.

The magic of the Nightshade was sentient, intelligent, powerful, and the Genii should not have been able to overcome it. It filled Van Bam with deep sadness to think of Marney and he knew that his old lover would have fought the Genii. But if Fabian Moor had been right all these years, if the Nightshade had left some magical residue in the psyches of the Relic Guild agents that exposed a weakness in its defences, then Moor had obviously found a way to extract it from Marney's mind. And that meant she had outlived her usefulness to the Genii. Van Bam pushed away an image of Marney suffering unimaginable tortures, though he knew that Fabian Moor would never have allowed her end to be quick and painless.

Whatever foul methods the Genii had used to grasp control of the Nightshade, their grip on Labrys Town was absolute. But the Genii's actions still left questions unanswered. Van Bam knew that Fabian Moor had reanimated at least two other Genii, but how many others did he not know of? The jar from the asylum had obviously been buried beneath the cell in which it was found. Samuel said that two golems had dug up the other from the river floor. But how had those terracotta jars got into Labrys Town in the first place? And now the Genii were here, what could control of the Nightshade possibly gain them? With no way out of the Labyrinth, all they had done was procured a feeding ground to sate their blood-thirst. Unless …

Unless they did know of a way out.

Perhaps their old ambitions were still alive. Perhaps they still coveted the subjugation of the Aelfirian Houses, and they had found a way to achieve it. Van Bam knew Fabian Moor had been using thaumaturgy to create personal portals, but to where? Maybe he had always known how to reach the Aelfir from the Labyrinth, but he and his fellow Genii were too few and weak to re-enter battle. Could it be they were waiting until an army stood at their backs – an army of gun-wielding golems a million strong – before setting their plans of invasion into action?

Van Bam looked back at Clara. Her colours were contemplative, and he felt an almost frantic need to know, *what had the avatar told her?* What could possibly be hidden in that warehouse?

Finally, their silent trek through a miserable landscape brought the Relic Guild deep into the southern district. The group stopped before a caged ladder that ascended high into the darkness above. Van Bam led the way up. They all understood that leaving the sewers was to leave relative safety. They would have to keep their wits about them; Labrys Town had become hostile territory.

The ladder led to a small, metal grille platform; and there, set into the dark stone wall, was an open archway leading to a narrow staircase. Illuminating the darkness with his glass cane, Van Bam began to ascend. The scrapes and shuffles of his colleagues' boots echoed in the tight space behind him.

The stairs finished at a dead end wall, but the brickwork carried the familiar maze pattern. Samuel affirmed that he sensed no immediate danger and Van Bam reached out, but paused before making contact with the wall.

With a pang of uncertainty, he wondered how deeply the Genii's influence had burrowed into Labrys Town. All the districts' energy came from the magic stemming from the Nightshade. Would the magic in this secret door still obey his touch?

Holding his breath, he pressed his palm to the pattern.

There was a click, and Van Bam exhaled in relief. A slim doorway swung outwards, and bright, blue-grey light flooded the stairwell. Turning sideways to slip through the gap, he exited into the southern district of Labrys Town, and the stink of the sewers evaporated in the fresh, chilly air of Silver Moon. Clara and Samuel followed, and the door closed and disappeared behind them.

Van Bam recognised the area. They had emerged at the back of a metal-works yard, in the heart of the warehouse region. The door that led to the sewers was hidden behind a false wall at the end of a supervisor's hut.

Here during the day, engineers built new trams, or repaired the old, or scrapped and recycled the decommissioned. Tramlines crisscrossed the stone floor, and against the rear wall, rusted metal parts had been dumped. The huts and workshops around the yard were shuttered and locked. The working day was long over, though the smell of hot grease still touched the air.

It felt good to be outside again. The sky was clear, full of stars. Even to Van Bam's inner vision, the cold disc of Silver Moon was bright and glaring after the dingy world below. Nonetheless, he kept his green glass cane illuminated under the brightness. After his and Clara's experience with Captain Jeter, he doubted its concealing light could hide them from the watchful gaze of Hagi Tabet. Fortunately, the eye devices in this area were mostly positioned within warehouses. The green glass cane would, however, hide the group from any warehouseman or tram driver working the nightshift.

'Come,' Van Bam said. 'We are not far from our destination.'

Unseen and silent, the three agents left the metal-works yard, and weaved their way through the streets and alleys between the warehouses. Clara and Samuel followed Van Bam, making sure to remain within his cane's circle of secreting light.

The further he travelled, the more concerned Van Bam became. The atmosphere felt wrong. The warehouses were vital for storing the food stocks and materials that ensured the denizens survived in their isolated home. Normally, there were security guards patrolling the area at all hours, and there was always a nightshift of yard workers. Yet the group passed no one on their journey, and not one light shone from a warehouse window. Van Bam could not even hear the sound of machinery, or the rumble of cargo trams. The southern district was too quiet. It seemed deserted.

Coming to the end of an alley, Van Bam brought the small group to a halt. Samuel moved up alongside the ex-Resident.

'We are close,' Van Bam told him, gesturing to the other side of the tramlines. 'The warehouse is on the next street.'

'Yes, I remember,' Samuel replied. 'You know, this place feels awfully quiet to me. Do you think something's happened to the denizens?'

'I would guess Captain Jeter has enforced a curfew.'

'Jeter,' Samuel growled. 'If we live through this, I think I'll have a little word with him.'

'Jeter might be easily fooled, but he cannot be blamed, Samuel. He is, and always will be, the Resident's man. There is no compromise in his devotion to the Nightshade.'

Samuel pulled a sour expression. 'So, the Genii get Jeter to clear the districts, and it's easier for everyone to search for us.' He scoffed. 'Nice to know we're still considered a threat.'

Samuel paused before speaking again, his face alive with remorse. 'Van Bam, if the Genii are already in the Nightshade—'

'Then Marney is dead,' Van Bam concluded.

Samuel nodded. 'I'm sorry.' He took a breath. 'We probably shouldn't be hanging around.'

'Agreed.'

'Wait,' Clara said. The young changeling's face was turned up toward Silver Moon. Her eyes were closed. 'I can hear something. A tram. It's coming this way.'

Both men stepped back into the alley.

'Stay in the light,' Van Bam reminded, holding his cane aloft.

A moment later, he too heard the sound: a distant rumble that was growing louder and closer. It wasn't long before the power lines began swaying overhead, and the sleek, blue and white striped body of a police tram trundled along the street. As it crept past the alley mouth, a police officer could be seen standing at the window staring out. Luckily, he was not wearing a receptor helmet and could not see through Van Bam's magic to the three agents hiding in the cane's light.

As the tram slipped from view, Samuel exhaled with relief. 'After you,' he said to Van Bam.

The group crossed the street and headed down an alley into a deserted street, flanked by terraced lines of warehouses. Innocuous looking, each shutter door was painted white, signifying the storage of metal ores. The Relic Guild headed straight towards the last warehouse on the right.

Samuel peered through the darkened window, checking for signs of life. Clara remained close by, still looking lost and contemplative. Van Bam faced the white shutter door and thought back to the last time he had been here.

The warehouse looked as rundown and abandoned as it had decades ago, somehow lonely sitting at the end of the terrace. Painfully, it reminded Van Bam of Marney. The last time he had come here was on the same day he had surprised her with a little attic apartment of their own. He almost smiled at the memory.

'Seems deserted enough,' Samuel said, turning from the window. 'I can't sense any danger, either.'

Van Bam nodded. 'Clara?'

Clara concentrated. 'I can't hear anyone,' she said. 'Or smell anything,' she added.

Van Bam stepped forwards and laid a hand against the shutter door. He felt the reassuring vibrations of mechanisms turning as it unlocked. As he raised it, the shutter made an obscene amount of noise in the stillness. The three agents stepped into the warehouse.

Van Bam experienced another jolt of nostalgia. The centre of the warehouse floor was etched with the faint outline of thaumaturgic symbols. Created by Hamir during the war, the engraving had become embedded with dirt over the years, and it must be scarcely discernible to normal eyes. But Van Bam's vision saw it clearly enough – the swirls and symbols of an impossible language. Whatever magic it had once generated had long since dissipated.

Apart from the engraving, the warehouse was as empty as it had always been. Behind a door on the far wall were the stairs that led down to the cellar. Near it was a large elevator platform that also descended there.

'Look at the eye,' Clara whispered. 'Something's wrong with it.'

Van Bam followed the line of her pointing finger.

There was a single eye device, positioned where it could observe the entire space. But the usually milky-white fluid inside was altered; it was now a distinct shade of pink – like milk powder mixed with blood – which rolled and swirled within the glass casing.

'I've seen this before,' Samuel said, 'back at my hideout.' He faced Van Bam. 'Why have the eyes changed?'

'Perhaps a reaction to the Genii,' Van Bam said. 'Let us hope it is a sign the Nightshade is fighting their influence. If not, Hagi Tabet could be watching us right now.'

Samuel looked to Clara. 'Underneath the warehouse, the avatar said, right? Something in the cellar?'

Clara nodded, but didn't seem sure. Samuel stepped quickly over to the stairwell door and rattled the handle. It was locked.

Extinguishing the light from his cane, Van Bam moved to the back wall and stood upon the elevator platform. He reached for the control box, and Clara and Samuel joined him.

The ex-Resident's thumb hovered over the down button. 'For what it is worth,' he said, 'be ready to defend yourselves.'

He pressed the button, and the elevator began its descent.

In the police headquarters, Captain Jeter stood in his office, gazing down onto the plaza of Watchers' Gallery, shadow-streaked in the light of Silver Moon. It was deserted, as were the streets of the entire town. Not even the trams were running tonight. The denizens were under curfew.

Jeter remembered how proud he had been the day he was made Captain of the Police Force. The Resident himself had bestowed the position upon him, and Jeter had sworn to uphold the laws of the Nightshade rigorously. Now he felt a fool. He had allowed a demon-worshipping whore to corrupt the old Resident. Under his very nose she had wormed her way into the Nightshade to spread her poison. And Jeter had let her slip from his grasp. Twice. She was still out there, somewhere, and she and her fellow demon-worshippers threatened the life of every denizen.

At the sound of a knock, Jeter turned, and Sergeant Ennis entered the office. There were dark rings around his eyes, and he looked dishevelled in his usually smart, dark blue uniform. At this moment, rest was an unaffordable luxury for the entire police force.

'Report,' Jeter said.

Ennis rubbed a hand over his ashen face. 'There was some trouble down Green Glass Row, sir – denizens breaking curfew.'

'It is dealt with?'

'Yes, sir. There was some violent protesting – three denizens were killed. But the deaths brought the crowd to order. As soon as we started shooting, most of them dispersed to their homes, though we still had to make several arrests.'

'Very good,' Jeter said and motioned for his sergeant to take a seat.

Ennis slumped into the chair wearily, and then frowned at his captain. 'Should I get you a doctor, sir?'

Jeter shook his head. He knew what he looked like, but he didn't care. His nose was broken, and the blood in his nostrils had dried to hard, sharp lumps. Bruises had manifested under his eyes, and the swelling gave him a deep ache, a constant reminder of his failure. He deserved the pain.

'How goes the search for Van Bam and Peppercorn Clara?'

'We're still looking for them,' Ennis said and he sighed. 'A patrol unit contained a small outbreak of the virus in the northern district, but they were long gone from the scene.'

'To be expected, I suppose,' Jeter grumbled. 'They feed and they disappear.' He stared down at his broken spectacles lying on his desk.

Van Bam had stood right next to him in the interrogation room, mimicking an officer, and Jeter had suspected nothing until it was too late. He should have known the possessed Resident would be able to use magic. Back at the very moment Van Bam had announced the revival of the Relic Guild, Jeter's suspicions should have been aroused. Everyone knew there were no magickers left, and the Relic Guild had died out years ago. If not through his newfound love of demon-worshipping, through the rituals of blood-taking, how else could Van Bam have come to possess such power? It all seemed so obvious now.

'Sir,' Ennis said, 'our resources are stretched. We have as many officers as possible out combing the districts, going door-to-door, trying to flush out the Relic Guild – but people are disappearing, and these random outbreaks of the virus …' He took a breath and looked down. 'Sir, the denizens know what we're up against. They're frightened.'

'With good reason,' Jeter said. 'Five bounty hunters I sent after Old Man Sam, Ennis. I'm yet to hear word from any one of them.' He shook his head. 'I should imagine he is reunited with his friends by now.'

He turned and stared out of the window again. 'I was only a child when the real Relic Guild walked our streets – and you, Ennis, were not even born. From the shadows, they watched over this town, protected us from the unseen. Now, these bastards are a perversion of everything the Relic Guild once stood for. They are an insult to the name, even if no less powerful.'

'Could they do it, sir?' Ennis said in a tight voice. 'Could they really bring the Retrospective to Labrys Town?'

'Yes,' whispered Jeter.

Behind him, Ennis swore softly. It was a hopeless sound, lost, resigned. Jeter turned to face his sergeant again.

'We have a duty to perform,' he said sternly. 'We will not fail the denizens, no matter how desperate our situation seems.'

'With all due respect, sir, what chance do we stand against the Relic Guild? I saw the aftermath of their virus at the asylum. I saw what they had done to people.' Ennis opened his hands helplessly. 'We're fighting with bullets against magic. The Relic Guild can hide within plain sight. They move without being seen—'

'Hagi Tabet can see,' Jeter snapped. 'Or perhaps you have forgotten, Sergeant?'

'No, sir,' Ennis replied quickly.

'Then calm yourself!'

Jeter tried not to groan as he lowered himself into the chair at his desk. He wasn't really that angry with Ennis; the man was only expressing the doubt felt by all the officers. Fear had spread through the ranks like the virus of the demon-worshippers. But Ennis needed to accept, here and now, that even though, in his corruption, Van Bam had been displaced, the Nightshade remained strong. Its eyes were on their side.

Adopting a calmer tone of voice, Jeter said, 'Hagi Tabet is watching over Labrys Town, and she does not sleep. She will not rest until her denizens are safe. And *you*, Ennis, will trust in our new Resident as I do. Understood?'

Ennis nodded and some resolve came back to his weary face.

'Then back to business,' Jeter said crisply, and he leant back in his chair. 'What of the homeless? They have been rounded up?'

'For the most part, sir,' Ennis said. 'We're using the jails and shelters to keep them off the streets, but we can't be sure how many are left out there.'

'Keep looking, Sergeant. Vagrants are easy pickings, and if they're infected with the virus, we could have an epidemic on our hands before—'

'Captain Jeter.'

The soft, lilting voice of a woman filled the office and interrupted the conversation. With a flurry of motion, Jeter jumped to his feet and saluted the eye device on the back wall. The action was quickly copied by his sergeant.

'Yes, Ma'am.'

'Rest easy, Captain,' Hagi Tabet said. 'There is some good news in these dark times.' She paused before giving a long, breathy sigh. 'I have located our enemies.'

She paused again, and the fluid within the eye swirled pinkly. Jeter frowned and lowered his hand. Had he detected amusement in the Resident's voice?

'Ma'am?' he said.

'They are hidden in a warehouse in the southern district,' she said. 'I have given the precise location to your Watchers. Now, go and kill the Relic Guild for me, won't you, Captain Jeter?'

'Of-Of course, Ma'am.'

'And, Captain … please don't let me down.'

The eye clicked and the fluid inside settled. The Resident had gone.

In the ensuing silence, Ennis turned to face his captain, his mouth open, speechless.

Jeter swallowed. 'Tell the Watchers to send that location to all patrol units, Sergeant. Gather everyone.' He clenched his teeth. 'The Relic Guild does *not* leave that warehouse alive.'

The elevator descended into the cellar. Immediately, the atmosphere felt eerily still, the air stale, as if undisturbed for a very long time. With his rifle in hand, its power stone primed, Samuel was quick to scan the area for enemies, but he detected nothing. The elevator platform touched base, but no one moved or spoke.

The cellar was deserted. Two glow lamps shed weak light; one was positioned at head height to the right of the elevator platform, and faced the other positioned on the opposite wall. Between the glow lamps, a rod of dull grey metal, no thicker than Van Bam's cane, rose up from the smooth stone of the floor.

Van Bam was the first to act. He strode over to the metal rod and studied it. Clara joined him, while Samuel went to check an open archway cut into the end of the left-hand wall. Through the archway was the dark empty stairwell that led back up to the warehouse. Samuel took comfort from knowing the door at the top was locked.

'Samuel, look at this,' Van Bam said.

There was an uncharacteristic edge of awe in his voice. Samuel holstered his rifle as he moved to see what they had found.

Van Bam was studying the tip of the metal rod, which was at eye level. It ended with a hollow diamond shape, giving the rod the appearance of a spear.

'The mark of the Thaumaturgists,' Van Bam whispered.

The diamond was positioned in line with the glow lamps, and their light met through its hollow centre. The thaumaturgic symbol served as a frame for what looked to be clear glass, but when prodded by Samuel, it proved to be flexible, gelatinous.

'It is perhaps best not to touch it, Samuel,' Van Bam warned. 'I have no idea what purpose this device serves –' he studied the length of the spear's shaft – 'but I do recognise the metal it is made of. It is neither solid nor liquid, and its colours …' He seemed in awe again. 'I observed Hamir use material like this a very long time ago, Samuel. You recall the automaton spider?'

'I'm not likely to forget it,' Samuel replied. 'But what's this thing doing here? Did Hamir make it?'

It was Clara who responded. 'No,' she said, 'but you're on the right lines.' Judging by the changeling's expression, she was once again on the edge of something just beyond the reach of her memory. 'Hamir didn't make this thing. But he did show Van Bam how to use it.'

Samuel looked at Van Bam, but the ex-Resident was fixed on the rod and made no response.

Clara's expression became wistful, and the ghost of a smile played on her lips. 'Thaumaturgy has memory, Van Bam. And it remembers its teachers.'

Samuel screwed his face up. 'What's she talking about, Van Bam?'

But his old friend didn't reply. Instead he passed Samuel his cane, and then reached out for the metal rod with a tentative hand. With almost dream-like slowness, Van Bam gripped the shaft. He gasped, his grip tightening as though the metal was charged with some intense energy.

'Van Bam!' Samuel shouted, but the ex-Resident raised his free hand to stop him from acting.

Van Bam exhaled a long breath, and smiled. 'I once helped Hamir do something extraordinary, Samuel.' His voice was distant. 'The magic in this metal remembers that help. It has been waiting for me.'

Samuel had never felt more bemused, and his anger rose. 'For love of the Timewatcher,' he growled, 'what's going on, Van Bam?'

'We shall find out. Perhaps the two of you should stand back.'

Clara showed no sign of moving, so Samuel took her by the arm and dragged her away from the diamond-tipped rod. As he did so, Van Bam withdrew his hand and joined them.

Samuel barely noticed Van Bam taking his cane back; he was watching, disconcerted and fascinated, as the spear of dull grey metal began to radiate light. It started as a faint glow that soon brightened to a rich purple flare. Samuel raised a hand against the light as it began flickering with rapid, blinding flashes. Through his fingers, he saw darker rings of purple shooting up the shaft to the top where it gathered, soaked almost, into the gelatinous substance within the diamond-shaped frame. More and more of the rings added light to the thaumaturgic symbol until the shaft was drained of the coloured light and the diamond blazed like the brightest star in the night sky.

Static charged the atmosphere, and the hairs on Samuel's arms stood erect.

At the sound of a sharp crack, the three agents flinched as one. It was followed by the low hum of energy building up. Two thin beams of purple light shot from the diamond and hit the glow lamps with a second loud noise. The lamps fizzed and buzzed before redirecting the light to the wall opposite the stairwell. Fractured into a multitude of searing, purple streaks that filled the cellar with a nauseating strobe effect, each beam focused on the centre of the wall. Wherever one hit, a patch of brickwork disappeared in a puff of dust as fine as tobacco smoke. Quick and fleeting, the beams continued to burn away stone until they had fashioned a neat rectangular area that resembled a dark doorway.

Samuel's mouth hung open. The beams of purple energy danced around the frame of the rectangle, as if keeping its shape open. Within the frame, the doorway was coated with a black substance that rippled like liquid glass.

'A portal?' Samuel asked no one in particular. His throat had gone suddenly dry.

In the flickering light, Van Bam's expression was just as astonished. 'Events unfold as they have to,' he whispered.

Clara was brave enough to step forward.

'Careful,' Samuel snapped as she approached the beam connecting the diamond with the glow lamps. But he needn't have worried; Clara seemed fully aware that energy capable of destroying stone would have no trouble with flesh. She ducked under the beam, and, flanked by the purple streaks, she stood with her back to her colleagues, staring into the glassy portal.

'Samuel,' she said softly, 'you told me the portal outside the Nightshade only goes one way, didn't you?'

Samuel shrugged. 'All right,' he told Clara. 'If you say I did.'

'That can't be right, can it?' She rubbed the cut on the back of her head. 'I mean – portals are two way things. That's how the Thaumaturgists designed them to be. Surely you know that?'

Samuel's confusion deepened, and he was relieved when Van Bam replied for him.

'Clara,' he said, 'I cannot pretend to understand the mechanics of portals, or the thaumaturgy by which they are designed, but I can assure you that Samuel is correct. Nothing can leave through that portal at the Nightshade.'

'I'm not saying Samuel's lying,' she continued, clearly irritated. 'I'm saying the entrance and exit aren't always located in the same place. But a portal always – *always* – has a way in and a way out. They can't exist without both. The avatar told me that ...' She spun around and faced her fellow agents. 'The avatar told me! I remember ...' Her mouth worked silently and her hands shook.

Samuel stepped forward, closely followed by Van Bam, and together they ducked under the purple beam and approached Clara.

Samuel gripped the changeling by the shoulders. '*What* do you remember, Clara?'

She shrugged him off and turned to the portal. 'This –' she pointed a finger at the dark, rippling doorway, and took a step closer to it – 'it's connected to the portal outside the Nightshade. It's that portal's exit – a way out.'

Clara spoke as if her statement should have been obvious to all. This was higher magic she was talking about, something neither Samuel nor Van Bam knew much about. But where Van Bam seemed eager to believe her, Samuel felt only scepticism.

'Just wait a minute,' he growled. 'Van Bam, what if the avatar lied to her? Fabian Moor could have created this portal. It might lead us straight into the Nightshade.' His face darkened. 'Or the Retrospective.'

'It might also lead us to the Aelfir who have been keeping us alive for the last forty years.'

'It does!' Clara said adamantly. 'It's the Labyrinth's backdoor. It was kept secret from you.'

Samuel checked an angry retort. He was as desperate as anyone to find help, to believe the avatar was on their side, and that this portal *was* the answer. But the pragmatist in him simply couldn't out-argue the cold, suspicious mercenary he had become.

Old Man Sam stared at the portal almost angrily.

'The only way to know for sure is to step through,' he said. 'And I'm just suggesting we think really hard before doing that.'

'What's left to think about?' Clara said. She seemed both irritated and overjoyed. 'I'm not afraid.'

'Perhaps Samuel is right, Clara,' Van Bam suggested.

Without looking back, she threw her arms into the air, made a noise of exasperation, and took another step closer to the portal. For a moment, Samuel thought she might leap forward and dive blindly into the glassy blackness. But she turned around, and her eyes flashed yellow as she glared first at Samuel, and then at Van Bam.

'The avatar is telling the truth. I can't explain it, but I just know it is.' Her face twisted into an almost bestial expression. 'And we're all going to die anyway if—'

She looked up sharply, sniffing the air.

At the same moment, Samuel's prescient awareness flared. Time slowed. He became connected to his environment with almost painful sensory perception. The flashes and flickering of purple light became measured pulses. A dull *click* was followed by the groan of hydraulics. The elevator platform began rising.

Samuel wheeled around, drew his rifle, and aimed it at the stairwell door. The power stone whined and glowed into life.

The ripping and tearing of wood came next: the door to the warehouse above being smashed from its hinges. Voices followed – loud, shouted orders – and then came the sound of heavy feet pounding down the stairs to the cellar.

Samuel tracked his aim along the stairwell wall, judging the position of the lead runner.

He pulled the trigger and the power stone flashed.

With a spray of stone, the bullet smashed through the thin wall, found its target, and the magic it contained ignited. There was a brief scream and a roar of fire. A figure, smouldering but not alight, tumbled to the foot of the stairs and fell through the doorway. He rolled from side to side, frantically trying to lessen the heat in his clothes. He wore the bowl-like receptor helmet of the street patrols.

Samuel's second bullet shattered the black glass and incinerated the person beneath.

Another patrolman stumbled against the doorway, already aflame. He must've been touched by the magic in Samuel's first bullet. The fire ate through his clothes, burned away his skin and muscle, and his skeleton crumbled to ash on the floor.

That first shot had left a gaping hole in the stairwell wall. The barrel of a rifle appeared through it and spat out a lethal projectile. Samuel's prescient awareness was one step ahead of the shooter, telling him which way to duck. The bullet missed the old bounty hunter, screaming past his ear. Someone grunted behind him. Samuel fired through the hole in the wall. The sound of shattering glass preceded the flare and fury of red flames, and the agonised screams of dying police officers.

And then the glare of Van Bam's magic streamed over Samuel's shoulder. It covered the doorway and the hole in the stairwell wall with a barrier shining green against the flickering beams of energy that cut purple lines through oily smoke and the stench of burnt flesh.

The shouts and footfalls on the stairs were muffled now. Two patrolmen arrived at the doorway, looking demonic and insect-like in their black helmets. They pounded the green barrier with the butts of their rifles, causing it to ripple like disturbed water, but they could not break through Van Bam's magic.

With his last fire-bullet spent, Samuel slid the rifle into the holster on his back, and drew his revolver. Up above, the elevator platform had almost reached the warehouse's upper level. There was no telling how many police were up there; how many officers Hagi Tabet had sent after them.

Through the pounding of his heart and the rushing of blood in his ears, Samuel became aware of a whimpering sound behind him.

Clara was down. Van Bam crouched over her, and she clutched at his shoulders, struggling to keep her breathing steady. It was difficult to see in the flashing light, but it looked as though the bullet aimed for Samuel's head had found Clara's hip.

Van Bam lifted her into his arms, and the changeling yelled in pain.

Samuel looked past them to the secret portal kept open by thaumaturgy.

'No choice now,' he said.

With a determined nod , Van Bam turned and carried Clara to the doorway. His stride didn't falter, and, as he neared, the glassy fluid bulged outward, enveloped them both, and snapped them back into its blackness away from the cellar into wherever.

Samuel stared after them as the surface became smooth once again. His prescient awareness felt as flat as it had in the presence of the Genii, and he hesitated to follow.

The barrier at the stairwell was failing now Van Bam had left the area; the patrolmen had created cracks in the magic, fracturing it into an ever-growing spider web. Above, the elevator had completed its ascent and was now beginning to descend. Samuel caught a glimpse of many booted feet standing on the platform. He turned to the portal.

Where else was there to go?

His revolver clutched tightly in hand, he took a step back. Then, with a deep breath, he ran forward, gritted his teeth, and fled into the darkness of somewhere else.

DEPARTURES

By the time Samuel met Macy and Bryant at the disused ore warehouse in the southern district, the sun had risen and cleared the boundary wall. The warmth and light of the early morning did little to alleviate the sombre silence hanging over the agents; they had each endured a miserable night of fruitless searching.

While Bryant studied the strange metallic spider, Samuel and Macy stood alongside each other, watching Hamir working. As aloof and detached as ever, the necromancer cradled Lady Amilee's leather-bound book in one arm while tracing a finger down the open page, evidently checking the design of symbols he had engraved into the warehouse floor against its contents.

The symbols formed a rough circle of interconnecting swirls and shapes carved an inch deep into the stone. They configured more into a meaningless pattern than the complicated language Hamir had hinted they represented. Samuel couldn't tell where the pattern began or ended – if it even had a beginning and end – but the necromancer seemed quietly confident with his understanding of the transcription. He stepped lightly around the rough circle, flipping back and forth through the pages of the book, pausing now and then to double check some detail or another, and gave the occasional nod of satisfaction. Samuel had little comprehension of what he was doing, and even less inclination to find out.

Beside Samuel, Macy snorted a breath. Her expression was pensive and she was grinding her teeth.

She and Bryant had spent the night trying to find Mr Taffin. They had looked in all his usual haunts, spoken to his known associates and employees, but no one had seen him since the morning before last, and the Twilight Bar was closed for business.

Samuel had gone to the apothecary shop in the western district. He had broken in and checked the apartment above, but Gene was not at home. Samuel had found evidence of a small struggle, though: a cabinet upturned, the mattress pulled off the bed, a few worthless ornaments smashed on the floor. Fabian Moor, it seemed, had captured his first agent of the Relic Guild.

'Do you ever wonder where he fits in to all this?' Macy said, nodding towards the necromancer. 'I mean, Denton says Hamir was around when he joined the Relic Guild, and he reckons Hamir hasn't changed from that day to this. He never ages, his appearance never alters – and he has always had that scar on his forehead.'

Samuel shrugged. 'To be honest, Macy, I really couldn't care less how Hamir fits in to anything. I've other things on my mind.'

She nodded, quiet for a moment, then, 'You know, Gene might be stronger than we give him credit for.'

'You really think so?'

Macy looked to the floor. 'Well, at least we can hope Fabian Moor is finding out he's a tough old dog after all.'

Samuel didn't know whether she was trying to hearten him or herself, but her words lacked conviction.

While he had been at Gene's apartment, Samuel had found a few strands of hair in the bathtub. It was enough to use in the spirit compass, enough to track the apothecary's location. However, when he placed the hair inside the compass, the usually trusty device remained inactive. Samuel and Macy both knew the most likely explanation: Gene no longer had a spirit left to detect.

Without looking up from his book, Hamir said, 'If you need a straw to clutch at, Samuel, please remember that the spirit compass works on simple magic. It might be blinded by the presence of a Genii.' He bent to wipe away stone dust from a groove in the floor. 'It doesn't change Gene's predicament, I suppose, but Fabian Moor might have reason to keep him alive.'

Samuel glared at the necromancer, trying hard to prevent images of Gene being tortured, infected, turned into a golem, invading his mind.

'What about the Nightshade, Hamir?' Macy said. 'Moor seems to think the Relic Guild has information that can show him a secret way to enter it.'

'It's improbable at best, Macy,' Hamir replied. 'You magickers don't control the Nightshade. In fact, it's very much the other way around.'

'But Moor believes we aren't aware of the information,' Samuel added, 'that the Nightshade left some residue of itself in our minds, some blind spot. Could he be right?'

Hamir considered. 'I suppose anything is possible where higher magic is concerned.' He sniffed. 'Thaumaturgy is a tricky beast.'

'You're telling me,' Bryant said.

Macy's twin was inspecting the metallic spider. He had stepped under its long, thin legs and was peering up into the grey and disfigured face of the golem that had once been Betsy.

To Samuel, the events at Chaney's Den seemed a long time ago.

Looking unconvinced, Bryant added, 'Don't get me wrong, Hamir – I trust Lady Amilee as much as everyone else – but this thing really doesn't look powerful enough to take down a Genii. It's so spindly and ... *weedy*.'

Hamir looked up from the book and stared at him for a heartbeat. 'Bryant, perhaps it would be best if matters of higher magic were left to me, yes?' His tone and expression were noncommittal, but Samuel got the impression he was offended. 'However,' Hamir continued, 'should I ever need advice on how to bash a head, be assured you'll be the first I ask. Now, if you please, step away from the construct.'

So saying, Hamir returned his attention to the book and the circle of symbols at his feet.

Bryant shook his head, gave the necromancer a sour look, and stepped over to join Samuel and Macy.

'This is going to be a long day,' he muttered to his sister.

'Yeah,' Macy replied. 'I almost wish I'd gone with Van Bam and Angel.'

Despite the situation, Samuel couldn't deny the touch of envy he felt at the mention of Van Bam and Angel. They had already left the Labyrinth, escorting Ambassador Ebril and his entourage back home. Samuel would have given anything to have gone instead of either of them, to see an Aelfirian House again, even one as apparently troubled as Mirage. Van Bam was a fair diplomat, but Angel was in no way a better bodyguard than Samuel. He knew it, and so did Gideon.

It probably amused the Resident no end to deny him the opportunity to leave the Labyrinth, and that was just one more needle in Samuel's eye.

But Samuel's bitterness and jealousy were futile; it wasn't as if he could change the situation. He knew Gideon had enough on his plate without finding time to deal with Samuel's resentment. Not only was one of his agents missing, but he also had a new political situation on his hands.

Word of Ebril's departure had already spread, and now the other Aelfirian refugees were demanding passage back to their respective Houses. If Gideon's diplomatic skills were half as bad with the Aelfir as they were with his agents, he could well alienate a few Houses by the end of the day. Samuel only hoped the guidance of Sophia could temper his caustic manner enough to salvage at least some degree of civility within their relationships.

Hamir closed the leather bound book with a snap.

'Hmm.' He pursed his lips and looked up. 'My interpretations are a little rough around the edges, but I think we are ready.'

Samuel didn't know if he was talking to the spider or the three agents lined up before it. By their confused expressions, Macy and Bryant were wondering the same thing.

Only adding to the mystery, Hamir began whispering in a quick and unintelligible language. His voice carried a strange and alien resonance, musical yet ominous. It seemed to swell in the warehouse, and Samuel shied from the sound, resisting the urge to step away from Hamir. It reminded him of things he didn't want to remember … and implied things he did not want to know.

Hamir's words were directed at the design of symbols on the floor. The more he whispered the alien language, the more the atmosphere changed, building a prickly energy that made the hairs on the back of Samuel's neck stand on end. The swirls and shapes of the interconnecting pattern seemed to grow, expand and rise up above the stone. They flared with purple light that quickly disappeared to leave spots and slashes on Samuel's vision. Hamir growled a final word, and Samuel was left with the impression that the symbols had somehow darkened, solidified, the light filling their shapes like molten metal.

Silent now, and with the book under one arm, Hamir approached the three agents. He paused before Samuel and produced a pair of goggles from the inside pocket of his jacket.

'Please, put these on, if you would, Samuel.'

Samuel accepted the goggles and stared at them for a moment. They were much the same as those used by welders, except for the lenses. Made from glass, the same shade of deep green as Van Bam's cane, the lenses were faceted, protruding from the frame like the eyes of an insect. Samuel looked at Macy. She shrugged. Hamir waited expectantly. Samuel slipped on the goggles.

Expecting his vision to turn green, he was surprised when instead all colour was drained from his world. His colleagues and the barren interior of the warehouse appeared to him in dreary grey. Samuel raised a hand before his face. His skin was the colour of a corpse.

'What's the point of these?' he asked Hamir, tapping a lens with a dead finger.

The necromancer didn't answer. The scar on his forehead burning brightly white, Hamir stepped past Samuel and headed for the spider.

The three agents turned to watch Hamir, as intrigued now as they had been confused. With his back to the group, Hamir stared up at his creation.

'This construct has been given one simple task,' he said. 'To capture Fabian Moor –' he motioned to the design of symbols on the floor – 'and bring him here to his prison. As with all spiders, the construct's best weapon is stealth. It is imperative Fabian Moor does not see it coming.'

He spoke in that strange, breathy language again; this time a single word carrying an instructive tone.

The goggle's faceted, insect-eye lenses, had not changed the colour of the spider. But with Hamir's command, its appearance wavered as though a veil of clear water had been drawn across it. The effect animated the face of the golem's head, making its features dance, almost appear to laugh. For the first time, the construct moved. It skittered as if flinching. The metallic tips of its eight legs ticked against the stone floor, and then were still again.

The legs began to fade. From the ground up, they vanished as if the spider's existence was being slowly erased, drained into nothingness. After its legs, the smooth lower hemisphere of its body came next. The golem's face was the last thing to disappear.

Judging by Macy and Bryant's noises of surprise, they too had seen the spider vanish.

Hamir, with his back turned to the group, held up a finger: a silent instruction to wait.

A few moments passed, and he said, 'Samuel?'

In the grey, empty space where the spider had stood, a patch of colour returned to Samuel's world: a blur of purple that expanded and thickened to a fat body of fog. Tendrils, eight of them, grew from the body, thin and insubstantial as they drifted down to touch the floor with puffs of smoke. The ghost of a giant spider formed before Samuel, its deep purple colour standing out in the grey like a single coal burning in a dead fire.

'I can see it,' he told Hamir.

'Excellent,' Hamir replied. 'To be honest, I wasn't sure the goggles would work.'

He turned to face the three agents, his hands clasped behind his back. 'Your job is to distract Fabian Moor, to make him believe you are the only threat he faces. But be warned – the construct will be single-minded in pursuit of the Genii. Do not get in its way.'

'Easier said than done, when we can't see it,' Bryant grumbled.

Ignoring the comment, Hamir continued, 'Once set free, the spider will be driven, fast, and it will take the shortest route to its prey. You will have a hard time keeping pace with it.'

He held up a hand to stave off another comment from Bryant. 'Fortunately, this is where Samuel's favourite little toy can be of use. Samuel, the spirit compass, please.'

As Samuel fished the device from his pocket, Hamir produced a phial and a small, slim pair of tweezers.

'Expose the interior, if you would.'

Samuel unscrewed the cap from the compass, and then pressed its face. It clicked and sprang up on a hinge, revealing the tiny, empty flat-bottomed dish beneath.

Hamir popped the cork from the phial and used the tweezers to extract a single hair.

'Before she turned into a golem, I had the foresight to cut a lock of hair from Betsy's head,' Hamir explained. 'It contains the residue of the magic which infected her – which is to say, the same magic that now resides within the golem's head. It should work in the spirit compass as any other organic material would.'

Samuel held the compass out, and the necromancer gently lowered the hair and coiled it into the dish.

Samuel pressed the face back into position and watched the needle. It ticked and turned until settling into a position that pointed directly at the smoky and purple spider ghost standing behind the necromancer.

'Got it,' he said.

'Good.' Hamir turned to face his construct again. 'Macy, be so good as to open the warehouse door, would you?'

With a frown, she complied. The shutter rattled up to reveal morning light. Instead of a rich golden colour, the light appeared decidedly sickly to Samuel's altered vision.

'Once released, the spider will not stop until its task is complete,' Hamir told them. 'It will allow you no time for respite, or to catch up should you fall behind. If you want my advice, it will be easier for you to follow underground.

'Now, are you ready?'

No one replied, which Hamir took as affirmation.

'Macy, please stand outside. Ensure no one strays past the door.'

She stepped out of the warehouse and disappeared from view.

Hamir drew a breath and barked a single, alien word at the spider.

Instantly, the purple ghost became a flurry of motion. Tendril legs rose and fell on the floor with the scrapes and chimes of metal on stone. Its cloud-like body turned towards the door. Without pause it sprinted forwards, out into the open. It headed straight across the street, and climbed up the wall of the opposite warehouse. Splinters of stone fell to the ground where the pointed tips of its legs dug into the brickwork.

In but a moment, the automaton spider had climbed the wall and disappeared over the warehouse roof, fast and eager to hunt down a Genii.

Hamir turned to Samuel and Bryant.

'Good luck, gentlemen. I hope you survive.'

Marney awoke to sunshine spilling in through the window. It bathed her face with golden warmth, dragged her up from the depths of dreams, and lit the darkness behind her eyelids with an orangey-red glow. With a sigh she reached out a hand, searching for a familiar body lying beside her; but her fingers only closed around a cold and empty space. She opened her eyes. The residue of Van Bam's emotions lingered in the bed, and Marney could still feel the touch of his lips upon her forehead: a farewell kiss to his sleeping lover.

Alone, she sat up. In the light of day, the rundown apartment above the bakery did not seem half as romantic as it had the previous night. Van Bam had most likely left the Labyrinth already, and Marney didn't know when she would see him again. She was glad he hadn't woken her. She didn't want to say goodbye face-to-face.

With weary acceptance she rose from bed, washed and dressed herself, eager to be away from the love nest that now seemed so dreary and soulless. No one paid much attention to her when she stopped to buy a muffin from the busy bakery below the apartment. With her breakfast in hand, she slipped out onto the street.

She decided to walk for a while before taking a tram to the Nightshade. It was too early for anyone to wonder where she had got to, and she was in no hurry to discover what new surprises the day would bring. Besides, the crisp morning air would help to lighten her melancholy. Blocking the swirl of emotions radiating from the denizens who flowed along the pavement with and against her, Marney ate her breakfast. The muffin was still warm from the oven, and the preserve inside was dark and sweet.

Strangely, as she walked and ate, her thoughts decided to turn back to her university days. Amongst the flowering memories, she was surprised to find the face of a young man waiting for her; a young man called Karlin.

Marney smiled sadly at the memory.

Karlin had been her first boyfriend. A sensitive soul, almost pretty, with his brooding features and long black hair, he had been conducting his final semester in music studies when he and Marney got together. He was a talented guitarist, a poet, a performer, and considered one of the cooler people among his peers at university. Marney could hardly believe it when she managed to catch his eye.

Karlin fell head over heels for her, adored her, and Marney lapped up his attentions. She loved the fact he was such a good musician; loved the songs he wrote for her, the way he looked when he sang them to her. Marney loved that her boyfriend played in bands; she loved following him to gig after gig, watching him up on stage in rough and seedy taverns, knowing the other girls in the audience didn't stand a chance with him. She loved that Karlin only had eyes for her as he performed. But Marney had never loved Karlin himself.

She supposed it was his presence that she found most attractive; his natural ability to command the attention of any audience. Karlin's aura took the spotlight away from Marney. She was happy and secure hiding in his shadow. Not that she was hiding from herself; she understood what she was – that being a magicker, an empath, was a dangerous thing to be in Labrys Town. Being around Karlin seemed to make it less dangerous, somehow. Maybe she manipulated his feelings for her without even realising it herself. Maybe she used him as a shield.

Marney had known all along it wouldn't last. Karlin often spoke of the future, of his dreams of playing the biggest stages along Green Glass Row. He always included Marney when he spoke of these things, as if they would be together forever, as if she would always be there to help him through the lows and celebrate the highs.

Marney always knew that one day she would have to leave him, and that thought haunted her every time she watched Karlin on stage, every time she pretended she was part of his long-term plans. She dreaded the moment when she would burst his bubble; the moment where an empath would look into the sensitive eyes of a creative soul, and feel every break of Karlin's heart.

Fortunately for Marney, that moment had been spared her.

Marney had been roused from bed one night by a voice in her head.

While Karlin slept beside her, the voice called Marney from her dormitory, down into the communal gardens outside; and there, a kindly old man named Denton waited for her.

It had been a strange moment, dreamlike and quick, barely long enough to leave a mark on Marney's memory. Quite literally, Denton had taken her by the hand, led her away from the life she knew, and propelled her into the shady world of the Relic Guild. Karlin never knew what had happened to her. Marney hoped he had found a new muse.

As she walked through the fresh morning, lost in her thoughts of the past, life suddenly seemed too complicated. She had found *real* love with Van Bam, and now he had headed off into the war. She would find no peace and security until he returned.

Was there even a guarantee he *would* return?

With this question burning unanswered in her heart, Marney stopped walking abruptly. She realised that she didn't know where she was.

She had been following the main street, intending to keep on it until she felt ready to catch a tram back to the Nightshade. But somewhere she had turned off into a dingy side lane. The disused buildings rose high on either side of her, tall enough to block the sun and plunge the desolation into shadows.

Why would she blindly turn into an area she didn't know? Denton had taught her to be wise to her environment, and all the bad things in the eastern district lurked in its side lanes.

Marney turned, planning to retrace her steps. But why did doing that suddenly seem like such a bad idea? She turned again, studying the way ahead. A curious feeling came over her; somehow she just *knew* that at the other end of this neglected lane, the answer to the most intriguing mystery awaited her.

Why would she think that?

Alert, Marney reached out with her empathic senses, searching for the emotions of anyone who might be in the vicinity. But she felt no danger, no mugger – or worse – watching her from the shadows. All she sensed was a light presence stroking her thoughts with threads of soft silk, egging her on, willing her to continue forward.

Marney smiled wryly; the presence reminded her of a long time ago, when a voice had called her from sleep and changed her world forever.

Emoting a cloak of concealment around herself, Marney walked to the end of the lane. There, she saw the Resident's personal tram waiting.

Its sleek and black body seemed to absorb the sunshine; the dull silver square on its side was like a metal eye staring back at her.

Hidden from the perceptions of others, Marney stepped from the lane and approached the tram. She laid a hand on the silver square, the door slid open, and she stepped inside.

'You know, you could've just shouted for me,' Marney said to Denton as she closed the door behind her.

Sitting on the bench seat, Denton nodded, said nothing, just crushed his hat in his hands.

Marney's smile faltered. A well-filled rucksack sat on the floor between her mentor's feet. With a frown, she took the bench seat opposite him.

'Denton, are you going somewhere?' she asked.

'Yes, *we* are,' he replied.

The tram moved off, and Marney placed her hands against the unpadded bench on either side of her, feeling the vibrations of wheels trundling along metal tracks. Denton's emotions were closed to her, and that was never a good sign.

'What's going on?' she said.

He met her eyes, hesitated, and then said, 'Gideon has been in contact with Lady Amilee.'

Marney nodded. 'Yes, Van Bam told me—'

'No, Marney – this has nothing to do with Ambassador Ebril. We have been given orders concerning the mysterious House where Fabian Moor was hiding.'

'The Icicle Forest?' Marney sat forward. 'It's been found?'

Denton shook his head. 'The Thaumaturgists have no record of it existing. They are worried, to put it mildly. They believe the Icicle Forest is a secret Genii stronghold hiding within the Nothing of Far and Deep ...'

He fell silent, lost to his thoughts.

Marney's mouth was suddenly dry. 'What is it, Denton?'

'Lady Amilee,' he said. 'She claims the doorway to the Icicle Forest must be buried so deep in the Great Labyrinth that not even she can see it. If anyone stands any chance of finding that doorway, then we must know the House Symbol. But ...'

'But according to Llewellyn, the only two people who knew that symbol were Ursa and Carrick,' Marney said slowly. 'And they're dead.'

'Yes. Yes they are.'

Marney shrugged. 'Then we'll get it from Fabian Moor. *If* we can catch him, right?'

'Perhaps. But we're not going to wait for Moor'

'What are you telling me, Denton?' She dampened the fear crawling up inside her. 'You said we have orders.'

He averted his eyes. 'Lady Amilee has given you and me a mission, but ...' He made a disgruntled noise. 'Forgive me, Marney, but I don't believe you're ready for this.'

'Denton ...' Marney wasn't sure what to say next.

Concern and uncertainty were etched deep into Denton's face.

Marney decided to project her own emotions to him, her fear, her confusion, how intrigued she was about what it was he did not believe she was ready for; but most of all, she projected her complete, unwavering trust in her mentor.

Denton met her eyes and gave a wan smile. 'Here,' he said, 'I have something for you.'

He dipped into the rucksack between his feet and pulled out what looked to be a leather girdle. He passed it to Marney, and she saw that it was a baldric holding two lines of six, slender throwing daggers.

'I sometimes forget how much you've learned, how much you've grown,' Denton said as she stared down at the knives. 'You really don't need protecting anymore.'

'Then stop stalling,' Marney said. She held the baldric up. 'Where in the Timewatcher's name are we going, Denton?'

Denton sighed. 'Marney, have you ever heard of the Library of Glass and Mirrors?'

'Of course,' she said. 'Everybody has.'

The Library of Glass and Mirrors was an Aelfirian legend, a fabled House that recorded history. But not just any history; the legends said it contained the historical accounts of every race and culture that had ever existed, did exist, or *would* exist. All stored in the Library of Glass and Mirrors. The past, the present, and the future – *everything* was known to its librarians.

Marney scoffed. 'It's a myth, Denton.'

'That's what I thought until today,' he said. He held up a hand to stave off Marney's incredulity. 'The Thaumaturgists consider it a dangerous place, and rightly so. They fear it, and have vowed to never use it themselves, but they have always known the Library of Glass and Mirrors to be real. And they know how to reach it, Marney.'

'If any record of the Icicle Forest exists,' he continued, 'then it will be stored at the Library. But the knowledge kept there makes it far too dangerous a House to have a doorway out in the Great Labyrinth, Marney. If we are to reach it—'

'Reach it?' Marney snapped. 'Denton, wait a minute—'

'Lady Amilee has given me a map,' he said sternly. 'It will lead us to the Library, but we must travel through various Houses first. The journey will take us into … into …'

'Where, Denton?' Marney demanded. She gripped the baldric tightly. 'Take us into where?'

Denton sat back and rubbed his face.

'I'm so sorry, Marney. You and I are going to war.'

CHAPTER TWENTY

LOST PATHWAYS

Fabian Moor stood within the confines of his silver cube. Mo Asajad and Viktor Gadreel flanked him. Together they faced a wall, which had cleared to shimmering air, revealing a scene of pandemonium.

A land lay beyond the cube, a land of sharp rock and scorched trees, buffeted by vicious winds. In the sky, clouds the colour of bruised flesh roiled like poison, spitting lightning at a barren terrain that teemed with corrupted *things*: *things* that roamed across the land, near and far, big and small, too many to count, each and every one of them a monster. Twisted bodies with too many limbs; hunched abominations with gaping maws filled with too many teeth; scabrous hulks with wicked thorns for hands. Of varying shapes and disfigurements, these perverted creatures stalked a broken landscape, fighting and existing without reason or conscience.

Despite the chaos and violence that reigned within their view, not one sound reached the ears of the Genii. They observed while surrounded by dead and eerie silence.

Viktor Gadreel made a low, grumbling sound. '*This* is what became of our Aelfirian armies?' he asked.

'Along with their realms, yes,' Moor replied. 'Disturbing, isn't it?'

Great beasts with elongated heads flew through the poisonous sky, gliding gracefully on leathery wings. They dodged the spears of lightning, and dived to attack shambling giants who swung laboriously at them with boulder-like fists on the end of tree-sized arms. Smaller creatures scurried around the feet of the giants; some fought among themselves, others searched for food, or so it seemed. In the distance, a hive of arachnoids exploded into life with sabre-legged defenders who met the attack of spiny, slug-like monstrosities.

Gadreel shook his head in wonder. 'And you say it was the Time-watcher who created this place?'

'The Retrospective, She called it,' Mo Asajad answered. Even she, in the face of this brutal scene, had lost her spiky argumentativeness. 'The corrosion of dead time. It serves as a reminder of what it means to be the Timewatcher's enemy.'

Gadreel scoffed. 'To think, She dared to call *us* evil.'

'Yes, the irony runs deep,' Moor said.

Gadreel looked at him, his one eye dark and unblinking. Dressed now in the cassock of a priest, the bald Genii was as hulking and powerful-looking as he had always been. It pleased Moor to have the old brute back at his side.

'It is just as I told you, Viktor—' He was cut off by a blinding flash.

Out in the cruel wilderness, a lightning bolt struck a giant, tore it apart, reduced it to a shower of bone and meat in which the smaller creatures revelled and fed.

Asajad made a small noise of delight at the spectacle.

'The Retrospective is an unimaginably huge realm,' Moor continued. 'These *wild demons*, as the humans like to call them, are vast in number. They will serve our purpose well, don't you think?'

Gadreel remained sceptical. 'All I see are beasts succumbed to mad-ness, Fabian. Even with our combined thaumaturgy, how can we hope to turn such mindless animals into a trained army?'

'We can't,' Moor replied. 'But there is one who could.'

Gadreel look at him sharply, angrily. 'You said he was gone, banished for good.'

'No, Viktor,' said Asajad. 'We said he was missing.'

With a smile, Moor turned from the Retrospective and approached the strange, tree-like creature standing at the centre of the cube. Its snake's nest of roots twisted and writhed on the silver floor; its ten-tacular branches held aloft the filthy magicker of the Relic Guild, the empathic human called Marney.

'They would have us believe that he is unreachable, lost forever,' Moor said as Gadreel and Asajad came alongside him, 'that only the Timewatcher knows his true location.'

'But some secrets aren't as well kept as *they* believe,' Asajad said. She stroked Marney's slack and unconscious face with a delicate hand.

Gadreel folded his meaty arms across his barrel chest. 'This *human* really knows how to find his prison?'

'As Fabian said, it is ironic,' Asajad sighed. 'The Timewatcher believed in equality, demanded that we treated Aelfir and humans as our peers.' She traced a finger down the empath's naked body. 'And now She will rue the day She ever trusted so lowly a creature as this.'

Gadreel nodded, clearly pleased.

'So long ago,' Moor said, 'we three endured tortures to preserve our essences, to escape the war against the Timewatcher, but history showed that we had died. It was all for this day, my friends.'

He took a deep breath and exhaled heavily, staring at the pale and pitiful magicker hanging before him. 'Soon, this empath will reveal to us the hidden location of Oldest Place, and the Aelfir will know the true meaning of horror.'

Viktor Gadreel grinned, and Mo Asajad closed her eyes as if listening to the sweetest of music.

Moor turned from the empath and the tree-like monstrosity, and faced the Retrospective once more. The silent images of mindless rage and lustful violence no longer disturbed him; they fuelled his blood with the roar of higher magic.

'The day has come, my friends,' he told his fellow Genii. 'Soon, Lord Spiral will stand beside us once again.'

ACKNOWLEDGEMENTS

When you get handed a ticket to the Biggest and Best Ride, you come to realise there are a lot of people who deserve your eternal gratitude. I would like to thank:

Mum and Dad for the life they gave me; Dot and Norm for the start they gave me (and sadness too that Dot never got to see the release of this book). My test readers: Kellie and Katy (the Almost Girls), Geoff, and my main man Trusty Mike. My agent John Berlyne for his perseverance and for unlocking the door I'd been banging on for the last ten years; and my marvellous editor Marcus Gipps who made me feel so welcome and special when I found the courage to walk through that door – this also goes for Gillian, Simon and Jen, along with the rest of the amazing Gollancz team.

Keith, Lesley, Helen and Kelly, the students I studied with and the students I taught. The T-Dog for keeping the faith, Stefan Fergus for his seal of approval, Miss Grumpy Bear (who doesn't scare me at all), and the staff of the Rendezvous Bar & Bistro for keeping me plied with coffee while I wrote a large chunk of this story. And my wonderful daughter Marney, whose birth disrupted the writing of this book, and who is still too young to read about the adventures of her namesake.

To each and every one of you, my thanks.

This book is dedicated to Jack, my wife and best friend, who supported me while I stood in line for the Biggest and Best Ride, and put up with my every shade and mood. I love you.

Turn the page for a preview of the sequel to *The Relic Guild*

THE CATHEDRAL OF KNOWN THINGS

TIME MECHANIC

At times, he played the long game in the strangest of places.

Above, the primordial mists of the Nothing of Far and Deep roiled beneath an angry sky yet to warm its cold days with the fire of a sun; a monumental dome of liquid slate devoid of nights filled with the ruby and silver glares of its moons. Below, unused time congealed into slabs of pulsing colour to create a landscape of blues and reds hued so variedly as to fill the spectrum between dusk and dawn. Raw thaumaturgy dashed the air like static, whipping, dancing, as free and wild as windborne snow. A hum, low enough to be felt rather than heard, vibrated and churned the volatile atmosphere, coaxing shape from shapelessness.

Hovering between the angry sky and the landscape in flux, Fabian Moor was exhilarated by the flakes of higher magic swirling around him, stinging his face, singing to his blood. An age had passed since he had last been able to enjoy the moment.

Defeat at the hands of the Relic Guild was far in the future, yet a distant memory now. Those petty, interfering magickers might have proved much more intelligent, problematic – even more powerful – than Moor had been prepared for, but ultimately their meddling had achieved nothing that hindered Lord Spiral's greater strategy. Yes, details had been compromised, planning required adjustment, new pathways needed to be found; but all the Relic Guild had really achieved was to buy themselves a little extra time. Just a few more years.

With a feeling of satisfaction, Moor looked to the northern horizon, and stared with wonder upon a column of energy that connected unstable land to swirling sky like an umbilical cord of liquid fire. Droning with a mournful song, blazing, spitting bolts of purple at the ground, the column snaked and twisted through the air like a whirlwind. The

First and Greatest Spell, that energy was called, and it bore a legend. It had been cast by the only creature of higher magic worshipped by all races: the Timewatcher.

The First and Greatest Spell would one day be contained within a building named the Nightshade. But now, in its raw state, the spell was an immense and untamed formation of thaumaturgy that inflated an ever expanding bubble within the Nothing of Far and Deep. It held aloft the sky while solidifying time into the founding stones of an intrinsic House that would come to be known as Labrys Town, a human haven surrounded by the alleyways of an endless maze called the Great Labyrinth. The creation of this House would prove to be the Timewatcher's grandest achievement, and her biggest mistake.

Among all the Thaumaturgists, only Spiral, the Lord of the Genii, had been able to match the Timewatcher's power; only his command of higher magic had been able to smuggle Moor back to this time, a thousand years before the Genii War, to when the Timewatcher's fabled First and Greatest Spell birthed the most significant epoch in the history of the Houses.

Moor's sense of wonder grew. In this time frame, the Aelfir were warring against each other, out among the plethora of realms, fighting in perpetual, bloody battles that never heralded a victor – a cycle of pointlessness that was already centuries old. When the Great Labyrinth was completed, The Timewatcher would use it to break that cycle, and spell the end of what the Aelfir would come to call the Old Ways. Moor understood what a privilege it was to be chosen to bear witness to such an important beginning, to such … *creation*. Labrys Town might give the Aelfir a common ground, give them peace, but that peace would not last.

And to think, in only a millennium, the Great Labyrinth would become the catalyst that caused The Timewatcher to lose so many of her children. Lord Spiral and his Genii were coming, and nothing would be the same again.

An itch crawled across his skin.

Hollowness gnawed inside him.

Fabian Moor sighed.

From the satchel which hung from his shoulder, he took a phial of blood and popped the cork with his thumb. He paused before drinking, staring at the phial and its contents.

A part of Moor had hoped that being present at this primitive stage of the Labyrinth's creation might ease his cravings; that the flakes of raw thaumaturgy, hissing in the air like a storm of static, might substitute the need for sustenance that ached in his core. He wondered: was this chronic need to feed on blood a weakness? Perhaps the virus that he carried meant he had become nothing more than vermin. Or did his condition make him greater even than the Thaumaturgists?

In the overall scheme of things, did it matter?

Lifting the phial to his lips, Moor drained the blood in one go. He was repulsed by how willingly he savoured the rusty tang as it slipped thickly down his throat, quenching his hunger, filling the void inside him. The phial fell from his grasp, and he watched it tumble down, end over end, until it disappeared into the fluxing landscape. There was no time left for musing and marvelling. Slowly, Moor descended. His eyes ever watchful, his instincts alert, almost fearful.

The purple fire of the First and Greatest Spell might have been providing the highest of thaumaturgy by which this House was achieving existence, but the Timewatcher's spell would not sculpt the final design. For that, the Great Labyrinth and its town required labourers ... of a kind.

Moor could see them as he neared the ground, hundreds, thousands of them, scurrying and lumbering and sliding over slabs and boulders that glowed blue and red. Radiating a vague violet sheen, the workers burrowed and dug, carved and built. Labouring tirelessly, in perfect unison, they hardened time to the black stone foundations of this House. Sculptors, creators, the builders of realms, these things were the Timewatcher's loyal pets. They were the Time Engineers.

Some of them appeared humanoid, hefting stone and laying brickwork; others appeared as giant slugs that devoured everything in their path to then excrete lines of dull purple jelly like icing squeezed from tubes. The last of them were arachnids, and they scooped up the jelly upon flat backs and carried it to the humanoids to use as mortar in their work. The Time Engineers needed no sustenance, no rest, and were unconcerned by the hostile environment. They would not stop building until this House was finished.

Moor spied an area of completed ground beside a wide chasm, and headed towards it. Landing near the edge of the chasm, he froze, tense and ready, as an arachnid scuttled towards him, back laden with purple mortar.

For the most part, Time Engineers were apathetic creatures, harbouring no prejudices, incapable of distinguishing between friend and foe. They understood only order and purpose. However, whether Moor be Genii, vermin, or a new and brilliant form of life, he remained fundamentally a creature of higher magic. If the Engineers detected his thaumaturgy, they would regard him simply as raw material to be mashed and ground into the foundations of Labrys Town.

The single arachnid didn't pose much of a threat. But if the one approaching detected Moor, it would summon its fellow Engineers, and one Genii could not stand against the thousands that would answer that call. Should he attempt to fight, they would alert the Timewatcher to the discrepancy, and Moor would have to flee before his lord and master's orders could be carried out. There would be no second chance. Subtlety was his best friend in this place.

Thankfully, the lone Engineer was focused on its current task. It did not pursue the Genii who had broken into this timeframe, but scurried up to the chasm and disappeared down into it. Relieved, Moor peered over the edge.

The fissure was shallower than he had expected, though it still sank into the ground a fair way. Its mouth might have been crude and ragged, but the further down the chasm reached, the neater and squarer its walls became. Moor could see Time Engineers working tirelessly, their violet glow lighting the depths. Some clung to the walls, smoothing and shaping; others worked at the very bottom, constructing what Moor supposed would be the partitions of interconnecting rooms.

Glancing nervously around at the forming landscape, ensuring no other Time Engineers were close by, Moor dipped a hand into his satchel again, this time producing a small terracotta jar. He ran a pale hand over the smooth and plain surface, feeling the charge of higher magic held inside.

The last of the Genii.

The other jars containing the essences of Moor's fellow Genii were already in place. Viktor Gadreel, Hagi Tabet and Yves Harrow now lay waiting among the bones of Labrys Town. This final terracotta jar contained the essence of Mo Asajad.

In Moor's natural time period, the war against the Timewatcher was over, and Lord Spiral had lost – or so his enemies believed. The rest of the Genii faced imminent execution, and the last of their allies among the Houses of the Aelfir had been vanquished. Every one of the secret strongholds Spiral had created within the Nothing of Far and Deep was being searched out and destroyed. There were no safe havens left for the only remaining Genii.

Moor could not take the other Genii to where he was headed; a tomb of his own awaited him, and his immediate future was too unpredictable to play minder to his comrades. The passage of time, while they lay hidden beneath the noses of their enemies, was the best weapon they had now. The higher magic that contained Asajad, Gadreel, Tabet and Harrow inside the terracotta jars was unstable; but with the energy of the First and Greatest Spell wrapped around them, they would be kept safe, kept strong, waiting for the day that Moor could return to reanimate them.

It was Lord Spiral himself who had taught Moor the forbidden thaumaturgy that had preserved the essences of his colleagues. Moor remembered the tortures it had inflicted upon them. He could not rid himself of the images and sounds of their suffering. Only Mo Asajad had refrained from screaming when Moor had reduced her physical form to ashes. She had glared at him throughout the process, gritting her teeth against the agony, and she had not stopped glaring until she no longer had eyes to glare with.

Moor studied the terracotta jar in his hands, struggling to understand why Lord Spiral had chosen Lady Asajad for the task. Her devotion to the Genii cause was pure, but Spiral was the only person Asajad would obey without question. When her essence was reanimated she would resent following Moor's orders. She would not function well within a group not under Lord Spiral's personal command. Mo Asajad lived to dominate, she craved control. She was an unhinged creature of higher magic, and Moor could foresee problems.

He circled a finger around the jar's wax seal.

It was not beyond the realms of temptation that he might compromise Asajad's containment device. He could hurl it down into the chasm, to the very bottom, where the terracotta would shatter and release the thaumaturgy it contained. And when Asajad's essence began its ravenous search for meat and blood and reanimation, the Time Engineers could have their way with her. They could recycle her thaumaturgy and grind it into the fabric of the Labyrinth. Getting rid of her now might cause fewer problems in the long run, Moor reasoned. And who would know what he had done?

No. Spiral had chosen Asajad, and Moor could not defy his lord and master.

Holding the jar securely in both hands, Moor stepped off the edge of the chasm and floated down.

Careful to keep himself away from the arachnids clinging to the sheer faces surrounding him, he continued descending until he neared the bottom. His earlier suspicions had proved correct; the Engineers were indeed segmenting the wide and long floor into rooms. The walls they had built thus far were incomplete, appearing as ruins. Moor wondered what manner of building would eventually rise from this great pit.

He landed in a half-finished room where a single humanoid Time Engineer, its glowing skin fractured by black lines like a network of veins, laboured away. The Engineer did not react to the Genii's arrival. It continued to build its wall higher.

Taking a steadying breath, Moor latched onto the thaumaturgy with which the First and Greatest Spell had saturated this land and flashed a quick command to the humanoid.

The Engineer ceased working and turned to face the source of the irregularity.

It had no features as such, just a swirl of black-veined violet where its face should have been. The glow of its body brightened and dimmed as though it was unsure how to proceed. Once again Moor touched the First and Greatest Spell. He didn't dare delve too deeply lest its power absorb his own entirely. He barely skimmed the surface, scratched down just enough to send the Time Engineer a simple but firm command which it could not refuse.

Moor placed the terracotta jar on the newly formed floor and stepped back. The Engineer stepped forward to kneel beside the jar. And then, just as the other Engineers had done for Gadreel, Tabet and Harrow, it proceeded to bury the essence of Mo Asajad.

It punched the floor, its fist sinking effortlessly into hardened time with a sound oddly poised between breaking glass and splashing water. The Engineer plunged its arm down to the shoulder before withdrawing it, leaving behind a perfectly circular hole. Moor held his breath as the Timewatcher's labourer picked up the terracotta jar and lowered it into the opening. The worker then began rubbing flat palms over the floor in circles as if washing it. Faster and faster it rubbed until, with subtle pulses of red and blue, the hole was filled and smoothed to black stone.

Moor relinquished his command of the creature. The Engineer turned away from him to continue working on the wall. Only then did the Genii sever his connection to the First and Greatest Spell; only then did he rise at speed, up past the arachnids clinging to the walls, out of the chasm and high into the blizzard of thaumaturgy.

Fast and silent, Moor continued to ascend, soaring towards the roiling slate-grey sky. To the north, the fire of the Timewatcher's mighty spell continued to drone and spit; below, the violet glow of the Time Engineers dotted the landscape. He did not stop rising until he came within several yards of the thick and churning primordial mists of the Nothing of Far and Deep. For a final time, he pushed a hand into his satchel and removed the last item, a simple wooden scroll case.

Moor slid out the scroll and unrolled it carefully, letting the case fall from his grasp. Upon clean white parchment were glyphs and symbols, swirls and shapes, strange configurations, written in black ink by a hand that Moor knew all too well. It was a complicated formula that decorated the page, more complicated than any other Thaumaturgist could create. These were the words of Lord Spiral himself, the language

435

of higher magic, and they were for Moor's eyes only.

This scroll was one of two that Spiral had left Moor before his defeat at the hands of the Timewatcher. The first had allowed Moor to travel back to this early stage in the Labyrinth's creation. But the second …

In this time period, Moor was as a single bee in a forest, a grain of sand in a desert, an unnoticed interloper, but he could only remain for a short while. He was not shielded from the raw elements as the essences of his comrades were in their terracotta jars. He was whole, alive, and if he lingered too long, the mighty thaumaturgy that had delivered him to this time would cease protecting him. The First and Greatest Spell would drain the higher magic from his body until only dust remained. Fortunately, Lord Spiral had given him a way out.

Moor began reading aloud from the scroll, the language of the Thaumaturgists hissing and sighing from his lips as quick and fleeting as the flakes of higher magic whipping around him. He intoned the words of his lord and master, his voice growing in intensity, barely able to contain his urgency.

As Moor recited, a grey churning disc appeared in the Nothing of Far and Deep directly above him. Growing darker and smoother, it swirled faster and faster until Moor read the last word and the disc collapsed into a portal, a black hole punched into the sky.

The scroll burst into flame, burning in a flash to ashes that blew from Moor's hand to be lost in the blizzard.

With his work done, the Genii gave a final glance below him to the landscape birthing a House. The Relic Guild would see Fabian Moor again, and at a time when they were not prepared to deal with him. Moor would return to wake his fellow Genii, and together they would search for Spiral. They would find the hidden prison that the Timewatcher would come to create for the Lord of the Genii.

All things were known in the end.

Moor rushed up towards the portal. Without hesitating, he flew into the black hole and disappeared from the Labyrinth. For now …